This Place is Home

Also by Irene Te

THIS PLACE IS MAGIC

THIS SONG IS OURS

THIS PLACE IS HOME

Irene Te

RABBIT YEAR PRESS
HOUSTON

For David and Owen, because home is wherever you're running around yelling while I attempt to write a novel

For a full list of all the clowns
involved in this circus, please visit
irenete.com

And for access to the confidential
dossiers compiled by [REDACTED],
keep dreaming, pal.

~ The Management

September

Transcript from the weekly K-pop news podcast **Omma Gosh!**
Season 5, Episode 38

Jooney Chun (Host): Folks, it's suddenly the end of September and I have no idea where the year went.

Maisie Chun (Co-host; Jooney's Mom): Jooney has no idea about anything. Been that way since he was a very little boy. (*pause*) All boys like this.

Freddie Dang (Co-host; Producer): Don't talk to me about boys right now. I'm still in mourning. I want nothing to do with any boys, ever. Forever. Until I'm dead.

Jooney: Okay, well what I should've said was, "Folks, it's the end of September and Freddie still hasn't fully recovered from the June announcement that Apollo's Max Lee is dating actress Hazel Lim."

Freddie: (*wailing*) Why does he get so mad when they ask him about her? He must really love her, this must be so serious—

Maisie: Better be serious. Those boys so old! Only one of them has a girlfriend! Hurry up!

Freddie: Auntie, you know they're not supposed to date. Fans like to believe they have a chance.

Maisie: (*snorts*) Well, they don't! Wake up! Go marry an accountant!

Freddie: An accountant. That's so specific. (*muttering*) But not a doctor...?

Jooney: Personally, I'm just tired of waiting to find out where Apollo's going next. They've been 'in talks' with a new agency for at least a month now, right? When did we first hear about that?

Freddie: Gosh, yeah. That was weeks ago. I have to say, Zenith is not where I expected them to go. Can you imagine if this goes through?

Jooney: As a reminder to everyone listening, Zenith Media is currently home to boy group W4VE and rookie girl group 2M2D. And look, don't yell at me for this, I'm just delivering a journalistic truth, but Apollo would be the biggest act they've signed since the late 90s.

Maisie: Ohhhh. That's right, this company, they also had Orion! Long, long ago. Old men now. Very old men. (*claps hands*) So it's good! This is a place for old men, Apollo gets along there just fine.

Freddie: (*laughing*) She makes it sound like Zenith is a retirement home for K-pop idols.

Jooney: They're not even that old, Ma. Most of Apollo is around my age.

Maisie: What do you want me to tell you, eh? You are very old. Hurry up with your life.

Jooney: Okaaayyyyy—

Freddie: If it wasn't for everything that happened over the summer, I bet Zenith would be yelling that they've hit the jackpot. Like Jooney said, this agency hasn't had a globally successful group since the Orion days. W4VE has always been pretty solid, and 2M2D had a fantastic debut in July. Adding Apollo to the lineup puts the company in a great spot. I mean, minus the scandals. They'll be dealing with those if the transfer goes through.

Jooney: Maybe they don't care. I'd say this is a massive win for Zenith even with one member dating and a few others about to enlist. We're talking a guaranteed hiatus, but they must be confident Apollo will pay back the investment.

Maisie: Of course! Worth the money! Kazu just has to take off his shirt, boom, girls throwing cash on the stage.

Freddie: Jooney, stop making that face. The lady's not wrong. (*heavy sigh*) I've said this before, but like, how could Apollo hit us with so many headlines on that same night? Remember how insane that was? Ari running away to sell waffles, the legal drama with their agency, then Max is dating too? What made them think I could handle this emotionally?

Jooney: (*chuckling*) It was a total PR meltdown. One crisis at a time, guys.

Maisie: Pfft. Why wait? Get it all done, wham. Nice to see some of them move out, find their own place. And I hope the Max boy brings his girlfriend to the big awards show this weekend.

Freddie: (*wailing*) I don't!

Jooney: I've gotta say, even with a dating reveal, the group's weathered it pretty well.

Freddie: Emerald hasn't.

Jooney: Yeah, yeah. True. Stocks majorly tanked over the summer and their CEO was asked to resign. I'm amazed there hasn't been more of a legal battle, but it seems like the boys wouldn't have agreed to finish out their existing obligations if they hadn't, I dunno, mended fences a bit since June.

Freddie: Apollo's still together and determined to stay that way. Which is great, because I just can't take any more drama, okay? I'm fragile. This is something I've learned about myself. Thanks, Apollo.

Jooney: I haven't given up on the Emma Han theory and I know I'm not the only one. Guys, she came out of retirement just to help Apollo break up with their agency. She's gotta be dating someone in the group. This would be the scoop of the century for me.

Freddie: Why does she necessarily have to be dating one of them? Let it go, Jooney.

Maisie: Blah, blah, blah. I just want to see some cute babies. Not asking a lot, okay? Apollo boys all old enough to settle down. Go settle down!

Jooney: Well, Apollo, if you're listening — you heard her!

Maisie: Jooney. Do you hear me? When I say time to settle down, are you listening?

Freddie: (*snorts*)

Maisie: Just kidding! Freddie and Jooney married ten years now!

Freddie: Ohhhhhhhhhhhhhh—

Jooney: —mmmyyyy godddd let's take a quick break with one of our sponsors...!

1

J IYEON FOUND THE SIXTH photo tucked inside the glove box of her car.

Six of these, so far. Pictures had also appeared inside a kitchen cabinet, plus the tiny closet in the entryway and the drawer where she kept her hairbrush. Then, Eunjae had hidden one in the pocket of a cardigan left hanging in her closet all summer, on hold until a chilly day when the season turned at last. Another was tied to the handle of an umbrella, a selfie they'd taken on her tiny excuse for a balcony after dark. It came out grainy and underexposed, and yet somehow sweeter for it.

Leaving the glove box open, she examined the latest photo. Printed on flimsy copy paper, it featured Jiyeon's right hand and Eunjae's left, both holding milkshakes. A single line had been scrawled underneath. "Sorry about our weird dates," she read aloud to herself.

It made her laugh, and suddenly Jiyeon was there again: hidden in a booth toward the back of a twenty-four-hour diner at 1:00am, trying to decide between blueberry cobbler or something called a peach melba. No one else had been around except a disinterested waitress and some teenagers sharing a stack of pancakes.

Over the summer, they'd grown accustomed to a pattern of late nights and early, early mornings. Times when they might slip through the world unnoticed, pantomiming a normal life. They couldn't be seen together in the broad light of day. They couldn't be caught, or else. Things were already unstable for Apollo. The need for secrecy intensified with every passing week.

Generally, Jiyeon was delighted to find these surprises he'd left behind. But she'd opened the glove box to dig out a business card, one that Eunjae had watched her toss in there, and she hadn't touched it since July. Even though Jiyeon promised to call the leasing agent for that retail space he'd found back in June. Even though she'd promised to make that call as soon as the calendar flipped to August.

If she told him about finding this picture in her glove box, Eunjae would wonder why she'd only discovered it now. He'd ask about it, of course. She didn't want to lie, but she couldn't bring herself to explain, either. Jiyeon retrieved the photo from the diner, dropped it gently into her bag, and snapped the glove box shut. The business card stayed where it was.

A pizza arrived fifteen minutes later. Jiyeon brought it in, realizing she was hungrier than she thought. Had she remembered to take a lunch break? She put her phone on a tripod and went to brush out her hair. It was beginning to unravel after so many hours at the shop, strands sliding free from the tidy braid she'd pulled together that morning. What a long day it had been. But she'd managed to get the rest of the afternoon off, and now Jiyeon had a full evening to catch up on laundry. Talk about a wild Friday night.

Fridays never really felt like Fridays in the traditional sense; Jiyeon worked every weekend, full shifts on both Saturday and Sunday until Denny returned from Seoul. She'd be up before dawn the next day, braiding her hair in front of the bathroom mirror, decidedly unglamorous in her Wanna Waffle t-shirt and battered sneakers. But on Fridays, she met up with Eunjae. They ate together, ordering the same food or similar. She'd arrange for his meal and he'd arrange for hers. It was a small thing, but it helped diminish the many thousands of miles between them.

Eunjae called not long after she came to sit at her tiny kitchen table, right on the dot at 4:30pm. It was 8:30 in the morning for him, and already tomorrow. He'd still be asleep right now if Emerald hadn't scheduled a meeting on extremely short notice. The whole day had been reshuffled to accommodate this change. At least they'd managed to make date night happen anyway. Date afternoon? Date morning? Whichever.

Jiyeon chose a slice of pizza. She held it up for him to see. "Here's mine. Did yours make it?"

"Ah, mostly."

"What do you mean, mostly?"

"Max went to pick it up last night," Eunjae replied, yawning, "and ate half of it on the way back. Said he was starving." He took a bite. "Breakfast pizza, though. It really is a thing."

His brothers always claimed to be starving. Also, of course Eunjae was content to eat the pizza straight out of the fridge. Maybe he was worried someone would beat him to the microwave and claim it for themselves. Shaking her head at this very plausible scenario, Jiyeon said, "It's definitely a thing. I've tried to get Denny to add it to the menu tons of times. Waffle breakfast pizza, you know? So fun."

"And he won't do it?"

"Just starts ranting that breakfast pizza is an abomination." Which was why Jiyeon had asked Max to handle the date night food delivery; she'd wanted to avoid another lecture on why waffles are not pizza and why pizza is not breakfast. A girl could only hear the same monologue so many times before going nuts. "Oh, but did they tell you what the meeting's about? Is it the public relations stuff?"

"Don't think so," Eunjae replied. "We picked a PR firm and Zenith sent approval, but now we're waiting for both agencies to agree on when the management should start and who's paying for it. Should be the only thing left, though. Hopefully we can sign in a week or two."

A thought occurred to him. He set the pizza down, trading for his phone. "I need to forward this email, hang on. It's from the shipping company. I think some of my stuff might get there before I do. Was it really okay to send it all to your parents?"

"Like they'd ever let you send your stuff to some storage unit. We'd never hear the end of it. Dad will just pile it up in my old room until you get settled. Besides, Denny told me you've got nothing but 'photography doodads' and 'overpriced denim.' It'd be different if you had furniture, too."

"Never needed to buy any," he admitted. "I've lived in the dorms since I started at Emerald and the rooms always came furnished, so yeah. I guess all I've got are cameras and clothes."

"You can just find everything else later on."

"Yeah. Denny says I need to prioritize a haircut, though. Direct order."

"Oh, sure," said Jiyeon. "He's the boss of everyone, our Woosung."

"It does get in the way at dance practice."

Eunjae often joked about keeping the same haircut until he turned eighty, and Jiyeon was late to realize that this meant never wanting anyone else to trim it until he was eighty. He kept letting it grow out so long that the strands had to be tied back from his face. "Go get a haircut," she told him. "It won't hurt my feelings, I promise."

"Can't. I signed away the exclusive rights."

He pronounced this with such mock solemnity that Jiyeon had to smile. "You're allowed to do that? Don't you belong to your fans? I figured you'd have to ask them before signing your life away."

"Yeon-ah. You're not a fan?"

"Well. Maybe just a little bit."

"So it's fine."

"It's nothing drastic though," she told Eunjae. "I might not be enough of a fan."

"Are you sure? I've seen the calendar in your kitchen."

"That's a low blow. Your brothers bought it, I can't be held responsible."

"But you left it up," he pointed out, "so you must be a fan."

Tacked above and to the left of Jiyeon's toaster, this calendar had been sold out since the previous Christmas. It contained a full year of Apollo's Ari, one photo for each month. The backdrops were exotic locales and sweeping vistas. The fashion came straight from runways in Paris and Milan. Eunjae's brothers contrived to find it on eBay for an exorbitant sum. Then they'd waited patiently for their chance to hang it on her wall and run. *You can't miss hyung if you're soooooo sick of his face*, Jesse had scribbled on the cover.

To grow so accustomed to the sight of Eunjae — what an unimaginable concept. At this point, he'd been gone longer than he'd ever stayed. But Jiyeon pushed this recurring sadness into the far corner of her mind. This was supposed to be date night, and he was stressed enough over the last-minute meeting. Eyeing the way he kept drumming his fingers on the desk, she said, "I bet it's nothing bad, Eunjae."

He sighed. "I hope it's not about Max again. They need to stop asking him when he plans to break up with Hazel. He's not getting any better at controlling his temper."

"When *is* he planning to break up with her?" Jiyeon mused.

"Your guess is as good as ours," said Eunjae.

"So much for it being a 'temporary arrangement.'"

On multiple levels, it still boggled her mind that Max had been willing to go so far for the sake of revenge. Angry at Jungwoo, he'd declared himself in a relationship with the same actress his brother had been secretly dating off and on for months. Jungwoo hadn't corrected the claim. And instead of denying it, Hazel had defied expectations by confirming the news as true. The two were now locked in a public relationship that continued to draw the ire of Apollo fans even as it complicated the group's future. At one point, Sunshines even staged an ambush outside Hazel's agency.

Eunjae viewed the reception of his brother's dating news as a preview of what could be expected, should he go public with his own relationship. She knew better than to ask how long they'd be hiding. Jiyeon also knew better than to suggest, again, that she could handle whatever backlash they might face as a result. Even if Eunjae could tolerate the prospect of fans raging about her on the Internet, she understood that this was also about Apollo. The group couldn't handle another wave of incendiary headlines. Not with new contracts and a new agency finally within reach.

So she kept quiet about it as Eunjae switched from video to a regular call, headed out to start his day even as hers drew to an end. She shut the blinds and left the lights off for a while. The dark softened perception and skewed distance, and if Jiyeon focused only on the sound of his voice in her ear, it was like a magic trick. He was here. He never left.

"A week still feels like forever," she said. "Tell Denny to change your ticket."

"Been asking every day since June."

She remembered the photo from the car, still sitting in her bag. Jiyeon went to find it. There was room on her nightstand, right next to his favorite camera and the pair of glasses he'd left behind on purpose. And she'd joked about treating these objects like collateral, hostages held until Eunjae's eventual return, but that was because Jiyeon didn't want to cry about him leaving. At least, not while he could see.

A year ago, she would've managed this better. Now, she was exhausted. But if they'd met a year ago, two years ago, would Jiyeon have stopped long enough to truly see him? It took being exhausted to recognize that when she was with Eunjae, the world went beautifully, blissfully quiet. Time slowed down. She could rest.

"Eunjae," she said, propping the photo against her bedside lamp.

"Mm."

"Thanks for all the weird dates."

"No problem. What about the car wash next? Aren't some of those open twenty-four hours?"

"Yeah, but whew," she replied. "The romance. It's too much for me, I think."

His laughter dispelled every doubt weighing heavily on her heart. Jiyeon held on to the warmth of that sound long after they said goodbye.

2

ALTHOUGH TABLES COULDN'T BE reserved in the Emerald Entertainment dining hall, the one in the back left corner was considered to be Apollo's.

Eunjae had no memory of how this table became their designated spot. Shoved right up against a window facing the building next door, it didn't offer much of a scenic view. Proximity to that window also meant sweltering through their meals in summer, then shivering side by side in winter. And they could've picked any other place to sit, but somehow they always ended up here. It was arguably the worst corner of the dining hall, but it was their corner.

Not for much longer, though. They'd finished almost all of their remaining contractual obligations. The members of Apollo had signed a provisional agreement with Emerald that would be in effect until the end of November, but most of the group — including Eunjae— had nothing more on the schedule after this weekend's performance. As soon as that was done, he'd be heading back to California with Denny.

Eunjae found it difficult to imagine *not* living here. Was it really happening? Would he really be allowed to go?

As he finished the last few bites of his lunch, lukewarm sunshine spilled through the window and onto the tabletop, balancing the cold fluorescent lights. There was something satisfying about the four sets of dishes arranged on green plastic trays, four key cards on green lanyards, four jackets in a pile on the far side of the bench. Eunjae stopped eating and took a picture.

He meant to send it to Jiyeon. This didn't happen because somebody had to hurry and catch Max's pencil before it rolled onto the floor, and then somebody had to intervene before Nicky got himself decked with a cheap book of crossword puzzles. Kei certainly wasn't lifting a finger. He had yet to even look up from his magazine.

"Look, why are you getting so mad at me?" Nicky had his legs stretched across his part of the bench, bright orange hair freshly dyed, an insouciant little smile on his face. "I'm only reading what other people wrote. It's not like these are my opinions."

Max tossed the pencil again. It hit the table with a violent thwack. "Fuck right off, hyung!"

"Okay, maybe it's time to get off Star-Connect," said Eunjae. "We've gone through a lot of comments already."

Without missing a beat, Nicky replied, "And we should go through some more. Like this one! Oh, this one is good." He cleared his throat. *"Shop window couple! This is a PR ploy and I'm sick of it. Max should be deported to Texas, there's no reason for him to be here anymore."*

"Texas...?"

"Shop window couple...?"

"It's what people say when the relationship seems fake," said Kei, turning to the next page. "Lots of Sunshines think you're just dating for the attention."

"Not everybody thinks it's fake. See, this one says Max's obsession with Hazel is the most romantic thing they've ever seen—"

A woman's voice cut in, disembodied, speaking perfect English. "How can he be obsessed with her?" this voice demanded, startling three of the four people at the table and sending one of them into gales of laughter. "He barely knows this Hallie person. I think Madison's right and we should sue. This has gone on too far, bubs."

Max gawked at Nicky. "Why the hell are you on the phone with my sister?" he exclaimed, leaping to his feet. "How do you even have Mikaela's number?"

"That's just how this works. If she's your sister, I have her number." Nicky's smile widened into a grin. "Isn't it so funny?"

"You're insane," hissed Kei, the magazine forgotten now.

"Nah. Mostly just bored."

"What the actual, honest fuck!"

"Stop shouting in public," scolded Mikaela. "And why's Dad saying you won't have Heather with you this weekend? Shouldn't you bring her home to meet us? You've been dating for months now, you're practically engaged—"

"Her name is Hazel! I've said that a million times, and there's no way in hell I'm bringing her with me. Give up! Get a life! Leave me alone!"

"Holly, Hannah, whatever. Don't change the subject, Max. Why do you think it's okay to shack up with some random actress you only met once?"

"*Shack up*—"

"I'm telling you that it bothers me. It's the most bizarre thing you've ever done in your whole life. I could accept some kind of one-night-stand situation, but this is pushing it."

Nicky had his head pillowed on both arms by this point, laughing himself hoarse. Kei seemed on the verge of fleeing the room. Fellow diners had started to take notice, the commotion drawing eyes and ears. Eunjae mopped up a puddle that sloshed out of his water glass when Max jostled the table. He whispered, "We need to take her off the speaker."

Max went a mile further and wrestled the phone away. "Bye!" he told his sister. "Go to bed! Goodnight!" He punched the button to hang up, then launched himself at Nicky, a dozen expletives poised to tumble out of his mouth. But that was as far as he got, because Denny materialized behind him, foreboding as a thundercloud blotting out the sun.

None of Apollo's other managers had ever been as efficient, or as frightening, as Denny Han. Persuading him to take the job was the smartest decision they'd made since debut. Under Denny's reign, the dorms became a bastion of structured schedules and flawless sleep hygiene. He delivered everyone to their events on time, in one piece, and appropriately clothed. The unbridled menace of his glare was enough to kill any suggestion of outlandish diet plans or stylist selections involving mesh. How they'd go back to living without him, Eunjae had no idea.

Now, Denny's gaze swept over the table, scrutinizing each of them in turn. A frosty silence descended, changing the barometric pressure in this corner of the room. "Moriyama," he said. "You've been known to read a calendar correctly. What's on the docket today?"

Kei sat up straighter. "Captain! We have a meeting in fifty-seven minutes, Captain!"

"Correct. Make sure Hong gets to the right conference room this time. You'll need to bring this one, too." He rousted Nicky off the bench while Kei's enthusiasm deteriorated instantly. "Help Moriyama with these trays. You're going from Point A to Point B, no detours. Until then, keep your hands where I can see them," he added, "or else."

"Oooh, or else what?"

"Try me and find out, bucko." Next, Denny pointed at Max. "Why are you here? You're supposed to be in the studio with Shakespeare. Working lunch, no breaks, no fraternization."

"Ah, Jungwoo goes by Orpheus in the song credits... not Shakespeare..."

"Everyone knew who I was talking about, Ryan!"

"Pass," said Max, matching Denny glower for glower. "I was down there all morning, okay? It's like being in goddamn jail. And I wanted to eat with Ari-hyung."

"What, like you can't do that separately? Not everything has to be a group activity. You guys can do stuff on your own even though you share a hive mind powered by one brain cell."

"But we won't see each other for a while," Max argued. "Everybody's leaving after the awards thing. You can't blame us for wanting to eat lunch together."

"Spare me the melodrama, Lee. You've been eating lunch together for more than a decade. It's not like you won't see Ryan when you move to LA."

"I won't be out there for another month!"

"Yeah, and I think you'll live. Start looking at apartment listings. Send him some weepy postcards from Florida. 'Day two of the struggle. Wish you were here. How about this coffee table from IKEA?'"

Kei wrinkled his nose. "IKEA."

Much to Eunjae's consternation, Denny motioned for him to get up. "Let's go. Founders just asked to see you upstairs in ten. I have no idea why, so don't ask."

"Whoa, whoa," said Nicky, in the middle of stacking lunch trays. "What about me? That's my son, Chief. His business is my business."

While their manager enjoyed a solid laugh over that assertion, Eunjae handed Max his pencil and crossword puzzle. "Don't let Jungwoo forget about the meeting, okay? Hyung loses track of time when he's working."

"I hope he forgets. I've seen enough of him today."

"Max, come on."

"I'm not going back down there," his brother insisted. "Jaehwan said I have to put in eight hours of songwriting every single day, but he didn't say which hours."

"Help Kei, then. Or go up to the conference room and see if you can figure out what the meeting's about." Everyone in the group wanted to solve this mystery. When pressed, not even Denny could provide much in the way of information. *Something about a change of plans*, he'd told Eunjae yesterday. *More vague than usual.*

A change of plans. This worried Eunjae, but surely anything major would be communicated with more urgency. Apollo was expected in Bangkok by Friday afternoon. Tickets were booked, hotel rooms arranged, stage outfits tailored and ready. And he wasn't the only one flying home when the performance was done; if the schedule was extended in any way, they'd all be affected.

He fell in with the others leaving the dining hall, Max at his heels. "You're going up, right?"

"Yeah," replied Eunjae. "To the top, I guess."

"Then I'll go with you. Keiichi can handle Nicky and Gyu by himself. I'd rather be at this meeting fifty minutes early like a fucking loser."

The lobby of Emerald's main building buzzed with activity. Paneled in dark wood, with a contrasting floor that gleamed like ice, it thronged with people coming and going. As they walked by, one of the receptionists called to Denny from the front desk, a frantic note in his voice.

"Manager Han, it's... um... well, it's another phone call."

Denny's expression hardened into a scowl carved from granite. He waved them on, striding to the front desk without further explanation. All they got out of him was, "The executive floor, Ryan. I'll meet you up there when I'm done."

Kei and Nicky veered off toward the exit. With Max, Eunjae walked past reception, aiming for the main bank of elevators. While they waited, his brother flicked through text messages, foot tapping on the marble floor.

"Zu says he just saw some board members coming in. What's going on? We agreed to having PR babysitters and they agreed to let us pick which ones. I thought that was the last thing left. What else could they want?"

Apollo had fielded multiple offers of representation since June. Many of these were generous, but none were entirely forgiving. The industry couldn't overlook rebellion, and the dating news had angered legions of fans. The group was expected to make concessions. For example, aggressive public relations management for the transitional period, plus longer if deemed necessary. And Apollo was prepared to negotiate, so long as their next agency agreed to sign all nine of them, together.

We belong to our fans, Jaehwan had reminded them all, back when the group started reviewing offers. *The least we can do for Sunshines is to stay together. They're afraid this is the end for us, but we can show them that it isn't.*

Some agencies were fine with keeping Max, but only if he dropped Hazel. Others just wanted him out of the group. A few felt that Apollo should continue as seven, without the two members who had dared to rock the boat. The victory they'd earned on that summer night continued to come at a price.

It was a price Eunjae remained willing to pay. His bags were packed, the majority of his belongings crated up and on their way across the sea. The future was a vast, unmapped wilderness, but going home was the most important thing.

One more week. Jiyeon was right when she said it still felt like forever.

3

E UNJAE EXPECTED DENNY TO steer him in the direction of the
CEO's office. Instead, they stopped at a door he'd never had cause
to open before, painted black and labeled EXECUTIVE LOUNGE.

Inside was a cozier version of the main lobby. The same dark
wood paneled the walls, polished smooth as glass. Rugs covered the
herringbone pattern on the floor, and on the largest of these, a frazzled
intern sat with his legs crossed. Two little girls stretched out beside him,
arms working and legs pumping. Eunjae hesitated on the threshold,
feeling like he'd stumbled into some kind of New Age aerobics class.

"It's so boring here," whined the older of the two; she looked to be
about five or six. Her leg struck out, aiming for the intern's unprotected
ribs. But Denny was there in a flash, blocking the child's foot with his
hand.

"None of that." He sat back on his heels, solid and immovable
as a boulder. "Sloppiest kick I've ever seen. You can do better." Denny
scooped up a tiny, discarded shoe. He returned this to its owner, then sat
and stared until it was restored to the correct foot. "Here," he said then,
motioning for the girls to stand up. "Let's fix your form. You want one

foot in front, like this. Hands up. Yep, like that. Fighting stance."

The intern was understandably alarmed. "Are you teaching them how to kick me...?"

"Cool it, Hwang. You'll only get kicked if you don't dodge." Denny went back to teaching. "Now, take a step back. Your foot needs to go from here to here. And turn your shoulders a little, put some power into that spin."

"We're spinning?"

"Mr. Police Guy, this is a spinning kick?"

"Right now it's a talking kick," came the reply, stone-faced, no inflection. "You wanna learn or not? I don't have all day. That guy doesn't know how to do this either."

The children gazed up at Eunjae. "Ajussi, you don't know about kicking?" giggled the younger. "Didn't you learn anything in school?"

"It's been a long time, and I didn't go to normal school."

"But where did you go to school?"

"Here. This was my school."

"This isn't a school," the older girl informed him right away. "This is Mommy's company. Do you know Mommy? Her name is Soyeon. She works at this office with Auntie. They make songs and stuff."

"I do know her. And I learned how to make songs here, but we didn't, ah, learn how to kick."

This triggered some loud whispering in Denny's ear. "Ajussi learned how to be pretty."

"And you'll know more about basic combat than he does. Think about that for a second."

Solemnly, the younger girl asked, "Can you teach him, too?"

And this was how Eunjae found himself learning how to deliver a proper windmill kick. When the lesson concluded, he stood at the window with Soyeon's daughters, waiting for the founders to arrive. Behind them, Denny gave Intern Hwang a crash course on keeping small children entertained with minimal resources: dos, don'ts, and key phrases for de-escalation.

Time ticked by and the cheerful patter of the girls' voices melted into the background. Clouds scudded across a sky that couldn't decide whether it wanted to be stormy or serene. Eunjae looked down at the place that had been his home since he was fourteen years old. The lounge boasted a panoramic view of the Emerald Entertainment complex. Comprising three separate buildings, only one had been around when the members of Apollo were recruited.

We helped them build this, he thought to himself. The second group to debut under Emerald, and the first boy group the label ever launched, Apollo had been there for every step of the agency's growth so far. But those days were done. Soon there would be parts of Emerald's history that Apollo never touched.

Finally, the founders arrived in a swirl of expensive perfume. The girls went to their mother as soon as they saw her. "Dad's waiting for you in the parking garage," Soyeon said, "so grab your backpacks and get going. I'll see you when I get home." She kissed each of them on the cheek. "Thanks for being so good today. I think you had some help, but everybody needs help sometimes."

"You need to help the pretty ajussi."

"Mommy, how come you didn't teach him more?" they heard the eldest complain, even as Soyeon led her out to the hall. "He needs to know lots of other stuff, too. Like, you gotta hit with your heel and not your toes. And you never do the spin with your eyes closed!"

She provided a brief demonstration. Denny saluted her.

"We kick to stay safe from bad people. That's what the police guy taught us."

"The police guy...?" murmured Haewon, listening to this exchange. Meanwhile, Eunjae took a seat, grappling with a renewed sense of foreboding. Why had they called him here? What did they need to say, and why couldn't it be said later, at a meeting that was important enough to upend multiple schedules? It couldn't possibly be good. He knew this for a fact when Soyeon asked Denny to stay as well.

"Me?"

"Yes, please." While Denny sat down next to Eunjae, Soyeon set her laptop on the coffee table. "I'm sorry you had to wait. Our last meeting went too long, and of course it's been crazy at home, too. I had to bring the girls with me today. Thanks for being so patient with them."

She pulled up a file. Haewon took over in the stiff, detached tone she always used with Eunjae and his brothers nowadays. "Prism should be in touch very soon. We've cleared everything on our end and Zenith is done reviewing the terms as well. Wise of you to request image management from a third party, but your choice was a surprise. They're known for being very... strict."

"We're aware of that," Eunjae answered politely. "Prism gets the job done. That's what we've heard from their past clients."

"Oh, they do. At any cost."

Soyeon shot her a quelling look. "We wanted to talk to you about the second season of *Sunshine 24/7*. As we discussed when you signed the provisional, the episodes were ordered shortly after the first season was released. But then they had all those strikes in Hollywood, and now there's a new production company attached. You remember all of this, right?"

Eunjae did remember. "I thought plans for that second season were on hold until we've finalized the new contracts with Zenith."

"Not anymore. In addition to a new production company, there's a new director on board. He'd been following the headlines about Apollo all summer, reading everything he could find about you and the Han family. How they took you in when you missed your flight, and the way they helped you... find the courage to fight your contract."

Soyeon swiveled the laptop screen so that they could see it clearly. "They've decided on some major changes. Since part of the premise involves surprising the members, we really shouldn't be giving you a preview, but I think it would be best to avoid any more surprises between us."

Surprises? Eunjae leaned forward, studying the screen. There was a photo on display: an old-fashioned American diner, flanked by palm trees, oddly familiar.

"Because he thought the story was so heartwarming, this new director proposed restructuring the show around all of the members working at a restaurant, just like you did. Originally, they had Apollo trying out a new job every twenty-four hours. Now it will be one job at a twenty-four-hour diner."

They clicked to the next slide. Now there was a sign lit up in curling blue neon letters: *Sunshine Diner*.

Denny's head snapped up. The concept on the screen bore an eerie similarity to Wanna Waffle, from the signage to the lettering, even the palm trees wrapped in string lights. Although the door wasn't orange, the overall impression was a close match.

In the corner was a prototype title card. *Sunshine 24/7*, Eunjae read to himself, stomach churning. *Apollo At Your Service*.

"They've scouted a location already. You'll be filming near Los Angeles for eight weeks. Since you're signed to the provisional contract until the end of November, we've reached an agreement with Zenith to split the costs for PR management during filming." Haewon crossed one ankle over the other. "It would benefit all parties if this went smoothly. Assuming everything goes well, the transfer and new contracts would be finalized in December."

Soyeon had noticed the look on Eunjae's face. She drew a breath, then exhaled slowly. Turning to Denny, she said, "The producers want you to join the main cast. You'd be on the show as both Apollo's manager and the restaurant manager. They'll be sending an offer within a day or two. If you don't have an agent, you might want to get one."

Denny stared at her, arms crossed, sunglasses slipping down his nose. "Me? Are you serious?"

"Just you," Haewon emphasized. "The producers pitched a concept that included the whole family, but we had to object. So did Zenith. We have to consider Apollo's image, especially after what happened this summer."

Here, she pinned Eunjae with a cool, calculating stare. "Your manager's sister is very pretty, isn't she? Best to keep her off the project. And just to be safe, no contact until this deal goes through. We'll be monitoring to make sure all members comply. You know how the fans can be."

4

"WE'RE CLOSING SOON," JEANNIE whispered, clinging to Jiyeon's arm behind the counter. "Why won't they leave? I played the Closing Countdown and everything. I did it just like the boss wrote in the giant binder with the Standard Operating Procedures. I was on protocol, and for what?"

Jiyeon gave the cash drawer a firm shove, listening for the harsh, metallic click that meant it was properly shut and wouldn't spring open again five minutes later. "Maybe they're almost done," she replied. "Let's give it until 8:00, okay?"

"Okay." Jeannie untied her orange apron, flinging it around her neck in a move she'd inherited straight from Denny. Then she scowled at the dining room at large, also very much like Denny. "I'm just annoyed. What's the use of Standard Operating Procedures when people won't operate, like... standardly?"

"Standardly?"

"You know what I mean! That's a real word, and don't play the dunce card with me, only I can play the dunce card, that's *my* strategy—"

"I promise I'll go over there and talk to them at 8:00, if they're still here. I won't keep you even one second later, and you can skip groceries if you want. Same for tomorrow night." Wanna Waffle had been closed on Mondays ever since Denny's departure. They'd extended weekend hours to help make up for it.

"You're not going anywhere near them," gasped Jeannie, mortified. "Those are Sunshines, the feral kind. They might try to bite you, and then I'd have to bite them, and that's the last thing I want to do when I've been working for twelve hours. I'm exhausted! I don't have the stamina!"

"Pretty sure your shifts are always six hours long, Jeannie."

"And it felt like double because we were so busy! Saturdays and Sundays were always busy, but now they're worse. I'm blaming Apollo."

Jiyeon zipped the cash envelope and didn't argue. It was fair to credit Apollo, and the subsequent media coverage, for the surge in customers. All summer, fans had descended upon Wanna Waffle in droves, crowding in to see the place where their idols had broken free of Emerald Entertainment. The restaurant was now an indelible part of Apollo's history.

While the initial furor had died down, Sunshines still arrived on pilgrimage with surprising regularity. They swarmed over the booths and tables, took photos of every plate and mug and potted plant. They posed in the parking lot outside the shop with photo cards in decorated cases, clutching light sticks, their arms full of Apollo merchandise. Some even arrived in outfits carefully curated to match what their favorite member had worn at one point or another. The more meticulous fans sought to sit in the same spots and order the same waffles, right down to the toppings.

Although Jeannie was quick to label them as feral, Jiyeon thought tonight's Sunshines were pretty mild. None of them had tried to approach her, for starters. She'd had her share of Apollo devotees desperate to wring Emma Han for information. These girls had attempted a few sly glances in her direction, easy enough to deflect. Small mercies.

In many ways, Wanna Waffle was nowhere near equipped for such an influx of customers. The pace had never been so hectic, the work never so relentless. Still, she didn't mind. There was a time when Wanna Waffle stood empty most days, and Jiyeon remembered it too well. Even on the most beautiful California mornings, when sunlight drenched the dining room in a wash of mellow gold, there had been something very bleak about it. The view from behind this counter hadn't always been reassuring.

Needs people, her sister Janie used to say, chewing gum and pushing an embroidery needle through the cuff of a sweater draped over her lap. *That's what's missing.*

Years had passed. Jiyeon was much older now, so it shocked her every time that same flare of irritation blazed up inside her chest. Sure, they needed people. They needed lots of people to make the restaurant less of a failure, that much was obvious. And in her eyes, it would be a failure for everyone in the family. Not just for their parents, whose money had gone into the walls and floors, into benches with tattered upholstery and a brand new sign to hang above the door. This failure would belong to all of them. The thought had been unbearable.

It used to make her crazy that her parents had made this investment, but it made Jiyeon even crazier that Janie could sit there, perched on her stool at the register, filling the petals of a flower with one neat stitch after another. How could her sister see a problem and feel no compulsion to fix it? But Janie was Janie, in the end, and Jiyeon was Jiyeon. She no longer needed this reminder from her parents every day of her life. And Wanna Waffle hadn't failed. Wanna Waffle was still here.

Still here, bursting with life. The shop felt so small, outpaced by its own growth. Reminded of the task she'd set aside when it came time to close up, Jiyeon leaned against the scrubbed countertop and traced the bounds of the dining room, eyeballing measurements. She ran aground on the same conclusion. "I've been thinking about what Dad said," she said to Jeannie, "and there's just no way. We couldn't fit more tables in here if we tried. We'd be at capacity, too."

Jeannie paused in the middle of refilling napkin holders. "God, I'm so glad. That's the best thing you've told me all week." She tore open another package, then whisked out the exact amount of napkins needed, no more and no less, with a practiced flick of the wrist. "I don't want more tables. More tables means more work for me. And I'm *over*worked okay? I'm *above* capacity."

"Hmm."

"Like, I wasn't built for that level of activity. That's not what I'm good at and I accepted it about myself a long time ago. I'm not like you and Denny. He wants waffle supremacy and you want a haircut palace. You guys are crazy, okay? You make me so tired. What's next? Another Wanna Waffle? I can't."

"If only," said Jiyeon, choosing not to comment on the haircut palace. "Denny's not interested in expanding, you know that. And if we did open another branch, he'd call it Wanna Waffle 2."

Jeannie dropped some napkins, aghast. "You can't let him do that. Forget about the salon, you need to come up with a better name than Wanna Waffle 2." She poked Jiyeon in the cheek. "If you guys open another restaurant, you'll make more money. I'll retire early and you can support me."

"One restaurant is hard enough to manage. I love this place, but I'm giving it back when Denny gets home." Jiyeon eyed the parking spaces in front of the restaurant. "We could look into outdoor seating. It might be doable." She took a pen from the jar next to Denny's gong, intending to scribble a note about permits and city requirements on the back of her hand.

"You don't have to write on yourself anymore," said Jeannie, clucking her tongue. "Just put it in your Notes app. Remember? You're here in the space age with us now?"

"Oh. Yeah, you're right." Jiyeon regarded her phone with a wariness that was deeply ingrained. She knew that it made sense to switch to an actual smartphone again, but her heart kicked up its pace when the phone was in her hand, and not necessarily in a good way.

She felt ridiculous. Most people thought nothing of their phones, which were more like appendages nowadays, integral to so many aspects of life. Shiny and new, Jiyeon's was an even flashier model than the one she'd urged Eunjae to borrow when he first arrived; he'd wanted to keep the original, out of what Denny called 'maudlin sentimentality.' So she'd gotten another, albeit reluctantly. Video calls, nicer photos, a staggering catalog of apps for every purpose under the sun — it offered these things, and more.

Jiyeon didn't want more. Against her own practical nature, she still found herself staring at this phone and craving *less*.

She typed out her thoughts on a potential patio, then checked her messages. Still nothing from Eunjae. She responded to a few tags on the Wanna Waffle account, careful not to stray into Emma's territory. Jiyeon avoided that old account, as a rule, and maintained a policy of keeping the notifications turned off. She never opened anything, no matter who it was from.

"Yeonnie," her mother called from the kitchen. "Hey, where's your dad, huh? Gotta go soon. Still need groceries for tomorrow."

Jiyeon peered through their main window, past the strokes of Evan's latest artwork on the glass. The sky had darkened to violet. Her father stood just outside the entrance, framed by palm trees marching in a row along the street. Their slender trunks swayed with the breeze as Joey made small talk with some ladies from Sunday night mahjong, not to be confused with the more dramatic ensemble from Thursday night mahjong. "He's with the Bright Valley bus," she told Lizzie, "helping them load up."

"And he's yapping," Jeannie chimed in. "Yap, yap, yap."

"Well, go tell him no more yaps. This guy! It's 7:55 already!"

Jeannie bounced over to relay this message, ponytail swinging. One of the ladies shot a pointed glance at the Sunshines leaving with their Apollo plushies and photo cards. The shop's regulars had grown increasingly discomfited by the wave of 'outsiders.' They complained that Wanna Waffle was crowded now, that their cozy brunch spot just wasn't the same anymore.

It wasn't the same. Jiyeon couldn't argue with that. But was it so wrong to make Sunshines feel welcome here? For the most part, they weren't any trouble.

The trilling of the shop's landline cut through her thoughts. "Wanna Waffle," she said into the receiver, her brain still making calculations. There was no response to her greeting. The line crackled and went dead.

Weird. Wrong number, maybe. Or a spam call. Jiyeon forgot about it within seconds, what with Lizzie emerging from the kitchen to ask about a ride back from her haircut later that week. "You should call Gloria, tell her you're coming," her mother went on. "Let somebody else cut your hair, yeah? Take a break."

"I just trimmed it myself last month."

Lizzie waved a dishtowel at her. "That boy is coming home and you don't want to look nice?"

"So you're saying I should make an effort?" Jiyeon asked, laughing. "And anyway, that boy needs a haircut more than I do."

"Ask Ryan if he thinks she needs to make an effort," teased Jeannie. "Bet he says nope."

"He's smart. Knows the right answer." Lizzie watched as the trio of Sunshines made their exit, still recording as they went. Then she bustled to the door and flipped the sign from OPEN to CLOSED. "Only joking! Pretty with no work, just like Mom." In Korean, she added, "But I'm not joking about taking a break, Yeonnie. You're working too much. And don't give up just because you couldn't get the place you wanted. Go tour some more, you'll find something else you like."

"I'll take a break when Denny's back from Seoul."

She wasn't giving up. Why did everyone act like she'd abandoned her own goals? Was that really fair of them when her to-do list was a million miles long? Keep the shop going, sell Denny on building a patio, pacify the grouchy regulars. Jiyeon was also supposed to pretend she *wasn't* crazy about a guy she found outside her family's restaurant. Otherwise, his career might go up in flames. And hadn't her own career gone up in flames? Didn't she put it to the torch herself?

Jiyeon stopped to hang her apron on its hook in the pantry. Life would balance out soon. There would be time to breathe, time to get back to the goals she'd set aside. They'd figure out what to do next. Things would go back to normal.

Normal was possible, right?

From the group chat shared by all nine members of Apollo

Nicky: 6 minutes late!

Nicky: Where is he? I expect Jess to be late, but not Ari

Jesse: omg why u only care abt the clock when u trying to murder us

Jesse: sorry we were late for the DEATH PARTY hyung

Jesse: sorry we didn't want to be PUNCTUAL about dying

Jesse: sorry we luv being ALIVE

Nicky: Hear me out… what if we crank the dance break up to 2x

Nicky: Then you'll really be living

Jesse: waaaaaaaaaaahhhhhhhhhh

Jungwoo: Ari, run while you still can.

Namgyu: ha! don't say that, I'll cry if ari runs away again…

Max: Where IS hyung?

Max: And why does it have to be a medley?

Max: We can never do just 1 song at these award things, it makes me insane

Jungwoo: Don't look at me. It wasn't my decision

Max: Yeah, but it was your idea

Max: And it's a goddamn stupid one, which is why I thought of you first

Kei: What a surprise, because you never think of him. You're not obsessed. Ha ha ha.

Max: That shit had Park Jungwoo written all over it

Max: Shut up Keiichi

Jesse: omg u guys should stop fighting

Jesse: what if the PR people read this chat

Jungwoo: That's true. Prism will probably request access.

Jungwoo: They'll be allowed to review almost everything we do and say.

Kei: And now they're coming with us to CA.

Jesse: i'm so scared tho bc everybody says prism is soooo mean

Jesse: why did we have to pick the scariest PR group ever

Max: Jesse for fuck's sake don't be dumb

Max: You'd rather have Zenith PR? Or Emerald?

Max: The agencies would just be looking out for themselves

Max: Hyung was right when he said we should hire someone neutral

Jesse: ari's a lawyer omg

Nicky: Isn't it so funny that Max hates corporations now

Nicky: He's still mad the Zenith rep said he should break up w Hazel

Nicky: Excuse me! That's true love!

Jungwoo: Is it?

Namgyu: awwwww!!!!!!

Max: (*7x angry face emojis*)

Jesse: fuck right off hyung!!!

Jesse: there, u don't have to say it bc I said it for u

Jesse: and anyway everybody has a luv story now and i'm soooooo sick of it

Jesse: first it was ari and now max

Jesse: or was it max first n then ari

Jesse: idk i'm OVERWHELMED

Nicky: It was Ari first

Nicky: Oh no, I missed my flight and I have amnesia!

Jungwoo: Geez, guys.

Nicky: Let me stay here! I'm just a sad K-pop man!

Jungwoo: No! Come back with me! wE'rE bEsT fRiEnDs

Jungwoo: That wasn't me… he took my phone…

Jungwoo: How do his thumbs move that fast…

Jesse: omgomgomg and then the captain

Jesse: RARRR WE CAN'T HARBOR FUGITIVES FROM

    THE LAW

Nicky: But daddy I love him!

Max: S

Max: T

Max: F

Max: U

Kei: Surprise! I hate it here!

Jesse: LOL LOL LOL LOL

Namgyu: awwwwww!!! but does anybody want something from the vending machine

Jungwoo: Is it the good vending machine?

Nicky: Who's paying?

Nicky: International Bank of Kazuhiko?

Kei: Actually… yes.

Nicky: OoOoOOOooHhhHHhh

Namgyu: ha! zuzu-hyung is the nicest brother, right? he's acting like a zombie for now but that's okay, he's just feeling so super sad. and when he's not sad anymore he'll remember about the money and yell at us. aww, i'll be so glad when that happens.

Max: Fuck this, I'm going up to find hyung

Kei: Another surprise! Ha ha ha.

Max: Why are you laughing like that? What a freak

Jesse: LOL LOL LOL LOL

Namgyu: but what if ari ran away again because they said he can't be with

Namgyu: haha!! oh man I almost typed it here!!!

Jungwoo: Not a reason to run. There's ways around that.

Max: You would know

Max: (*7x eyeroll emojis*)

Nicky: Quit talking and let Gyu clean out the vending machine

Nicky: Focus, Hong Namgyu

Nicky: It's a game

Jaehwan: ?????????

Jaehwan: It's not a game!!!!! Give the wallet back and go downstairs!!!!!

5

AFTER HOURS, THE EMERALD lobby lost its aura of frenetic activity. The lights were dimmed and the main entrance locked. In the lower levels, some trainees might still be taking lessons, and the studios could be busy at any time of the day or night. But in this part of the agency's domain, business had concluded.

Eunjae trudged past the security guard on duty, keeping his head down, eyes on an email. It was from his younger brother, Ezra, just three lines long. The last was a question: *When will you be back in LA?* He read without comprehending, feet shuffling along on autopilot. There were a lot of questions hanging in the air. At least he still knew the answer to that one. The filming news had thrown a number of plans into disarray, but he could still go home.

Behind the reception desk, voices rose and fell. Did anyone know of a good, last-minute birthday present? Was it still raining out there? Everyday, normal concerns. Perhaps that was why Eunjae only felt worse after overhearing the conversation. He'd love to trade his own concerns for the everyday, normal variety.

And just to be safe, no contact until this deal goes through. We'll be monitoring to make sure all members comply. You know how the fans can be. Every time he remembered that conversation with the founders, and the conversation he'd need to have with Jiyeon, Eunjae found his thoughts falling into a familiar pattern. It wouldn't be so hard, running away from here. To slip through the doors and blend in with the stream of commuters on the sidewalk, borne away on a tide of strangers. He could buy a ticket online, board the plane, and leave all of this behind. But it only seemed easy on the surface.

There was no future in running away. Eunjae rounded the corner and waited for the elevator, composing and deleting entire speeches in his head. Soon, he'd have to tell Jiyeon everything. Worse, he couldn't even tell her in person.

He was sick of being so far away.

"Excuse me," Eunjae heard someone call out, along with the tread of stiff leather loafers on the lobby floor. The remaining receptionist on duty beckoned to him from the other side of the desk. She must be new; he didn't recognize her face.

"I'm so sorry to bother you. You're Ari, right? From Apollo? I know your manager said he wanted to handle these calls personally, but he didn't answer when I tried his cell." She glanced at the phone, where a tiny red light flashed above a button labeled HOLD. "I'd keep trying, but this lady sounds so upset. She won't stop asking for you. What should I tell her?"

A terrible clarity took hold. *Your manager said he wanted to handle these calls personally.* Just yesterday, Eunjae had watched Denny dealing with this same issue. He knew now, without a doubt, that it would be the same person waiting impatiently on the line.

She won't stop asking for you.

"It's okay," said Eunjae. "I'll talk to her. You should go."

"Are you sure? Manager Han told us—"

"Don't worry. Your family's waiting, right? I overheard, sorry."

The receptionist bowed, peppering Eunjae with further apologies as she gathered her things. He noticed all of this, and made the appropriate responses, but it was as though someone else acted in the scene while he watched from far, far away.

Eunjae brought the phone to his ear. "Mum," he said, dully. The word felt wrong, like a note sung off-key.

She preferred acting to singing, but Leila had a lovely voice, clear and cold as a winter's day. His mother could deliver any line with the musicality of flowing water. And when she was angry, her words took on the weight and pressure of water, as well — a freezing river, unhurried but inexorable.

"Finally," said Leila. "I've gotten so tired of calling and calling and calling. Did you know I've been trying since June? As soon as I heard the news, I was on the phone. And I can't count how many emails I've sent. I've even mailed letters, Ari. The slow way. How can it be so difficult to speak to my own son?" A hollow laugh. "It's unbelievable."

"If this is about Ezra, you can leave it to the school like we agreed. They know how to contact me directly."

"Your brother? He's fine. For now, at least. Ask me again when you've finished ruining your career and Blackridge sends Ezra home for good. I doubt it will take much longer. The tuition there is no joke, my love."

"He won't have to leave Blackridge. I wouldn't let that happen."

More laughter, joyless and sharp-edged. "When will you wake up?" Leila asked. "You can't keep pretending that everything will work out. Zenith thinks you're damaged goods. Why else would they drag their feet like this? The other boy is dating, so what? It's you. You're the one they don't want."

"That's fine. I don't regret what I did."

"You don't even understand what you did. Stop playing games and let me fix this before it's too late. They don't even know the whole story yet. It'll take just one tabloid reporting that you've thrown it all away for some girl in California—"

A bolt of bright scarlet lanced through Eunjae's head, tinting his vision, slashing his composure to shreds. But he never heard the rest of what Leila had to say, nor did he ever have the chance to respond. Cool fingers pried the phone from his grasp. The call came to an abrupt end.

"It's alright," said another voice he knew. "I've got him. Oh, were you about to leave for the day? Go ahead. Thanks for working so hard."

Eunjae looked up. Red faded, reverting to the lobby's pale neutrals and lush, saturated greens. Clicking heels announced the receptionist's departure, leaving him with someone unexpected: Jaehwan, cropped hair hidden under a baseball cap, his jacket speckled with raindrops. So he hadn't imagined it. His brother was here, and not just on a screen, or as the disembodied voice of Eunjae's conscience.

The world righted itself. "Hyung? But how? I didn't think we'd see you before we left."

"I can't stay long," Jaehwan admitted, "but I had to be here. Won't have another chance for a while." A smile softened the contours of his face. He slung an arm around Eunjae and guided him back to the elevator. "It's good to see you, Ari."

6

T HE ELEVATOR MADE ITS descent. Jaehwan watched the display flashing overhead, from L1 to B1 and then to B2. "Sorry to interrupt, by the way," he said. "Can't have you throwing a phone at the wall. Wouldn't be a good look."

"Sorry, hyung." Haltingly, he explained that it was Leila who called, and that Denny must have blocked her past attempts at getting in touch. "I haven't talked to her in years. I wasn't ready for it."

They stepped out when the doors opened on B3. Jaehwan kept his arm around Eunjae's shoulders, hanging a right instead of continuing down the long hall. "That wasn't your mom on the phone. I'm your mom, and I'm standing right next to you. Why would I bother calling? You think I've got that kind of time? Use your head, kid."

Eunjae managed a miserable nod. He was grateful for Jaehwan, whose presence was a comfort he'd sorely needed, but Leila's words were now buried in his heart like shards of ice. His mother knew about Jiyeon. All too soon, profound relief gave way to deep, pervasive dread. It sparked an irrational urge to dial Jiyeon's number, to hear her voice on the line and confirm that she was okay, as if Leila might have harmed her already.

At the next juncture, his brother mentioned that he'd ordered dinner. Denny had gone to meet the delivery driver. "He's taking the news better than you," Jaehwan remarked.

"That's usually how it goes," murmured Eunjae. Denny was unshakable.

"Best manager on the planet. I owe him my firstborn child."

"Ah, but wouldn't that be Nicky...?"

Jaehwan chuckled at this. "No returns or exchanges."

These basement floors were a warren of practice rooms and recording studios. Apollo had their own designated space, the door marked with their logo. Since debut, it had served as their second home. They'd eaten here, slept here, triumphed and failed here. It rarely went unoccupied for long. But the next time they worked together, whether in units or with all nine, the members of Apollo would be signed to Zenith. They'd never have a reason to practice here again.

Their last dance practice in this room. It saddened Eunjae to think of it. And yet, the sadness came with another realization: this was just a room. What warmth it held came from the presence of his brothers. It only felt like home because they were here with him.

No other groups were at this end of the hall, tonight. Jaehwan grimaced at the noise level. "Maybe I'll turn around now," he muttered. Scraps of arguments leaked through the gap in the door, all the various conflicts growing more tangled by the second. Interwoven through the racket was Kazu's mournful howling, louder than all the rest. He'd reverted to Japanese, as he often did under stress, and Eunjae thought he could pick out the words *I just want to go hooommmeeeee.*

"Shit," said Jaehwan. "He was supposed to stay in Tokyo all the way through January."

"I hope we can make it to the wedding, at least." Kazu's cousin was getting married in November. She'd invited the whole group. "Now he'll barely get two weeks at home before we start filming."

"So that's settled, then? This is definitely happening?"

"Doesn't seem like we have much of a choice."

In their provisional contract with Emerald, there was a clause stating that the members couldn't be forced to participate in anything; they were free to opt out of scheduled activities if they wished. For a price, of course. Rejecting a gig could be costly, whether it was a few hours on stage, a day on a variety program, or eight weeks filming a show. Brand sponsorships might be withdrawn. In this case, the production company could sue for financial losses incurred when the stars backed out or postponed filming.

"It's not what anyone wanted or expected right now. We've had to deal with worse, though. Two months is better than four. And I know it won't be easy on you or Jiyeon, but that's one less thing for you to worry about. Can you imagine if the agencies let them cast the whole family, including her? You'd get yourself caught after one episode. I'd bet money."

Eunjae was spared from having to admit that Jiyeon didn't even know about the show yet, or the agencies' demands. For this, he could thank the sudden cessation of Kazu's howling. He'd gone silent on the other side of the door.

"Oh, god. That's the sound of him giving up." A tremendous, world-weary sigh. "Let's go scrape Zu off the floor. It'll be just like the good old days."

Jaehwan went striding through the door and was almost immediately overrun. Eunjae had to laugh, hanging back as the others cycled from shock to disbelief to pure elation. It took a while for Apollo's leader to break himself out of the pile of shouting, whooping brothers. At long last, he made it to where Kazu had collapsed in the middle of the room.

"Up you go," said Jaehwan, hoisting him off the floor. "They'll still let you fly out for Mika's wedding. Very few people are stupid enough to get on the wrong side of Tachibana Group, and by that I mean the wrong side of your aunt."

Excitement fizzled out into a collective shudder. Kazu's aunt was terrifying.

"Filming wraps in November," Jaehwan continued in his most soothing tone. "You get to be home for Christmas this year."

"You don't know that for sure, Hwannie. You don't know anything for sure. Nobody does. Life is the worst."

"You're the worst. Thought you were supposed to be the leader right now."

"I quit. I need to go home. I missed my mom's birthday again."

"Yeah, and who ran away from home in the first place? Wasn't that you? Came all the way to Seoul to be a teen father—"

"Not *my* father," said Kei, under his breath.

Nicky lounged on the bench beside Kazu. "Oooh, not anybody else's father either, right? I didn't miss any scandals? You know I hate to miss a scandal."

"Nicky."

"What? Hear me out, leader-nim. He could've had a fling or something. Teenagers do that."

Jungwoo hid behind his notebook. Eunjae longed to do the same. "Oh my gosh," said Jesse. "Ohhhh my gossshhhh—"

"Awww! Hyung really was that young before, I forgot he was a teenager long ago." Namgyu patted Kazu on the head. "It was just so long ago, though. Nobody's brain can remember that far."

Jaehwan squeezed his eyes shut, summoning patience from some ethereal plane. Then he glared at the lot of them. "Missing one. Where's Max?"

"Here. Found him wandering around upstairs."

Denny had entered the room with a level of stealth more commonly attributed to cat burglars and assassins. Behind him, Max spotted Jaehwan and attempted to bolt. This attempt failed. While the others clamored over the bags containing their dinner, Eunjae tried to remember the telltale signs of cardiac arrest. How did Denny manage to sneak up on him so often?

"Ryan." A pair of chopsticks passed back and forth across his field of vision. He looked down to find a plate under his nose, loaded with food. Denny had a drink for him, too. "Eat," came the gruff command. "You're running on empty."

He had no appetite, but Eunjae did as he was told. In his head, he worked on how to properly apologize for the myriad ways in which his fame complicated the lives of those around him. Was there anything that it couldn't ruin?

"Hey," said Denny, reading his mind. "Quit blaming yourself. You don't get to take credit for every catastrophe. I'm the one who should be sorry, yeah? Yeonnie told me you don't talk to Leila. I was supposed to have that handled."

In a rush, Eunjae said, "It's okay. That's... I mean, she's my mum. She should be my problem and nobody else's."

"Nah. She should figure out what I mean when I say 'by appointment only.'" Denny confiscated Jesse's cup before he could trip and spill its contents on an unsuspecting Jungwoo. "It's my job to screen your calls. I'm your manager until the end of November."

"You're my friend," said Eunjae. "A really good one. Thanks, Den."

A grunt. Translated into words, it meant something along the lines of, "You're welcome." But then he also went on to say, "You know that nice lady who raised you? We should look for her. See how she's doing."

"Miss Vivi?" Her name came with a rush of memory, images bound up in songs and stories, in the scent of lemon soap. Just like always, it hurt to think of her. It hurt less, though, and in a different way.

"Bet I could track her down. Just say when."

Jaehwan clapped his hands, calling the room to attention. "One last dance practice," he announced. "Let's make it count."

Thunderous applause. "Shine bright!" Jesse yelled.

"SHINE BRIGHT!"

Kazu's face crumpled again. "Shine bright," he echoed, sniffling into Eunjae's shoulder.

"Here's what's happening: you'll go shoot the second season for eight weeks. We're negotiating for reasonable hours and time off in November for the wedding in Tokyo. Cameras in common areas only. If we can swing it, those stop rolling by 10:00pm. No guarantees, though." He rubbed at his temple. "Just keep your heads down. Do what Prism tells you to do. We hired them to help us, so let them do their thing."

"Yeah, Max. Do what Prism tells you to do. Break up with Hazel and give her back to Jungwoo so we can all live in peace—"

"Why the fuck should I break up with her just because they want me to? It's my life."

"Don't break up with her, then," snapped Kei. "Do whatever you want. Just don't drag the rest of us into the mess with you." With a clatter of cutlery, he added, "You too, Ari. They want you to stay away from Emma-noona, so listen to them. It's just for two months. Put up with it."

Jungwoo murmured that a workaround was more than possible. He offered the words as reassurance, but Eunjae stared down at his plate, not trusting himself to speak.

"Keiichi, be nice," Namgyu said, appalled. "It's just too sad. I love them so much. They belong together."

"We belong to our fans." Jaehwan issued this reminder with gentleness, even a measure of regret, but his words bore the honed edge of a knife. "They got us this far. They've believed in us all this time. We promised them we'd stay together, and we will. We'll make that happen no matter what."

Notifications

Today

7

"I'll be right there, honey. This phone never rings until I've got someone in the chair."

"I'm fine," Jiyeon called back, tucking the phone away. "Don't worry about me."

At Gloria's, Jiyeon was always eight years old again. Time began evaporating as soon as she walked in. She'd imagine the years drifting to the floor, clipped away with all her split ends. Then the elapsed decades would be swept aside, along with an inch or two of Jiyeon's hair, and she'd leave the salon feeling so much younger. Lighter, too. Brand new.

She wasn't supposed to get a haircut today. In fact, she came here specifically to give her mom a ride back to Ivy Lane, nothing more. But of course Gloria and Angie weren't going to be satisfied with that. It had been a long while since she came for a visit. Hence, the interrogation.

"How old is he?" asked Miss Gloria, sipping at her afternoon Diet Coke from the gas station down the street. "This new guy."

"We're the same age, Auntie."

Gloria allowed this to percolate for a moment. The answer seemed to have met her approval, because she moved on to the next question.

"And he's from around here?"

"Sort of. San Bernardino. That's where his family lives."

At almost the exact same moment, Jiyeon's mother piped up with, "No, no. Australia!" Confused looks all around. Then, in the spirit of clarification, Lizzie added, "But right now, in Seoul. Just for a short time. Coming back soon!"

"San Bernardino," Jiyeon said again, cutting a meaningful glance to her left. Lizzie sat under the dryer with a novel she absolutely wasn't reading, ankles crossed, not noticing that she'd said a tad too much.

"Well, that means I don't know him," Gloria exclaimed from the chair on Jiyeon's right. "And you didn't even bring him to meet me!"

"Don't mind her, sweet girl. She only retired from cutting hair. Still meddling full time, as you can see." This came from Gloria's daughter, Angie, who had returned from booking an appointment over the phone. She smiled at Jiyeon in the mirror, switching out a comb for the scissors in her apron pocket. "You met this guy at the restaurant?"

"Yeah. He was in town for his sister's wedding."

"Lucky, then." Angie trimmed another layer, judging the length with a practiced eye. "Sounds like he came in for waffles and won the lottery instead."

"Oh, very lucky. And so lost! The amnesia—"

"The amnesia," Jiyeon hastened to say, "is something Mom saw in a drama. Have you seen that one? It's called *I Loved You*."

Angie nodded, recognizing the title instantly. What followed was a merciful reprieve from the topic of Jiyeon's love life. She enjoyed ten whole minutes to regroup while the other three discussed amnesiac corporate heirs, tragic deaths, and carousels on the beach. It was a much-needed break. Answering questions about Eunjae was stressful, and since the salon was empty, its proprietors had plenty of time to wring all the gossip out of her.

She'd never meant to fall out of touch with Gloria and Angie. When Jiyeon did have a day off, like today, she'd find herself too exhausted to get through more than a few chores or errands, whatever needed to get done. The social call and inquisition were long overdue. And she'd missed this place, too. It remained one of her favorite places in the world.

Gloria's salon was in a strip mall a few blocks from Ivy Lane. For as long as Jiyeon could remember, it stood sandwiched between a bakery on the left and a rotating selection of retail ventures on the right. When she was a child, that side sold electronics, a sign for TV repairs permanently mounted in the window. Now it was a boutique selling novelty soap. But G & A Salon was still the same, down to the potted palm out front. Four-year-old Denny had named it Polly for reasons he refused to divulge. Although it wasn't the same plant from back then, the name hadn't changed. Everyone just kept calling it Polly.

She loved being here. If Eunjae planned to keep the same haircut until he turned eighty, then Jiyeon planned to get her hair cut at the same salon until she turned eighty.

On the topic of Eunjae, she hadn't heard from him since very late last night. He wasn't usually so quiet. But she did know that they'd had a surprise visit from Jaehwan, plus the flurry of preparations before they left for Bangkok. She'd wait to ask how things were going. In the meantime, her break was over. "Tell me his name again," prompted Gloria. "Your dad told me, but you know my brain these days."

"Ryan," Jiyeon replied, having rehearsed for that one. She frowned a little at her reflection, swathed in a black nylon cape from the neck down, most of her wet hair twisted up in alligator clips. That Joey Han. She'd need to have another talk with him at dinner later, and then again at every dinner, forever. What else had her father been telling people?

Confirmed: neither of her parents could keep a secret to save their lives.

As if on cue, Lizzie chimed in. "Ryan Kim! That's his name." At least she hadn't blurted out the actual name. Jiyeon made up her mind to just take what she could get.

"There it is! Ryan! That's it. I knew it started with an R." Gloria relaxed into her own chair, sun-browned face sporting more freckles than ever. She seemed smaller, too. More than a decade had passed since Jiyeon outpaced her in height, but this was different. It was a reminder that time and its relentless current slowed for no one. Not even Gloria, larger than life for as long as Jiyeon could remember.

Angie's scissors made a satisfying *snick*, cutting another overgrown layer. "And he's been away for a while? This Ryan of yours."

"Uh-huh. For work."

"For work? What kind of work?"

She'd settled on a stock reply for that one as well. "Customer service."

"And he sings!"

"For fun," Jiyeon said, fighting the urge to fidget in her chair. But she couldn't help adding, "He's really good at it."

"Well, that's wonderful." Angie gave Jiyeon's cheek a gentle pinch. "Hey, you know what else Joey said? He told us you'll be opening your own place soon. I was so excited! You were just a tiny thing, the first time you asked how much it costs to buy a salon. You sat right here and told me it was your dream. 'It's the big dream of my life, Auntie Angie.' Gosh, you were the cutest."

They traded smiles in the mirror, and it was so easy to see all her past selves reflected there. Jiyeon was eight, nine, ten, listening to all the aunties chattering while Gloria or Angie cut the split ends out of her hair. She was sixteen, and this was her part-time job: sweeping up after the stylists, running towels through the wash, unboxing product shipments. She was in that first year of cosmetology school, working here whenever she wasn't in class.

She closed her eyes, soothed by the brush gliding through her hair. For the longest time, she'd wanted a place just like this. For the longest time, she'd toiled toward the opposite.

"I thought I found a good spot," she said, "but I missed my chance. I'll look again when life settles down a bit."

"You'll make it happen. No doubt in my mind." Angie unclipped another section. "Ryan's back on Sunday, isn't he? You must be so happy."

"Did my dad tell you that?"

"How'd you guess?"

Jiyeon needed to have such a long chat with that man. "Yeah, Sunday. Denny, too."

"It's been months and Mrs. Le is still talking about seeing your brother on the news," said Angie. "Mentions it every time she comes in. And she asks why the famous girl doesn't work here anymore. Why can't she have the Instagram girl cut her hair? Famous Emma Han. That's what she calls you."

"I think I said two sentences on camera," Jiyeon pointed out, laughing. "Denny had more screen time than I did."

Gloria whistled. "What a story! Just imagine, finding a movie star on the sidewalk like that. I'd marry him on the spot. Take me back fifteen, twenty years—"

"An idol, Mama. The boy they found, he's an idol. A pop star."

"Movie star, pop star, idol star, who cares? I know an opportunity when I see one. If not him, then the other guys. Didn't his band have something like six or seven members? Eight?"

"Nine," said Lizzie. "So many! Very good boys, most of them."

"Most of them?"

"You know which ones I'm saying, Yeonnie!"

"See?" Gloria sang out. "Lots of choices! Marry one of them, then get a big divorce, make some cash."

Angie chose to ignore the bit about big divorces, although she did mouth an apology at Jiyeon. Out loud, she said, "Your brother's the one who found him, right? Dennis Han, adopting an idol off the street. I almost fell off the couch, hon."

8

Y OUR BROTHER'S THE ONE *who found him*. Jiyeon wrestled with a moment of dissonance so strong that it threatened to undermine her composure. This, even though it had been her idea to change the story, to make this crucial revision to the evening when she first met Eunjae.

Retell, reframe. She'd wanted to give the press and the fans and every other prying eye just one less thing to latch onto. There would be no avoiding the speculation, which was logical on top of being inevitable. But if it was Denny who found Eunjae instead of Jiyeon, the story took on a different cast. People jumped to unexpected brotherhood instead of summertime romance. And that was safe, because no one could know the truth.

"An idol," Gloria mused. "That's a tough job. Same for your boyfriend, Miss Emma. Customer service! All day, dealing with crazy people. We get some coming in here now, they want a haircut, then they say they don't like it. 'I want a refund!' How? You want me to give back your hair? Too late! We threw it in the trash!"

Lizzie giggled at this, loud enough to be heard above the dryer's dull roar. Angie rolled her eyes. "And she said that, too. Thankfully the lady thought she was joking."

"I wasn't!"

"I know, Mama."

Gloria clucked her tongue. "I'm too old to be talking to stupid people."

"Our Ryan Kim, so good at that!"

"He's good at talking to stupid people?"

"You know my meaning, Yeonnie! Ryan says nothing and they tell him everything." She crossed one ankle over the other and told Gloria, "When you meet him, you'll see."

Her mother wasn't wrong. However, Jiyeon would be happier if she'd copy Ryan Kim and switch to saying nothing. *Read your book*, she pleaded with Lizzie telepathically. *What if I can't bring him here? What if they have to wait years before they can meet him?* While she didn't think Gloria and Angie would trumpet the truth about Eunjae's identity to the world at large, it felt wrong to burden more people with a secret like this. Besides, the risk increased with every person who knew. The fewer in the loop, the better.

It hurt, though. Jiyeon hadn't anticipated how difficult it would be, keeping quiet about someone who meant this much to her.

She checked her phone. There was a message from Eunjae, asking if he could call.

Almost done, Jiyeon wrote back. *Everything okay?*

I guess? Don't worry. No rush.

Talk had turned to gas prices, grocery prices, the rising cost of rent. The salon needed new flooring and half the pipes were on the fritz. Angie bemoaned the astronomical quotes they'd received from contractors. "I can't decide which is cheaper," she said, unwinding the cord on a hair dryer. "Getting everything fixed? Moving someplace new? Who knows."

Jiyeon forgot about the text she'd been typing to Eunjae. "You'd leave? But you guys have been here forever."

"Well, there's nothing we've built here that we couldn't bring with us," said Miss Gloria. "It's the people, sweetheart. Not so much the place." She pursed her lips. "What a lot of junk we'd have to pack up, though! I think we should stay put. Who cares if it's falling apart? I'm falling apart. We can do it together."

Jingling sleigh bells filled the salon with a burst of unseasonal holiday cheer. Gloria had these tied to the door handle year-round, fastened with a red bow, and now the chiming announced the arrival of another customer. He stood on the threshold beaming at them, cutting an impressive figure in his slate gray suit. Jiyeon turned to look, then just as abruptly turned away, back to the mirror and her own strained expression staring back in the glass.

"Oh!" Angie cried out. "You're here! And Emma's here!" Her face fell. "Oh, no. Okay, let's calm down. Let's just take some deep breaths and figure this out."

Of course her ex-boyfriend would come in for a haircut today, of all days. And of course Arthur would come to this salon, because he'd been coming here for almost as long as Jiyeon.

"You won't make any trouble for my girl, will you, Mr. Hong?" Gloria inquired. "We didn't know she'd be here today. I would've rescheduled you."

Arthur only grinned. "What? 'Course I won't," he replied. "Ouch, Miss Gloria."

"Ouch! That's what you'll say if you make her mad!"

"I'm not mad," said Jiyeon. She bit back a sigh. "Hi, Arthur."

Happiness brightened his face, which wouldn't be out of place in any Korean drama searching for a leading man. He'd grown into the chiseled good looks of an orphan hero, morally upright, stricken with a tragic backstory. Not that Jiyeon could picture Arthur and tragedy on the same page. She'd spent years of her life watching sadness roll right off him, repelled by his radiant positivity.

"Hey, Emmie," he replied, upping the wattage on his grin. "Look at that. I knew I was getting here early for a reason. How's everything? It's been forever!"

"It's been two weeks."

"That was just a text, though. I haven't *seen* you in forever. When's Dee-dubs back from his big adventure?"

Angie's expression turned quizzical. "Dee-dubs…?"

"He means Denny. D for Denny and W for Woosung."

"Yeah," said Arthur, as if this should've been patently obvious from the start. "Dee-dubs."

"Back on Sunday," chirped Lizzie.

"And Ari too, right? Man, I really hope I get to meet him this time—"

Gloria narrowed her eyes at both of them. "Ari? Who's that?"

"A friend. Denny's friend. He's coming for a visit."

It took a second, but Arthur got the hint. "Yeah! Great guy. Can't wait to see him." He angled himself toward Miss Gloria, lowering his voice as if imparting a secret. "Ari's my pen pal."

"Your pen pal." That was the first Jiyeon had ever heard of it. "Really."

"Well, we send emails. Same difference." He went swiping through the calendar app on his phone. "Dinner! Next week, maybe. I'll take Ari to that new place with the giant basket of zucchini fries. It's cool if I borrow him, right? Denny won't flip out? I know they're best buddies and all."

She blinked at this. "Oh, sure."

"Wait," said Arthur, bouncing into the chair next to Lizzie's. "I'm being a jerk. You can come too, Emms. You get along with Ari, right?" Pleased with these arrangements, he moved on without waiting for her to confirm or deny. He chattered with her mother until Gloria returned to the original subject.

"Okay, we met the old guy already," she said, gesturing at Arthur. "When will we meet the new guy? Soon?"

Arthur swiveled back to Jiyeon so fast that there had to have been some danger of whiplash. "New guy?" he exclaimed. "Who?"

A fist rapped on the front window. Gloria waved to the couple who ran the bakery next door, on their way home for dinner. "You could've gotten a big, big divorce from this one," she whispered, pointing at Arthur. "Why didn't you just wait? Marry first, then break up. Didn't I tell you that before?"

Angie shushed her. Jiyeon tried to decide between laughing or crying. Her hair was dry, so she shrugged free of the cape, standing up to shake clipped strands onto the floor. "It's nobody you know, Arthur."

"I might," he argued. "Try me."

"Why? You've been out on dates, haven't you? And I've never been in your business about it."

Primly, Miss Gloria reported that Arthur had, in fact, gone out for drinks with Felicity Wen. She'd heard it from Felicity's mother while they both waited in line at Lowell's. The grocery store: a whirling nexus of Lemon Grove gossip, second only to either of Wanna Waffle's weekly mahjong nights.

Lizzie made a tutting noise. "Felicity Wen! Much younger than you! Why take a baby for drinks? Arthur, you are a very nice boy most of the time—"

"Most of the time? It's not all of the time?"

"Most of the time. Not this time. Our Woosung, he graduated the year before her, eh? Find somebody your own age!"

Jiyeon hugged Angie and then Gloria. She promised to come back for a haircut in six weeks instead of sixteen. Arthur couldn't wheedle her for information anymore, since his own haircut had begun, but he'd texted twice from the chair by the time she reversed out of her parking space. There was another message when she pulled away from Ivy Lane, her mother waving from the front door. Jiyeon dismissed the notifications and called Eunjae from the car as she headed home at last.

He answered on the third ring. "Yeon-ah."

"Hey," she replied. "Can you hear me? I'm driving. You're on speaker."

"I can hear you." A significant pause. "What's wrong?"

"Hmm?"

"Ah, you sounded a little upset..."

"I'm fine," Jiyeon lied. *Not upset, just annoyed.* Her irritation with Arthur wasn't even worth mentioning. "I thought something might be wrong over there, since you wanted to call."

Another pause. "Sort of," said Eunjae, with a sigh. And then he told her about the show.

Sourced from internal correspondence between Prism Strategic Management, Emerald Entertainment, Zenith Media, and production company Studio 77 ahead of filming for the second season of Sunshine 24/7

SUBJECT: Re: Re: Re: Risk Assessment - Emma Han
FROM: xxxx@global.prismstrategies.com
TO: xxxx@emerald-ent.co.kr
CC: xxxx@zenithmedia.co.kr, xxxx@prod.studio77.com
ATTACHMENTS: EH_RISK_ANALYSIS_V3_092123.PDF

Good day,

As requested, please see the attached update to our team's comprehensive risk assessment of Emma Han. This version includes new metrics based on analysis of fan discussion in public forums such as social media and the Star-Connect app from June 2023 to the present. We've taken the liberty of incorporating metrics derived from engagement spikes on Emma's legacy content during recent message testing; see Appendix F for full report.

Summary:

- Subject is Emma Jiyeon Han, hairstylist previously serving celebrity clients, lifestyle/beauty influencer and content creator (@jiye_unnie)

- ~980 followers at present, peaked at ~1.7 million

- Account inactive but not deleted

- High engagement during active years

- Strong visual branding and multimedia storytelling skills

- Proven aptitude for building rapport with core demographic of women aged 18-40

- Personal ties to Apollo members

- Projected risk level of **<u>78-85%</u>**

While the Prism team is sympathetic to valid concerns raised by both agencies, our position remains unchanged. In-depth analysis suggests that ***complete exclusion of Emma Han poses higher risks than controlled inclusion***.

As seen in the aftermath of her interactions with Apollo in June, fans are prone to fill in the blanks with rumors and speculation. When not provided with a structured and plausible story, the public will invent one. Any level of concealment, whether intentional or perceived, is liable to damage the group's image.

Our proposed solution is a proactive reframing of Emma's brand, public persona, and connection to the group through her supervised involvement on the set of *Sunshine 24/7*.

<u>Primary Recommendations</u>:
- Creative consulting role on production team, off-camera, minimal screen time

- Emphasis on professional distance over personal relationships

- Cross-platform rebrand: @jiye_unnie –> @emmajhan

- Pre-approved, curated content only

We are confident that Emma's skills and platform can be leveraged to benefit the group, build trust in the show's authenticity, and boost agency-approved messaging. Your support is appreciated as we work to regulate all narrative arcs which overlap with the Apollo brand, especially at such a crucial junction.

Best,
XXXXXXXXXXXXXXXX

Senior Storytelling Strategist
Entertainment Division
PRISM STRATEGIC MANAGEMENT
+ 82 2-555-XXXX
XXXX@global.prismstrategies.com
www.prismstrategies.com
"Every angle in the best light"

- - - - - - - - -

CONFIDENTIALITY NOTICE: This message may contain sensitive and privileged information. Any unauthorized review, use, copying, and/or distribution is strictly prohibited.

9

DAWN WAS JUST A blue haze on the horizon when Jiyeon clocked in for Thursday's opening shift. In the dining room, shadows settled among the tables and stacks of chairs, steeped in the restaurant's signature aroma of waffles and maple syrup. A pale orange glow peeked through the gaps between window shades. She propped the back door open with a gigantic wooden wedge, provenance unknown. Like so many things at Wanna Waffle, it had been there forever.

As sunrise gilded the sky, she helped her father move a succession of potted plants outside, some grown so large that Joey needed both arms to carry them. "I feel like these are multiplying," Jiyeon mused, watching him lumber out of the restaurant with a fern straight out of the Jurassic era. It seemed even more massive than the last time they did this. Her dad continued humming to himself, setting his cargo on the asphalt with great care. He patted the fern's leaves as though it were a puppy.

"Got a good deal the other day," Joey said. "Orchids on clearance, just forty cents at Lowell's! Not bad, huh? Picked a nice one for Ryan, too. He can put it in his new place. Easy to take care of, orchids. Perfect for beginners."

She smiled at this. "Oh, sure. He'll love it."

Once they'd arranged all the plants in a row, Joey paid a visit to each one, pouring a silver stream of water from a pitcher reserved for this purpose. Jiyeon had no doubt there would be at least three new plants next Saturday. And there would be a fresh argument about what to call them; her dad insisted that each plant deserved a unique name, but Lizzie thought that was overly ambitious. She insisted that they should all just be named Charles. It worked for Jane Austen and it would work for Joey Han.

Coffee grounds, fried dough, damp earth. Jiyeon breathed in the scent of a new day and wondered when these sensory details had become such a bone-deep comfort. Her sixteen-year-old self had loathed getting up before the sun for her obligatory shifts at Wanna Waffle. She'd counted the hours until she could toss that orange apron on a hook and spend the rest of her day elsewhere. Now Jiyeon found herself wanting to stay right here, where everything felt worn and weathered, as familiar as the future was uncertain.

She snapped a picture of the fern for Eunjae. He wouldn't see it right away, late as it was in Seoul right now, but it might cheer him up. He'd been quieter than usual since he called about the show.

By Jiyeon's estimation, things could be a lot worse. *Sunshine 24/7* would film a little over an hour away, in Monroe. Eunjae wouldn't be in another country anymore. And the production team had decided on shooting at a renovated diner rather than turning Wanna Waffle into a stage set. They could carry on with business. It was Denny she worried about. He'd told their parents that he planned to do the show, that he'd stay with Apollo through November as originally agreed, no matter what that entailed. But she knew that this plot twist gnawed at his conscience.

Even as Eunjae felt guilty about Denny being drawn into this situation, Denny felt guilty about being away so long. The shop meant just about everything to him.

Just then, Lizzie poked her head out of the kitchen, whipping up some muffin batter. "Yeonnie, tell me again when your brother will be on TV. Next month?"

"No, that's just when they'll start filming. I don't think anyone can watch the show until next year. January or February, maybe."

Jeannie poked her head out for the express purpose of tattling. "She's talking about it on the phone. I saw the earbuds go in."

"I'm not talking about anything!"

"Better not be," warned Jiyeon. "You could get Denny in trouble."

Morning traffic rolled to a stop on the boulevard. Music poured through someone's car window, heavy on the bass. Taking the plastic pitcher from Joey, Jiyeon circled around to the front of the shop, where a few more plants took pride of place next to the orange door. Once she'd watered these, she went back inside, finally remembering to send that fern photo to Eunjae. That was when Jiyeon noticed the two missed calls from her agent. What could Colette want from her at this hour? They hadn't spoken in months, what with Emma going into sudden retirement.

Actually, this was... a ton of notifications. Her phone kept buzzing. Every time it went off, Jiyeon's fingers itched to toss the thing into the oven and crank the heat as high as it would go. It didn't help that two of the newest messages were from Arthur. And she had an email from someone named Eric at Prism Strategic Management, whatever that was about.

No way did she have time for this right now. There was an endless checklist in her mind: bring out more coffee cups, take down the chairs, an Apollo sticker to scrape off the wall behind Table 6. And she kept finding things to do, a bevy of small tasks that kept her occupied until the shop opened thirty minutes later. Between the morning and lunchtime crowds, it was 2:00 in the afternoon before Jiyeon had a chance to just sit for a second.

She started with Eunjae's text from the airport, saying they were off to Bangkok. Then there was another missed call from Colette and a second email from Prism. "Hold on," she murmured. Wasn't that the name of Apollo's newly hired public relations firm?

The shop's land line went off. Jiyeon answered, but just like the other night, no one was there. This had Jeannie rushing over in a panic. "That's it. We need to tell Denny. Yesterday someone called to confirm he had our address right. Isn't that what a search engine is for? Why are they calling? What if it's a stalker? Is this a Code Blue?"

Movement caught Jiyeon's eye through the dining room window. "It's not a Code Blue," she said, trying to sound as confident and reassuring as possible. And there was something more she wanted to add, but the words evaporated soon after.

There was a boy on the sidewalk outside Wanna Waffle. Words were printed in a band of black across the front of his shirt. Jiyeon could only read the fragments that said -RIDGE and PHYS ED. Unaware that she'd spotted him, the boy pored over his phone, thumb punching the call button. In the background, she heard the shop phone ringing, ringing, ringing. Was he the one who'd been calling recently?

And it couldn't be Eunjae, of course not. Eunjae was taller, had grown into his proportions, and this boy's hair was much shorter. A crew cut, tidy and practical. But the color of their hair was the exact same: golden brown, with natural highlights that bleached to brighter strands of blond after enough time in the sun.

Jiyeon's legs brought her to the door, seemingly of their own accord; she couldn't recall standing up. Through the stained glass panels, the boy's image refracted into shards of color and light. She waited for him to look up from his phone. If she could just see his face, she would know for sure that this wasn't a dream. Would she wake up at any second, feeling foolish?

But when the boy looked up, Jiyeon saw a younger version of Eunjae. This was his brother, here at Wanna Waffle when he should be at his boarding school on the other side of the world. She turned the knob and propped the door open with her foot, feeling like it was June again, feeling like she'd stepped through time. What a disorienting sensation.

The boy jumped a little when he saw Jiyeon. She called to him from the doorway. "Ezra?"

He shied away, just a half step backward, and almost bumped into another figure approaching from the parking lot. The man's hair and eyes were much darker, the set of his shoulders wider, but the familial resemblance was clear: this could only be Eunjae's father, Simon. With a few more years of growing, the teenager would likely match him in height.

"That's her," Ezra mumbled to his dad. He turned to Jiyeon, stuffing both hands into his pockets. "You're my brother's girlfriend, right? We came to see him. Is he here yet?"

10

A POLLO'S ARRIVAL IN BANGKOK unfolded in the usual dizzying blur. Eunjae waved mechanically as security staff herded them past a legion of Sunshines bearing gifts and handmade signs. Then he took refuge in the minibus waiting on the curb, ears ringing, assailed by flashing cameras. While their driver navigated a gauntlet of vibrant, bustling city blocks, Eunjae kept both eyes glued to his phone. How many times had he read and reread these texts from Jiyeon? *Ezra's here*, the first one said. But how could his brother be there? Why?

He needed to call her. First, though, Eunjae had to talk to Ezra. He'd do it as soon as he made it off the bus and into his hotel room. Each additional second spent in traffic felt excruciating. He tensed every time someone honked a horn or roared past them in a thick cloud of exhaust. Max shot him several glances from across the aisle, curiosity morphing into open concern. Denny looked over just once. Judging from his expression, he'd gotten the same news.

Gridlock slowed their progress to a glacial crawl. Eunjae dispatched a terse email to his father and triple-checked the Blackridge academic calendar. Meanwhile, the delays just kept rolling in. Their destination was mired in chaos, fans clogging every pathway to the main entrance. Multiple idol groups like Apollo were staying at this hotel, and although it wasn't supposed to be a known fact among anyone's fans, word had gotten out long before the planes touched down. It seemed as though decades elapsed before things settled down and the room keys were doled out at last.

Eunjae practically sprinted out of the lobby. "Ya, slow down," Kazu admonished him. "What's gotten into this kid?"

"We're supposed to take the stairs to the service elevator on the fifth floor," said Kei, hooking a finger in Eunjae's collar and reeling him back in. "Evasive maneuvers. Weren't you listening when the Captain gave orders?"

"Sorry. I'm just... I have to make a call. It's important."

Kazu jumped to conclusions immediately. "Yikes. Young love."

"Don't smile like that. Creep!"

"What? I think it's cute!" But then the mood collapsed. "Ari's headed home soon. I'm glad he gets to stay there longer than I do." Kazu's voice wobbled. "My mom—"

Jungwoo interrupted this gloom-filled speech. "Watch out. Kei's little fan club is in the building. They're dancing backup for Athena's stage tomorrow night."

Squinting at the teenagers headed their way, Eunjae thought back to some announcements made by Emerald last month. The agency had named the trainees who would debut next year, in the wake of Apollo's departure. "They'll be in one of the new groups, right?"

"Yeah, and they're in love with Keiichi. He's oblivious, of course."

Kei turned his head sharply to the right, catching his admirers off guard. The girls shrieked in unison. Then they spiraled into a bout of frantic greetings, bowing to their seniors as etiquette required. The one with the most composure managed to thank Jungwoo for a song he'd written for their EP. "We really hope they'll let us have that one," she said, pointedly making eye contact with everyone except Kei. "Could you please tell Max-oppa that I have an idea for the English part?"

"Lucie, he went up the stairs before we did. Why didn't you just tell him then?"

"We don't talk to oppa outside the studio."

"His girlfriend's too scary," came the unanimous verdict. "We don't want her to get the wrong idea." And then the trainees excused themselves, scurrying away like their lives depended on it.

"Why couldn't you be girls?" Kazu complained. "I'd rather have daughters. And what's wrong with you, Keiichi? Try smiling next time. It won't kill you."

Kei's expression made it clear that giving out smiles for free was a ludicrous concept, off-camera and outside of work hours. This earned him a scolding that lasted all the way up to the tenth floor.

Eunjae stopped in front of his own room, key card in hand. Even the highest-quality soundproofing often proved no match for the sheer decibel range of Denny's voice; he could hear him in there, deep in conversation.

"Look, that's up to Yeonnie," he was saying in Korean, as Eunjae crept inside. "Obviously I'd be happier if she didn't." He paused to glare at the fancy leather office chair parked at a desk in the corner. It was the kind that swiveled, rolled, and reclined to a hazardous angle. Eunjae expected to find Denny with a screwdriver and four sets of confiscated wheels by tonight at dinner. But that part about Jiyeon... he had to hurry and talk to Ezra. Then he'd call her right after.

He maneuvered his suitcase through the narrow entryway. Denny paced to the window, every step producing a faint tremor. "What? Yeah, of course it'll be okay. It's one bad review. That's not enough to tank the whole restaurant."

At this point, they both heard a theatrical gasp from Jesse in the hallway. "Ohhhhh my gooossshhh. It leaked already? Is it hyung's fault?"

"I resent that," said Nicky. "I've been a perfect angel. I could've gotten Jungwoo to board the wrong plane two different times and I totally didn't. Ask the Chief, he can vouch for me."

"Aww, Jungwoo could've gone on an adventure!"

"Jungwoo can go straight to hell," grumbled Max. "Hyung, are you okay in there? You looked all weird on the bus."

Denny threw the deadbolt. "Alright, keep it moving, Lee. You could go a full hour without Ryan if you put some real effort into it." Then, as Max argued through the door, he motioned for Eunjae to get going. The room had balcony access, so he tiptoed out there, wincing at the immediate blare of traffic from the streets below.

He had Ezra's phone number but couldn't remember the last time they'd actually talked. Christmas, maybe, a year or two ago. Eunjae did the math again, puzzling out time zones. They'd flown out from Brisbane, since Ezra spent school holidays with Simon. Would his brother be awake if he called right now?

But he was just stalling, delaying an uncomfortable task. Bewildered as he was by Ezra's actions, and as vital as it was to learn the motivation behind them, this wasn't a conversation Eunjae wanted to have. It was difficult to avoid blaming himself for what felt like the dozens of different ways he'd fallen short. Why was this the first time they'd be speaking to each other in so long? Why hadn't Eunjae done a better job of keeping up with his brother, of reaching out more frequently? He was older. He should've taken the initiative.

He thought he knew what to expect, and what he'd say, when

his brother picked up. But Ezra's voice came down the line and it was no longer the high, piping voice of a child; it didn't match Eunjae's memories whatsoever. He gripped the balcony rail, stunned by this revelation. He'd listened to his own voice on enough occasions to realize that they sounded very much alike. His brother, his echo.

An echo, but only in the most superficial sense. Ezra had words of his own.

"I tried to ask when you'd be in LA. You didn't write me back. It's not my fault you won't talk to Mum or Dad, either. We're supposed to be your family and you don't tell us anything. They didn't even know you have a girlfriend."

Eunjae had plenty of reasons for not talking to his parents, and now he knew exactly how Leila found out about Jiyeon, but this was hardly the time discuss either topic. "Look, I've had a lot of things come up over the past week. I'm sorry I didn't reply. It doesn't change that you showed up out of the blue. Why? Are you in trouble? Do you need something?"

"I can't come visit you unless I'm in trouble or I need something?"

"No, that's not what I said—"

"I guess Mum was right. She said you'd be mad, and you are."

"Ezra, I'm not—"

But his brother was gone. He'd ended the call.

11

At 6:45 the following evening, Jiyeon pushed her feet into a pair of flip-flops, then hurried downstairs. Her food had been delivered. She kept Denny on the line as she took the steps by twos, all the way down and all the way up again. Busy arguing her case, Jiyeon didn't even look up to admire the clouds shrouding the sky in sweeps of blush and lavender, gauzy as cotton candy.

"Like I said, they're offering more of a consulting role. Not even full-time hours."

"That's still too much," her brother said. "You can't be backstage at the clown convention *and* running the shop *and* starting a new business from scratch all at the same time. Something's gotta give, Yeonnie."

Jiyeon reached the landing. She walked the last few yards to her apartment and let herself back in, plunking the bags down on the counter with a thud. "I could help you. I *should* help you. It's my fault they want you for the main cast, isn't it? You were covering for me. And if I'm on set, I can manage the diner a couple days a week. That gives you time for Wanna Waffle."

"Sure, sure. These yahoos would take care of themselves while I was gone. They'd get along great and nothing would be on fire."

"Emerald staff can be with Apollo on your days off," Jiyeon replied, sorting out the various components of her meal. "Eunjae said they're sending people over."

"Yeah, okay. And does he know about your devil's bargain with Prism?"

"Devil's bargain? Really?"

"You know that's what it is!"

Whatever he wanted to call it, the offer relayed by her agent sounded a lot like the tidiest solution to a number of Jiyeon's problems. They'd proposed a behind-the-scenes role for Emma Han, wanting her help in recreating the atmosphere of Wanna Waffle in an authentic way. She'd be in the background, not part of the main cast. The job did involve some content creation, but her on-camera appearances would be limited to a few interviews.

Most importantly, she could take some of Denny's workload. She had the training and professional experience to sub for him as diner management. Her brother would have more days off, more time at the shop. Jiyeon saw no reason why both of their dreams should be sidelined.

It worked for her. She saw this as a worthwhile risk, but Eunjae wouldn't see it that way. He'd likely reject this plan outright.

"Denny, you can't say anything. Let me talk to him first."

"Why would I mention it? They're working tonight. The last thing I need is Ryan having a mental breakdown on stage. This guy's wearing at least fifty pounds of sequins as it is. He'd go down and stay down."

"So you think I should wait to tell him?"

"I think you shouldn't do this, period," Denny exclaimed. "You were paying attention, right? You know the premise? They want *Apollo* running a diner. That's gotta be the second funniest joke anybody's ever told. The second worst idea anybody's ever had. The most questionable concept imaginable. A disaster on eight pairs of legs, with eight pairs of empty eyes—"

"Let me guess. It's the second funniest and the second worst 'cause my idea took first place."

"Bingo." But in a much more subdued tone, he added, "Look, noona. You definitely shouldn't do it just to help me out. You've picked up enough of my slack."

"Helping you out is one of the few reasons why I'd ever agree to do something like this."

The line went quiet. Jiyeon checked the time, saw that it was 7:00, and told Denny she had to go. It was Friday for her, Saturday for Eunjae. Date night.

She switched out her phone for the laptop waiting on her desk. The call connected, showing the back of Eunjae's head. Nicky could be heard cackling from just beyond the frame. It had to be Nicky. No one else in the group laughed like that.

"Hyung, she asked you to help? This isn't a trick?"

"I've never tricked anybody in my life. That's just paranoia, my son. Wow, the forbidden romance is really getting to you." Nicky waved at Jiyeon on his way out. "One Bangkok breakfast delivered to this dope over here, just like you asked. That'll be three easy payments of $3,999, okay? Wire transfer, hard cash, gold bars—"

Eunjae got up and shut the door. "Sorry. I wasn't expecting Nicky to take over room service."

"I thought he'd come up with something better than room service." Bangkok was a foodie's paradise, and Nicky was Apollo's most adventurous eater. She figured he'd know exactly what to bring back for Eunjae. "He promised to behave. I paid him in gossip."

"From mahjong night?"

"It's our most dramatic night. Thursday though, not Sunday."

Jiyeon pried up the lid on the largest of her takeout containers and savored the ensuing cloud of fragrant steam. Pad Thai from the place two blocks down from Wanna Waffle; he must've asked Denny for a recommendation. Mindful of what her brother had said, she decided not to open with the offer from Prism.

"Found another one," Jiyeon said, holding up the seventh picture he'd hidden in her apartment. A Polaroid had been taped inside her limited edition Apollo calendar. She'd flipped the page from September to October, since the month was winding down, and there it was: a photo of Wanna Waffle's orange door. Her left shoulder was in the frame, and a length of wind-blown hair.

He smiled. "That was a good day."

"October might be my favorite calendar page, by the way."

"Oh, no. What am I doing in that one?"

"You're in a wheat field, wearing the best trench coat I've ever seen. You've got flowers, too. A huge bouquet."

"So that's why it's your new favorite," Eunjae replied, laughing. "The flowers. I just happened to be there."

"No way. It's my favorite 'cause of the puppy."

"There was a puppy?" He paused, sifting through his memories for this particular absurd photo shoot, and then he said, "There *was* a puppy."

"Uh-huh. So you're carrying this big, rustic bouquet and also a Dalmatian. You look like your name might be... Stephen."

"Stephen."

"Yeah. And you're on your way to apologize to some farmer's daughter, or ask for her hand in marriage. Or both."

Another pause. "First the apology, then the proposal?"

"Hmm. First the puppy, then the flowers. You'd have to play the rest by ear."

"Ah. Maybe I'm apologizing for the proposal."

She snorted. "Sorry to bother you, but please marry me."

"I apologize for inconveniencing you with my feelings," Eunjae rattled off in Korean. "I know that I'm still lacking. Even so, I sincerely wish to spend the rest of my life with you. Please look with kindness on my hopes for the future."

Laughing, Jiyeon almost spilled her drink. "What do we call this? A propology?"

"Hey, that's pretty good."

"Your random superpower."

"Don't forget the weird dates," he said, taking the tiniest, most cautious sip from his cup of coffee. "My other specialty."

"Well, I can't complain."

She watched him reach into a paper bag with the air of someone dipping their hand into a basket of writhing snakes. He withdrew that hand almost immediately as tumultuous bickering erupted outside his hotel room door. Jiyeon shook her head. More brothers, of course. Between them, they somehow had so many.

In typical Apollo fashion, the others let themselves in without knocking. "Ari, guess what? You left your key card in our room! It was in Nicky's bag. Haha!"

On the screen, Eunjae mouthed a silent apology. She stifled a sigh and carried on with dinner. Something she'd learned during these months he'd been in Seoul: privacy came at a premium, and that was true whether Eunjae was in the same room or an entirely different country. This might never change.

"Hyung, did you see this shit in the Prism email?" Max caught sight of Jiyeon over his brother's shoulder. "Oh, Emma-noona. Hey."

She raised a curtain of noodles, miming a toast. "Florida Man. Hey."

He gawked at her. Jesse jostled him aside. "I think my rating should be higher," he fretted, plopping into Eunjae's lap. "Doesn't this make me seem boring? Noona, tell me I'm not boring. Like, I'm at least more interesting than Keiichi."

"It was a risk assessment. You want a low rating, not a high one. Idiot!"

"Oh my gosh, he's still soooo mad that his number was higher than Nicky's."

Eunjae leaned sideways to avoid getting elbowed in the eye. "Everyone's number was higher than Nicky's."

"That's how you know this is all bullshit."

Kei rolled his eyes at Max. "Whatever you say, Mr. 92%."

"Aww, but is it true that we won't see you until December?" Namgyu and his mop of lavender hair suddenly monopolized the screen, brows drawn, mouth turned down at the corners. "It's just too awful. Ari should fight them about it. I never fight with anybody, but I'd help him. And we'd win! I just know we would. I'm good at winning."

Jiyeon processed these words. She met Eunjae's panicked gaze. "Until December...? Why would it be that long?"

"Hyung, you didn't tell her yet?"

"Of course he didn't. That's just how he is. Remember when Ari didn't tell us about that clause in our contract?"

"Shut the hell up, Keiichi."

"Oh my gosh. Ohhh myyyy goooosshhhh, noona looks so mad now, she's about to break up with us—"

"Hmm. Yeah, I guess I should've realized I'd be dating all of you."

Jesse's wail shifted to a higher key, evolving from 'police siren' to 'mournful banshee.' Meanwhile, Eunjae grabbed the laptop and ran. He reappeared a moment later. Clamoring voices continued to leak through the hotel room walls.

Jiyeon set her chopsticks down. "Are you sitting in the bathtub?"

"Ah... yeah." Eunjae yanked the shower curtain shut, as if it might provide an additional line of defense. He sagged against the cold porcelain in despair. The directive from both agencies came out in a torrent: they wanted zero contact between Emma Han and any member of Apollo until filming was done and the group signed with Zenith.

"I'm sorry," he said again, hanging his head. "I thought we could talk about it when I got home. And I know this doesn't make it any better, but keeping it from you... that's not what I was trying to do. I just... I'm sorry. I messed up."

She leaned back in her own chair, the meal forgotten, date night disintegrating perhaps beyond salvage. So the agencies wanted her gone, but Prism didn't want her as a free agent. Too dangerous. They'd engineered a compromise.

Her temper flared. Not at Eunjae, because Jiyeon couldn't be angry with him for keeping a secret when she had a few of her own. She understood why he'd been putting it off instead of coming clean. Jiyeon didn't blame him, but the situation triggered her sense of injustice. Why was it so hard? Would it ever just be normal?

Minutes ticked by as they sat together, an ocean and a full day apart. Darkness seeped across the apartment windows like ink diffused in water. The night seemed to expand, its borders encroaching on every pane of glass.

But on the screen, mid-morning sunshine slanted into Eunjae's hotel room. Suddenly the distance felt tangible — no longer a series of numbers or a difference in hours, but a physical and impassable barrier. A divide between one world and another. The unwelcome realization struck fast and lodged deep, fleet as an arrow, accurate to a cruel degree.

Eyes burning, Jiyeon rested her cheek on the tabletop. Eunjae reached for her on reflex. But she was too far away to hold, and this would be the case for another twenty-four hours. It had been like this for months.

In the end, she couldn't bring herself to talk about Prism's offer. Jiyeon kept imagining Eunjae on stage at that awards show, forcing a smile, determined not to ruin the performance. Her fingers went to the elastic looped around her wrist, seeking comfort in the mindless habit of twisting it inside out, then back again.

"You're mad," said Eunjae.

"I'm not. I'm fine. I miss you, though."

He sighed. "You don't even know how much I miss you. I'm not great with words or I'd tell you all about it. But I'll be there tomorrow, okay?"

"Okay," she murmured, closing her eyes. "With flowers and a puppy, right?"

"You have to ask?"

Jiyeon lifted her head. "Kidding! Please don't bring a puppy. I never paid a pet deposit."

"How much is it? Maybe I need to see the lease."

"Oh, goodness." She sat up to find him smiling at her. It was a fragile smile, but he was trying. She could try, too. Jiyeon ran her thumb over a section of elastic that was beginning to fray. "See you tomorrow, Ryan Kim."

"Tomorrow," Eunjae replied, "with flowers. And a puppy."

This video begins with a prime view of the Han family's kitchen floor. The linoleum features a pattern so scuffed and worn that it's difficult to tell if those are curling vines or thin, fluted leaves. But that is the hem of Mrs. Han's long skirt, and when she swings the phone upright, we see Ezra's face taking up the whole screen. His eyes widen. "Um, is that recording?"

"Yes, yes," says Mrs. Han, transferring the phone into his care. She turns it around so that it's her face smiling at us now, a dimple in one cheek like all three of her children. Indicating the precise spot where she'd like Ezra to stand, she tells him, "Right here, okay? Later, when they come in, you stand here and get the video."

She bustles away, but Ezra stays in place for a while. Slowly, he pans to his left, where Evan and Mr. Han have been tasked with hanging a hand-painted banner above the TV. One corner keeps fluttering down. Jeannie supervises from the dining table, by turns laconic cheerleader and whiny critic.

Ezra pans to the right. We glimpse Jiyeon on the couch, legs tucked beneath her, watching the proceedings with amusement. Her phone screen brightens with a notification as Ezra zooms in to capture the words on the banner: *WELCOME HOME, OUR BOYS!*

There's something about this that holds Ezra's attention. He lingers on it for a long beat, conversations flowing around him. Then, Jiyeon says, "Five minutes. They're at the light on Linda Vista."

Mrs. Han flies out of the kitchen, giving orders left and right. Lights wink out in rapid succession. Ezra backs up, wedging himself between a cabinet and a rather magnificent potted ficus. Caught up in the confusion, he bumps into the tree. This video ends and the next one begins.

It's dim, but not too dim, since no one thought to douse the light on the back porch. Jeannie is heard whispering, "Auntie, why are we hiding, though?"

"So we can pretend we're not home."

"But they know we're home. Like, that's why they're coming here and not somewhere else." She goes quiet. "Ugh, I used my brain. You guys need to stop me from doing that so much, it's not good for me. It's affecting my morale."

Mr. Han's reply is muffled, indistinct. Jiyeon moves to Ezra's side in the darkness, turning him so that the camera points at the apartment's back entrance instead. He murmurs a question and she responds, "Hmm. I've just got a feeling."

Sure enough, the glass doors leading to the patio slide open just a crack, allowing a sliver of moonlight to illuminate the gloom. Mrs. Han stifles a shriek as a megalithic figure shoves the blinds aside with a clatter. This giant hefts four pieces of luggage over the threshold in a show of brute strength.

"Unlocked! What are you people doing? That was a classic Red Protocol. Did you learn nothing in the last home invasion drill? Are you even doing the home invasion drills?"

Mr. Han throws his head back and lets out a great, booming guffaw. Jeannie complains that she's off the clock and this is too much. The invader is met by both parents, one laughing, one scolding. Ezra takes a tentative step out of his hiding spot just as someone rushes past him in a blur. He follows, finding a sight line through the vertical blinds left swinging in her wake. This is how he manages to record his brother catching Jiyeon in an embrace that lifts her right off the ground.

She's thrown her arms around him. Eunjae has his face buried in her hair. Even after he sets her down, it seems they will never let go of each other.

Just before the video ends, we see that Denny took all the luggage because Eunjae needed both hands for an enormous bouquet of flowers. Poking out of his duffel bag, we see a stuffed animal purchased at the airport. It's a puppy.

12

EUNJAE COULD OPERATE ON minimal sleep while still retaining nine years' worth of song lyrics in his brain. He'd survived experimental stage outfits, a fan who tried to clip some of his hair with nail scissors, and the time Apollo's mascot nearly shoved him into a plume of fire. On tour, he lived through jet lag so severe that it started to feel tangible, lost sleep layered on his skin in concentric rings. Still, he functioned somehow. Could he manage to catch his own girlfriend alone for even five full minutes, though? No.

So what have you accomplished in life? joked the voice of Invisible Jaehwan, still very much present in his mind on a daily basis. As he did his part to demolish a tray of brownies, Eunjae had to admit that Invisible Jaehwan made a good point there.

Mrs. Han was in the process of loading Jeannie and Evan with at least a week's worth of leftovers. Mr. Han could be found in his recliner, dozing through the nightly news. The apartment's ancient and little-used dishwasher had been pressed into service. Eunjae lingered at the dining table, cocooned in the sound of churning water. Finding time alone with Jiyeon had been next to impossible so far, but the same was true about catching Ezra. It didn't help that, despite traveling all this way, the latter seemed hellbent on avoiding him.

"Just try," said Jiyeon, during a lull in her ongoing argument with Denny. For most of the evening, the siblings had been debating the pros and cons of adding outdoor dining space to Wanna Waffle. They had yet to reach any kind of resolution. "You should talk before your dad comes to pick him up. He came to see you, didn't he? Ezra could've turned us down when we invited him, but he wanted to be here."

Eunjae glanced at the front door. His brother had vanished through it, mumbling that he'd wait for Simon outside. Glumly, he replied, "That's hard to believe."

But he went anyway, shrugging into his jacket and rehearsing what to say. It was late, but the air hummed with muffled strains of music. There was a party still going full swing at the complex across the street. Ezra slouched against a pillar, wrapped in his maroon Blackridge sweatshirt, watching people come and go. He turned when Eunjae called his name.

It was undeniably strange to see each other in person. The last time they met, Apollo was on tour. He'd invited his brother to the Singapore concert. They all went to dinner afterward, Eunjae caught up in the group's usual tangled knot of conversations and quarrels, while Ezra tried to follow along like a spectator at a tennis match. He came alone despite the offer of a second ticket for a friend.

This was his brother, by blood and not by contract. And yet they were strangers to one another, standing three feet and entire universes apart. Eunjae couldn't rid himself of the fear that he'd left it too late. Now Ezra was here and even just having a conversation with him seemed like an insurmountable hurdle. With every breath, he became more certain that he was unequal to the task. Where to begin? How?

Ezra spoke up first. "You shouldn't be out here. Dad's on the way and you hate seeing him."

"I don't care about that," Eunjae replied. "Haven't had a chance to talk to you yet, and now you're about to leave."

"You've been busy with everyone else."

It was a cold night, for this part of California. The sneer on Ezra's face made it feel even colder. Eunjae stepped in front of him, forcing eye contact. "Did you come here just to pick a fight with me? I don't understand."

"I came here to talk to you about the show."

"What do you mean?"

The teenager stared back, perplexed by this reaction. "The show you're filming with Apollo. I'm supposed to be on it, too. They talked to Mum and she wanted to sign the papers already, but I told her to wait until I could ask you about it." Ezra's gaze tracked the sweep of headlights rounding the bend, cruising Ivy Lane in search of a place to park on the curb. "I thought... maybe you wouldn't be okay with it."

"I'm not," Eunjae answered immediately. It was a knee-jerk reaction, a response so obvious that his brain could produce it even in a state of shock. "This can't happen. You're only fourteen."

"Weren't you fourteen when you left?" Now there was something accusatory about his tone. His hands curled into fists, hinting at emotions kept carefully submerged. "Never mind. This is your new life and I'm not part of it."

"That's not true."

His protest made no difference, despite its sincerity. "Don't lie," snapped Ezra. "It's okay if you don't want me here. We just have to get along on camera."

The world came grinding to a halt. "You said she hadn't signed the papers yet."

"She did it today. They wanted an answer."

"Ezra, no." *No, no, no.* The word ricocheted around his skull. This had to be a nightmare. Eunjae would wake up soon, surely.

The next pair of headlights belonged to their father's rental. Eunjae saw Simon at the wheel and wanted to drag him out of there, make him answer for this mess, but the impulse died fast. What would that accomplish? His dad had never opposed Leila in anything. If she wanted Ezra on the show, Simon wouldn't be the one to stop her.

He heard the passenger door slam shut. "Mum said we're coming back in two weeks," his brother said, rolling the window down partway. "Guess I'll see you then."

They left. Eunjae stumbled into the apartment, head spinning. He had no notion of how much time passed before Jiyeon found him there, standing in the entryway, one second away from unblocking his mother's phone number. He needed to call her. This couldn't be allowed to continue.

Jiyeon was at his side in a flash. "What happened? What's wrong?" Then she noticed the name on his phone screen, grabbed his hand, and rushed him into the bedroom she once shared with Janie.

In the dark, Eunjae panicked as history repeated itself. She'd done this on the night they first met. Was she about to lock them in again? This was going to get him killed. His brain filled with horrific scenes involving Denny and Mr. Han chasing him into the street, one of them swinging Jiyeon's trusty softball bat from high school. Mrs. Han would aim that deluxe annotated Jane Austen omnibus directly at his face.

"We can't keep doing this," said Eunjae, dropping his voice to a whisper.

Light flooded the room and its pair of twin beds, the high school mementos, Janie's travel souvenirs. The boxes he'd shipped from Seoul were piled next to the bookshelf. "Doing what?" Jiyeon asked him. Eunjae struggled to reply. His problems receded on an ebb tide. She was here. He was home.

Her hair was an inch or two shorter. His had grown far too long. It wasn't summer anymore, and they'd spent so much time apart that the feel of Jiyeon's hand in his was something new and novel. And yet, it felt just the same. Like a puzzle piece slotted into place, like a habit so ingrained that he couldn't remember forming it. Every thought slid right out of his head. Eunjae flipped the light switch. Then he kissed her the way he couldn't, with everyone else watching earlier — flush against the door, her fingers curled in the collar of his shirt.

"When you said we can't keep doing this," she murmured, breathless, "is that what you meant?"

Right, his life was actually in mortal danger. "Ah, no."

"Okay. 'Cause there's a door like this at my place, too."

Something had to be off with the central heating. Eunjae reflected on the number of occasions when this particular room had felt like the warmest one in the apartment. Right now, for instance.

Forcing himself to get a grip, he recounted the conversation with Ezra. Jiyeon listened without interrupting, but she was furious long before he finished. "Why would Leila sign off on this? He's so young." She answered her own question a beat later. "Well, I guess that's never stopped her before."

"She's punishing me. I know she is. It's not about Ezra at all."

Her fingertips grazed his jaw. "Hey," Jiyeon said, gently. "It'll be okay. Whatever happens, Ezra's not doing this alone. He has you."

"Yeah," he replied, "for all the good that'll do him."

"Don't say that. He couldn't find a better brother if he tried.

You're like a professional brother, and you sing a little. We could get you business cards."

She said it so confidently. Eunjae found himself laughing in spite of everything that seemed to be going wrong. "Might be a bad idea. Turns out I know how to be everyone else's brother, but I don't know how to be his."

Jiyeon tipped her head sideways, considering. Her earrings caught the light: tiny red flowers with rubies for petals, peeking through strands of wavy hair. "That's okay," she answered. "You can learn."

He could learn. A simple, indisputable truth. She had such a gift for changing how he saw himself, for illuminating the path ahead with just three small words.

"What about your mom, though? Is she really coming back with him?"

Eunjae managed a miserable nod. "That's what he told me."

"Then I need to be there with you," said Jiyeon. "They offered me a spot on the production team. I'll tell my agent to accept."

October

13

J IYEON TOOK ANOTHER SIP of coffee and watched her boyfriend sign autographs in a grocery store parking lot. This was an odd way to start her day, but the next two months were bound to be odd all around. Maybe she'd look back later and see nothing unusual about this morning. Maybe she'd start to see it as normal.

"Ryan just *had* to get out and take pictures," Jeannie huffed, slouching in the back seat with the grocery bags and a hunted expression. "He just *really* needed to do it, like he's never seen pumpkins before."

"He's seen pumpkins before, but probably not this many."

Like most American grocery store chains, Lowell's transformed into a pumpkin wonderland as soon as the calendar flipped from August to September. Pumpkins spilled out of wooden crates and galvanized metal tubs. They formed a maze leading up to the entrance, arranged in a jumble of sizes, representing every gradation of orange. Some were yellow or white, or even green. This year, they had a whole row of towering sunflowers marching along the back wall. Herbs and potted plants were nestled into every space between.

"Does he know it's even worse inside the store? Pumpkin pie, pumpkin scones, pumpkin ravioli, pumpkin spice popcorn..."

Jiyeon shook her head. "Nope. Didn't wanna risk it."

"Until now. The call of the pumpkins was just too strong." Jeannie sipped at her own drink, a fizzy concoction flavored with yuzu and lavender. "Hope it was worth it. Like, I'd better see Ryan's crazy good pumpkin photography in *National Geographic* or something."

"I'm honestly not sure if he ever made it up there."

They'd agreed that Jeannie would be the one to run in for the last minute groceries, but Jiyeon hadn't been around to see when the ambush happened. She'd embarked on a mission of her own: investigating the waffle place that opened in this shopping center last month. By the time she got back, Eunjae was on the grassy median between two parking spots, mask dangling from one ear. He still had the book he'd planned to read in the car, an old paperback from the *Molly Merriweather* series. Autographs signed, he made polite conversation with a pair of moms pushing shopping carts. The mom on the right gazed at him tearfully, hands clasped to her chest. The baby in the lefthand cart might have seen Jiyeon's desperate dive into the driver's seat. She hoped he was the only witness.

This ended their streak of going undetected. Of course it would happen on their last morning in Lemon Grove, running one more errand for the shop before they made the drive to Monroe. It was supposed to be a quick stop, in and out, then back to Wanna Waffle with blueberries and powdered sugar. If she approached him now, explanations would be in order. Better for the fans to think he'd come here on his own. Better for Prism to be under that impression, too.

"And he just left the car unlocked?" Jeannie groused. "That's a major security flop."

"He locked it. Eunjae has my spare set of keys, remember? You know he's been borrowing the car to practice driving with Denny."

"Still!"

"Still what? Come on, let's see if this is any good." Jiyeon brought out a Styrofoam container full of spoils, setting this on the center console so Jeannie could share. She'd ordered two kinds of waffles from the menu, plus three drinks, and got a good look around while she waited.

The place was nowhere near the size of Wanna Waffle. They had one long table and some bar seating, along with two more tiny tables outside. But everything was crisp and new, the interior designed to maximize every bit of natural light: pale yellow walls, honey-toned wood, shimmering white tile. Above the counter was a digital menu. Orders were taken through self-pay kiosks, eliminating the need for human interaction. They'd covered the back wall with an art piece made of moss, and neon signage spelled out the phrase, "Love you a waffle lot!" You'd be insane not to post about it on social media.

"Don't you dare," Jeannie hissed at her. "Don't even joke about it! Denny can never know you went in there, and he definitely can't find out that we tried the enemy's food! That's how we get banished!" She glanced over her shoulder as though he might be watching their every move. "No, wait. What's the word for when the pope does it?"

Jiyeon unwrapped a plastic fork. "Excommunicated."

"Excommunicated. That's it."

"We should've looked into this place sooner. There are other brunch spots around here, but this is the only one specializing in waffles like ours does. I'll just tell Denny it was research." She paused. "No, reconnaissance."

"You're being super chill for somebody who might have to watch Ryan get abducted by soccer moms."

"He won't get abducted by soccer moms." Jiyeon turned halfway in the driver's seat. "Hey, why are you so grouchy? Are you in another group project for class? Is that the problem?"

"No! I mean, yeah I'm in another group project, I'm always in a horrible group project since my professors hate happiness, but that's not it." Jeannie stabbed at a chunk of waffle, bottom lip wobbling. "Do you have to do the show? Can't you just stay here? Not even Ryan wants you to go up there with him."

"You both know why I'm doing it. I'll help out and Denny can drive down here more often. I wish *you'd* stay here. It'll be rough juggling the show and going to school at the same time, even if you're only doing weekends on set."

"Don't you think I know that?" Jeannie exclaimed. "It's the dumbest thing I've ever signed up for! I'll have to do so much work! But I have to do it, I can't let you go alone." She sniffled a little. "You'd never let me do something like this alone. You'd be really stupid with me. We'd be really stupid together."

"No question. But I won't be alone, Jeannie. I'll be fine."

Swallowing her first mouthful, Jeannie argued, "No way. Apollo doesn't count, they're just boys."

"Don't you collect those cards with their pictures on them?"

"I'm allowed to have a hobby! Evan's been collecting Godzilla action figures since we were three. Is that any better?" More sniffling, paired with reluctant chewing. "Oh my god. This isn't buttermilk, it's cornmeal."

"Uh-huh. The menu said cornmeal waffle with blueberry compote. This other one is their standard buttermilk, though."

"With what? Like what's the topping?"

"Mascarpone cream."

"Mascarpone?" The anguish intensified. "No! It wasn't supposed to be good! I was supposed to hate it! Can you tell the boss I tried really hard to stay loyal? I tried so hard that I ended up eating everything." Around another bite of waffle, she said, "But what choice do I have? I need to eat or I won't have energy. I can't be here for you if I don't have energy, so I have to keep eating. I'm eating because I love you."

Jiyeon wanted to crowd into the back with Jeannie and give her a hug. But the impromptu fan meeting had ended, and here was Eunjae loping to the car, already apologizing before he'd even finished folding his legs into the passenger's side. "I should've stayed in here," he groaned.

A petulant huff from Jeannie's corner. "Yeah! What were you thinking? Come on."

"The light was nice. Didn't want to miss it."

"You always say that! Just wait 'til Denny finds out! But he can never find out, so here's the deal: we won't tell the boss you were seen in the wild, and you won't tell the boss we consorted with the enemy. Got it, Ryan?"

"Consorting with the enemy...?"

"That was research." Jiyeon handed him their third drink, a house-made lavender lemonade. Then she backed out of the parking spot, conscious of the morning ticking away. There was no scenario in which her parents would say their goodbyes in a timely manner.

"Waff.le," said Eunjae, sounding out the shop name printed on the cup. "Wait, am I saying it right? How do you pronounce this? Waff-leh...? Or maybe it's more like waff-lllllll...?"

"It's pronounced 'rigmarole,'" Jiyeon replied, adopting her brother's exact phrasing and disgusted tone. Both passengers agreed that she got it exactly right. "Oh! They have this thing they do for customer loyalty," she went on, cruising through a green light, "and it's an app that tracks reward points. We have loyalty cards, but what about reusable coffee cup sleeves with our logo on it? Cute and simple. You buy one and then the next time you come in, you'll get a discount on your drink. Isn't that a good idea? I think our regulars would love that."

"It's great. And you could do something similar for your own place. You'll have a lot of clients coming back." There was such an undercurrent of pride in Eunjae's voice. She did her best to smile through the wave of guilt. How was she ever going to tell him about the salon? He'd take it so hard.

"You think everything she says is great," Jeannie pointed out, eyes rolling heavenward. "And why shouldn't you? She's the best. Why do you even get to be with her? You're not special or anything, Ryan. Jiyeon took you in off the street, but I was here first."

"That's true. You were here first."

"I was the original charity case, okay? Me."

"Right. Of course."

"They've been helping me forever. So I'm helping them back, forever. I'll keep doing it even though it makes me so tired. Like, I'm agreeing to work double time so I can be on your show, and I'm not making that sacrifice for you. Why would I?"

Eunjae nodded. "Ah, yeah. I'm just some guy."

"Exactly. And I'm not doing it for Jaehwan even though he's my bias and always will be." Jeannie speared another bite of waffle, balancing the container in her lap. "This is a Code Violet. *Again.*"

"Code Violet. Don't think I've heard that one before."

"It's when anybody with the last name 'Han' needs me for something and I cry about it. I cry about it a lot. And then I get up and help them since they've always helped me."

Jiyeon braked for a stop sign. She was the one who'd be crying, at this rate. "So that's what it means. I always wondered."

"That's so nice," said Eunjae, turning in his seat to smile at Jeannie.

She kicked the back of his seat. "Stop that. Don't praise me when I'm just being a brat. That's uncalled for, you're not even playing fair."

"Sorry! I'm really sorry—"

"I need to roll my window down and scream."

Before any screaming could commence, Eunjae resorted to an age-old trick that always worked with his brothers. Pulling the plastic lid off his lemonade, he passed it to Jeannie as a peace offering. "Give it a try. It's pretty good."

"Like I want to drink idol backwash! Backwash is still backwash even when the spit came from someone almost as hot as Jaehwan!" Swiping the lemonade, she added, "I'm not into you, Ryan. That's not why I'm accepting this. Please be aware that I'm not interested."

"Good to know," said Jiyeon, trying not to laugh. "We'd have to talk if you were."

Noises of deep disgust emanated from the back seat. Up front, Eunjae fiddled with the vents. "Isn't it warm? Maybe I'll roll my window down, too."

"Oh, 'cause you need to puke? Same." But Jeannie took a huge gulp anyway, and by the time they parked in the lot behind Wanna Waffle, her tantrums had evaporated along with three quarters of the lemonade. Jeannie never raged for long. She wasn't kidding about her limited energy reserves.

Groceries were stowed, bags loaded into the trunk. Evan came to shake their hands and Jiyeon promised to text Jeannie when they made it to Monroe. There was a second trip to the car; her parents insisted on sending them with enough food for an expedition to the South Pole. Then they had a moment to themselves while Denny loitered in the dining room, forever coming up with 'one last reminder' about running the shop while he was gone.

Eunjae took a picture of the weathered doorstop. "Eight weeks," he said. "Seems like plenty of time for things to go wrong."

"It'll go by fast. We'll be alright." Jiyeon had expected more resistance from Eunjae. He'd certainly objected at first, but his protests didn't last. Maybe he was just too worried about Ezra. Maybe it was the impending arrival of Leila, or the prospect of navigating two months in close proximity to his family after years of separation. She figured it was all of the above.

Jiyeon dropped the car keys into her pocket and hugged him, hard. "I'll kick your mom into next week," she offered, her voice muffled by Eunjae's sweater. It finally got a laugh out of him.

"I'd owe you five more songs."

"Works for me. Then you'd have to stick around."

His hand came to rest against her hair, fingers combing through the waves she'd left loose. "I'm doing that anyway."

14

I T WAS A STRAIGHT shot from Lemon Grove to Monroe. Simple enough for someone with just under two weeks of driving lessons under his belt, according to Denny's estimation. Eunjae was entrusted with the keys and promptly panicked, but the drive was uneventful. He forgot to be nervous behind the wheel.

The season had shifted, and signboards for oranges and pie now trumpeted Halloween festivities. Even so, Monroe remained largely unchanged since that first date with Jiyeon, late in July when summer was still very much alive. These were the same weathered bricks and painted benches, the same tidy squares of lawn and window boxes overflowing with flowers.

He'd greeted this morning with dread. Returning to Monroe felt less dreadful than anticipated, though. Brighter memories flickered in his peripheral vision: blueberry muffins, crates of lemons, a yellow dress. This was a place where they'd been happy. Eunjae felt Jiyeon's hand on his shoulder, just her quiet way of saying that she remembered, too.

"And the baskets?" Denny intoned from the passenger seat. "What's the rationale there?" He pronounced the word *baskets* like it carried the same negative weight as credit card debt, or termites, or arsenic.

Eunjae didn't need to check the rearview mirror to see Jiyeon's reaction. He could feel the force of her glare from the backseat, and she probably looked just like her brother in that moment, arms crossed and spine straight, mouth turned down in exasperation. "What's wrong with the cute baskets? Everyone likes them. We've gotten nothing but compliments."

"We did fine without serving toast triangles in baskets."

"It's a nice touch."

"It's straight up tomfoolery."

"Why not set ourselves apart from other local places that do breakfast and brunch? Eunjae sent me pictures from a few cafes in Seoul, they serve the food in all these fun ways—"

"Ryan put these ideas in your head? You're taking business advice from a singing waiter?"

A deadly silence. "Sorry, what did you just call him?"

"You heard what I said!" The grimace on Denny's face could've been carved with a sculptor's chisel. "That was too much of your own money to spend on nonsense. You needed that for your salon."

"I didn't mind spending it," his sister replied, fuming, "and I've still got enough left."

Eunjae hurried to distract them. "That sign up there. It's where we turn, isn't it? To get to the house?"

Gradually, the town had reverted to a patchwork of fields and citrus groves. Homes were larger here, spaced farther apart. Their sedate faces peeked out between fences and rows of trees. He motioned at a historical marker well on its way to being swallowed by the surrounding greenery. "Langley House," Jiyeon read out loud. "Yeah, that's it."

"Hang a left, Ryan. There should be a gate."

And what a gate it was, towering over them in glorious swirls of wrought iron, flanked by palm trees and wild honeysuckle. Eunjae gazed up at the place where they'd be living until the show wrapped in late November. Langley House presided over a wide, sweeping drive, draped in shreds and tatters of morning mist. He counted two floors and a round tower, all roofed in rosy Spanish tile. There was something watchful about the arched windows and doors. The house radiated an expectant air, as if waiting to decide how it felt about them.

"Wait a second," said Denny. "You'll need the new code."

"You had them change it again?"

Eunjae received a grunt in reply. Meanwhile, the cell signal must have seen drastic improvement. Three phones went off, buzzing like hornets as an influx of messages went through at once. Jiyeon reached for hers and grabbed the wrong device by mistake — her battered flip phone, no sim card, dead battery. This still went with her everywhere despite the fact that her digital life had migrated to the newer phone months ago.

For a few seconds that seemed to stretch forever, Eunjae kept his foot on the brake and watched her hold that old phone in the palm of her hand, running a thumb over a scratch marring the screen. An emotion flickered on her face, there and then swiftly gone. She switched it for the newer model, swiping past a solid wall of notifications on the lock screen. Eunjae wanted to say something, but in the end, he didn't.

The gates swung inward on silent hinges. Vans and pickup trucks jammed the driveway. Crew members had been on site for days, gearing up for filming to begin. The grounds thronged with people carrying crates and cables, ladders and sound booms. Eunjae steered the car down a narrower, unpaved track that branched away from the main drive. Rounding the corner, the back of the house came into view. The walls of this wing were sun-warmed adobe. "Dates back to the late 1870s," Denny informed them. "Everything else was built later on, when the family hit it big."

After the mini history lesson, Eunjae was directed to park under a tree. His terrifying driving instructor only made him redo the job twice. Jiyeon was the first to climb out, protesting Denny's tyranny the whole time.

The sheer size of the property became evident. They glimpsed a tennis court and the high walls of a kitchen garden in the distance. Not far from where they stood, another building crouched beyond a tall, manicured hedge. Much smaller than Langley House, it appeared to be some sort of cottage.

"Look at the light," Eunjae said, helping with the bags. The sun was finally coming through the fog. Transfixed, he took a few photos with his phone. "Wish I had my camera."

"Let's find it. You put it in the duffel bag, right?"

A deafening series of chimes struck the air, startling both of them. The doorbell. Then came footsteps and shouted greetings, the rumble of suitcase wheels on polished floors. "Helloooooo," someone hollered. "We're heeeerrreeee!"

It was Jesse's voice, bounding through the house as though his words had sprouted legs. But it was someone else who came dashing down the hall ahead of him: a ball of wispy white fur, ears unfurled like the wings of a plane, sporting a collar of shiny red leather. Jiyeon tugged on Eunjae's sleeve. "Is that... a dog?"

Denny muttered something unintelligible. A prayer? An oath? Mystified, Eunjae said, "But none of us has a dog."

Afterward, he would struggle to sort out which new arrival slammed into him first. Was it the puppy, flying down the hallway in a fluffy blur? Or was it Jesse, squealing in excitement, a beret balanced on his bright, blond head? Either way, it reminded him of being at the beach, bowled over by a rogue wave.

They had no time to recover. This was a rogue wave made of brothers in flashing sunglasses and ripped jeans, designer coats and Italian leather boots. Namgyu smothered both of them in a bone-crushing hug. Nicky strolled in behind him, walking backwards for some reason, followed by Kazu with a Vuitton bag meant to carry at least two large toddlers securely through TSA. He also had Max in a headlock.

"Those girls will have a full album before we do," Kei complained, his words reverberating in the house's cavernous foyer.

A frowning Jungwoo rolled his suitcase over the threshold. "We've got plenty of songs."

"Would you fucking drop it already, Keiichi? We're producing two tracks for them, not twenty."

"Sit down," Denny commanded, cutting the reunion short. He pointed at the puppy. "And you don't have the security clearance required for this meeting. Out."

Jiyeon held tight to the wriggling bundle in her arms. "I don't think she'll give away any state secrets, Den."

"Irrelevant. It's a historic property, yeah? No pets allowed."

"But she's so cute! Don't you think she's the cutest, Captain?"

Their manager would not be swayed. "All contraband pets will be addressed at a later time."

"Contraband!" Jesse cried out, clapping his hands. "Connie! That's what her name should be!"

"Hey, now. We agreed on her name. It's Uyu."

Jiyeon blinked at Nicky. "Milk? That's what you guys named her?"

"What? When did we give the dog a name?"

"Worst! Zuzu is the worst!"

Lip curling, Kei said, "That's not *my* dog. Leave me out of it."

Denny went into a spate of thunderous throat-clearing. Spying some production assistants through a window, Eunjae took the puppy from Jiyeon, crossed to the door, and poked his head through. It was easy enough to secure a temporary dog-sitter, and without having to offer Namgyu's suggested salary of a big hug and one million dollars that he didn't have. He returned just in time to learn that the day's agenda had been revised to include actual filming.

"They want footage of all members arriving together, including Ryan, so you're getting back in the car with your suitcases. I'm heading down to the diner with noona. Won't be back 'til later tonight. Keep the shenanigans to a minimum," he warned, with an extra glare for Nicky. "You're with Eric for the rest of the day."

"Oooh, Eric!"

"Boss, who's Eric?"

The doorbell went off again. "That's Eric," Denny replied. "Punctual, at least. I'll give him that. Moriyama, there's a box on the coffee table. Make yourself useful."

Kei hopped up, pleased to have been assigned a task. He distributed a stack of training manuals thick enough to be textbooks, each one stamped with a name, the Prism logo, and the company's motto: *EVERY ANGLE IN THE BEST LIGHT*. Eunjae caught Jiyeon staring at her copy. She glanced his way and mouthed the word, "Wow."

But then she was gone, off to the diner with Denny. He heard Eric talking to her at the door just before he came in. Something about a separate meeting to discuss the rebrand. What rebrand?

He'd have to ask her later. If his brothers were a wave crashing to shore, Eric was a meteor reducing the house to a blackened crater. "Apollo," he exclaimed, as though addressing thousands in an arena instead of eight exhausted idols squashed together on a couch. "What an honor. I'm Eric, your dedicated storytelling specialist from Prism Strategic Management. How wonderful to meet in person. So much better than a Zoom call. Don't you agree?"

Namgyu's grin went a bit lopsided. "He's Eric from the computer?" he whispered in Eunjae's ear. "I thought he looked totally different then."

Eunjae nodded. He'd been thinking the same. Eric had a friendly face, pleasant and unremarkable, like someone you'd find in a stock photo. Glasses perched on his nose, thick lenses in tortoiseshell frames. But the Prism rep they'd seen on screen had never worn glasses, and although that guy's name was also Eric, he'd been older. The hair was different. This Eric's hair was darker, smoothed back with copious amounts of gel. Or was it just Eunjae's imagination? There had been so many virtual meetings with Prism. It was all blurring together in his memory.

Eric continued gushing about how thrilled he was to work with them. He did this in a seamless mix of English and Korean, passing out business cards and revealing the Apollo concert tee under his blazer. "Huge Apollo fan here! You have no idea! Now, Prism values the production team's creative integrity, so I won't be on set every day. I'm always here for you guys, though. My whole job is to make sure Apollo gets through this without any issues, media-related or otherwise. Feel free to give me a call, message me on the Prism app, or text my direct number any time you need me."

Kazu scratched his head. "Yikes. There's an app, too?"

"Um, but is it just you?" Jesse ventured. "Is there another Eric?"

"Oh, definitely. We've got a whole team out here for Apollo!"

"And you're all... named Eric...?"

"Yes," came the cheerful response. "That way, we foster an ongoing, unbroken circle of trust, even if it's not a team member you recognize. Prism policy. The name's actually an acronym."

Nicky balanced the training manual on his lap, eyes shining in a way that would've had Jaehwan calling for a straitjacket. "So every letter stands for something, then? I need to know, Eric. I'm here to learn."

"Of course! E-R-I-C: evaluate, reposition, influence, control. Isn't that awesome?"

"Awesome," muttered Max.

"Control," echoed Eunjae.

Their new publicist nodded with such enthusiasm that it made him look like a bobblehead toy. His smile rivaled the noonday sun. "Absolutely. So! Are you ready to get started?"

From the air, Monroe is a tiny storybook town, its streets and houses nestled within a valley dappled green and gold. To the northwest, deep, glittering blue breaks the pattern of vineyards and citrus groves. This is Lake Monroe, dotted with pedal boats, reflecting fluffy clouds that drift across the sky. And farther along the curve of a one-lane road, Langley House awaits, elegant in the morning light.

Text pops up on the screen, styled to look like handwritten notes. We learn that Langley House is an iconic example of Mediterranean Revival architecture. Until 1998, it belonged to the Langley-Trujillo family, early settlers to the area. Passing decades have seen the house become a home, a hospital, and a movie set, by turns. Financed by the Langley citrus fortune, it's a historic property that operates as a vacation rental and event venue.

Palm trees frame a shot of the house's regal exterior. A fountain splashes in the courtyard. Further footage shows off Langley House's eight bedrooms, its garden of heirloom roses, the sprawling grounds that include a pool and tennis court. A sentence unfurls in flowery script: *Isn't this the perfect palace for eight princes to call home?*

These eight princes are ferried to Langley House in an SUV that could be mistaken for a miniature ocean liner. Gravel crunches as the vehicle progresses through the gate and up the driveway. The house is greeted with a chorus of oohs and aahs. And then, rather than rolling to a stop at the entrance, the SUV... keeps going.

A giant, animated exclamation point appears above the car. Inside, the passengers have fallen into uncharacteristic silence. Mouths hang open. Confusion reigns. Jesse looks from the house to the driver, then back to the house, eyes bugging out behind sunglasses with pale blue lenses. The episode cuts to an interview segment in which Jesse announces that this house is haunted, without a doubt. The vibe is so, so creepy. The vibe is *paranormal.*

Back in the SUV, the members murmur amongst themselves. Namgyu is certain this means they're about to go play tennis first, or take a fun guided tour. Kei crosses his arms, a sour, distrustful twist to his mouth. Meanwhile, Kazu relaxes and says, "Oh, we're parking in the back. That's all."

And it seems like Apollo's interim leader may actually be right for once, because the driver does seem to be aiming for the other side of the main building. He steers around the corner... and cruises right past the back door, too.

Max leans forward, alarmed. And in the middle row, wedged between Nicky (chuckling to himself) and Jungwoo (craning his neck for a glimpse of the rose garden), Ari sits back with a heavy sigh. "Oh, no," he mutters. "Please tell me that's not the place."

"What? Where?"

"The little house," Ari answers, pointing straight ahead. "See?" As one, the members lean over to look. Nicky hoots with glee. Kazu assures them that this can't be it.

Alas, this *is* it: a tiny guesthouse taking up a corner of the Langley House gardens, enclosed by a low boxwood hedge. The cottage looks comically small from here, as the SUV rumbles over the last few yards. Namgyu whimpers, "Aww, do they hate us? Is that why they're making us sleep in a shed?"

"Nobody's making you sleep in a shed, my son," Nicky replies. "Don't you even worry about that. I'm here to make sure you sleep outside, that's a promise."

"Awwww!"

"Ya, cut it out. Nobody's sleeping outside."

The driver pulls up in front of a trellis twined in ivy. Kei levels a scathing glare at the back of Kazu's head. "Of course somebody's sleeping outside. There can't possibly be more than one bedroom."

Helpful pop-ups tell us that he's right about the number of bedrooms. Other features include one bathroom, a pull-out couch, and a loft with two narrow beds, but we'll get to all that good stuff later. For now, the members of Apollo disembark, then follow a well-trodden path to the cottage they'll be calling home for the next eight weeks. Birds chirp. Uyu squirms out of Jungwoo's grasp and races ahead, barking madly, a cotton ball on stubby legs. What a stylish red leather collar! Is that Prada?

Every effort has been made to welcome the new tenants. Eight pairs of slides wait in a line, in eight different colors. Yellow roses grace the kitchen counter. Beside the vase is a wooden tray loaded with chocolate chip cookies, freshly baked. But not even the warmest welcome can distract from the reality that this is nowhere near enough space for eight people. The living arrangements will be snug, to say the least.

Max is the last to enter. He looks around and blurts out, "Well, [BLEEP]."

15

THEIR FIRST FULL DAY was long. The second day was even longer, and the third felt interminable. This was the last desperate scramble to get the set camera-ready, every chair and salt shaker and coffee mug arranged to the producers' satisfaction before the soft opening next week. While Apollo recorded interviews and posed for promotional photos, Jiyeon divided her time between prepping the diner... and spending hours sequestered in a trailer with Eric.

On Monday afternoon, they went through her personalized Prism handbook, page by excruciating page. Analysts had also prepared a list of posts across Emma Han's social media platforms, all of which had been deemed 'tangential to the desired narrative arc and updated brand imagery.' Jiyeon archived each of these offending posts by hand, trapped in Eric's office for most of Tuesday morning. Wednesday's meeting began with an overhaul of her various profiles and ended with a lecture on Prism's content approval process. It came with a visual guide printed on shimmering, pearlescent cardstock, like a wedding invitation gone wrong.

She much preferred working at the diner. Consulting for the

production, Jiyeon had pored over countless emails, restaurant supply catalogs, and interior design journals. She'd also seen enough vinyl swatches for one lifetime. But there was a sense of fulfillment in watching everything come together, even if entering Sunshine Diner was like stepping into a strange, alternate reality. Wanna Waffle, but not quite.

Denny was often there as well, training staff, sorting out the logistical details of opening for business. She'd hear her brother in the kitchen and feel a little less homesick. Once, he happened to walk by while the set designer scratched some random initials into a few of the tables; the production wanted that lived-in look, but on short notice. Jiyeon thought she might have to pop Denny's eyeballs back into their sockets afterward.

As expected, she rarely crossed paths with Eunjae. The film crew kept the guys on a packed schedule: a tour of Monroe, a day helping out in the citrus groves, several excursions into the countryside to film ad segments for sponsors. They were recorded playing tennis and splashing in the pool. Eunjae sent messages that Jiyeon waited to read until she was alone, but someone was always hovering nearby, close enough to read over her shoulder. One of the Erics, usually.

Case in point, she had an Eric at her heels all the way out the door on Thursday evening. It was the same Eric they'd met on Sunday. Jiyeon told no one except Eunjae, but this was the Eric she liked the least. He didn't give her the creeps, like Tuesday Eric, and he didn't monologue about algorithms and data like Wednesday Eric, and yet he was still the worst. She couldn't explain why.

"Don't forget," he said, trotting after Jiyeon as she left the diner. "We'll want to make this switch as soon as possible. And I know changing your handle is a big deal, Miss Han, but trust me when I say that this is for the best. Not just for the show, or for Apollo, but for you and your evolving brand."

He called Denny and the Apollo members by their first names, but she was always Miss Han. It was a way of keeping her at a safe remove, a benign and manageable distance.

"The new username is memorable and ultra professional. I think it'll be perfect." Eric grinned. Today his glasses had teal frames to match his teal Prism fleece. "Have a wonderful night, Miss Han. See you tomorrow!"

Jiyeon didn't want to see him tomorrow. She didn't want to see him ever. It was good to finally leave, headlights cleaving the dark on that one-lane road out of Monroe. As soon as she made it through the gate, Jiyeon turned away from the great, shadowy bulk of Langley House and went to find Eunjae.

The guesthouse glowed, string lights dancing gently, every window shining. Jiyeon hunched her shoulders against the cold. It really felt like October out here, the kind of October she'd only seldom experienced in California. It was because of the cold that she endeavored to walk faster. But Jiyeon slowed as she approached the ivy trellis, realizing that someone else was coming down the path: a woman who stepped gingerly from one stone flag to the next, avoiding the slivers of grass between each paver. Her heels would sink into the soft earth if she wasn't careful.

From the tennis court, the thwack of a ball; from the patio, scraps of a discussion conducted in low, cautious murmurs. Apollo almost never interacted at such a controlled volume. Meanwhile, the woman's perfume floated over on the wind, something strong and floral that tickled Jiyeon's nose. She almost sneezed. This didn't happen, but what a story: meeting Leila for the first time and immediately sneezing on her.

Because this was Leila, no question. Jiyeon could see it even in the dark. Eunjae and Ezra had inherited echoes of her beauty. She wore it with ease, fully aware of its power. And it was a beauty that arrested the senses, a beauty that made you stop and stare, but nothing about it invited you to linger. Perhaps that was the most discomfiting part of seeing Leila in the flesh. Not the obvious similarities between mother and son, but the differences between them — the sight of a face Jiyeon loved so well, but devoid of any gentleness or warmth.

It hurt. Did Leila smile like this when she sent him off at the airport, all those years ago?

There was a moment when Jiyeon considered retreating. She had no desire to meet Eunjae's mother, not if she had to feign politeness the entire time, and definitely not at the end of a day that had exhausted her on so many levels. This felt like the universe kicking her while she was down. Her presence had been noticed, though. It was too late to back out now.

Leila extended a hand in greeting, and while her smile didn't warm more than a few degrees, the spark in those eyes was anything but dismissive. It was a look of wordless appraisal, of curiosity and calculation. But it was nothing Jiyeon hadn't endured before, so she clasped Leila's hand in return and didn't flinch.

"What a surprise," said Leila. "I didn't know you'd be here. Ari never mentioned it, of course. How lucky that I ran into you. Are you just visiting?"

She weighed the merits of lying. How might Leila's demeanor change after learning that Jiyeon would be around, involved in the show, for the full duration of filming? She wasn't likely to approve. And yet, it was even less likely that they could avoid each other for long. Ezra was required to have a parent or legal guardian on set, since he was still a minor, and Jiyeon would be forced to interact with Leila many more times in the future. It was inevitable.

"They hired me as a creative consultant, part time," she answered, at last, "and I help my brother with the diner management."

"Oh, I see. Behind the scenes. It makes sense that they'd want to involve you." Leila's brow furrowed. "But Emma, this probably takes up so much of your time. Don't tell me you've put your life on hold for a man. You'll regret that. Take it from me, love."

"I haven't—"

"Good. Never do that, okay? A talented girl like you. So much potential! You can't always let his career be more important than yours." The smile softened. Now it conveyed sympathy and was somehow worse to behold. "Weren't you planning to open your own salon? I heard that's been your dream since you were little."

Jiyeon didn't know how to respond. The lady hasn't said anything malicious, and opening her own salon was certainly the dream she'd chosen for herself in third grade. There was no crime to report, no lie to call out. So why did it feel like she'd been wronged?

A strong gust whistled through the trees. The moon emerged from behind a bank of clouds, thin and sharp as a sickle. Leila squeezed Jiyeon's hand in farewell. "How lovely to meet you. Let's talk longer, next time."

Yes, so lovely. "Goodnight," said Jiyeon. "Take care on the road, it gets pretty dark out here."

"It does. This is truly the back of beyond." Leila turned to add one more thing, moonlight painting the strands of her silver-blonde hair. "Maybe you can help, Emma. I'm sure Ari would rather listen to you than me. He's angry, you see, because he thinks I forced Ezra into doing this. I didn't. His brother wanted to be here." Wry laughter. "Ezra's more like me. He knows a golden opportunity when he sees one."

An opportunity. Was that all? Did Ezra really go to so much effort just for a few guest appearances on Apollo's reality show? Jiyeon couldn't bring herself to believe it.

Footsteps caught her attention. Eunjae cut across the lawn, his gaze flickering from Jiyeon to Leila and then back to Jiyeon again. His mother paused beneath the trellis. Framed by the arch and its tendrils of green vines, she said, "Don't look so horrified, Ari. I didn't tell her any embarrassing stories about you."

He gave a curt nod, coming to stand beside Jiyeon on the path. "Okay."

"I'm so glad I came by. I've been dying to meet Emma. Have a wonderful night, you two."

A minute passed, then two and three, before Leila's rental car vanished around the bend. Eunjae and Jiyeon were long gone by then. There were cameras mounted under the eaves, but none were aimed at the right side of the guesthouse, so that was where they went. "Are you okay?" they asked each other at the same time. Eunjae launched into an apology. Jiyeon insisted that she was fine.

"Are you okay?" she repeated, bringing her hand up to his cheek.

His fingers closed around hers. "I'm okay." And then he pulled her in, held her tight. It had been days since the last hurried embrace. Jiyeon leaned into it with everything she had.

"I should've walked her out," said Eunjae. "Then you wouldn't have met her on your own like that. I'm sorry."

"Not your fault," she replied. "And anyway, I'm fine."

"What did she say to you?"

Ezra's more like me.

Weren't you planning to open your own salon?

But how did Leila even know about that? Somewhere in Emma's posts, maybe? Jiyeon felt for the hair tie on her wrist, worrying at the stitches holding it together. "I think I ruined her night," she said. "She didn't know I'd be here."

Eunjae sighed, sounding defeated already. "It was better when she didn't."

16

E UNJAE AND HIS BROTHERS hadn't lived in such close quarters for a long while. At least four or five years had passed since any of them shared a dorm with more than one other member, and even then, the space was split into separate bedrooms. The older brothers were accustomed to living alone. Needless to say, co-existing in this cottage would take some adjustment.

Or a lot of adjustment, Eunjae thought to himself, waking to a maelstrom of noise. In the kitchen, Kazu had their sole hair dryer blasting like a jet engine. Max and Kei had revived an age-old argument about how many alarms a person should be allowed to have on their phone between 6:00 and 6:30. At what point did this practice go from precautionary measure to full-blown psychological warfare? And Jungwoo needed his toothbrush out of the bathroom, but Namgyu was still in the shower, warbling his way through a favorite ballad.

"Just go in," Nicky bellowed from the patio. "Everybody's seen everybody naked by now. Who cares?"

Frostily, Kei reminded them that the place was rigged with cameras and all of these were rolling. Jungwoo shouted back that the door was locked.

"So pick the lock. Here, want me to do it?"

"Sorry, but why the hell do you know how to pick a lock? Why do I still have to keep asking this question?"

Kazu switched the dryer off. "Quit standing around, we've got less than an hour!"

"You're one to talk when you take forever to get ready."

"Deadbeat dad."

"The worst."

It was enough to justify remaining horizontal for the rest of the day. Eunjae contemplated burrowing into his sleeping bag and waiting for the floor to swallow him whole. Then he wouldn't have to figure out which brother made off with his toothpaste. Nor would he be forced to referee the inevitable wrestling match when Max and Kei reached for the hair dryer at the same time.

He did sit up, though. Jiyeon might have texted him back. It wasn't possible to have a proper conversation in person, not last night and not this morning either. Nor could he call her without being overheard. They'd resorted to messages instead. Eunjae hated communicating like this, as if they were still long distance when Jiyeon was no more than ten minutes away from him at most, but what choice did they have?

Your dad's here too? she'd typed an hour ago. *For how long?*

Until this is over, I guess, Eunjae texted in reply. An airline pilot one year shy of retirement, his father had rearranged his work schedule to join Ezra in California. This was the news his mother brought with her last night.

Jiyeon's response popped up right away. *Is your brother staying with him or Leila?*

Good question. Ezra's riding with us today. I'll have to ask.

The custody agreement between his parents was pretty clear-cut: for most of the year, Ezra lived with their mother in Singapore, where he attended Blackridge as a weekly boarder. He spent his term breaks with Simon in Brisbane and stayed at school or with friends when Leila had business in Sydney. She performed on stage with a theater company several times a year. Maybe his parents would stick to the same pattern here, Ezra shuttling back and forth between them. But did it matter? Was one option any better than the other?

Eunjae drew his legs in before Jungwoo could stumble over them. Waiting for his turn in the bathroom, he'd launched into a lightning round of cleaning. "Oh, you're awake. What do you think of these?" His brother hummed two melodies, varying by a single note. "First or second?"

"Second," said Eunjae.

"Max thinks so, too. And that's not for our next album, by the way," Jungwoo made a point of adding, for the benefit of every camera hidden in the living room. The rights to any songs they wrote during this period could be claimed by Emerald, according to the terms of their contract. But Zenith would expect a comeback from Apollo as soon as possible, ideally before Nicky and Namgyu announced enlistment dates. The group didn't want to risk these new tracks reverting to their former company when the transfer went through.

His phone buzzed. *Speaking of your dad,* Jiyeon said, *he just got here. And I think he's scared of me?*

Just doesn't talk much. I had to get it from somebody

You talk to me a lot, she pointed out. *You must be a fan, kinda.*

Big fan, he typed back, smiling. *So drastic*

Don't be like this when I can't get you back for it

And then she had to go because Eric was calling again. Good

timing; the scuffle over the hair dryer was underway, as if ordained by fate. He squeezed past Max and Kei in order to wash his face and brush his teeth at the kitchen sink. Then, while Kazu braved the task of rousting Jesse out of bed, Eunjae changed into the first few things he pulled out of his suitcase. It didn't really matter what he wore. According to Denny's schedule, they had stylists deciding the wardrobe again today. He added a jacket for the early morning chill and called it good.

"Hyung," said Max, cornering him by the refrigerator. "We need to talk. Don't worry about the cameras. They can't catch anything we're saying."

Eunjae couldn't really catch what Max was saying, either. That had to be the loudest hair dryer in existence. "What did we need to talk about?"

"The way you'd better fix your face if noona walks in while we're working."

"Fix my face...?"

"He means," said Kei, berating him over the dryer's deafening roar, "that you're a terrible actor. You'll be a total weirdo whenever you see her, and that's how you'll get caught. You get caught, Sunshines find out we've got two of you idiots dating, and we lose our deal with Zenith."

"Get off him," barked Max. "Go finish your stupid hair. Hyung, just be normal. You're so obvious. Try harder, that's all I'm saying."

"Try harder to fix my face. Okay."

"Ha! Fix his face! Is that what you just told him?" Namgyu strolled in, shirtless, chugging black coffee out of a travel mug. He tried the English phrase a few times before switching back to Korean. "Fix your face, fix your face. Aww, there's nothing to fix there, Ari."

Nicky popped his head into the cottage. He'd wrangled the dog into a track jacket that matched his own. "Hey, Ari Junior's here."

"Don't call me that," snapped Ezra.

"Ari the Sequel."

"Stop."

"Okay, so Budget Ari—"

Ezra whirled around to confront him, but Nicky had taken off again, hooting with laughter, running another lap around the property with Uyu on her leash. But the name changed yesterday, didn't it? Wasn't she back to being Marshmallow now?

Eunjae held the door open in case his brother wanted to come inside. The kid didn't move an inch. "That's what you're wearing?"

"Ah, yeah. Why?"

"You look like a walking laundry basket," sniffed Ezra, "but whatever."

"They'll have us change when we get there."

A shrug. "Okay."

Since this topic wasn't going anywhere, Eunjae decided to change tack. "I saw the schedule. Did they give you the interview questions in advance?"

"They did. Why?"

"Just wanted to make sure. I asked them if they could. I know you've never done anything like this before."

"It wasn't a big deal. All the questions were pretty boring." Ezra shoved his hands into his pockets. "Mostly they just want to know about you. Story of my life."

He said this with such bitterness that Eunjae took a small step backward, bumping into an incensed Max. He'd heard everything from 'walking laundry basket' onward. It might have ignited the umpteenth brawl of the morning if not for Denny's arrival. He surveyed the scene, colossal and unimpressed, a portent of inescapable doom.

"So," said their manager. "Three fully dressed, three half-dressed, one in a stolen bathrobe, one in a towel. Par for the course."

"Zu counts as half-dressed, right?" mumbled Kei. "Grandpa's not even wearing a shirt under that jacket."

"It's zipped up all the way," Kazu exclaimed in his own defense.

"Should you get a trophy or something?"

"I should get a trophy," whined Jesse. "Why am I awake right now? This can't be legal."

"Just get in the car, Ahn."

"But Captain, can we bring the puppy?"

"Oh my gosh! Oh my gosh can we *please* bring her—"

Denny rejected the notion outright. Then came his requisite speech about appropriate behavior in moving vehicles, similar to the safety demonstration provided by flight attendants. Herding Apollo out of the guesthouse, he warned that none of them would survive a scenario in which he was forced to pull over. No hostages would be taken. They'd enter an era of martial law. Guillotines, Catherine wheels, imprisonment in a tower accessible only by moat — the works.

The ruckus carried on, but in whispers. Somehow it was even more chaotic than bickering at the regular volume. Could Namgyu quit monopolizing the bathroom? Was it truly necessary for him to perform a full drama soundtrack while he was in there? And on that note, could Jungwoo please change the horrible goddamn lyrics he'd added to the one song yesterday? Why was he like this? What kind of fucking monster? But also, could Max refrain from using that kind of language around today's youth? There was an *infant* in the van with them!

Buckling his seatbelt, Ezra muttered, "I get it now. You tried to quit your job so you wouldn't have to live with these losers anymore."

It was like someone punched an invisible mute button. Mouths hung open all around.

"The hell's his problem?" Max complained, breaking the stunned silence.

"Ha! But that's so funny! Extra, extra funny, since I was born a winner. I've never lost at anything in my whole life!"

But Ezra had produced headphones from his backpack, a gigantic, noise-canceling pair with cushioned ear pads and flawless sound. He spent the rest of the drive ignoring them as if his continued existence depended on it, or he might become a loser by breathing the same air.

Eight weeks of this. Eunjae longed to crawl back into his sleeping bag and just stay there.

*A series of videos filmed by **Emma Han** on the set of **Sunshine 24/7: Apollo At Your Service**. Select clips were later approved for use as teaser posts on Apollo's official channels.*

Emma walks through a space outfitted in muted pastels. "Welcome to Sunshine Diner," she says, holding the camera with a practiced hand. Apollo's logo pops up first, outlined in blue neon. Then we see walls hung with posters of crashing surf, towering redwoods, a field of California poppies. But on the wall behind the counter is a gallery featuring doors in an array of shapes and sizes and colors, and one of these is a familiar, beloved orange.

"Guess who took this picture?" Emma asks us. She points to some text on a tiny card, mounted just beneath the frame. It credits the photo to *E. Song.* "That's my favorite one." The photo, or the photographer?

She turns the camera to show the room at a wider angle. There seems to be a plant in every corner, some of these even hanging from the ceiling. Cozy booths are tucked along the perimeter, upholstered in vinyl. Bar stools line a counter with shiny chrome trim. This counter anchors the space, housing the register and an espresso machine, brand new and terribly impressive. The floors are black and white tile, and Emma shares that these were chosen by the owner to match the diner's original look. The place has been around since the mid-1950s.

Next, we overhear an argument between Emma and the owner of a booming voice who absolutely does not want to open the windows due to established security protocols. After a bit of back-and-forth, Emma is told that she can lift the blinds if she wants to, when has she ever listened to him, it's her funeral. So she does, and the glow of an idyllic autumn morning transforms the entire scene. The pastels become soft and luminous. The booths are striped in pale blue, just like a cloudless midsummer sky.

In the video that follows, it's about an hour until call time and the blinds have been drawn again. Jungwoo is wedged into the back booth with Kazu and Jesse. The latter gossips freely as he pretends to study a menu. "And then he was like, 'You tried to run away so you wouldn't have to live with these losers anymore.' I'm not making it up, that's really what he said, hyung. Ask Zuzu. He was there."

Kazu gathers his hair into a bun, messy in just the right way. "I was? When did this happen?"

"Ohhhh my gooossshhh. Woooorrrsstttt."

"I think he's jealous," says Jungwoo, flipping his menu. "That's what we were talking about in the other van."

No context is provided for this snippet of conversation. The three look up when Emma approaches, then attempt to chat with her all at once.

"Noona, is the Captain just bluffing? Will there really be a quiz? I'm amazing at quizzes. That's how I got scouted, you know. I was on a quiz show."

Emma replies, "A quiz show. Huh."

"Sit down for a second," says Kazu, interrupting. He indicates the empty space next to Jungwoo, right across from him. Emma obliges without pausing the video. We're treated to a scenic view featuring Apollo's father figure, so solemn, the picture of parental concern. "What did that woman say to you last night?" he asks her. "Was she rude? You should've called me. I was right there."

Jungwoo laughs out loud. "Don't listen to him. He would've been useless."

"Call someone else," Jesse concurs, eyeing his eldest brother with pure, unfiltered derision. "Oh my gosh, Zu. Like, what would you do if Leila showed up and noona called you? Lay down and play dead or something? You think that lady's scarier than Jaehwan-hyung, you'd be crying, you'd be *paralyzed* with fear—"

A whistle pierces the air. It's Denny, mustering the troops. "Get in here. Mission brief."

"Didn't we already have the mission brief?" This is from Ari, now standing beside the booth with his hand outstretched. He's offering it to Emma, waiting to help her up from the bench, but Jungwoo reaches across and latches on first. Laughter rings out.

"Did you see hyung's face when you did that?"

"Yikes."

There's a grin in Jungwoo's voice. "Oh, sorry. Thought you were here for me."

"Ah, no."

"Woooooowwwwwwww—"

When footage resumes, we've moved to the diner's

gleaming, newly renovated industrial kitchen. Multiple conversations are underway. Kei praises the Captain's decision to have them come in for 'intensive diner boot camp.' Nicky giggles over an email from Prism, tickled by whatever he's found there, while Max is hunched over his phone. He's typing at a furious rate.

Our captain bangs a wooden spoon on the countertop. "First, some housekeeping. As you're all aware, my sister decided to fall for a celebrity paralegal."

"Sorry, what did you just call him?"

"You heard me," Denny retorts, continuing over his sister's protestations and the roar of Apollo members laughing their heads off. "As I was trying to say, it's all hands on deck, no errors, no exceptions. Take this seriously. Sometimes the best place to hide is right in plain sight, but that won't work unless every last clown in this room pitches in at 150%. Don't let Ryan's ill-advised relationship hit the news cycle."

"Ill-advised?"

"Noona, if you're just gonna repeat everything I say like a parrot—"

"Oh, like Miss Gloria's parrot that used to give you nightmares, and then you'd come into my room crying in the middle of the night—"

Nicky applauds, positively alight with joy. "I'll take a large popcorn. Put it on my tab."

"Sit down and find your knitting needles," Denny snaps at him, "or I'll find them for you."

"Oh my gosh—"

"The crew's getting here in less than forty-five minutes and only three of you can handle a griddle without incident. So we'll be working on that, but you need to remember what I've told you."

"Captain! You said that pancakes are inferior to waffles, Captain!"

"And I'm right," says Denny, with a snort. "Subpar texture. Structurally unsound. Poor syrup retention. It's a flawed food on multiple levels, but that's what they put on the menu. What else? Speak up. Don't let Moriyama hog the one lonely brain cell."

"Oooh, about pancakes or dating scandals?"

Jungwoo raises his hand. "Never let the film crew catch them alone."

"Correct. Under threat, converge en masse."

"Me, me!" Jesse squeals. "Run interference! Deflect suspicion with nonsense!"

Emma has forgotten about her phone. The camera's pointed at the floor. "We'll be fine," she insists. "I won't even be here half the time."

"There's the other half of the time," says Ari, with a sigh.

"Nice to see that Ryan's eyes are only 79% empty this morning. Downright refreshing." There's a rush of air, the rustle of fabric; Denny has started tossing aprons at Apollo members. "Yeonnie, listen. You're gonna need all the help you can get. I see nothing wrong with mobilizing these yahoos for the war effort. Think about their skills: singing, dancing, shouting, generating chaos, vapid small talk, minor acrobatics. It's the most efficient use of existing resources, yeah?"

Nicky's knitting needles click and clack. "Chief, don't forget that Max can steal girlfriends. That counts as a skill."

"You can fuck right off, hyung—"

As all semblance of order goes up in smoke, Ari reaches over and cuts the video.

17

S HE'D REGRET IT LATER, but Jiyeon had to ask. "Erin. Is that an acronym, just like Eric?"

Today's Prism lackey had wispy bangs and a long, thin face. Pearl earrings, teal dress, nude pumps. Smiling, she said, "You're so observant, Miss Han. E-R-I-N stands for almost the same thing, except for the last letter, of course."

"Right. What does the N mean?"

Erin smiled, baring teeth that were a dental and orthodontic masterpiece. "Neutralize."

Well, that was pleasant. Jiyeon went back to combing through outfits, perusing the rack labeled 'Emma' with one eye on the clock. She was supposed to film an interview soon. An hour had passed while Erin held forth on the kind of tone and body language that would best align with Emma's low key, minor supporting role. No deviating from the script. No referencing Apollo members by name or hinting at personal ties. The fans were much too suggestible. They could take the smallest detail and run wild with it.

"You should show some emotion, but don't go overboard. You love your brother, you love your family, you love your family's cute little restaurant. Apollo? Fun people. Very talented. If the producers push you for it, you can say the members are sort of like brothers to you."

"Oh, sure. They're like my brothers," said Jiyeon, "except I don't love them."

"Perfect! Such a professional. You'll sail right through this." Erin summoned the stylists. "Okay, we'll do these earrings with the flowers. Her followers will remember those. We should throw them a bone, but let's go with plain black for everything else, like the regular diner staff. Get us more of that by tomorrow."

Jiyeon changed into the clothes that Erin wanted her to wear. She let them plait her hair into Emma's old standby, a braided bun. She still opted for the same style multiple days a week, working at the shop. It was almost possible to believe that this was an ordinary shift. Here she was, dressed for work. Unfortunately, having to answer interview questions ruined the mirage.

She'd just finished when the cameras reoriented themselves, fixed on the main entrance. Jiyeon realized that the producers were directing a new arrival. "Great energy there. I think that'll work, Mr. Hong."

"Oh, it's just Arthur," came the breezy reply. Jiyeon ducked behind a partition. She'd forgotten he was scheduled to come in today.

At the apartment on Ivy Lane, in the bedroom she shared with Janie, there was a corkboard covered in pictures from high school. These were crowded with the youthful faces of old friends. In the largest, Jiyeon had her eyes closed, laughing. The joke was forgotten, the moment lost, but the boy beside her remained frozen forever in a dramatic pose: down on one knee, brandishing a fake sword. Arthur Hong, hero of the hour. The star, the protagonist, the main character.

And here he was now, polished on the outside, virtually unchanged on the inside. If Jiyeon didn't know him so well, she'd assume that the producers had dressed him to fit the image of 'respectable attorney' before recording his interview. He always looked like this, though. The impeccable tailoring and jubilant expression were just standard Arthur.

He hadn't seen her yet. There was still a chance to put this off a bit longer. But Jiyeon found her escape route blocked by Eunjae, who exited the kitchen at the same time she tried to enter it. He caught her by the shoulders to prevent a collision. The touch was swiftly withdrawn.

"Sorry," said Eunjae. "Didn't want to ruin your clothes." Indicating the pancake batter spilled all over his apron, he added, "I'm kind of a mess right now."

"That's okay. I'm the one who almost ran you over." Were they being overly familiar with each other? Did she have a stupid smile on her face? Jiyeon backed up another step. She said, "You look like a successful diner employee."

"I know," he replied, laughing. "Some of the batter even turned into pancakes."

"See? You're hired."

"Emmie!" Arthur's polished shoes came tapping across the floor at a clip. "Yes! You're here!"

Jiyeon turned to greet him, accepting the inevitable. She felt Eunjae's hand at the small of her back. He'd forgotten himself for a second. "Yeon-ah," he whispered. "Is that Arthur? *My* Arthur?"

"Oh, he's your Arthur now? Really?"

Cameras pivoted in their direction, magnetized to Arthur's every move. "Hang on. Are you...? Have we...?" Arthur dropped his voice, nudging Jiyeon with an elbow. "Emms, is this Ari? *My* Ari?"

"He's your Ari? Since when?"

Her comment was lost in a flurry of exuberant greetings. Eunjae came forward and Arthur grabbed him in a hug. "This is him," he yelled at the top of his lungs. "This is my pen pal!"

Brothers tumbled into the room. Their presence went unnoticed. Arthur and Eunjae were absorbed in conversation, the former yammering away about how exciting it was to meet in person, and wasn't Monroe just a hidden gem, and wow, the bird-watching around here! The lake life! Just excellent!

The cameras ate it up, but Max stepped in front of Jiyeon, convinced that this stranger might trample her by accident. "Who's the fucking Disney prince?"

"That's the lawyer," said Kazu, snapping his fingers. "Right? The guy who helped Ari with the contract?"

Jiyeon was now surrounded by men in pastel diner uniforms. She wondered how they'd managed to elude Denny's watchful eye. "Uh-huh," she answered. "Arthur Hong."

"Ding, ding, ding," said Jesse, giggling. "Yay! Zuzu was right about something!"

"He's a Hong, too? Aww! We need to be best friends!"

Nicky popped up. "Hear me out, Gyu. Cage match, no weapons, last Hong standing. Wouldn't that be a fun game? Wouldn't it be so funny?"

"Shut up," Kei hissed at everyone in general. "Why are you so loud?"

As for Jungwoo, he tapped Jiyeon on the shoulder. "You dated him, didn't you? Before?"

"So what if she did, hyung? Why do you care? What does it matter, that's over now—"

They scrambled when Denny showed up, ordering them back to the perils of new hire training. A producer pulled Jiyeon aside. "Emma, could we see you again around 2:30? Then you and Arthur could interview together. Unless… well, would that be awkward? Given your history."

"It's all good," Arthur answered for her. "We get along fine, no worries."

"Great! I think we'll do a solo interview and then get you in there with Ari once Apollo's done in the kitchen. Okay with you?"

"Yes! Can't wait!"

The producer scurried away. Eunjae said he'd better get going as well. "The boss sent me out to find something and I never came back. Don't remember what it was, anymore. I'm in for it." He went on to apologize for not being able to hang out longer.

"No worries, buddy. I'm out here for the whole weekend. Thought I might as well, since I've never been to Monroe. Heard the farmer's market is epic." Arthur whipped out his phone, swiping to a calendar app. Meetings, appointments, and social events were arranged in color-coded blocks up and down the grid. "Let's see. That's on Saturday. Hey, if you've got a couple hours free, we should go! The stalls stay open until 8:00."

"Ah, I could try. Think we're only filming in the morning."

Pleased as punch, Arthur tried to wrap an arm around Jiyeon. "You too, Emmie. Come with us. It'll be fun."

"Can't, sorry." Sidestepping out of reach, she explained, "I take over for Denny on the weekends."

"Whaaaaat? So I'll end up missing him?"

This was unacceptable. Arthur marched to the kitchen, determined to at least say hi to Dee-dubs. "Oh, quick question. I meant to bring this up when I ran into you at Gloria's, but you were getting a haircut, and then I was getting a haircut, and then the aunties… yeah."

"Sure. What's the question?"

"I just have to know if you changed your mind about that place because of me."

Jiyeon frowned. "That place... what place?"

"The salon. You were thinking of signing a lease, right? In that new shopping center? Your dad told my dad. Then I started worrying that you turned it down just to avoid me, since that street is on my Monday-Wednesday-Friday running route."

Arthur prattled on about his daily jog, the sanctity of his morning routine, and that one time Jiyeon switched gas stations because they bumped into each other there. So dramatic! She heard just a fraction of what he said. The pounding of her pulse was suddenly so loud, even louder than Apollo's raucous laughter in the other room. And up ahead, Eunjae faltered in his steps. He forgot himself again, forgot that the cameras were rolling, turning to Jiyeon with a dozen questions in his eyes.

There had been so many chances to confess. Busy at the shop, she'd missed her shot at that retail space when the leasing agent called in August. Someone else snapped it up within the week. Other units were available, with more square footage, but that wasn't what she wanted. She let it go. Every time she tried, Jiyeon couldn't bear to break this news to Eunjae.

"It didn't work out," she made herself say, because Arthur was still waiting for a response. "That wasn't anything to do with you, though."

"Oh, okay. I feel better. Ari, did you know she wants to open a salon?"

"Yeah," said Eunjae, quietly. "I did know that."

Memories of summer rushed by in reverse. It was September, August, July. It was the second week in June, and they were at Lowell's for the evening grocery run, waiting another five minutes while her dad combed the aisles for steel-cut oats. Eunjae had a map pulled up on his phone. Typically so mindful of maintaining space, he'd never chosen to stand so close to her before. Within seconds, she forgot every item on the shopping list.

See? It wouldn't have the best view, but it faces west. You could watch the sunset.

She'd felt the shift when it happened, like a tremor in the earth, like the first breathless drop on a roller coaster plummeting from the sky. Something had changed.

How stupid of me, Jiyeon remembers thinking. What would she do when he left? Because he would leave, of course. There was no Ryan Kim. He was a story she made up inside her head. His secret would catch up to him eventually, regardless of what it may be. Secrets had a way of doing that.

How stupid of me, she thought to herself now. *Why didn't I just tell him?*

18

THEY FILMED FOR TWELVE hours straight, 7am to 7pm, on opening day. Eunjae learned that he preferred waiting on tables to working the register. Kei discovered a newfound talent for flipping pancakes onto the ceiling, and everyone realized that Jungwoo had more fluency in English than he'd ever let on. Overall, the producers called it a resounding success.

The cast and crew piled into the main house for a celebratory meal. Even then, the cameras kept rolling. The footage was too good to miss: Kazu's gallant offer to pay for dinner but not delivery; the subsequent mix of applause and vehement booing; Nicky using an app to detect ghosts while Jesse cowered in the butler's pantry.

Eunjae willed himself to forget that they were still recording. It wasn't easy. He'd always been slow to adapt to the sensation of being filmed, like the high whine of a mosquito in his ear. Everywhere, the telltale gleam of a lens. Always, the knowledge that every move he made and every word he spoke could be cut and pasted into a story someone else was telling.

I'm sneaking out, said Jiyeon, texting from a different room. Three dots appeared at the bottom of the chat as she typed another message, but then they'd fade as she debated what to say. Eventually, she settled on just one more line: *I'll let you know when I get there.*

Eunjae wanted to cut through the living room, the kitchen, the phalanx of cameras. He wanted to walk outside and catch her before she made the drive back to Lemon Grove. They'd barely spoken since Friday. She'd covered for Denny all weekend, wrapping up staff training before the diner welcomed its first batch of real live customers. Apollo was busy too. There was always something going on. Whether he could see Jiyeon from across the room or they were standing right next to each other, it didn't matter. They were ships in the night. Having a proper, private conversation wasn't possible under current circumstances.

Drive safe, he sent back. It wasn't what Eunjae wanted to tell her. But going out there to say goodbye would draw too much attention, be too difficult to explain. He needed to be Ari right now. Apollo's Ari had no reason to leave his spot on the stairs and chase after Emma Han.

Why didn't she tell him about the salon? This question had plagued him ever since. And yet, didn't it make sense that Jiyeon hadn't said a word? For months, their relationship had revolved around Eunjae's problems, Eunjae's career, Eunjae's family appearing from the ether and imposing themselves on his life. When would she have had a chance to confide in him? Maybe if he'd been close by instead of thousands of miles away. Maybe if they hadn't spent more time apart than they were ever physically together, she would've told him the second it happened.

He should've asked her about it. What was wrong with him?

Eunjae got up, typing as he went. Just one word: *wait.* He knew there was a side door that led directly into the rose garden, and he could reach Jiyeon from there. If he hurried, if she saw his message and delayed leaving for a few minutes more, Eunjae could apologize. He just needed to make it outside without being detected, and his attempt was almost successful. But the conservatory wasn't empty, for a change; Kazu flagged him down, asking if he might lend a hand.

"That dummy Hong Namgyu went and did it again," he grumbled, gesturing at crate after crate of fresh flowers. "I'm done with this kid. I mean, what are we supposed to do with these? I sent him to help pick up dinner, not buy a whole farm stand." Kazu rubbed at the back of his neck, at a loss. "Kept saying Jiyeon loves flowers."

"She does," said Eunjae.

"Good, because there's more in the van. Got a minute? It'll be faster if we're both bringing them in."

Eunjae scanned the makeshift parking lot, just visible over the rose garden's ornate fence. Jiyeon's car wasn't there. He'd sent his message too late.

He'd hesitated too long. Now she'd be gone until Wednesday night, and even talking on the phone was difficult to manage. At almost every hour of the day, Eunjae was surrounded by cameras, brothers, or a combination of the two.

Well, so much for that. Stifling a sigh, he said, "Yeah, no problem. I'll help."

Kazu led him to the van, complaining every step of the way. "He just really, really wanted to go. But I didn't even give him money, Ari. I thought, what would Hwannie do? Step one, he wouldn't send Gyu with the credit card. So I gave it to the intern, right? And how do you think that went?"

"The intern had your card," Eunjae guessed, "but hyung remembered his wallet this time."

"Yeah! And why does he even have a wallet? You know his bank balance is usually zero. I swear he wouldn't know a budget if it punched him in the eye."

They trekked in and out, the stars cold and bright overhead. Midway through, Eunjae's phone went off, rattling with a barrage of new messages. These weren't from Jiyeon, but from Arthur.

>> *Hey! This is so crazy but I met your mom and dad just now!*
>> *We're all at the same hotel!*
>> *And I met your little bro at the diner*
>> *Great kid*
>> *Had tons of questions about my job*
>> *College and the bar exam and stuff*
>> *Maybe he wants to be a lawyer!*
>> *He can be my apprentice*

Eunjae locked the screen. "We should get these in water." The flowers were in galvanized buckets or bundled into paper-wrapped bouquets. He knew they'd fade quickly without tending.

Langley House had two kitchens, one older and one newer. They hauled everything into the nearest, drawing the cameras' attention in the process. Kazu ranted about extravagant spending habits and the folly of purchasing products that weren't even on sale. When interviewed about his latest impulse buy, Namgyu stated simply that money should be spent on whatever gave you the most joy. Why would you hold on to it and be miserable? So silly. Haha!

"Lay off him, Ueda," Denny boomed from across the hall. "He's stimulating the local economy. Shopping small and all that."

"Yeah, leave hyung alone. He's my nicest brother and he's allowed to never have any money if that's what he wants."

"That's right," Nicky drawled, ambling by with his phone on a selfie stick. "Stay broke, Hong Namgyu!"

"Awwww!"

"Oh my gosh. Nicky's on Star-Connect! He's doing a livestream!"

"Idiot. We're not supposed to do that without asking Prism first." Kei stomped out. "I'm telling the Captain."

"Hey, keep it down. I'm trying to see how long it takes for Eric to figure out what I'm doing. Don't you guys want to know if he's worth the money? I'm doing us a favor." Nicky went back to grinning at the thousands and thousands of fans watching his broadcast. "PR hasn't caught me yet. Isn't that so funny?"

Eunjae allowed the noise to wrap around him like a blanket. Brothers locked in debate, brothers laughing at shared jokes— it was a comfort, the soundtrack of his life for well over a decade now. There was so much he didn't know. He could see Ezra on the far side of the living room, noting the easy way he had with strangers, not a shy bone in his body. What else had he inherited from Leila?

At the very least, Eunjae knew what to do with these flowers. He used to watch Miss Vivi take care of the bouquets his mother brought home from performances, holding the stems under running water, cutting at an angle. Later, as he got older, he'd been allowed to help. She'd have the radio going, humming along. *Never forget to do this part,* Vivian used to say. *It helps them last longer. You can't just throw them in water, see? Some extra work gets the job done right. That goes for lots of things in life.*

"Here, Ari," Kazu said, joining him at the sink. "Show me how to do that. Somebody found me another pair of scissors."

"Ah, thanks. It's pretty easy, hyung."

They trimmed flowers side by side, the others coming and going as they pleased. Kazu admonished them for not helping and received all manner of excuses in return. Jungwoo and Max were the only two who didn't make an appearance.

"They're secretly borrowing the piano," Jesse whispered, the next time he dropped by. "We told Eric it's a song they wrote for Emerald, and then we told the Emerald people it's a song they wrote for Mika's wedding, and then we told the Zenith people it's not even a song." Tempestuous sighing. "I don't get how you can keep your big, dark secret all the time, hyung. Are you okay? Is the stress clogging your pores yet?"

Eunjae reached into the bucket at his feet, ready to trim another bunch. Water dripped onto his shoes. "Dark secret...?"

"I hope you and dark-secret-noona stay together forever, it's great since it isn't happening to me, like it's *adorable*, but it's totally not my thing."

Kazu flicked water at him. "Quit running your mouth," he hissed. "There's three Erics here."

Jesse scampered off, whining, Marshmallow running along at his heels. Or were they back to Uyu now? The dog had gone through more names than Apollo had gone through hair colors, collectively. Kazu shook his head as he watched them go. "We're lying to everybody. It's crazy."

"The new agency will want an album right away," Eunjae replied, stripping leaves from a long, green stem. "We wouldn't get any kind of break if Zenith knew how many tracks we've actually finished."

"I know that. And don't get me wrong, I want to go home. I'll lose it if we have to jump straight to promo after this. But it just seems like everything is harder than it has to be, you know? Make the agencies happy, make the publicist happy, make the fans happy. Why's that so hard? And when do we get to be happy? We won't live forever. We should be happy while we can."

Kazu filled a glass pitcher, holding it under the faucet. "Hwannie's right. He always is. And I know we said we'd stay together, but what if we end up hating each other? What if forcing this to work is the reason we fall apart?"

19

"LET ME KNOW WHEN you're done jailing baked goods," said Denny. "It's about time to get started."

Jiyeon looked up, holding a glass pastry dome in one hand. Her brother had interrupted before she could cover some muffins arranged on a wooden platter. These were massive, wrapped in fancy parchment paper, and much too appealing to keep in the regular case.

"I know you think this is stupid, but they'll sell faster. Just watch."

"No doubt," he grunted back at her. "Those suckers will definitely sell. You've trapped them. They can't get away now."

Jiyeon set the dome over the round tray, rolling her eyes. "Denny."

"What? I'm telling you that I get it. There's big money in nonsense. Did you see how much cash these hooligans took home in tips yesterday?"

It was a pretty substantial amount. Jiyeon used the hem of her apron to scrub a fingerprint from the glass. "They won't get to keep any of it, though. It's all going to charity. Nonsense for a good cause."

"You know who could use a good cause? Prism. And then maybe they'd quit redecorating my restaurant with Apollo propaganda."

He wasn't talking about this restaurant. Upon returning to Lemon Grove for her two days off, Jiyeon found the shop papered in life-size posters of Eunjae and his brothers. Sunshines hit the place like a tornado, taking hundreds of photos and videos, driving business through the roof.

Her parents were thrilled, at least at first. The regulars came away more disgruntled than ever. Tuesday's weekly bingo game was delayed by almost an hour. Jiyeon ended up staying later than planned so they wouldn't be understaffed for Waffle Wednesday.

In a perfectly cordial email, Eric had explained that encouraging this level of fan activity at Wanna Waffle was a win for everybody. It gave Sunshines a dedicated place to express their enthusiasm for the group and the forthcoming show without actually turning up on location in Monroe. After all, that was both a safety and privacy hazard. Plus, the shop made more money as a result. Wasn't that great? Mutually beneficial.

Jiyeon understood the logic, but she had to draw the line at replacing Evan's window art with a high-resolution vinyl wrap featuring all nine members. She'd rejected that offer on the spot. Denny would've gone nuclear if he got to it first. Arguably, he was going nuclear anyway.

"I've got Thursday mahjong threatening to move somewhere else, and we've gotten more bad reviews on top of that. The week isn't even done yet."

"We'll have Dad talk to the Thursday aunties," said Jiyeon. "He'll smooth things over. I had Jeannie reply to the reviews, too. One of the couples came back already and gave us another chance."

"You comped the meal?"

"Of course I comped it."

"Good. Fine." Denny surveyed the dining room like it was a

battlefield and he had the unfortunate honor of leading the last, suicidal charge. He tracked the towheaded figure of Jesse, wobbling out of the kitchen with too many trays. "Explain something to me. How's it possible that Ahn can sing and walk at the same time, but talking and walking is too much? What's the math there?"

"Hmm. Fair question."

Under normal circumstances, she'd expect a slow day. Raindrops pearled the windows and thick, gray clouds skulked on the horizon. It was the sort of weather that made people want to stay home. But it would be a full house, Jiyeon knew, because the producers engineered it that way. Scarcely a quarter of the diner's customers were honest-to-goodness civilians who wandered in off the street. The rest was a curated mix of paid extras and specially chosen guests. On the first day of soft launch, the production invited a group of local citrus farmers. Yesterday, it was a busload of ICU and emergency room staff, fresh off the night shift. No fewer than three nurses had cried on Eunjae. Jiyeon missed the whole thing.

Jiyeon missed Eunjae. She missed him all the time, but he was right there, reporting for Denny's mission brief.

When she came back to Langley House, there were flowers waiting in her room on the second floor. The attached note said they were a gift from Apollo, and yet the Polaroid taped to the jug could only be from Eunjae. It was a picture of lemons, stacked into a small pyramid, like a miniature version of the one they'd seen in July. He must've found it at the farmer's market on Saturday, with Arthur.

She turned away, intending to take up her post in the kitchen, but then there was a tug on her sleeve. Eunjae had followed, skipping the rest of Denny's lecture. "Emma," he said, because at least one camera was on them, bearing witness like an unblinking, lidless eye.

Oh, how strange, to hear him use that name. How jarring. But she wasn't Jiyeon here, and he wasn't Eunjae. It would've been dangerous to forget.

"Ari," she replied, doing her best to sound as normal as possible. "Need help with something?"

"Ah, yeah. Do you know if we have any extra chairs? They're saying we'll need more at Table 5."

"Oh, sure. I can show you."

They crossed into the kitchen. Perhaps deeming the interaction too boring to record, the camera focused its scrutiny elsewhere. And since the support staff was out there with Denny, Jiyeon and Eunjae were actually... alone. For the next six or seven minutes, anyway.

He motioned for her to duck behind the long prep table that divided the room. "Let me borrow one of your earrings. If anyone comes in, I was helping you look for it."

"Funny how we keep losing things," Jiyeon mused, removing an earring. She dropped it into Eunjae's open palm. His fingers closed over hers, warm and reassuring. And he laughed just like she knew he would, but his worries still won out in the end.

"I'm sorry," he said. "I should've asked you how it was going, with the salon. You probably thought I didn't care."

"No, don't be sorry. I'm the one who should be saying that. And I never felt like you didn't care." She'd never doubted this. He just didn't pry into her business; it wasn't in his nature. And if they were being as fair as possible, he didn't need to pry. She'd gotten into the habit of telling him almost everything. Keyword: almost.

As Emma, she used to share myriad details about her life to thousands of strangers daily. Clinging to her secrets was a hard habit to break.

Losing that retail space had hurt so much, for reasons that Jiyeon still couldn't bear to hold up to the light. Every mention felt like salt in the wound. While her parents and her brother and even Arthur were bringing it up all the time, Eunjae had done the opposite. She'd been so relieved.

Jiyeon didn't want to think about it. Nor could she stop thinking about it, but Eunjae had enough going on. The last thing she wanted was to drag him down even further. He would've been so disappointed that the lease went to someone else, and Jiyeon said this to him at last, admitting why she'd chosen to keep the bad news to herself.

"I knew you'd be upset, so I kept putting it off. That's why I couldn't be mad when you didn't tell me about Emerald. I wasn't telling you everything, either. I didn't want you to worry."

Eunjae frowned. "Let me worry. Isn't that part of the job?" Although their time was running out, he held on to her hand. "This is the first job I've ever gotten to choose for myself. Good or bad, I'll be here."

Crying would be a bad idea. How would she explain that? Jiyeon hadn't cried in August, when she drove by and saw a brand new sign above the space that might have been hers. She was late to call about it. This was her fault. Now she was here, crouched behind a table, succumbing to the pressure of all these tears she hadn't shed.

"That place... it could've been great, for me."

"I know. But we'll find another one, and it'll be even better."

The truth spilled out. "That's not what I want."

"What do you mean?" Eunjae asked, searching her face, trying to understand. Jiyeon wished she could help with that. She didn't understand what she meant, either, or why she felt lighter after the words were spoken.

That was when they heard it: Arthur Hong's altogether too peppy 'good morning!' as he came striding into the diner. How odd. It was a Thursday, bright and early. Arthur should be at the office. Besides, he'd finished his interviews over the weekend.

"DEN-DEN!" he bellowed. "Oh man, look at this guy. He could crush my skull so fast. Isn't that wild? I remember when he was only this tall. Tiny! Can you believe it?"

"No need to explain the passage of time, Hong. Take it down a notch."

Nicky's squealing carried through the walls. "Oooh, Den-Den!"

"He had these yellow binoculars, right, and he'd go on patrol—"

"Awww!"

"Chief, I can't clock in yet. I need this intel. Where are the yellow binoculars now? Do we have photographic evidence? How long have you been calling him 'Den-Den' and why hasn't he done anything about it yet? What kind of dirt do you have on our manager? Is the dirt for sale—"

"Kim Ahnjong."

"Ssshhhh. Not now, I'm taking notes."

By this point, Eunjae had rushed to the storage shed to pick up an extra chair. Jiyeon longed to stay in the kitchen, perhaps hide in the pantry while she was at it, but it came off more suspicious with every minute they were both gone at the same time. So she put her earring back in, returned to the dining room, and braced for impact.

The booths were filling fast. Arthur lifted his voice above the din of customers asking for menus, high chairs, selfies with the diner's handsome staff. "Oh, Emmie! There you are. I was looking for you. Guess what?"

Jiyeon eyed him warily. "What?"

"I'll be here every week now!" he crowed. "The producers said I can be a recurring guest!"

"I'll be here every week now!" he crowed. "The producers said I can be a recurring guest!"

20

J IYEON MADE CHANGE FOR a twenty and watched her current boyfriend chat about life goals with her former boyfriend. The pair sat together in a diner booth as every window filled from pane to pane with sunset hues: peach, rose gold, fiery orange. Would this eventually be normal, too?

It was Friday, and it should've been date night, but they'd have to take a rain check yet again. She still had a few hours left on her shift. Meanwhile, Eunjae's was done. He'd be leaving soon, and Arthur would tag along, off to grab dinner with everyone else who wasn't working late. They'd started staying open until 9pm as a trial run for Sunshine Diner's twenty-four-hour operating schedule.

Jiyeon smiled at the next person in line, and the next, and the next. The routine was simple, easy, repetitive, but moving to one of the griddles might be a better option. In the kitchen, she wouldn't have a front row seat while everyone else got to spend more time with Eunjae than she ever did.

At least she had Jeannie, here to help out for the rest of what promised to be a hectic weekend. She came over to stand behind the counter during a lull, glowering at Arthur. "So *he's* the one getting a date night instead of you?"

"Uh-huh. And he even brought his scrapbook."

"Not the scrapbook," Jeannie groaned. "Are you serious?"

"Just the first volume. He's got four now."

"No! I'm tired just thinking about that. Why's Arthur always so… Arthur?"

"Hmm. 'Cause he's Arthur? That's my best guess."

"Okay, but why? Like who told him he has to be this way? I'll never understand."

In addition to two different planners and his trusty calendar app, Arthur maintained an exhaustive list of personal goals. He kept this list in his head, but it also existed as a scrapbook, the pages crammed with accomplishments. This ponderous tome had existed since before Jiyeon even met him; she remembered Arthur bringing it to class for a project when they were in seventh grade, the year he transferred from private school to public.

Nobody ever made a peep about the scrapbook situation, even if they thought it was a bit odd. Arthur was friendly, athletic, a go-getter. Plus, he enjoyed something akin to celebrity status. Driving into the city, you might see his father, Arthur Senior, grinning down at you from a billboard advertising the Hong & Hong law firm. In the foreground, two knights went head to head in a medieval joust, locked on a collision course. TURN THAT CRASH INTO A CROWN — CALL KING ARTHUR TODAY.

If you called 555-ARTHUR, you could hire Lemon Grove's premier personal injury lawyers. If you called Arthur Hong, Jr. on his blue flip phone, you could get yourself invited for dinner, or video games, or a random pool party. He was popular from the moment he showed up, but not even his burgeoning social calendar could derail him from that list of goals, the many quests he aimed to complete. Because there was always a quest, with Arthur. Somewhere to be, something to achieve, someone to help.

Right now he was on a mission to dictate his entire autobiography in one sitting. Eunjae listened with genuine fascination. He paged through the scrapbook, asking questions, examining class photos and timeworn articles about the high school debate team. Twice, Arthur had summoned Jiyeon to confirm the details on an anecdote or provide the name to go with a face. If she wasn't in the room, he'd text her. *Emmie, where did we go for that field trip in junior year? Hey Emmie, come here for a sec.*

Emmie, Emmie, Emmie. Between Arthur and the multiple daily emails from Eric, she was ready to stick her phone under a tractor wheel, climb into the seat, and throw the whole thing in reverse. There were tractors aplenty in Monroe. It could be arranged.

The third time he called her over, several members of Apollo had joined in, waiting for the van. Ezra hovered on the periphery, neither joining the group nor straying from it. He inched closer when Arthur pointed to the scrapbook and said, "Emmie, look. Remember this?"

It was a picture taken near the end of their last year in middle school. With everyone lined up alphabetically by last name, Jiyeon and Arthur should've had Shannah Henderson standing between them, but she was absent that day. They posed together, holding artwork in black frames. Arthur was two weeks shy of saying goodbye to his braces for good. Jiyeon had embraced a short haircut, the shortest haircut of her life thus far, and she'd ironed all the waves out.

"Sure, I remember," she replied, with a wry smile for her younger self. "I kept my hair like that for a month, and then I realized it made me look too much like Janie."

"Who's Janie?"

"Their sister," said Eunjae. "We've never gotten to meet her."

This was news to Kazu, who sputtered that he had no clue there was a third Han sibling. And she was the eldest? And she lived in Spain? What? Jeers and booing all around.

Arthur spoke over the din, a long-suffering look on his face. "Yeah, but tell them why your hair is short. Wait 'til you hear this, guys."

They clamored for the story. A camera floated over, then another. She shrugged and gave them an honest answer. "Arthur said he liked my hair, so I cut it."

"Woooooowwwwww."

"Scary," Jungwoo commented in Korean, punctuating with a nervous laugh.

"See? This is what I've been dealing with. How long have we known each other, Emms? Eleven years? Twelve? She's broken my heart so many times. I've lost count, to tell you the truth." He jabbed a finger at the members. "So if you're getting any ideas, don't."

As one, Apollo turned to the camera. In perfect chorus, they said, "We belong to our fans."

A certain teenager proclaimed this to be creepy. At the register, Jeannie was fuming. "There was more! Tell them!"

"Arthur said he liked my hair and I should never cut it, so I cut it."

Max paused in the middle of clearing a nearby table. His scowl could've been the inspiration for any gargoyle perched on the spires of Notre Dame. "Why were you going around telling her what to do?"

"Hey, I was fourteen. What did I know?"

Ezra rolled his eyes. "I'm fourteen and I've never been dumb enough to tell a girl what her hair should look like."

"Yikes," said Kazu.

"Embarrassing," muttered Kei.

Ever the peacemaker, Eunjae tried to redirect the conversation by asking about the artwork. "You drew houses. Was this an art class?"

"No," Jiyeon answered. "Eighth graders were required to do a service project, so we decided to help renovate the rec room at Golden Grove. It's a retirement community. They send a bus to Wanna Waffle once a week for bingo and brunch."

"It was cheaper if we painted the art ourselves instead of buying it," Arthur put in.

Their teacher had written the prompt on the board: *East, west, home is best*. She'd asked them to think about the difference between a house and a home. Golden Grove was a place of residence, but was that enough for it to be *home* in the truest sense? They'd read *The House on Mango Street* and *Bridge to Terabithia*, books about staying home and leaving home and everything in between. Was home a physical place? Was it in your head, or maybe in your heart?

After some debate, the students had voiced their wish to turn that rec room into a happy, comforting space. Something that evoked the homes their new friends at the retirement community had left behind. A house was not the same as a home. On this, they could agree.

Some classmates drew mansions and others drew castles. Her friend Sylvia drew a houseboat. Instructed to draw a place that felt like home, Jiyeon went with... a plain old house. Four walls and a roof, some windows and a door. Straightforward, practical. Overly simple compared to Arthur's three-story townhouse with its neat hedges and rooftop garden, and he made sure to tell her so. But she'd never understood the appeal of stairs, and why did your garden need to be on the roof? Gardens grew just fine on the ground, too. If she had a garden, or if Dad had a garden, that's where it would go.

Joey would grow all kinds of things, Jiyeon reasoned at the time, but this was her drawing, so she added flowers. And a tree, throwing its long shadow on the grass. On its branches, she built a treehouse for Denny. Well, it was more of an observation deck. A lookout. Her brother had new binoculars, real ones, and he'd love being up there. For Mom, a real driveway and a new car, bright red, super fast. She sketched out a lawn that had enough room for Janie to turn as many cartwheels as she wanted. The latest phase was gymnastics.

For herself, Jiyeon borrowed her favorite thing about Miss Gloria's salon: the door. It used to be yellow. Although they'd painted it a different color the year before, because the landlord insisted, it was always going to be yellow in Jiyeon's memory. That's how it looked when she came to get her hair cut for the very first time. That's how it still looked, in her heart. She didn't want to copy it exactly, though. To make it her own, Jiyeon colored it orange.

Oh, goodness. Arthur had plunged her into the past again. In the present, he'd moved on to describing the house he planned to buy before he turned thirty. But Eunjae glanced up from the scrapbook to smile at her, and it wasn't the smile he used when others were around, so careful and polite. It was the smile she knew.

"I like your house," he said, only for Jiyeon to hear.

She smiled back at him. "Thanks. I like it too."

"Here, on the windowsill. Apple pie?"

"That's what windowsills are for."

"You're right."

The warmth of that moment was short-lived. His brothers were debating where to eat, a discussion that inevitably drew Eunjae into its chaotic orbit. Arthur had produced his curated list of local restaurants, ranked and annotated. As for Ezra, he drifted away, feigning boredom.

He aimed his phone at the light fixture hanging over the register. "It's a Sputnik lamp," he remarked, when Jiyeon attempted small talk. "That's what those are called, with the arms sticking out like that. I looked it up and it's pretty old." Then he opened the Instagram app, intending to post the photo.

"Instagram," she murmured. "I didn't know you had an account."

"I made it yesterday."

"You're kinda young for it, aren't you?"

"You just have to be thirteen," Ezra replied. "I've been fourteen since April."

"Hmm."

"I followed you. Did you see?"

She checked. Sure enough, there was the new follower notification, buried in Emma Han's standard avalanche of likes, comments, and tags. Jiyeon went to Ezra's profile. The last line in his bio read, *Managed by Mum @l.goldsmith*. She went over the words two more times. Then she switched over to see what he'd posted so far: a carousel of photos from the past two weeks on set, innocuous, mostly buildings around downtown Monroe.

"Mum says it'll be good to have social media," said Ezra, "so people can get to know me."

It's not good, her brain screamed in protest. But freaking out was the best way to put an end to this conversation, so she managed a wan smile. "You like scenery, huh? So does Eunjae. Never has any people in his posts."

"I saw that. I didn't follow him, though. He wouldn't follow me back." He gripped the back of a chair, knuckles briefly showing white. "Apollo's only following each other. "

Followers. That number had skyrocketed into the thousands and his account was less than a day old. It made her feel sicker than ever. "You have a good eye," she said, trying to stay calm, trying not to think about all the pitfalls waiting for someone so young on an app like this. "Do you like taking pictures?"

"You mean like Eunjae does?" Ezra shook his head. "I'm not that serious about it. It's his thing, not mine." He shifted from one foot to the other, two spots of bright color blooming on his cheeks. "I didn't want to mention him. In my profile, I mean. Mum told me I had to say that Ari from Apollo was my brother, or else nobody would care about me, and I figured she was right. I'm not... It's not because I'm trying to copy him or whatever."

"Sure. I get that. Believe it or not, I only started posting on Instagram 'cause of my sister. Janie had the account first. Then she got bored and moved on, but I stuck around." The admission tasted bittersweet, the way talking about Janie often did. "Nobody remembers that this used to be her thing. I never thought it would be mine, either."

"I want something that's mine," Ezra said then, something fierce burning behind every syllable, something that struck a chord in her heart — a familiar tone, a note that echoed, ringing like the high, piercing chime of a bell. Jiyeon knew that wish. She understood it much too well. And she wanted to stop Eunjae from leaving, she had to tell him what she'd just figured out, but there was no need to look for him at all. He'd overheard, and he was here, expression etched with revulsion and cold fury.

"Mum let you do this? What was she thinking?" There was no disguising the raw emotion in his tone. It shocked Arthur into silence. Brothers froze where they stood, alarm written large across each of their faces. Jiyeon reached for Eunjae's arm, a foolish move, caught by the cameras.

"Delete this. You're too young, you've got no clue what you're getting into."

"I'm keeping it," Ezra shot back. He lifted his chin, hands curled into fists. "You can't stop me."

An excerpt from **Molly Merriweather and the Timeless Prince,** *second in a series of children's books* (Molly in Time) *by Robin Ayres*

"You can't stop me."

These were the first words Molly Merriweather ever exchanged with herself. Not in the mirror, speaking to her reflection, and not in her mind, a silent show of defiance. She had fallen sideways through time again, tumbling eight years into the past, and this version of Molly was only eight years old.

"That's not how it works," the child went on. "We can't ever change what we already did. As soon as we make the choice, it's already too late."

"I know that. You don't have to explain."

Molly was instantly sorry for snapping at her. It made her sound like even more of a child than the one sitting up in bed, wrapped in a nightgown two sizes too large. This girl still had her mother downstairs, surrounded by books and papers, exhausted but perfectly safe.

The younger Molly didn't know any other reality. Puzzled, she said, "Then why did you come here? You know what Mama told us. We can only change Right Now, and this isn't Right Now for you."

Right Now for Molly, aged sixteen, was a place where Mama had vanished. If her eight-year-old self hadn't chosen to replace one gear in a machine's stuttering clockwork heart, her mother might have stayed. There would be no voyage to an island long since wiped from every map. She'd be at home. She'd be part of Right Now instead of Once Before.

If this Molly didn't make a different choice, only Never After was left. For both of them, that long passage into the future would lead to places where Mama remained lost. It was so hopeless to imagine those different, fragmented futures coming together at this juncture, united by a single tragic thread: every Molly in every timeline would lose the person she loved most in the world. Every Molly would make the same mistake.

The rules existed, set in stone. To break them was to risk making everything worse, splitting the long river once more. Molly couldn't explain the weight of this choice or the consequences of making it. That would go against everything her mother ever taught.

"I really am sorry," said the other Molly. "Time's already split. My future isn't your future. Even if I make a different choice, it won't change anything for you."

Molly choked down a sob. *Don't you see?* she wanted to shout—

21

THERE WAS NO ACTUAL garden at the Monroe Garden Inn. They made up for it with window boxes and containers, as well as two very small but very lovingly tended flower beds outside the lobby. Eunjae was willing to wager that the inn's profusion of terracotta pots held more plants than most full-sized gardens.

A strong breeze rustled through the foliage. Hours deep into a quiet Thursday evening, moonlight dripped from every petal and leaf. He climbed out of the van as soon as their driver hit the brake. This was Ezra's stop, not his, but he always walked his brother upstairs when they dropped him off.

On any other night, Eunjae would've paused to admire the contrast between the geometric lines of each planter and the wild profusion of greenery within. He'd be wishing for his camera. Even now, it was easy to compose the image in his mind, to choose the correct angle and frame the shot. Much easier than sorting out his emotions.

Eunjae kept returning to that moment with Ezra, rewinding and replaying the words that were said. But the memory had sharp edges. Regardless of how gingerly he held it, there was no avoiding the sting.

He wanted to get going, but a scuffle ensued in the van. "Aww, I want to go," said Namgyu, unbuckling his seat belt. "Hang on, Ari."

Kei blocked the exit with his leg. "Why do you have to go with him? Hyung can handle it by himself. He takes the kid up every night without any help from you."

"I know."

"So stay in the car."

Namgyu hopped out with the energy of a gymnast sticking a gold medal landing. "Next time," he told Kei, cheerful as anything. "Don't worry, okay? You're always so worried. It's really cute. I love it so much. But I'm the oldest here, and Ezra's the youngest, so he's my responsibility too."

They looked over at Kazu, snoring softly, long limbs splayed all over the passenger seat. He'd fallen asleep the second they left the diner. "Gyu really is the oldest right now," muttered Kei. "Good luck to us all." But he joined them a second later, and he didn't close the van door, avoiding the noisy process of sliding it open or shut.

Ezra stomped ahead of them, past the pool and down a breezeway lined with potted herbs, mint and thyme and lemon balm. They took the exterior stairwell to the inn's third floor, Namgyu chatting amiably while his companions walked in silence. "It's so nice," he mused, as a breeze ran its fingers through the plants, stirring up a fresh, vibrant scent that belonged more to summertime than autumn. In careful English, Namgyu added, "Do you like it here, Ezra? I like it here."

Ezra shrugged, tepid and noncommittal. "Guess it could be worse."

"What did he say? He talks so fast."

"He said it could be worse," translated Eunjae. Namgyu's expression contorted into one of pure bafflement. Why point out that things could be worse? That wasn't any fun. Of course they could be worse, but they weren't, right? Things were mostly good. What if they all focused on that part instead?

Kei shook his head. "We should all be like you, Hong Namgyu."

"What? That's so crazy. You should be like you. I think you're the best. And Ari's the best, and Zuzu's the best, and Nicky—"

"Is insane."

"Awwww!"

When they reached the stairs, Ezra threw a sullen glance in Eunjae's direction. "I can go up by myself. If you just want to yell at Mum, she's not back until Monday."

Naturally, his mother wasn't here to answer for what she'd done. Eunjae had to say something, though. She had no business putting Ezra on that app and his father had no business sitting around, letting everything just happen without lifting a finger. Pointless as it may be, he'd tell Simon what was going on. He shared custody with Leila. Surely that amounted to some form of authority over a fourteen-year-old's social media use.

Let's try talking to Ezra about it, Jiyeon texted twenty minutes ago. But why was this a talking point? It shouldn't have happened. The kid didn't need a public account watched by thousands of strangers.

Simon must have been watching for their arrival; he answered their knock right away, offering the usual polite greetings. "Out late tonight," he observed, while Ezra skulked into the hotel room, tossing his jacket onto a chair.

"We went out for dinner," Eunjae replied. "Can I talk to you before I go?"

His father responded with a nod. Now that they saw each other nearly every day, Eunjae often found himself comparing their interactions to the years spent trading concise, clinical emails. In retrospect, the emails were a lot wordier. Dad wasn't the type to use a full sentence when a monosyllable would do.

"We'll wait for you in the car," said Kei. To Simon, he bowed and said, "Goodnight, sir."

"Goodnight. Thank you for bringing him back."

"Aww, I wish we didn't have to bring him back. Too bad there's no room left in our little shed." Namgyu pantomimed eight men plus one teenager attempting to coexist in a cramped cottage, packed like a fancy can of sardines. The performance could be compared to an avant garde interpretive dance sequence. "Too many brothers!" he clinched, in English.

To Eunjae's surprise, Simon laughed. What a rare sound. Had he heard this very much as a child? He couldn't recall.

Ezra didn't laugh. His expression crumpled, collapsing inward. He reeled away as if he'd been slapped. "He doesn't have too many brothers. Why do you guys always say that?"

"Oh no, I really need to get better at English," Namgyu whispered to Eunjae. "What's he saying?"

There wasn't any time to translate. Dry-eyed, Ezra sucked in a shuddering breath, then railed at Namgyu with everything he had. "Eunjae doesn't have too many brothers! The only brother he's got is me. Just me, but he doesn't even care!"

Simon admonished him to calm down. His words fell short of their mark. "He'd rather have you," Ezra yelled. "I wish I'd figured that out before I came here. I wish I'd never tried!"

Rendered speechless, Namgyu reached out to him, poised to move in the direction of the attack when just about any other person would've flinched away from it. Kei intervened, predicting correctly that he'd just keep trying.

"That's enough," said Eunjae. "Fight me all you want, but leave everyone else out of it. They haven't done anything wrong."

"Yeah, of course not. They can't do anything wrong and neither can you. You're perfect, and millions of people love you, and I owe you for a million things I never even asked for. I get to go to a school that I hate so much. I have lots of friends because Mum tells everybody I'm related to you. People forget my name but they never forget yours. It's all because of you, you, you."

A school he hated. Friends who didn't feel like friends. How could Eunjae even begin to fix this? How much sooner could he have fixed it if they'd only talked more? "Ezra, I'm sorry—"

But there was more. "Your dream came true just like that. Someone flew you to another country just to make you famous. You're so special that our nanny went crazy and tried to kidnap you—"

"Ezra!"

He felt terrible and he sounded terrible, the fury burning so brightly in his voice that everyone recoiled from it. "Who told you that?" Eunjae demanded of his brother. In hindsight, he'd already known the answer.

Ezra bolted out the door and into the night. Eunjae lurched after him, apologizing to Namgyu as he went. But then his father told him to wait.

"What?"

"Let him go. I'll talk to him when he comes back."

"You'll talk to him? You expect me to believe that?"

"I will. He never runs far. He's a little bit like your mum," Simon added, with a rueful smile, "and a little bit like me. I never run far, either."

The light of a street lamp sliced through the blinds, carving sickly yellow lines into the opposite wall. Eunjae turned the knob, wrenched the door open. He'd heard Ezra's last sentence, the one that came out in a sob as he fled the room: *I should've known that you don't need me.*

"I'm going. This is my fault."

Simon winced. "It isn't your fault." Four words with an impact of four tons, uttered many years too late. Eunjae left anyway, pelting past his father, rushing out before Namgyu and Kei could hold him back.

The property was small, just two buildings and an office, a courtyard and the parking lot. There weren't many places to hide, not unless Ezra strayed past the bounds of the hotel and into downtown Monroe. It didn't take long to find him, but Eunjae stopped short of calling his name.

He kept to the shadows, beyond his brother's line of sight. Who was he, to fix this? What did he know?

Kei dashed down the steps, catching up easily. "We should go, hyung. You'll only make it worse if you chase after him like this."

"Give Ezra some time," Namgyu concurred. "You can try again when you're not upset."

An image flashed in his mind: his brother's jacket draped on that chair, forgotten. Eunjae found that he couldn't speak without his voice breaking. "It's cold," he said. "He'll be cold out here."

"He was pretty mad. Probably won't even feel it. Trust me, I'm mad at you idiots every minute of every day. You could drop me into a blizzard and I'd feel nothing."

"Aww, Keiichi. You're not mad at us every minute. That's just too crazy. Don't try to be all tough right now. If you feel bad, just feel bad."

Kei opened his mouth, then closed it again. Finally he said, "You're right, Gyu. I do feel bad. I feel awful."

It was Namgyu who led him away, meeting no resistance. But the bright fragrance of everything green and growing, confined to pots and yet flourishing— it was too much, suddenly. Eunjae stumbled, thinking of Ezra somewhere near and all alone.

Surrounded by friends, yet all alone.

Growing and growing, all alone.

22

Max was waiting on the patio when they got back, huddled under the string lights with Uyu. Bundled up in his grubby hoodie, he'd wrapped himself and the dog in an additional layer of blankets filched from the Langley House linen closet. Fuzzy socks and scuffed blue slides completed the ensemble.

"Don't go in," he warned. "Eric showed up an hour ago."

Namgyu took the puppy from him. "Which Eric? Ha, they're so hard to keep track of, I don't know how anybody does it."

"Vanilla."

"Great, the first one. He's worse than every other Eric." This was significant coming from Kei, the world's most ardent devotee of vanilla as a flavor. "He's even worse than Creepy Eric and Professor Eric combined."

"He wants to see you next, Zu."

"What? Why? I haven't done anything!"

"Well, somebody fucking did. There was a leak today. Prism's losing it. And you're supposed to be leader, so Eric's asking for you."

"A leak? Is it from the show?"

"Yeah." Max shifted uncomfortably in his lawn chair. He glanced at Eunjae for a second, then chose to focus on the fire pit, where a few embers still smoldered. "Sorry, hyung."

"Sorry for what?"

Kei consulted the Internet and came up with a grainy clip of Max at the diner, stepping in so that Jiyeon wouldn't be trampled by an overenthusiastic Arthur. "Our knight in shining armor, Max Lee," he read out loud. Then he was too busy rolling his eyes to get through the rest of the caption, so they crowded around to see for themselves.

"It doesn't show Jiyeon's face," said Kazu.

"Doesn't matter. Look at the comments, everybody's saying it's Emma Han. Something about the way she did her hair."

"People have known about her being here since the first week. It's not like Prism wanted it to be a secret."

Kei sighed out of exasperation. "Again, doesn't matter. This video proves that she spends at least some time with us on set. They didn't want her on camera for this exact reason. Look at the fans flipping out."

He was right. The situation could very well deteriorate from here. But what Eunjae found most concerning about the footage was the angle from which it was filmed. Only Max was recognizable, the video cropped to reveal just the back of Jiyeon's head and half of Arthur's suit jacket, but you couldn't get that angle without standing in a certain spot. It was filmed from behind and to the right of Apollo, toward the back of the group. And this was worth investigating, but Eunjae didn't have the energy just then.

It had been such an endless day. Exhausted, heavy-hearted, all he wanted was ten uninterrupted minutes in the shower and another five minutes to reply to Jiyeon's messages. He'd tell her goodnight even though she wouldn't see it for hours. Then he'd try and get some sleep himself. Maybe the morning would bring a miracle, or at least a measure of clarity.

But their one and only bathroom was occupied, of course, and although it was Eunjae's night to take a twin bed in the loft, Jesse had beaten him to it. He was up there snoring, dead to the world. Nicky slept in the other bed and it was Jungwoo's turn in the master. At this rate, any remaining bunks would be outside, on the lawn. But with Eric and Kazu in the living room, even the sleeping bags were off limits. Bad timing. Bad luck, bad news, bad everything.

Eunjae backtracked out of the tiny cottage, which now felt more claustrophobic than ever. He let the door shut with a bang. Then he closed his eyes, sagging against a brick wall long since leached of any warmth. Three weeks in and he was ready to call it quits. November and freedom seemed eons away.

But it wasn't freedom, right? That was an illusion. Their time here would end and Apollo would sign with Zenith, a two-year contract, maybe three. How many similar situations waited down the line? This mess with Ezra, and having to hide his relationship with Jiyeon — those problems wouldn't mend on their own. Time might heal some damage, but not all of it.

"Hyung. You okay?"

Eunjae opened his eyes to find Max staring at him, mouth pinched with worry. Namgyu watched from a few paces away, Uyu curled up in his arms, while Kei scrolled social media with an air of disinterest. He was listening, though. They all heard it when Eunjae said no, he wasn't okay, not really. His brother hated him, his parents were irresponsible, and Eunjae was just as bad, because why hadn't he done a better job with Ezra? If he hadn't tried to run away from his audition back then, Vivian wouldn't have gotten fired. Ezra would've had her in his life. He wouldn't think she was a terrible person who— no, that was too difficult to say, he couldn't repeat it. But what if he'd fought back? He never fought Leila, he just sat around being useless. Useless, that was the word. A great word for how Eunjae felt right now. And it was Friday, and Friday was date night, and he'd failed every date night for the past three weeks.

It was a deluge of words. He could've kept going, but it hurt too much. And then Eunjae wondered if there was any point to saying more, or saying anything, period. These were his problems. Why force them on his brothers? Why upset the dog? She whimpered, sensing his distress.

"Shit," said Max. "Okay. You want ice cream?"

Kei lowered his phone. "Ice cream? Are you serious? It's 10:45."

"We need car keys. Hang on, I bet Nicky stole some—"

"Ha! Ice cream, that's such a good idea. Ice cream fixes a lot of things. We can all go tomorrow! Everybody can feel better. Doesn't everybody just want to feel better?" Namgyu returned the dog to Max, giving her one last good scratch behind the ears. "Let's do this, guys. New plan! You two go inside and tell Zuzu it's past your bedtime. I'll stay with Ari. We'll go take a walk."

This announcement sent Kei reeling out of his chair. His voice ratcheted upward, bordering on shrill. "A walk? To where? Right now? It's pitch black out here! And neither of you has any sense of direction! Ari couldn't find the airport and ended up living with strangers for two weeks!"

"Phew! Take a deep breath. Nobody's going to the airport! Gosh, that's so far away, why would we go there? We can just walk around until Ari isn't so sad anymore. You know Jaehwan-hyung always says taking a walk is a good idea."

"He says that when he's mad! 'Take a walk, Max!' is just code for 'Go away before I wring your neck, Max!' and everybody knows it!"

"Wow, what the fuck? He's told your ass to take a walk, too. Hyung's told you that a million times. Why am I the example?"

Kei ignored him, gesturing wildly at the night in general. "Take a walk? At this hour, in a weird town, in a foreign country—"

"Aww, it's not even a foreign country for Ari. This is his country now, he's moving here. It's home." Namgyu grinned. "I've got this. No more tears! Big Brother Hong is here!"

"Who taught you how to say that in English?" Kei exclaimed.

Max went back for his blanket. "I'm going with you. Walking is stupid, we can just borrow one of the vans. It's freezing out here."

"Aww! It's not that cold, I think it feels nice!"

"Respectfully," said Max, "you'd be wearing shorts in hell, hyung."

"Ha! That's so true!"

"It's not true. Gyu would never end up in hell."

Max shot him the most withering glare. "It was a goddamn joke, Keiichi. But don't worry, because I'll explain it to you when we're both in hell, I'll even talk slow so you'll get what I'm saying—"

"Go ahead and explain it now. Aren't we in hell? This is hell for me! I hate it here!" Kei turned to Namgyu. "You can't take Ari and go walking around in the damn countryside. That's insane. You're being insane, okay?"

A light flared up in Namgyu's eyes. Grabbing both younger brothers, he said, "You're being insane, *Namgyu-hyung*. Walking is stupid, *Namgyu-hyung*. But that's okay, *Namgyu-hyung*. You're my big brother and I'll listen to you, *Namgyu-hyung*."

"Oh, shit," muttered Max, because they'd done it now. This was not a brother who pulled rank very often. When he did, you were screwed.

Eunjae berated himself for not agreeing to the walk as soon as it was suggested. "You're my big brother and I'll listen to you,

Namgyu-hyung."

"Ha!"

"I'm sorry, Namgyu-hyung."

"What for? Silliest thing you've ever said."

Eunjae prodded the other two with his foot until they got the hint. This resulted in the weariest, most begrudging sigh he'd ever heard, but Kei broke first. He mumbled, "You're my big brother and I'll listen to you, Namgyu-hyung."

"There we go. And what about our knight in shining armor, Lee Seojin?"

"Yeah, yeah. You're my big brother and I'll shut up now, Namgyu-hyung. Go take a goddamn stupid walk, Namgyu-hyung."

"Aww! See, that wasn't very hard. I knew you could do it. Gosh, I'm so lucky. I have the best baby brothers ever." He took Eunjae by the shoulders. "Anyway! Ready?"

"Ah, yeah. I'm ready."

Max and Kei shuffled indoors. There was some grumbling about serial killers potentially lurking beyond the property's walls, but the matter was settled, and Namgyu had won. "Goodnight!" he called after them. "Love you so much!"

They set off toward the tennis court. The grounds were cloaked in deep blue shadow. Soon, some of these trees would be bare, the roses withered by frost. Eunjae imagined the house's grand facade hung with holiday lights. Time kept flowing, whether it did so at a trickle or swept through like a riptide, dragging him under. Where would he be, when the season turned again? What else would change? In the stillness, his thoughts were much too loud.

He looked to Langley House just once. Simultaneously comforted and concerned by the dim glow of Jiyeon's window on the second floor,

Eunjae hoped the day's troubles weren't keeping her awake. But he didn't send a message; he kept going, letting his brother steer the course.

Namgyu hummed a ballad as they walked. He didn't speak again until they came to the property's edge, Monroe slumbering in the valley below.

"You'll listen to what he said, right?"

The only brother he's got is me! Just me, but he doesn't even care!

Eunjae swallowed hard, throat aching. "You mean what Ezra said, hyung?"

It's all because of you, you, you.

"Aww, no. I already knew you were listening to him. But did you hear your dad when he said this isn't your fault?" Namgyu reached over to ruffle his hair. "Make sure you listen, okay? Because it isn't your fault. Everything can't be your fault, Ari. That's a lot."

The world went blurry. "Yeah. It is a lot."

"I know it's rough right now, but guess what? It's never that way forever. The bad stuff comes and goes." Again, the weight of Namgyu's arm around his shoulders, warm and reassuring. "When it's over, everything good is still right here."

***From the footage that eventually became Episode 5 of
Sunshine 24/7: Apollo At Your Service** (after considerable
editing)*

The episode opens with pumpkins. The sheer number of these is distracting, but we can't overlook the hayrides, the haunted house, and two enormous inflatable slides gently swaying in the wind. Monroe's annual Fall Festival is the total package, an autumnal entertainment complex that simply screams, "America!"

On this chilly Friday night, there are toddlers running around with gourds, parents pushing strollers, roving bands of children destined for a violent sugar crash. Lights beckon from the midway, and every ten minutes we hear the clanging of a bell as draft horses pull a wagon around the fairgrounds.

"There's also a petting zoo," Denny informs the camera in dire tones. Screams ring out; they're filming him in front of a ride meant to look like a Viking ship. It swings in an ever-widening arc, back and forth, as tinny music pipes through the speakers.

Jesse dashes by just then, clutching a bouquet of candied apples on sticks. Denny watches him like a spectator pre-gaming the apocalypse. He turns back to the producer and says, "Hazard pay. I deserve it."

Meanwhile, the members of Apollo take turns posing with a scarecrow whose misshapen head and menacing smile would be right at home in anyone's nightmares. They exclaim over every single baby dressed as a pumpkin. They're collectively mystified by funnel cakes. They want to do all the things.

"I'm sure the boys will be fine," the producer replies, laughing nervously. "Look at them. They love it."

Denny laughs himself hoarse. Then, the video suddenly plays in reverse. Jesse runs backwards across the screen, and scenes from the festival blink past in a blur. Night brightens into day. Now Apollo gathers in front of the boathouse, dressed for work, admiring their surroundings. It's late afternoon and the lake shimmers under a flawless blue sky.

Jungwoo stands at the railing with Namgyu. "Look, hyung," he says. "They have those boats here. Remember when we did that variety show in Japan?"

"Aww! That was the best time ever!"

Here, the episode cuts to a clip of this show, in which Apollo played a game yet to be surpassed in chaos. We're presented with sixty seconds of carnage as the members careen around a lake on pedal boats shaped like swans. Bodies fly through the air, clad in neon life jackets, arms and legs flailing. Jaehwan gives orders to ram someone's boat head-on. His eyes glitter, beautiful and utterly without mercy. Our final image is of Nicky boarding another vessel, a move stolen from pirates terrorizing the high seas. He flips Kei into the water while a roaring Kazu threatens to string him up like a flag.

"That was so much fun," gushes Namgyu, the winner of that game. "I hope we get to play again!"

Although we won't be seeing a repeat of Apollo's nautical disaster, it looks like a competition is at hand. The producers explain that the prize is two glorious days off for the whole group, but only if everyone succeeds at their assigned task. "Secret missions," grumbles Kei, lips flattening into a grim line.

"Secret missions," Max concurs. He pulls a granola bar out of his pastel yellow hoodie and takes a bite. When he extends this bounty to the brother nearest at hand, the offer is declined. Ari seems to have lost his appetite.

They're called in order by age, eldest first. Kazu enters the boathouse while the others confer amongst themselves. Only Nicky is quiet, industriously tapping away at his phone. This behavior hasn't escaped Denny's notice, but he doesn't intervene. For now, he just glances at a text message and announces, in response to Namgyu's repeated requests, that zero K-pop people will be operating watercraft without training or proper licensure. "Over my dead body, Hong." ("Awww...")

Kazu emerges, deep in thought. Nicky goes in right after him, receives his mission, and... strolls back to the group, behaving in perfect compliance. Wait, really?

No, not really. Thanks to an enterprising cameraman, we get to observe a master at work. Nicky approaches the members one by one, pressing them to reveal their secret missions. The goal: win two days off. The strategy: find the easiest mission and give it to their weakest link, Ari.

Again, it's Kazu first. "Okay, keep yours," Nicky tells him. "Nobody wants to do that one."

"What? Why not?"

"They want you to find birthday presents for Max and Keiichi, but you can only pay in vegetables. Terrible mission. You're the only one who could make that work, so keep it." Nicky waves him away. "Gyu, what's yours?"

There's some resistance. Namgyu knows you can't win if you're disqualified for breaking the rules. But Nicky points out that the rules never explicitly said to keep the missions a secret. They never gave that to him in writing, which was their first mistake. And wouldn't it be sad if they *all* ended up losing just because *some* brothers always have to be the winner? Namgyu surrenders. We learn that he's been tasked with assembling a five-course meal using free samples from market stalls. Then he needs to get somebody to eat the feast he's put together.

"Eh, that's rough. Have fun with that." The same verdict is issued for Jungwoo. His mission is to spend an hour integrating the full choreography of Apollo's debut single, *U SHINE*, into his regular work duties. If anyone asks what he's doing, he has to start over. And Nicky is endlessly amused by this, but it's Max's mission that takes the cake. While working their pancake stall at the fall festival, he's supposed to quote some of Apollo's English lyrics to their customers. He's required to do it with a straight face, and he doesn't get to choose which lyrics. This means "Baby, can I waste your time?" is fair game.

"Who'd you piss off?" Nicky asks, once he's finished laughing himself to tears. "Aren't you supposed to be popular in America? Don't they love you here? Maybe one of the producers has a crush on Hazel."

"Shut the hell up, hyung." But despite the vitriol, Max

appears to have accepted his own doom. Shoulders squared, he says, "You want us to get the time off, don't you? And you promised to help me with Ari. I'll take care of my end if you take care of yours."

"Oooh, relax. I'm on it, buddy. Your favorite brother is in good hands. I'll be your knight in shining armor—"

Nicky takes a punch to the arm. He doesn't care; everything is just so funny. He's still wheezing when he gets to Kei. "Let's see. You need to thank a member every time a customer thanks you." The prospect makes him giggle. "You've got the worst luck. That's a bad fit for you, but Ari could manage it. I might come back later."

"Get him to switch with me now. Mine is stupid. They want me to thank you guys, for what? Stealing my silk pillowcase? Ruining my life?"

Nicky grabs Kei's face and plants a big, sloppy kiss on his cheek. "You're welcome, my son. I know I bring you so much joy." He traipses away. In the background, Kei might be breaking out in hives.

Last to receive his mission is Jesse. Based on the spring in his step, he's hit the jackpot. He refuses to be manipulated into swapping missions. "I know mine's the easiest!" he wails. "That's why I'm keeping it! I'm just supposed to pretend I don't know how to do basic things until someone else gives up and does it for me. I do that anyway! This is my chance, you can't stop me, I'm *locked in*—"

Apollo's youngest member kicks up such a fuss that Nicky lets it go. He's not about to compromise his agenda, so he'll switch with Ari himself. "Getting ten people to ask for a selfie, that's brainless. I'd just be bored," he confides to the camera, "and I'll be chained to a griddle until 6:00, anyway. Now, writing my name on every order without getting caught? Way more interesting. They should've specified which name, though. They might regret that later." Nicky grins. "Hey, you got all of that, right? When I made my rounds?"

The camera shakes. "You knew I was filming?"

"Oh, yeah. Wait, were you trying to be sneaky? That's so funny. Aren't you the same guy who's been selling our used water bottles to fans online? Can you believe I've never told anyone about that? By the way, for a small monthly fee, I won't say anything about your other secret, either."

"My other secret? What are you talking about?"

But Nicky's long gone. We'll never know, and neither will this guy.

23

At Lake Monroe, the air hummed with all the candy-fueled energy you might expect from the weekend before Halloween. The water was a mirror, its gleaming surface burnished to a high, golden shine as the sun dipped below the horizon. Hay bales and ornamental wheat sheaves lined the sidewalks.

They'd been in the thick of this autumn extravaganza for hours. The producers had Apollo running a stall at the festival's sprawling lakeside market, a pop-up version of Sunshine Diner. The guys took turns dishing up pancakes and working the crowd, cameras ghosting behind them every step of the way. Their stall was such a hit that Jiyeon lost track of time.

She lost track of Eunjae, too. It was ages before she realized that he was still out there on the nearest dock, surrounded by tourists. He'd offered to take one family's photo, according to a report from Jesse, and then the requests wouldn't stop coming. Selfies with the photographer were in as much demand as the photographer's services.

"He's gotten ten people by now, right?"

"More than ten. Ari's good to go."

"Good to go for what?" asked Jiyeon.

"Nothing," came the weirdly synchronized reply.

"Huh. Okay."

Jeannie focused on crowd control. Nicky handled the griddle, as usual, while Max and Jesse stacked pancakes on paper plates. They needed to survive being jammed into this stall with one another for thirty more minutes. Then they could close up shop at last. It would amount to a lot of disappointed people in line, but the producers wanted more footage of Apollo enjoying the event.

When would she have a chance to talk to Eunjae? He'd gotten back late last night, and he'd been so quiet since then. Jiyeon had no idea if they'd have time tonight, either.

"I need to get out of here," she sighed, without really meaning to complain out loud.

"Ooooh, me too," said Nicky. "But here's what else I need: the scoop. And the cameras just left, so let's get into it while we can. What's with you and Arthur, ajumma? Tell me. I'm all ears."

"Nothing's going on there."

"Exactly. Nothing. No chemistry."

"Why would they have any?" Max groused. "That's done. They broke up twice already."

"Did you hear that, Jess? Bark, bark, bark. I thought the dog was here."

"He does sound like Snowball, oh my gosh."

"Whoa, whoa. Her name's Uyu. That's a flat fee of $499 if you're changing it again."

Jeannie leaned forward as though reporting the latest twist in a journalistic investigation. "They didn't have any chemistry back then, either." And when Jiyeon turned to her, eyes wide, she only doubled down on that assertion. "What? It's true! You have loads more chemistry with Ryan than you ever did with Arthur. You have more chemistry with literally any member of Apollo. I should know. I've seen it."

Max stared at Jeannie, slack-jawed. "Gross!"

"Everything I'm saying is true. The equation works perfectly if you just switch out Arthur. Like, who was that photographer man? Phillip? Jiyeon and Phillip, cute. Jiyeon and Colin, also cute. I sorta thought that might go somewhere. Jiyeon and Arthur, though? Not cute."

"Oh my gosh. Ohhhhhh my gosh. Who do I tell? I have to tell somebody—"

"Who's Phillip?" Max demanded. He almost dropped a pancake on the ground. "And who the hell is Colin?"

"Excuse me, have you seen our dog? Bark bark bark—"

Jiyeon hastened to explain before the argument spiraled into a full-fledged brawl. "They used to work for me. Phillip was my photographer and Colin helped with editing all the videos." She aimed a puzzled glance at Jeannie. "You thought I might end up with Colin? Really?"

"He had a nice car!"

"Jeannie, he was married."

"Just barely! They weren't even married for a whole year yet!"

Nicky clanged his spatula against the mixing bowl. "Okay, people. This is hard for me to say, because I'm very, very interested in all of this new information, but let's focus up. She still hasn't answered my original question."

"Why did we get together? I guess it just happened."

She fell into a relationship. She didn't fall in love. That much became obvious early on, and yet she'd forced herself to avoid thinking about it for years. Who even fell in love, anyway? Was that something that happened in real life? It seemed like fiction, an urban legend passed down through the ages. A phenomenon that skipped her and happened to other people instead.

Jiyeon had dated as a teenager, sure. It was never long-term, never serious, and never Arthur. Romance fell to the wayside as she juggled cosmetology school with shifts at Gloria's, but she was too busy to care about it much. Then came the big clients, the early years on social media, the later years when her life online went spinning out of control. Arthur had waited through all of that. It felt less like a love story and more like a foregone conclusion. He was the obvious answer she'd been dodging for years and years. Everybody told her so.

Her mood guttered like a candle flame. Jiyeon didn't want to talk about Arthur, or even think about Arthur, or read the eleven text messages he'd sent her between last night and this afternoon. *Hey Emms, did you ever change your username? I was talking to that guy from Prism and he made some good points. Emmie, look at this spot by the new grocery store. Much better than what you were looking at before. Emmie, you should go look. Emmie, Emmie, Emmie.*

"There's not much else to it," she said, eager to move on. "Arthur planned this thing for my birthday. There was a food truck, and all our old friends were there from high school."

Jeannie huffed at this. "So what? Ryan got you that little trophy from Lowell's."

"He did." And she smiled at the memory, which was a personal favorite.

"You went out with him because of the food truck, or what?" From the expression on Max's face, it was clear that Jiyeon's response might alter his opinion of her forever. "It'd have to be one hell of a food truck, noona. That guy's a freak."

"He said it had always been me. There were a lot of people watching. I guess I felt like I had to. Or that I should? Like it was the thing I was supposed to do?"

Nicky winked at a customer, who stuffed another few dollar bills into their tip jar, mesmerized. He thanked them profusely. Then he turned to Jiyeon and said, "Ajumma, that story was even more boring than I expected. Let's talk about this instead: how do you feel about the chemistry between your boyfriend and your ex-boyfriend—"

Max seized the spatula and shoved it into Nicky's mouth, attempting to put an end to that line of questioning. Jiyeon responded, though. "I know he likes Arthur. It isn't easy for Eunjae to make new friends, so I'd never tell him to stop. Things are hard enough, yeah? Why add more to that?"

Their last ten minutes went by without incident and staff offered to handle the rest. Max and Jesse were chomping at the bit, eager to buy churros and carve pumpkins. They ran ahead, taking Jeannie with them. The cameras trotted to catch up. Where did Eunjae go? She'd looked for him by the water, but he and Denny weren't on the dock anymore.

Jiyeon was still weaving through the crowd with Nicky when Arthur made his grand entrance. He galloped into the festival square on horseback, no less. "A horse," she murmured, watching this spectacle unfold. "Where'd he get a horse?"

Her companion finished sending a flurry of text messages, cackling all the while. "Never mind about that for now. Hear me out, okay? Let me just throw this out there. You said things are hard, but do they have to be?"

"Hmm? What do you mean?"

"I mean that it could be easy. We just choose the harder way, thinking it's the only way, or the only right way. Your forbidden romance, for example." Nicky pulled up an image on his phone: four guys who were obviously idols, their hair and clothes emblematic of the late '90s. "This is Orion. They were huge back then, the biggest moneymaker Zenith Media ever had, but they didn't even make it to their fifth year before the first dating scandal hit. Amazing, right? I wish we could've matched them for speed. I've been so bored all this time, ajumma, you've got no idea."

"I feel for you."

"You should. Nothing's worse than being bored. But anyhow, my point is that this guy," he said, zooming in on an Orion member, "also had a forbidden romance. She was an idol, too. That's the Holy Grail of forbidden romances in this business, okay? He went all out. Eyes on the prize. Experiment! And guess what? He didn't try to hide it."

Jiyeon saw Jungwoo waving to them, appearing and disappearing as he waded through the crush of people. She'd catch a flash of his hair, dyed a deep burgundy, the same shade as red wine. Then she would lose sight of him again. The crowd had swelled after sunset, with many drawn to the festival's evening performances.

"Did it work?" she asked Nicky. "Was the group okay even though he went public?"

"Oh, yeah. Two more albums. Seven years. They even got married. You know our bigwigs at Emerald, the founder noonas? They went to the wedding."

A group of preteens in soccer uniforms streamed around them, headed for the midway. Jungwoo reached them at last, saying they should head in that direction as well. "Hey, was that Arthur just now?"

"On the horse? Uh-huh." Jiyeon decided to avoid the midway. She wanted to be wherever Arthur wasn't. "You guys go ahead. I'm gonna look for Eunjae."

"Wait," Jungwoo blurted out. "I know where he is."

"He does." Nicky gave a thumbs-up with one hand while holding his phone with the other. Was he recording this? For what? "Rock and roll, son. Don't keep the Chief waiting."

"And this is all you want from me? You swear, hyung?"

Nicky promised him that this was it. No strings attached, no fine print. They couldn't torture the info out of him, that's how seriously he took this business. To Jiyeon, he said, "Listen, ajumma. I'm not about transparency. I like secrets, same as you. But that was one time in history when telling the truth actually worked out for somebody, so I think it's worth a look. I like to study the ways, even if they're not necessarily my ways."

Still recording, Nicky indicated that she should leave with Jungwoo. For some reason, the latter was struggling to make eye contact. "Sorry about this," he said. "I mean it. And can you tell Ari, too? Make sure he knows. I'm really sorry, but I don't have much of a choice."

She blinked at him. "You're saying sorry in advance? For what?"

"This." His fingers closed around Jiyeon's wrist, transforming their interaction into a classic Korean drama scene. The only thing missing was a ballad playing in the background. "Come with me."

24

"D ON'T ASK QUESTIONS, RYAN. Just get in the boat."

It wasn't the strangest directive he'd ever gotten from Denny, but Eunjae was perplexed nonetheless. Had the plans changed? Why had he been brought to the lake on his own? Last he'd heard, the crew wanted Apollo to gather at the midway. There, they would find out if they'd gotten the weekend off.

"Take this," Denny said now, passing a reusable grocery bag over the side. "Should have everything you need, and then some."

Eunjae stowed this mysterious cargo at his feet. "Don't we have to pay to ride these?"

"Already done."

"This sign says the attendant has to explain the safety measures—"

"The attendant," Denny replied, "is indisposed."

"Right. Okay."

"And there's nothing to explain, anyway. One, wear your life vest. Two, don't fall overboard. Easy."

A cheer rose up from the fairgrounds, cresting the hill and reaching Eunjae as a muffled roar. While he adjusted the straps on his life vest,

Denny checked his watch. Then he dispatched a text message, muttering to himself about the death of punctuality as a character trait. Also, he mumbled something about a horse. A horse...?

Another minute ticked by. A couple approached the dock, but Denny redirected them. Planting himself in front of the ticketing booth, he said, "Temporarily closed. Low level biohazard situation."

The next would-be boating enthusiasts were dismissed in a similar manner. Eunjae checked his phone, noting that the group chat was suspiciously quiet. And there was nothing from Jiyeon, even though the stall should be closed. Where did everyone go? Maybe they were headed here. He waited, watching the water, listening to the creak of wooden planks as Denny paced the dock. It was a moment of much-needed tranquility after everything that happened with Ezra, who wasn't here tonight. Not feeling well, according to their dad, when he called the producers that morning. Understandable. In a lot of ways, Eunjae wasn't feeling well either.

"Any minute now," said Denny. He motioned at the boats. "Ever tried one of these?"

"Ah, yeah. We were filming for this show in Tokyo and we had to race swan boats for one of the games."

"And you all made it out alive. Miracles do happen."

Eunjae reflected on the experience. The members had somehow gotten the idea that they were supposed to sink each other's boats instead of competing to see who could cross the lake at the fastest speed. To this very day, Nicky insisted he had nothing to do with that crucial bit of misinformation.

"I got lucky," he concluded. His partner was Namgyu, and they had yet to invent a game that his brother couldn't win.

Another pair came down the hill. This time, Denny didn't warn them away. "Finally," he grunted. "Better stick to songwriting, Orpheus. Can't say you have a promising career in delivery services."

"Jungwoo did his best."

Eunjae leaned so far over the side that he almost tumbled onto the dock. That was Jiyeon. She climbed in next to him, snatching the second life vest from the floorboards. "This is the one we're taking? Did it have to be the most boring boat they've got?"

"Boring?"

"You heard me."

"Have you seen the rest? They look deranged."

Their boat was a plain, boxy variant designed for practicality over whimsy. The others were shaped like swans, but also ducks and flamingos, even a dragon. Jiyeon argued that the ducks were cute. Denny countered that their eyes were big, empty, and psychotic. Meanwhile, before making the return jog uphill, Jungwoo paused to apologize.

"For what?"

"I hope you never find out." Somehow, his expression came across as regretful and wistful at the same time. "Anyway, have fun. Maybe Max will stop yelling in the chat about all the date nights you've had to miss."

"He's been yelling about that?" In the group chat? When?

But Jungwoo took off in a hurry, shooed into the night by their manager. On the seat next to Eunjae, Jiyeon braced her feet against the pedals as their boat slipped free of its moorings. Her brother made short work of the knots.

"Forty-five minutes, Yeonnie. I've made the arrangements." He pointed at Eunjae. "Don't drown. We're driving tomorrow."

They did get the weekend off, then. That was good news. Mission accomplished, Denny turned to go. Eunjae called to him at the last second.

"Boss," he said. "I know it's too busy right now, but I thought... if you're still offering, I do want to find her. Vivian, I mean."

His manager slowed to a stop. Trading a loaded glance with Jiyeon, he replied, "Changed your mind, huh?"

Eunjae nodded, although it was more complex than just changing his mind. He supposed it was also a change of heart. "I won't bother her. I'd be happy just seeing that she's out there, and knowing she's okay. If we could find her, that would be enough."

A snort. "*If* we can find her? Ryan, come on. Believe in the network. Trust the resources."

Jiyeon reached for Eunjae's hand. "Of course we'll find her. Don't worry." And then they were off, pedaling slowly, the shoreline receding behind them.

The seats were cold, no cushions, but they found a blanket in the bag Denny had packed. Folded into a tidy square, it was the most glaring shade of yellow known to man. "Vacuum-metalized polyethylene," Eunjae read out from the label. "Windproof, waterproof, heat-reflective. Designed to boost odds of survival and rate of rescue."

"Oh, goodness." Jiyeon peered inside, examining the rest of their provisions. "Why did he think we'd need a fire-starting kit...?"

Out on the water, the night felt impossibly vast, its edges distant and undefined. This was the most solitude they'd managed in ages. There were no brothers and no producers and no cameras. They worked the pedals, finding balance, falling into a rhythm underscored by comfortable silence. The breeze had died; they pedaled to the center of the lake, until the fairgrounds felt like a world removed, and then they allowed the boat to simply drift.

Eunjae had a hundred, hundred things he wanted to tell her. The words that tumbled out were not his first choice, but also felt like the only choice.

"Ezra thinks I left because this was my dream. Mum told him it's what I've always wanted. And he thinks Vivian tried to ruin that for me, that she's this terrible person."

"But that's not true," Jiyeon said. "Did you say that? Did you tell him?"

He shook his head. "How?"

"He'd listen, Eunjae. Give him a chance—"

"I can't!" He stared out at the lake, tracking moonbeams as they skipped like stones across the surface. "It's like Ezra's had a different mum all this time. He doesn't see what I see. Even if he doesn't believe me, there's no going back. He'd never be able to look at her the same way again. How can I be the one to tell him? Why does it have to be me?"

Jiyeon didn't have an answer for that. Of course not, because who would?

"What if Mum's doing it again? Everything she did with me... all the choices she took away... what if she takes them from Ezra, too?"

Without hesitation, Jiyeon replied, "She won't. You'd never let that happen. *We'd* never let that happen."

If they floated any longer, they'd drift off course. He missed a beat, leaving her to handle it alone for the barest fraction of a second, and the boat listed to the right immediately. Eunjae hurried to pick up the rhythm. As usual, he was the one who slipped and lost balance. He was the one holding them back.

She didn't call him out for it. She just kept going. When strength was needed, when there was something to be solved or mended, it was her hand that held them steady. And did she have a choice? His brother, his career, his relationship. Across the board, Eunjae had no idea what he was doing.

"Your brother deserves to know what really happened," Jiyeon said, her gaze locked on the opposite shore. He heard her sniffling. "Tell him the truth. I know he'll believe you."

"He won't. He hates me."

"Ezra doesn't hate you. That's not true, either." Her eyes were bright with tears. She regarded him with such sorrow that he wanted to apologize for being the cause of it, no matter how unintentionally. And then she said, "Lose the vest."

Eunjae thought he must have misheard her, what with the sudden, deafening roar of his pulse. "Lose the vest," she repeated, shrugging out of her own. "It's in the way." A tear rolled down her cheek. Jiyeon scrubbed at it with the heel of her hand. Fiercely, she said, "Please. I need to hug you. No one will see, it's dark, and it doesn't have to be for long—"

Eunjae tossed the vest. He pulled her in close and held her so tight that she lost track of what she was saying. And he didn't have a clue about tomorrow, but in that moment there was only clarity. A certainty that endured without faltering or fading. Here was a fixed star on an ever-changing horizon. Here was the lamp in the window, leading him home.

Much too soon, their boat reached the shore. The lights and noise of the festival surged up to meet them. They had to get up, return to reality, but the idea of resuming that charade left him sick at heart.

"Yeon-ah. Let's just run away."

"Where would we go?"

"Anywhere. The moon. San Bernardino."

She laughed. "Oh, sure. *Ryan Kim: The Origin Story*. Good choice."

Water lapped against sun-bleached boards. On the dock, Jiyeon said, "I know it won't be easy, talking to Ezra, but Leila's kept enough from him. He needs to hear your side of the story. We can't control what happens after, but I think we need to trust him."

She reached with her free hand, pulled the elastic out of her hair, and slid the faded black band onto Eunjae's wrist. After so many years, the flowers were more pink than red, worn in the sun too often and thrown into the wash by mistake dozens of times. "This thing's gotten me through a lot. Take it with you."

Eunjae protested immediately. He tried to give it back, but Jiyeon stopped him, smoothing the band where it had twisted. She tugged at the cuff of his sweater until the elastic was hidden from view. Overwhelmed, driven by impulse, he leaned in to kiss her. "Let's run away," he said again, his mouth on hers. "Let's just go right now."

"I want to. I think about it more than I should." In a whisper, Jiyeon said, "Feels like I'm going insane."

"We're in a forbidden romance. I think we're supposed to feel insane."

"So it's fine, then?"

"It's normal."

Months ago, Jiyeon wrapped her arms around him in a parking lot, saying goodbye. For Eunjae, it was a lesson in two parts. He learned that goodbye could be harder than he'd ever imagined, and he learned that holding her close was the easiest thing he'd ever done. Easier than breathing. This made it difficult to leave her, every single time.

Reluctantly, they stepped apart. Arthur came down the ramp just seconds later. "What are you doing?" he demanded. "How could you be so careless?"

25

WHEN THEY WERE SIXTEEN, maybe seventeen, Jiyeon and Arthur helped at a restoration project hosted by the Lemon Grove Historical Society. Back then, a portion of each weekend was for volunteer work. Their service club had a packed schedule. On that particular Saturday, Jiyeon climbed a rickety ladder to scrub a row of windows caked in grime. She did it because it needed doing. Also, she did it because Arthur told her not to.

She still remembered his reaction, when one of the rungs snapped and she'd come close to falling. He'd been worried, yes, but also livid. The same emotions warred in his expression right now. But what right did he have, to be so upset about this, to scold her for being careless? When did any of this become Arthur's business?

As usual, his presence brought the past into sharp focus, overlapping it with the present in a way that made Jiyeon feel trapped. She was sixteen and Arthur was saying that he loved her. She was twenty-six and painfully aware that she didn't love him in the same way.

Fighting to keep her anger in check, Jiyeon said, "Please just stay out of this."

"I'm supposed to stand by while you get yourself into this much trouble? You could've gotten caught, running off like that." Arthur proceeded to list the consequences of getting caught, as if they weren't well aware. Apollo fans would be furious. The guys could lose the contract they were so close to signing, and the damage to their careers could be irreparable.

"Wait. You said we could've gotten caught." Eunjae frowned, studying Arthur's face in the gloom. "How long have you known about us?"

Arthur had the grace to look wildly uncomfortable. "A few weeks."

"Who told you?"

"I promised I wouldn't say."

"Arthur—"

"I promised!" He rubbed at the back of his neck. "Does it matter? Look, Ari. This came out of left field for me, but... I'll be honest, man. I thought you'd think twice before getting involved. If your fans find out, they could make Emmie's life a living hell. Stalking, death threats, harassment. I figured you'd never put anybody through that. I really thought you'd know better."

Even as this admonition stunned Eunjae into silence, it stoked Jiyeon's temper into a roaring blaze. "We're done here. This conversation is over."

She took Eunjae with her. Arthur jogged to keep up. "Hey, let's just calm down, okay?" He said this in his most placating, most infuriating tone. It made her anger burn higher and brighter, the fury escalating to a fever pitch. How was it that he could know her for over a decade without ever learning what *not* to say?

"I'll calm down when you leave. Go home. Tell them you can't do the show anymore. I'm serious, Arthur. I've had enough."

"Would you just let me explain? Don't be like this, don't do that thing where you try to take care of it all on your own. You never ask for help even when you need it."

"And do you think it's helpful to scold us like we're little kids? We both knew what we were doing, when we made this choice. I thought I was choosing to be with him, and only him, but so many people keep getting involved. That's not normal."

Normal. Eunjae flinched at the word she'd chosen. Instantly, she was sorry. Jiyeon ran up hard against her own exhaustion, a solid wall built with bricks she'd laid by hand. She was so tired. She didn't want to talk about this anymore.

Farther down the path, Apollo had congregated near the water, loaded with souvenirs and midway prizes. She could tell they were worried, but although she was grateful that they cared, it was just more weight to bear. Another row of bricks. Jiyeon stepped aside so that Eunjae could be drawn into the fold once more. Brothers slung their arms around him, veterans at concealing fatigue with jokes and laughter. He was the only one who couldn't manage a smile.

The guys filmed their final segment of the day. Arthur joined her on the sidelines, more determined than ever. "You left this kind of life," he persisted. "Said you were sick of living every second on camera. You didn't want it anymore. Now you're willing to do it again, just for him? I don't understand."

"You don't have to understand. For the last time, this isn't your problem."

"How can you say that? I know it's over between us, but you're still my friend, and so is Ari. I'm just worried. This could be bad for both of you."

"So we should break up? Is that where you're taking this?"

"I never said that! Emmie, come on." Arthur sighed, pacing to the edge of the dock. "I guess I was pretty hard on him earlier, but I've got nothing against Ari. I'm not saying you shouldn't be with him."

"Good," Jiyeon retorted, "since you'd have no right to say it."

"Could you just let me talk? I want to help you!" He rubbed at his temple the way he always used to when they'd argue, like her stubborn defiance had given him a headache. Then Arthur said, "You guys have to keep this a secret, don't you? I could help you hide."

She stared at him. "What?"

"The fans won't think you're dating Ari if it seems like you're with me. Solves so many problems. That's why they asked me to stay on. We don't even need to pretend, they'll just edit some footage and make it seem like we're together. It won't be real. It's just for optics."

"Optics."

"And it would be a lot safer," he pressed on. "You could still be with him, but no one will suspect that anything's going on—"

Well, there was only one answer. Jiyeon cut him off, unwilling to hear another word. "No," she said. "We won't be doing that."

"Why not? Apollo's PR guy said it was a great idea."

So he was good buddies with Eric, too. "And where did this idea come from, originally? The same person who told you I'm with Eunjae?"

The look on his face was enough to confirm her suspicions. Over the course of their long relationship, as friends and then more, Arthur's thoughts and motivations had always been as transparent as Jiyeon's were opaque. The pieces fit. He'd met everyone in Eunjae's family because he was staying at the same hotel. He'd brought her a 'solution' which involved active deception, the telling of a continuous lie. Arthur, who felt morally compromised by even the smallest, most harmless fib. Arthur, who couldn't even lie about his schedule for the sake of a surprise birthday party. She knew him too well. He didn't come up with that plan on his own.

"Next time you hang out with Leila, ask her why Eunjae has her number blocked."

There was no attempt at denial. "She's just worried about him. That's his mom. It's only natural."

"Not everyone's mom is like yours or mine. Leila's been a lot of things, but she hasn't been his mom."

Jiyeon started walking away, but Arthur pursued. "You know what I said, when I found out you were dating him? I told her that it couldn't be true. You don't do stuff like this. It's just not like you."

"It's just not like me to do what, Arthur?"

"To... to be like this!" he exclaimed, hands thrown up in exasperation. "Sometimes I don't even recognize you. You've been with Ari for what, a few months? But you're willing to be here, wasting your time working backstage on a reality show when you could be doing your own thing. You've known what you want out of life for as long as we've been friends, and that's what you should be doing right now, you should be out there going after your big dream. I thought that was the plan. I can't believe you'd change it for a guy. You definitely weren't about to change anything for me."

She read the hurt in his expression, the struggle to find order and meaning in a world that had flipped upside down, gone off track. She made note of the stubborn set to his jaw as he waited for her to acknowledge that she had, indeed, lost her mind completely. Her priorities had gone out the window. He was right and she was wrong. Wrong for not being the same girl he'd met in middle school, wrong for growing into a shape that was new to him. Jiyeon heard everything Arthur was trying to say. She even heard the things he refused to say out loud.

The water was cold, but shallow. Jiyeon shoved him into it.

"It's your turn to listen. Plans change. This isn't what I expected, but I've found something good and I won't let go. And maybe I seem so different 'cause you never really knew me. You just thought you did."

He grabbed hold of the deck, splashing her shoes and the cuffs of her jeans. Jiyeon crouched down to look him in the eye. "I'm not done yet. It's not my place to tell Eunjae that you can't be friends. If he still likes you after this, that's his call. But if you ever nag him about his mom or his job or anything else, you'd better hope I don't find out. You don't know the whole story. You don't have any right."

Arthur lost his grip on the sodden boards. He slipped below the surface, then popped up and scolded some more. "Emmie, do *not* push his mom into the lake. I'm serious! I know that look! Geez, you really haven't changed much after all, I take it back—"

Jiyeon ignored him. Apollo and the film crew had come to investigate. "Arthur fell in," she said. "Can you help? He'll need to borrow a coat, at least. And I have some beach towels in my car. I'll go get them."

Denny snorted, but the guys were already on the move. Namgyu shucked his jacket and went pelting down the dock. Nicky jogged after him, catching Jiyeon's eye as he passed. "Hurry, Zu," he bawled over his shoulder. "Arthur can't swim!"

"What? Are you joking?"

There was another splash, the sound of a heroic, if unnecessary, rescue. Eunjae pushed through the jumble of people and equipment to reach her, but Jiyeon was searching for a face in the crowd. Sure enough, she found him: Eric in his teal jacket, the Prism logo clearly visible on his chest. She could hear Denny already, berating her for the lack of subtlety, but she didn't care. When Eric noticed her staring, Jiyeon stared right back.

From the group chat shared by eight of the nine members of Apollo, originally named Talking Behind Ari's Back *by someone who thought it would be so funny. This has since been changed to the less incendiary but far more boring* Group Chat 2.

Kazu: Anyway the suits are purple and we have to wear them or my cousin will kill us

Kei: Wrong chat, old man.

Kazu: Wait, what?

Kei: Did you seriously type half of that in the other chat and half of it in this one?

Kei: Do you use your phone blindfolded?

Kazu: This chat was at the top of the list!

Jesse: omg can't believe we have a secret group chat now

Jesse: get me out of here, i can't keep secrets, i don't have the willpower

Jaehwan: ?????

Jesse: just kidding, don't kick me out, I need the info

Jaehwan: You know what? I'm muting this. I don't want to know what you people are doing. I'm on vacation. This is not my lookout right now.

Jaehwan: Godspeed, Kazuhiko.

Namgyu: awww! nobody deserves a vacation more than leader-hyung, i love that he's on vacation, i can't wait for my turn

Kazu: What

Kazu: No come back

Max: Can someone explain how Jungwoo knew before the rest of us did

Max: Why tf was he included

Jungwoo: What plan? Nicky was blackmailing me!

Nicky: Ooooh it's busy in here

Nicky: Jungwoo, nice job

Nicky: I like the part where she grabbed your wrist right back

Jesse: omgomgomg REVERSE WRIST GRAB

Nicky: No time for a back hug? What's another small betrayal after the big betrayal?

Max: What the FUCK hyung

Jesse: REVERSE!!!

Jesse: WRIST GRAB!!!

Jungwoo: I told him I was sorry…

Kei: Why can't they just take the deal? Isn't Eric right? It would be easier if everyone thought noona was with Arthur.

Nicky: Oooooh and then if Ari's caught with

her, I could have another scandal!

Nicky: *Emma Han Leaves Lawyer Boyfriend for Lawyer Idol Who Was Also Her Boyfriend!*

Nicky: *Ari's Not Your Angel - Love Triangle Cheating Scandal 2025!*

Namgyu: aww, nicky's smiling so big right now! he's so happy!

Kei: Okay, never mind. That's worse. Not sure the "plan" is any better, though.

Nicky: Hey, have a little faith in me

Nicky: I did my research

Kazu: Hang on, who grabbed what now?

Nicky: This plan will work

Nicky: This plan will break Eric's soul

Namgyu: haha! omg!

Jesse: basically what happened zuzu is that jungwoo grabbed emma noona's wrist in public like it was a drama or smth

Jungwoo: Because Nicky made me do it!

Kazu: YOU DID WHAT

[*Denny has been added to the chat*]

Denny: Who dragged me into this nonsense?

Kei: I did, Captain! Hyung's being a psychopath, Captain!

Denny: Not exactly breaking news.

Kazu: THAT IS YOUR BROTHER'S GIRLFRIEND

Nicky: YEAH MAX

Max: *(8x angry face emojis)*

Max: *(6x knife emojis)*

Jungwoo: I apologized! To both of them!

Jesse: lol lol lol when eric sees this

Max: Who the hell cares about Eric

Max: Ari was losing his shit the other night and I can't blame him

Max: He ran away last time

Max: What if hyung just quits for good this time?

Max: We're doing this to help him

Nicky: Bark bark bark yes we are, my son

Jesse: but omg hyung why u blackmailing other hyung

Jesse: what did he do this time

Jungwoo: I didn't do anything!

[*Jiyeon has been added to the chat*]

Namgyu: aww!!! yay!!!!

Jiyeon: why am I here?

Denny: Mission brief, Yeonnie.

Nicky: Whoa whoa whoa

Nicky: Chief, are you saying it's a go

Nicky: Are you making me the happiest man alive

Denny: I'm authorizing the use of lethal force.

Denny: If Eric's busy with your nonsense, maybe he'll leave the shop alone.

Jiyeon: wait, eunjae says he's not in this chat

Max: We'll tell him tomorrow

Jesse: omg yeah we keep secrets now noona

Jesse: we all have a traitor face like jungwoo hyung

Jungwoo: Okay…

Max: I don't! (*6x angry face emojis*)

Nicky: Okay okay I'm ready

Nicky: Hear me out, ajumma

Nicky: Eric wants the fans to think you're dating Arthur

Nicky: No scandal since he's a civilian

Max: Yeah he's a fucking loser

Nicky: Great idea, but mine's better

Nicky: Ultimate misdirection

Nicky: Sunshines can't say you're dating Ari if it looks like you could be dating all of us

Nicky: We could be GREAT ex-boyfriends

Kei: What kind of goal is that! Idiot!

Nicky: They'll be so confused

Nicky: And it would be so funny

[*Ari has been added to the chat*]

Denny: Lee, you can't keep cracking under pressure like this.

Jesse: omgggggg

Max: Hyung needs to know!

Ari: I need to know what?

Nicky: I'll tell you when I finish leaking this
    video of Namgyu

Kei: Insane! Goodnight!

Jiyeon: i think

Jiyeon: that this might be the longest night
    of my life

Kazu: YOU'RE THE ONE LEAKING THE VIDEOS??????

26

The sticker was huge, with a font to match, and printed on vinyl so offensively neon that it left an afterimage every time Eunjae blinked. *PLEASE BE PATIENT*, it read. *STUDENT DRIVER*. Denny slapped this warning onto the bumper of his SUV with the air of someone performing a crucial civic duty. Then he tossed the keys to Eunjae and said, "Let's go. Ten points if you don't terrorize any pedestrians today."

"Are you fucking kidding me?" Max exclaimed, advancing down the driveway in his pajamas. "You can see that from space!"

"Good. Even aliens deserve to know that rank amateurs are on the road. Communication saves lives." He lowered his sunglasses. "And why are you here? Need something?"

Eunjae knew better than to respond if their manager asked this question. It wasn't meant to be answered because you absolutely didn't need anything. If you needed it, Denny would've gotten it to you already, along with an instruction manual and concise verbal directions for its use. And if the sunglasses came down half an inch? The wisest course was to turn tail and run.

He figured Max knew better, too. They'd been under Denny's watchful eye for months now. And maybe Max was aware, but awareness didn't stop him from declaring that he did, in fact, need something. He pointed to the bumper sticker and said, "Take this off before he gets bullied. Nobody likes a student driver."

"They don't have to like him. They just have to avoid him. So get back in the house and enjoy your day off, yeah? Have some breakfast. Get online and order some age-appropriate sleepwear."

Max didn't budge. He didn't even respond to the comment about his garish cartoon pajamas. "Hyung, are you really letting him do this to you? You don't have to. I'll just grab that stupid thing and go."

Chuckling, Denny urged him to try it and lose a hand. Eunjae hastened to intervene before his brother could take the dare, since he'd never known Max to not take the dare, and he'd never known Denny to not deliver on a promise. "It's okay," he said. "I mean, I am a student driver."

"Incredible. A statement founded on logic." Denny pushed the sunglasses back into position. "Go inside. I got a text from Miss Lim's manager. Someone's coming by with that stuff in about an hour, give or take. We're heading out and I won't be around to handle it for you. Play nice." Those last two words were punctuated by the passenger door slamming shut, a signal that there would be no further discussion.

Hearing the message loud and clear, Eunjae hustled to take his spot behind the wheel. "Hazel sent him something?"

"Clothes. She wants them in coordinating outfits during that wedding weekend in Japan."

"Don't you think we should stay, then? What if Max throws everything into the fountain?"

Another door slammed. His brother claimed the back seat and

buckled himself in. "No way am I staying here. Find the gas pedal, hyung. Get me the hell away from this place."

For a moment, the car shook as though an earthquake had ripped through the valley. It wasn't an earthquake, though. It was just Denny. "You're scared of her," he said to Max, laughing, "and it's fair, 'cause I've seen Hazel's knife work. That's two of you being sensible for a change. Less than five minutes apart, too. Somebody pinch me."

"I'm not scared of her! I just don't want to see her. You never know with Hazel. She said it'd be someone else bringing that stuff, but I wouldn't put it past her to show up anyway. I'll pass. It's bad enough that she's coming to the wedding."

More of Denny's explosive laughter. "Fine, I won't kick you out. Can't blame you for prioritizing survival. But you won't make a single noise the whole time Ryan's driving, yeah? Not one word. This is a distraction-free learning environment."

"I won't distract him—"

"Correct. You'll comply with the directive unless you want Miss Lim to know your exact location. I'm talking latitude, longitude, and approximate miles above sea level. Full coordinates. Don't test me, Lee."

Max clamped his mouth shut. Eunjae took his foot off the brake, but then the doors opened again, and four additional brothers squashed into the SUV. They wanted a ride into Monroe. They wanted a ride all the way to LA. They wanted to stop for donuts, coffee, scrambled eggs. No, they wanted tacos. But actually, what about crepes?

An ominous *thunk*: Denny engaging the locks. "Great. Today's lesson is parallel parking. The goal is 85% accuracy, and now I won't need to use these cones I ordered online. You guys are pretty sturdy. You can do the work of a safety cone, no problem."

The silence that followed was deeply unnatural. Eunjae checked the rearview mirror, concerned. Maybe he'd imagined his brothers piling in. But no, the seats were occupied. His passengers were just... quiet. Trapped. Regretting their life choices.

He eased the car down the driveway, through the iron gates, and onto the narrow road that led to town. The fields were wreathed in fog. Sporadic sunshine burned through the mist, flooding groves and pastures with a haze of gold. Visibility was limited to five or six feet ahead, and although Eunjae knew the route, his grip tightened on the wheel. He'd never driven in these conditions before.

Denny's voice cut into his thoughts. "Just follow the dotted line, Ryan."

"Sorry. I should speed up a little, too."

"You're fine. Watch the road and stay in your lane. Eyes front, lights on, wheels on this side of the line. Nothing to it. And quit acting like you don't know how to drive. Sure, the fog makes it hard to see. But you manage every single day with all that hair flopping into your eyes, so how's it any different from this? Low visual acuity is the norm, for you."

Max couldn't take it. "Hey, he gets enough shit from Ezra. Don't pile it on."

That complaint got him a reprimand, since he'd agreed not to talk, but Eunjae only sighed. "Wish I knew what to do about him," he said, braking at a dilapidated stop sign.

"Why should you have to? Your parents fucked up, but that's on them." Max leaned back, stretching his long legs as far as the space allowed. "And also, Ezra could shut his mouth sometimes. It wouldn't kill him."

A grunt from Denny. "Would you like to be the pot or the kettle in this situation?"

That broke the spell. After not talking, bickering, or even daring to breathe for a record six minutes, the others reverted to their old ways in an instant. "Never mind about the kid for now," said Kei. "Are we seriously going through with this? Those videos of Gyu and Jungwoo are all over the Internet. I'm shocked Prism still let us have the day off."

Patiently, Denny explained that the circus had rolled into town and wasn't going anywhere. This was the world they lived in. It was a clown game played with clown rules, and you could only win using clown tactics. But Kazu was not aware that a video of Namgyu had also been leaked. What? When did that happen?

"He posted both of us last night," Jungwoo replied.

"I thought we were doing those one at a time!"

"Quit yelling, Zu. What's it matter if the posts are making us look good? Isn't that what the agencies want? Prism should be paying hyung a salary with benefits."

"They should," Nicky giggled. "One leaked video and I rebranded Max into a gentleman. Not even just a gentleman, but a *perfect* gentleman. None of the Erics can even compete. And have you opened Star-Connect today? Exactly, you haven't, because you can't. We tanked the servers. Sunshines are nuts over Namgyu buying out that farm stand. The guy's a hero. He's saving the American agricultural industry."

Kazu was aghast. "They're calling him a hero for paying full price? He maxed out his credit card! Again!"

"The fans don't care about that, Zu. They want to be lucky, lucky Emma Han. They want flowers from Hong Namgyu. They want to *be* the flowers. And who made that happen? Me. Eric's taught me so much about manipulating people—"

"Don't you mean manipulating perception or something?" Kei cut in, revolted.

Eunjae merged onto the highway, setting a course for Lemon

Grove. "Boss, should we call her now?" They had an hour left to go, with most of his brothers present and unable to walk out in a huff. It was a good time to talk. Denny made an agreeable noise, still a grunt but in a less forbidding key.

Jiyeon's voice came through the car's Bluetooth connection, nice and clear. "Who am I talking to? Ajussi, are you in the car?"

"Oooh, I can be. What's your best offer?"

"Kim Ahnjong."

"What? Time is money, Chief."

"Her time is money, too," said Eunjae.

"Oooohhh—"

They heard Jiyeon talking to someone, a muffled conversation over clinking dishes and the faint hiss of a faucet running. She came back to the phone and said, "Sorry, I had to get out of the kitchen, it's too crowded in there."

"Good turnout, Yeonnie?"

"Uh-huh. I think I've got this in the bag. But anyway, I've been thinking about Nicky's plan. It's an interesting plan, and I like it better than Eric's, but one meddling ex-boyfriend is enough for me. No offense, guys."

"She's talking about Arthur? Why? What did he say to her?"

Kei rolled his eyes. "Could you keep up with the weird plot twists, Grandpa?"

"Nicky was telling me about this member of Orion who dated and went public—"

"See? I've been useful. I'll bill you later."

"She should bill you for interrupting her."

Max snickered at this. "Wow, hyung. You finally figured out how to make Ari mad. Not even Jungwoo could do it."

"Eh," said Nicky. "It's fun, don't get me wrong, but I'd have more fun if I could make him jealous. Wouldn't that be the real prize? I'll get there, don't worry."

Denny issued a stern and highly specific reminder of the dark fate that would befall everyone in the vehicle, if he had to make Ryan pull over. All conversation ceased.

"Anyway," Jiyeon went on, "I think things worked out for Orion 'cause the fans didn't feel ambushed. They felt like they were part of the story from the beginning. She was an idol too, so people saw them together even before the dating news, when their groups had overlapping schedules. Maybe Sunshines could get used to seeing me around."

A few beats passed. Eunjae was instructed to practice changing lanes and managed it well enough. Then Nicky said, "Sounds great to me. I've got a whole album full of Ari 'seeing you around' if you want access. Family discount, ajumma. Don't miss out on this goldmine."

"The hell do you mean by that?"

"You've been recording him? You've been recording all of us?"

"To be clear," Jiyeon cut in, "no more leaked videos. We make new content featuring all of you, hosted by me. I won't hide anymore. We're not announcing anything, that's not the point. But the agencies wanted me invisible, Prism wants to control how I'm seen, and I just don't think that's right. Think about it, okay? Gotta go." But then she came back on the line to tell Kazu not to wait up. "Eunjae's staying with me for the weekend. I'll give him back by Monday."

"What? Hold on—"

Too late. She'd strategically ended the call. Eunjae rushed to change the subject. It was now or never. "Jungwoo," he said, eyes fixed on the road. "The wrist grab, it's what Nicky told you to do, right? You wanted him to stay quiet about something."

"Um... right."

"Because you got an offer from Emerald and you didn't want us to know."

Denny crossed his arms, staring straight ahead, his expression inscrutable. Everyone had gone quiet again. A deeper silence this time, overpowering even Max. In fact, Max was the quietest of them all.

It took Jungwoo several tries, but eventually he managed to reply. "I didn't want *you* to know," he said, with a sigh. "I wasn't ready to tell anybody, but especially not you."

"Sorry, hyung. I know I forced you into that."

"It's okay. I would've had to bring it up soon, anyway."

It stood to reason that Emerald would want to keep Jungwoo. Privately, Eunjae had been waiting for this to happen. Having guessed the secret didn't make his feelings about it any less complicated, but he understood why the news had been difficult to share.

"I didn't give them an answer," Jungwoo went on to say.

Kei lifted his head. "Why not? There's only one answer. The deal with Zenith is for all nine of us. You can't stay with Emerald, that isn't an option, and what about our songs—"

"Keiichi." Kazu's voice was stern, inflexible. His weariness felt tangible. "Not now. Just... please. Not now."

27

A T LANGLEY HOUSE, THE view from Jiyeon's window encompassed the back half of the property. This included the gardens and tennis court, with Apollo's cottage buried amid the hedgerows to the right. Most mornings, she'd see three figures sprinting up and down the paths: Kazu, Nicky, and Namgyu, up at dawn for their daily run. Jungwoo sightings were common as well. He had a favorite bench in the rose garden, and he'd sit there with his guitar and a cup of coffee, notebook close at hand.

The rest of the group was fond of sleep and rarely made an appearance before lunch. Jiyeon envied their ability to stay in bed. A month after moving into this room, she'd maintained her habit of waking early even when it wasn't necessary. Sunlight soaked through the sheer curtains, working better than any alarm clock. Despite the day off, she'd gotten up at the usual time.

It had been a productive morning, to say the least. Jiyeon felt as though she'd been awake for days. After helping with post-breakfast cleanup in the kitchen, she threw herself into preparing for a meeting with Eric. When she checked her phone, a message from Eunjae was waiting to be read. *Hey, good luck. Kick Eric into next week.*

She smiled, typing as she left her room. *More like next year.*

Jiyeon had never met with multiple Erics at once. They'd always maintained a quota of one Eric per visit, as if gathering in greater numbers might implode the space-time continuum. She'd whiled away many dull presentations by imagining the Erics spontaneously combusting if they ever laid eyes on each other. But today there were three of them in the library, wearing serene smiles and Prism baseball caps. The one in the middle had been at the lake last night.

As if a council of Erics wasn't enough, they'd also brought an alternate Erin. Cozy in a teal sweatshirt, she sat beside the fireplace, laptop balanced on her knees. She'd taken the last available chair, meaning Jiyeon would have to stand. Original Eric shuffled some papers, maddeningly cheerful as usual. "Good morning, Miss Han! Isn't it gorgeous out there? If you'll hang on another minute or so, we're waiting on one more."

Jiyeon made a slow circuit of the room, perusing the bookshelves, peering through glass cases at Langley family memorabilia. The library served as a repository of yellowing documents and photos in tarnished silver frames. Here was someone's wedding band, and a cameo locket left open to show the tiny picture tucked inside. Portraits of long-dead citrus barons were also in ample supply.

So many objects, so many stories. She wondered what all the sad-eyed women were thinking, when they posed for these photographs in their best dresses and lace mantillas. She wondered if they thought of this place as a house or a home.

"Am I late? I never thought I'd run into traffic in a little town like this."

Leila, with her cosmopolitan accent and supermodel smile, hair swept into a chignon. Of course she'd be the final addition to this meeting. She shut the door behind her, trailing the scent of expensive perfume. The Eric on the left surrendered his chair without hesitation.

They traded pleasantries. Jiyeon crossed to the stained glass windows. She'd always loved the panels in their door at Wanna Waffle. She perched on the sill, finding comfort in the play of color and light. Her sister would call it a good omen. A sign or a message, like the universe sending courage when she needed it.

"Why don't we get started?" Eric flipped to the next page in his sheaf of papers. "You've got great timing, Miss Han. There's some exciting stuff in the works. Can't wait to hear your input."

The other Erics concurred. Erin tap, tap, tapped on her keyboard. "We've got an awesome opportunity for you. We took an idea from Leila and ran with it. That's why we invited her to sit in. Oh! But did you want to go first? You're the one who called the meeting."

Another idea from Leila. Great. "No, go ahead. Let's hear it."

There was a short debate over who should do the honors. In the end, Leila took the lead. "I just couldn't stop thinking about your salon. I see how hard you work every day, and you never seem to have a minute for yourself. When you're not here, you're helping your parents. You should be chasing your dream, Emma."

Erin chimed in, some saccharine nonsense about Leila being so supportive. She even threw in a joke about Jiyeon being lucky to have such a fantastic future mother-in-law. So they weren't even bothering to feign ignorance on that front. Good to know.

"To that end," said Eric, taking over, "we'd like to start the next phase of your rebrand. Now, you've done an amazing job developing this warm and relatable online persona. Your clean record has definitely made a positive impact. Thanks to these leaks, fans are now aware that you interact with Apollo on a regular basis. They're not upset about it, which is a welcome surprise. Love being wrong, let me tell you!"

Erin nodded at this, fingers hovering over the keys. "Sunshines currently don't perceive you as a threat. That's been our trajectory all along, but we need to reinforce it more than ever. You're not looking for romance, you're looking to level up as a professional. The guys are fun, but you've never lost sight of your goals. That's the angle."

Here, Eric set some pages on the coffee table, showing Jiyeon that they were commercial property listings. "Our goal is to present you, Emma Han, as the strong and independent young lady that you are. Career-focused. Driven. Starting this week, you'll be dropping a lot of your diner shifts to work on a fresh content push. We'll roll out new posts as a counter to the videos that went viral. Erin has you scheduled to tour three spaces available for lease, all very well-suited for a salon."

"We've also got a few partnerships for you." Erin listed a real estate brokerage, a cosmetology school, and an interior design studio. Solid choices. Prism had clearly been working on this gambit for weeks.

Jiyeon slid down from the windowsill. Fighting to keep her emotions in check, she took up the printed listings, skimming through descriptions, scanning the numbers for square footage and monthly rent. "You want me gone," she observed, wryly.

"Yes!" Leila replied. "We do. We want you out there, making that childhood dream come to life! You deserve to have this chance. To be honest, it's what I wish I could've had, when I was your age. I was so young when I got married, and then Ari came along. It was years and years of getting him to lessons, finding tutors, singing competitions. I gave it everything I had. I had to give up on my career, my big dreams." She sighed. "I'm so happy, Emma. I helped my son, and now I can help you."

I helped my son. Jiyeon took a breath. She counted to ten. "Hmm."

"Now, I know you're a huge help to your brother, but Prism has a replacement lined up for you. Everything's covered. You can focus on Emma, Emma, Emma and finally get your business off the ground."

"Thanks, Leila. It's so nice of you to care about me like this."

"Of course I care!"

"What if we toured these places together?" said Jiyeon, flipping the switch, putting on her sunniest smile. "I'd love that. Wouldn't you?"

"It sounds lovely. Wouldn't you rather go with Arthur, though? Childhood dream, childhood friend. Those go together, don't they?" Leila looked to Eric for backup. "I'm no PR expert, but I've been learning."

"You're my star student," Eric assured her. "Mr. Hong would be the perfect special guest for these posts." To support this assertion, the bonus Erics produced content calendars, updated metrics, samples of captions and topics to pursue in her quest for the ideal salon space. Jiyeon stopped them midway through.

"I won't bring Arthur with me. I understand what you're going for, but I think it would be confusing to include someone from my past in a content series about my future. It's not the creative direction I want to take."

Jiyeon kept talking so that no one had a chance to object. "This works out pretty well, really. At breakfast this morning, we were talking about some posts I could put together for the show, in collaboration with Apollo. I'll have more time for both projects if someone's covering me here."

Eric's smile wavered. "The production approached you with this?"

"Uh-huh." Well, after they heard her pitch, and after she'd made them waffles using the batter recipe that Denny kept under lock and key.

Worked like a charm. As their dad was fond of saying, waffles made the world go 'round. He was right, but if Eric hadn't figured that out yet, was it Jiyeon's problem? She didn't think so.

Leila's languid posture didn't match the glint in her eyes. "Isn't that a bit risky?"

"It's very risky. That's why the agencies pushed back on your involvement, initially. We'd have to meet with them—"

"Both agencies want the group's reputation to stay positive. Isn't that why Prism was hired? It also seems to me like Emerald and Zenith would benefit from keeping Sunshines happy. Apollo belongs to their fans, and this is what fans want most right now. They send messages asking how the guys are doing, if they're okay, if they're getting enough rest. There's been so much secrecy around this second season. Sunshines wouldn't be so desperate for leaked videos if we took them behind the scenes a bit more."

Jiyeon returned the listings to Eric. "The Emerald founders are executive producers on the show, aren't they? I have an appointment with one of them tomorrow. You're welcome to sit in if you'd like."

The shock on Eric's face was well worth preserving in an oil painting. "You scheduled directly with Soyeon? That's very difficult to do."

"I know a guy," said Jiyeon.

Specifically, she knew nine guys. Once they'd processed what she said to them in the car, getting an email address for Soyeon was easy. And Prism knew how to tell a story, how to bend the light and alter what was visible, but she could do that just as well. It had been her whole life, once.

Jiyeon had no desire to bring Emma back for good, but she saw that Emma could *do* something good, one last time. She would tell this story, not just for Apollo and their fans, but also for herself.

28

"Jungwoo has an offer from Emerald?"

Jiyeon sat for a moment and considered this news. Hiding with her in the kitchen at Wanna Waffle, Eunjae worked on a stack of waffles, his late dinner after a day of driving brothers around like a taxi. He said, "They want hyung to stay. Nicky found out somehow, so the usual stuff happened."

"Oh, sure. The usual blackmail. Very normal."

"Very normal. Very Nicky."

An hour after closing, the shop felt like an isolated bubble, a vessel set adrift. The shades were drawn, the doors locked. Jiyeon took up some silverware rolled into a napkin, one of many such bundles she'd been assembling when Eunjae and Denny arrived. She unwrapped a fork and had a bite of waffle, too. Pioneered by Jeannie, this was a new addition to the menu, mochi instead of their signature buttermilk. She liked it. Hopefully they'd have customers who felt the same way.

Eunjae sipped from his water glass. He'd need a trim soon, she thought to herself, absently. Apollo had a wedding to attend next weekend. She'd better get to it within the next few days. "He didn't want to tell me," she heard him say. "Worried I'd be mad."

"Are you mad?" she asked. He shook his head, because of course he wasn't.

"This is what he's always wanted. Jungwoo picked Emerald because they encourage their groups to self-produce, and because of Haewon-noona. He wanted to learn from her. I know he still does."

Jiyeon understood that Haewon was the other half of the duo behind Emerald's founding. A gifted songwriter and producer, she was the genius behind nearly every hit song released by her former girl group, Jewell. Years of going uncredited had spurred Haewon to help establish a company that favored strong lyricists and composers. The industry regarded her as a legend.

Cautiously, Jiyeon voiced the concern weighing heaviest on her mind. "Eunjae, what if he accepts? What would that mean for the rest of you?"

"I don't think Zenith will like it. The original deal was for nine members."

"Could Jungwoo work as a producer and just sign a separate contract to perform with Apollo?"

He sat back, pensive. "It's possible. I guess it would depend on how hyung negotiated the contract. The problem is that our songs are written and produced by Jungwoo, mostly, with some help from other people in-house. If we wanted to keep using his songs, Zenith would have to license them from Emerald. They'd own the rights."

"And you'd want to use his songs, of course." Without him, Apollo would have a different sound. "So your new agency would have to pay, or give you songs by someone else."

"Yeah," Eunjae replied, sadly. "If Zenith offered him a producer deal, he'd probably take it just to stay with us, but we're slowing down.

This is our tenth year coming up. Apollo won't be releasing songs very often, not with hyungs enlisting. Jungwoo's writing for new groups at Emerald. There's more demand for his work, more creative freedom."

He lapsed into silence, as he was wont to do after speaking so much. Jiyeon let him be. Painful choices loomed ahead, choices between growth and stagnation, loyalty and independence. There would be sacrifices regardless of the path they chose.

Jeannie strolled in, finished with the last of her closing duties in the dining room. Sensing the somber mood, she fished around in her apron pockets for some soda candy and dropped a few pieces on the table. "This isn't a breakup, right? You're okay, Ryan, but if she says it's over then you'll need to choke on that candy. House rules."

"Oh, goodness."

"Ah, no. It's not over." But then Eunjae set his fork down with a clang. He looked up at Jiyeon, suddenly mortified. "Wait. You *should* break up with me. I didn't even ask how it went today. Sorry, I know I keep doing that."

"How it went with what?" Jeannie asked. "And by the way, could you quit shoving Arthur into lakes when I'm not there to watch?"

It was Jiyeon's turn to apologize. She promised to wait for Jeannie next time, then summarized the meeting with Prism. As he listened, Eunjae's mortification intensified. They were forcing her to take tours? Even worse, it was his mother's idea? No, this wasn't right. He'd go back and read Jiyeon's contract again. He'd find a way to get Leila on a plane and out of this country.

"Don't send her away just yet," Jiyeon replied. "I need her to come with me."

"Yeon-ah."

"I mean it. Trust me on this."

A chuckle from Jeannie. "Gonna grill her, huh?"

"You bet I'm grilling her. What if she knows how to find Vivian?"

"I'll ask, then," said Eunjae. "You shouldn't have to deal with that."

"It's fine. If Leila's messing with me, then she has less time to mess with you."

"Messing with you is exactly how she messes with me," he argued. "She knows it. She's figured out that it's the best way to upset me, when she won't fight me directly, when she goes for you or Ezra instead."

Scooting out the door, Jeannie whined that she was bluffing, they could never break up, she'd never be okay again if that happened. Meanwhile, Jiyeon's parents returned from the evening grocery run. Denny strode in behind them, carrying Lowell's bags, arguing with their father.

They sounded like a pair of thunderstorms dueling for supremacy. Joey defended his choice to decorate the dining room with life-size cardboard cutouts of Apollo, sent by Prism earlier in the week. Denny wanted these removed, pulped, and recycled into something functional. Napkins, for example.

"We need napkins. We *don't* need effigies of Ryan and his associates."

"Effigies," murmured Eunjae.

"You heard him."

They got up to help, unloading egg cartons and orange juice, milk jugs and whipped cream. Starting this week, Wanna Waffle would be open on Mondays again. It was the only way to ensure that regular patrons could continue to reserve tables for their bingo nights and committee meetings. Every other day brought a deluge of Apollo fans, leading to long lines and a dire shortage of space. Prism loved it, the agencies loved it, and the production loved it even more. Interest in the show kept soaring to new heights. Business was better than ever, but at a price.

They got the groceries stowed in record time. True to form, Denny cast about for something more to do. The group's hectic schedule meant that he wouldn't be back to Wanna Waffle for almost two weeks. "If nothing else, this latest round of shenanigans kept Eric distracted for a while. He almost forgot to ship the merch for that event he wants us to host."

"Sorry, Den. I'll talk to them again."

"Don't worry about it. This will be over soon enough."

The lights clicked off. Denny and Joey resumed their squabble in the twilight, the argument going strong right up until the former left in his SUV. That was when Lizzie came to Eunjae with an envelope. "How's little brother? Having fun? Good actor?"

"Well," said Eunjae. "Better than me."

Jiyeon pointed at the letter. "Does everybody have a pen pal? Am I the only one who doesn't?"

"Yes, yes. Give it to Ezra. When he was here, we talked about Jane, yeah? Her letters. Writing letters all the time, that lady."

"Jane. Ah, you mean Janie? In Spain?"

"No," said Jiyeon, passing him the car keys. "Jane Austen. They're on a first name basis."

"Makes sense." He slid the letter into his pocket, taking care not to bend it. "Thanks for writing to him. You didn't need to do that when you're so busy here."

"He wrote to me first! Of course I'm writing back!" Lizzie explained that they'd received a thank you note from Ezra, mailed out from Monroe weeks ago, but the shop was indeed very busy. She'd taken forever to write her reply. "Likes to write letters. Told me they have no phones at school except weekends. Computers just for class, homework, that kind of thing. So, the kids write to each other instead. Sent you a card for your birthday, didn't he? That's a very sweet boy, same as you."

Eunjae went quiet again, waiting while Jiyeon locked the shop's back door. She didn't know it at the time, but they were both mulling over this new detail about Ezra, and her mother's words as well. *That's a very sweet boy, same as you.*

It was long past sundown. The city had stripped the palm trees on the boulevard, preparing to install lights for the coming holiday season, so the darkness was more complete than usual.

"Yeon-ah."

"Hmm?"

"I'm leaving for that wedding next Thursday. I know it's short notice, but would you come with me?"

At first, Jiyeon thought she'd misheard. "To Tokyo? I don't have an invitation. And what about Eric?"

"He'll have a lot to say, like he did about Max bringing Hazel. No media coverage allowed, though, and Zu's family takes the security really seriously. Not that Prism could stop us from attending as private citizens. Here, you do have an invitation."

He showed it to her, attached to an email. Kazu's cousin had even written a note, addressed to Jiyeon and scrawled elegantly on monogrammed stationery. *Faster than the post*, it read. *Won't you please join us?* At the bottom, she'd signed it 'Mika' as though they were old friends.

Eunjae turned to her in the dark, Ezra's letter crinkling in the pocket of his coat. Softly, he said, "Taking your girlfriend to a wedding... that's a normal thing, isn't it? I've had to say no to a lot of those. But this time won't come again, we've only got right now, so I want to try. I want to be there with you."

Normal things. So sharp was her longing in that moment, so boundless and deep, that it left no room for any other thought. "I'll go," she told him. It was an easy answer to give.

"You will?"

"I will." She laughed. Why did he look so shocked? "I don't have a dress. I'll have to find one."

He raked a hand through his hair, embarrassed. "Sorry, I didn't even think about that part. Is it too late? What can I do?"

"Eunjae. You asked me to a wedding and now you're apologizing for it?"

"I am." Now they were both laughing. Switching languages, he said, "I sincerely apologize for causing concern. I requested your company at a formal event without considering the inconvenience this might cause. I will reflect deeply and take responsibility for my actions. Please continue watching over me with warmth and kindness."

"You should ask Eric for a job. Senior Apology Composer. Lead Atonement Officer." And she could've come up with more, but she kissed him instead.

He was right. They only had right now. This time wouldn't come again.

November

Transcribed from a livestream by Emma Han (@jiye_unnie)
on the official Star-Connect channel for Sunshine 24/7:
Apollo At Your Service

Emma appears on camera, dressed in a Sunshine Diner t-shirt. She's pulled her hair into a ponytail that has just the right amount of volume. How did she do that? I mean, look at it.

"Hey! So over the weekend, I mentioned that I'm still getting tons of questions about that video with the wrist grab. I've asked Jungwoo to help me explain."

The screen floods with emoji reactions as Jungwoo joins her in the frame. Sunshines inundate the chat with heart eyes and roses and all-caps screaming. Oppa looks adorable in his uniform! Oppa seems kinda shy today, what's going on?

Jungwoo tells the fans that he's just embarrassed about the video. "I didn't know any of you would see that," he says. "Sunshines, I'm sorry. You know you're everything to me."

For the benefit of viewers who don't speak Korean, Emma provides a quick translation. The fans are swooning. Someone types that they always knew oppa wouldn't go for someone like Emma; the next three lines are just people announcing they've hit Block and Report.

She doesn't miss a beat. "Okay, before we get into it, let's start with this: did you always want to be an idol? Was this your dream?" Speaking to the audience, Emma adds, "I'm just curious. I know you're the experts, but I haven't known Apollo as long as you. And I'm kinda trying to figure out where to go with my own dream, so this is like research."

Oh no, what's going on with her dream? Girl, are you okay? What about the salon? Their concern is a surprise to her, but she's clearly touched by it.

In the meantime, Jungwoo replies, "I don't know about being an idol, maybe not that specific, but I've wanted to write songs since I was a kid. My mom was watching a drama, *A Rose in Winter*, and there was a song that played at the end. I thought it was the saddest thing I'd ever heard."

Max interrupts. "And that's how you decided what to be when you grew up? What the hell, hyung?"

"And do you remember the song?" Emma asks, redirecting a distracted Jungwoo.

"Oh, yeah. Of course I do. It's *Last Goodbye* by Jewell."

Emma smiles. "I hope you get to do what you love for years and years." She sounds so sincere. The fans repeat the sentiment. "Are you ready to tell them why you grabbed my wrist at the festival?"

"Nicky made me do it," Jungwoo replies right away. This triggers an outpouring of sympathy in the chat. Of course it was Nicky, that makes perfect sense. But for every Sunshine who quickly accepts that explanation, there's another who refuses to entertain it. What is this slander? Nicky is an angel! Nicky is above reproach!

"And why did I grab your wrist right back?"

He bites his lip, more hesitant to answer this question. "I was going the wrong way."

Wow, look how he was able to admit that! Oppa's so honest! Emma reads through the comments. She blinks, then starts laughing. "They wanna see another wrist grab."

"What? Really?"

"Uh-huh." She lowers her voice so that the camera won't catch what she's saying. We get to watch Jungwoo's expression go from disbelief to denial to deeper embarrassment. "It's for the fans," says Emma. "You said they're everything to you."

Sunshines echo this a hundredfold. Oppa did say that! Didn't oppa mean it? Surely he wouldn't lie. Boys only lie in real life!

Jungwoo doesn't last long under this full-scale bombardment. He exits stage right, sighing, and Emma follows him into the kitchen. Apollo member Ari stands at the sink, scrubbing an oversized pan that won't fit in the dishwasher. He gives Emma a questioning look.

She points at Jungwoo, who sighs again. "Sorry, Ari. Anything for Sunshines."

"Ah, what do you mean—"

The sheet pan slides out of his grasp, hitting the sink with a clang. Water splashes onto the floor. Sunshines are screaming in the chat, ecstatic. Jungwoo just grabbed Ari by the wrist! Cue the ballad, trigger the slow-mo! Some of us have been waiting to see this moment for years!

The camera swings low, pointed at Emma's shoes. She's laughing so much that she almost dropped it.

29

C OMING BACK FROM THE weekend was painful, and the days that followed were strange ones. Monday's shifts were rearranged to accommodate celebrity guests flown in from Seoul. Then the weather forecast prompted Emerald to move a photo shoot. They shuttered the diner, announced an obscenely early start time, and threw the whole production into chaos. This was how Eunjae ended up in full kit on a Tuesday morning, sprawled on the wing of a vintage plane. The concepts for Apollo's annual *Season's Greetings* calendar were always... interesting.

This year-end gift set for fans was a time-honored tradition among K-pop groups. Jiyeon's special edition Ari calendar had been part of the previous holiday season's merchandise, which included a planner and stickers as well. Eunjae had heard from their other manager, Nami, that this year's box came with a miniature sundial.

Zipped into a pastel blue jumpsuit, he was told to pose with a citrus crate and got a splinter as a souvenir. That wasn't fun. Neither was the part where they wanted him tossing an orange and catching it, alluringly. He knew what they were asking for, and Eunjae could do it, but that didn't stop him from wanting to melt into the concrete floor. Ten years in the business and he remained so easily embarrassed.

Whenever the photographer didn't need him, he wandered around taking pictures himself. The staff had scouted a derelict hangar for part of the shoot. There was beauty to be found in its steel bones, in the panes of cracked and clouded glass. A ruined roof left the interior open to the sky. At the right hour, the place glowed from within, shot through with cold October sunlight.

On the drive back, Eunjae swiped through his pictures and sent some to Jiyeon. Her schedule had also flipped upside down since that meeting with Prism. She'd be around a little bit longer and he wanted to see her.

He got out as soon as the van came to a stop. Staff directed them to the main house, promising a breakfast buffet. Eunjae witnessed the tail end of a quarrel on the way in. "You're not supposed to be leaking videos anymore," Kei said, exasperated as usual. "Quit coming up with insane ideas for them. I'm sure noona doesn't need help."

"We're collaborating. And I'm the one who said telling the truth might be worth trying sometimes. I was the inspiration."

"It might be worth trying *sometimes?* Are you listening to yourself? Psycho!"

"Call me names all you want, but if you don't get your post done before we leave, we'll have to get you at the wedding."

"Do you have to sound like you're planning a murder?"

"Do you have to be a fake snob? If you were a real snob, you'd appreciate my vision."

Kei accused Nicky of conflating insanity with artistry. Nicky declared that His Royal Highness the Dark Prince Adrianos was an enemy of the arts. If you wanted to escalate a conflict, all you had to do was mention the time Keiichi voiced the lead in a popular anime franchise. Eunjae knew he'd have to step in before it got any worse.

As it turned out, he didn't have to. Jiyeon heard their bickering and came to mediate. She popped up between them, held up her phone, and flipped the camera around. Nicky broke into a grin mid-sentence. Kei's grumpy expression became a look of practiced indifference, transforming him into the cool and unsmiling crush who neither knew nor cared that you existed. All nine members of Apollo were conditioned to drop everything for a selfie.

Jiyeon glanced at Eunjae. "Huh. That really does work."

"It's pretty reliable."

"Well, well," Nicky said, loading a plate with food. "Ajumma, nice to see you. Keiichi here would like to volunteer for your next post—"

"Don't listen to him, I'm not volunteering for anything!"

"You can wait if you want," said Jiyeon, pouring Kei a glass of orange juice out of sympathy. "I've been reading what your fans have to say and most of their requests are really simple. Nothing crazy."

Kei was visibly relieved to hear this, but Nicky filed an objection. "Define crazy, though. For example, it wouldn't be crazy if I knocked into him right now and he spilled that juice on your dress. That's such a plausible scenario. Accidents happen, you know? Then we film him while he panics." A beatific grin. "You want authenticity? That's authentically Keiichi."

"You're not spilling anything on her dress," said Eunjae.

"You used to have a sense of humor, Ari."

This got Kei started on why there was nothing humorous about what hyung just said. Being funny wasn't the same as being a complete lunatic. The bickering resumed as Eunjae and Jiyeon left the dining room, seeking sanctuary. "There's a crane in the driveway," she told him.

"Please tell me you guys are going up on cables next."

"Hope not." Finishing his breakfast as they walked, he said, "Ezra had a letter to send back. Still won't talk to me, but Dad brought it last night."

"It's cute that he wrote back again." Jiyeon paused to fix the patch on his chest, embroidered with his stage name and slightly crooked. "Hey, about Ezra... I think I found something. I'll show you later."

Outside, they found her brother and a terrified stylist. "The beret is for what purpose?" Denny inquired, scowling down at a tablet screen. "And for god's sake, don't say sun protection."

"I guess... well, I guess there isn't a purpose, Manager Han. It's not really there for, um, utility?"

"Correct."

"So we should use something else...? Would you like us to pull a different hat, maybe...?"

Denny regarded the stylist through sunglasses tinted darker than the void itself. "If you know what's good for you, Yee."

"Y-yes, of course! New hat! Different hat, more sun protection!"

"Great. Moving on, who approved platform soles on these boots? Ahn can barely survive Earth's standard gravity. That's sabotage, plain and simple." Swipe, swipe. Denny's sunglasses slipped down the bridge of his nose. "Justify the decision to wrap Ryan in random fabrics. I'll wait."

Jiyeon chose to interrupt before the stylist dissolved into a quaking pile of bones. "What's going on out here?" she asked her brother, squinting at the Langley House lawn. People scurried about with their arms full of daisies and sunflowers, mums and marigolds, yellow petals everywhere. Configurations of white vases were laid out on the grass.

"Poor logistics, that's what's going on. These people invent rigmarole but can't execute it."

Those were words on the grass, Eunjae realized. The display would be photographed from above. "What do the flowers spell out? Do you know, Boss?"

A snort. "*The sun is always shining*. Dumbest slogan I've ever heard. Yeah, pal. That's how the sun works." He stalked away, bellowing that anyone dressed like air crew for Candy Land Airlines was due for a wardrobe change in thirty minutes. "And quit carrying that dog everywhere, Ueda. Muscles atrophy with disuse."

Complaints rang out. The puppy was tired. The puppy deserved a hammock, a stroller, a palanquin carried by uniformed security officers. Their little Haneul was a precious angel, why should she have to walk? And so on.

They spent the next twenty minutes watching interns arranging yellow blossoms. Sometimes a voice would shout instructions from the crane, directing staff to move this vase or that one until the photographer was satisfied. Brothers came out of the woodwork and Jiyeon stepped back to get them on video. She'd taken to collecting random scraps of B-roll, banking the short clips for later use. "You look more like mechanics," she mused, " but these are supposed to be flight suits, right? So you're pilots."

"It's whatever you want," Nicky answered. "You like pilots? We can be pilots. You like hot mechanics? We'll fix you up, three easy payments of $3,999. Oooh, or we could be hot janitors—"

Kei pushed him away, nauseated. "Please shut up. It's bad enough that I have to wear this." His flight suit was a very pretty shade of lilac. Jiyeon liked it and made a point of saying so, but he only heaved a sigh. It was just some cheap polyester blend. Noona didn't have to be so nice about it.

"Ya, ajumma. You still filming? Remember my appearance fee runs by the minute during peak season."

Max demanded to know what the hell he meant by 'peak season.' Jiyeon promised that she was aware of the pricing. "You guys mind if I knock out some of my posts? Thought I'd start with Kazu. Where'd he go?"

"Oooh, but our dark prince said he's going first—"

Kei dragged Kazu back to the group, then bolted out of range in a shameless bid for self-preservation. This didn't save him from the sight of what their eldest brother was wearing under the flight suit. More accurately, what he *wasn't* wearing: a shirt.

"Ah, hyung... is the zipper stuck, or...?"

"Yeah fucking right," Max exclaimed around a mouthful of croissant. He was on his second or third helping of breakfast and showed no signs of slowing down.

Jiyeon cleared her throat. "I think you lost something."

"Who, me?" Kazu looked down. "Like what? Oh, the dog! No, Haneul's fine. The interns are giving her a bath. She got mud on her little paws."

The floodgates opened. Was he allergic to decency? Did hyung need a ride to the nearest bordello? Why did he think this was a photo shoot for an adult film poster? And the dog's name was Gelato. How was that so hard for him to remember?

Jiyeon backed away slowly. "Hmm. This won't work. Too many brothers."

"Sorry," said Eunjae. "Maybe tomorrow?"

"Yeah, I'll try again." But she didn't put her phone away just yet. "Okay, come look before you go get changed."

She had screenshots saved to her camera roll, taken from the

Blackridge Academy website. Ezra featured in each one. He posed with his group on a field trip, and with a crowd in the school's pavilion. Jiyeon had cropped Leila out of the frame, leaving only an elbow and the brim of her hat.

"I know I don't have a lot here. I felt bad searching through the school newsletters like some kind of stalker. It's just that I've been thinking about this a lot, and then I kept coming back to what my mom said on Saturday night. You know, when she said Ezra's just like you."

"Make sure she never tells him. Being just like me is the last thing he wants."

"Don't you see it, though? He's in a uniform most of the year, but when he gets to choose, he copies the way you dress."

Eunjae looked again. Realizing she was right, he said, "Same kid who called me a walking laundry basket."

"Same kid who doesn't hate you. It's the opposite, Eunjae. And I know 'cause I used to do this with Janie. She was everything I wanted to be, and everything I didn't want to be."

Her gaze turned inward for a moment. "Sometimes, Ezra's just like you... but he's also just like me."

30

THERE WAS A POLITE way to wake your brother at the crack of dawn, and then there was the Apollo way: flipping the lights on, whipping the covers off, and shaking the victim until they rolled onto the floor in a bundle of blankets and thrashing limbs. The alternate method involved everyone piling onto the mattress while singing ballads at top volume. Joints popped. Bones were crushed. There was a lot of yelling, swearing, and frantic kicking. Eunjae didn't think Ezra was ready for that, so he went with the milder version.

"Time to get up," he announced, seizing the kid by one shoulder and jostling him mercilessly. Ezra tried to break free, but Eunjae handled it with the cool detachment of a veteran. He'd dealt with worse. For example, you practically needed body armor if you planned to interrupt Jesse's beauty sleep.

Ezra squinted at him. "Why are you here? What time is it?"

"Early. Come on, they're waiting for us."

"Who? The film crew?"

"No. Hurry, everybody's ready except you."

"Ready for what?"

Eunjae scooped up a pair of sweatpants folded neatly on top of the dresser. Passing these to Ezra, he replied, "Just get up. You'll see."

His brother stayed with Simon in adjoining rooms, the closest you could get to a suite at the Monroe Garden Inn. Eunjae cut through the connecting door, a grumbling teenager at his heels, and didn't expect to find their father waiting by the exit. He'd transferred his coffee to a travel mug. Tucked under his arm was a novel and a box of granola bars, unopened. "I'd like to go," he said. "If you don't mind."

Eunjae shrugged. Upon evaluation, he didn't mind if Simon wanted to linger on the periphery like a ghost. He was used to it.

Three minutes later, he'd gotten Ezra into the van, Dad following through downtown Monroe. The buildings were submerged in a cold, clinging mist. Kazu suggested that they run to their destination instead of driving. Nicky and Namgyu voted yes. Jungwoo had his headphones on and heard none of it. As for the driver, Max refused outright. "Pass. The high school's seven miles away and I'm freezing."

Ezra rubbed the sleep out of his eyes. "The high school? Why are we going there?"

"We've been borrowing their track. It's so nice! I love it there. You'll love it there, too. I know you will." Namgyu offered Ezra a sip of some terrible green drink. He'd either forgotten or didn't care that the kid couldn't understand a word he was saying. "You'll run and run and run, and you'll be so tired that you won't be mean anymore. You just won't have the energy for it. Aww, I can't wait! I'll love you so much when you aren't mean anymore!"

"He's kidding," said Nicky, winking. "Gyu loves everybody, even you."

"Ha! That's true!"

They pulled up to an empty campus, but it didn't stay that way for long. Denny showed up with Kei and a gaggle of production staff. Jesse shambled after them, zombielike, whining nonstop.

"You said I could sleep in," he wailed at their manager. "Why would you lie to me like this, what happened to *respect*, what happened to having *morals*?"

"I did say you could sleep in. Feel free to crash in the van."

"Why does that sound like a trap?"

Denny hefted a giant case of bottled water onto his shoulder. "It's not a trap. You're done growing, right? I know how tall you are," he said, "so I won't have to measure you for a coffin. Gets you another two minutes."

"Waaaahhh—"

The members fanned out to do their stretches, cameras rolling. Ezra received a shoddy explanation of how wind sprints worked. He didn't seem to believe they'd be engaging in such insanity until the others took off running. Eunjae went with them. He guessed, correctly, that his brother would follow. There was nothing for it except to join in.

Half an hour later, the sun crept over the horizon, revealing that most of Apollo had collapsed on the field. Brothers sprawled on the grass like beached whales. Eunjae limped over to the bleachers, breathing hard. He watched Ezra take a granola bar and some water from Simon before coming to sit on the bleachers as well. Although this was an unexpected development, Eunjae said nothing.

"I get that you're mad at me," said Ezra, "but this was too much."

"I'm not mad at you."

"Don't lie about it. I know you can't wait for me to leave. You and everybody else."

Eunjae bent to tug at a shoelace until the loose knot came undone. Then he tied it again, tighter. "I couldn't wait for you to get here," he said. "That's what I remember."

He was twelve, and he'd long since resigned himself to being his parents' only child. But Ezra came home from the hospital, a squalling bundle immediately transferred into Vivian's arms, and Eunjae was no longer alone.

"I thought we'd do everything together. I made this list, and I'd put stuff on it almost every day. Miss Vivi helped me think of ideas." Eunjae cracked a smile, thinking back on what he'd scribbled there. "She kept having to tell me it might be a while before you could do a lot of those things. I said I didn't mind waiting."

Ezra sat up, keeping his back turned to Eunjae. The sharp ridges of his shoulder blades poked through the fabric of his shirt. "And then you left," he said, embodying everything it meant to be fourteen and angry, fourteen and confused.

Over by the van, Eunjae saw Jiyeon sifting through the trunk of her car, a telescoping phone mount tucked under one arm. She would know what to say. She would ford this river, brave the crossing, and she'd do it both swiftly and surely. Clumsy by comparison, Eunjae could only wade into the water and fight the current as it tried to drag him under. His first instinct was to apologize. He went with honesty instead.

"And then I left."

It wasn't what he wanted to do. At the same time, he'd struggled to imagine another future. For so long, Eunjae had prepared to leave, his days structured around that imminent departure. Leila attacked the goal with every tool at her disposal, every ounce of her trademark tenacity. He was around seven or eight years old when he stopped having any time to play after school. It started with the voice lessons. Then came piano, Korean language tutoring, longer sessions with a vocal coach. The lessons were private, one-on-one. Other kids were a mystery. They lived in a universe separate from his own.

And then Vivian was gone, vanished overnight. A new nanny was hired for Ezra, but Eunjae had little to do with her. The schedule became more grueling than ever. His mother bowed out of a stage role in order to manage him directly. *I don't trust anyone else to get you where you need to be*, Leila would say, eyes flashing with rekindled rage any time he dared to ask about Miss Vivi.

"But I didn't stop asking," Eunjae told Ezra now. It had been his one act of rebellion, during those dark months between the first audition and the second. Even at the airport, poised to board that flight to Seoul, he'd pleaded with his mother to bring Vivian back.

"They'd let trainees call home once a week. I called just to ask Mum about Vivian. Sometimes she told me that Miss Vivi was gone, that she went home to her family. Sometimes she said that you were happy with the new nanny and didn't need our old one anymore."

What he didn't share: finally, maybe two months in, Leila began passing the phone to Simon when he called. If Eunjae planned to drone on and on about that woman like a broken record, he could save his breath and go practice instead. Didn't he want to debut? Could he be invested in his own future for a change? If she'd been blessed with even half his talent, if she'd received even half the amount of support, what could she have been? His attitude disgusted her.

Dogs barked from a nearby yard. The wind picked up slightly, sending up an eddy of dry leaves that swirled along the pavement. Eunjae waited. The story had to be told, and he'd done that, but the telling left him feeling like an empty shell. He took a deep breath, and then another. He watched the clouds go scudding across the sky.

Ezra took a deep breath, too. "I didn't know," he said, his voice barely above a whisper.

"It's okay. I should've told you."

"I feel stupid. I should've been asking a lot of questions, like when you got into that big mess with your contract this summer. That's when Mum started acting... weird. She kept saying you were ruining everything. And I believed whatever she said to me, I just believed her and didn't try to find out more."

"Why wouldn't you believe her? She'd never given you any reason not to, right?" And try as he might, he couldn't keep the bitterness from coloring his tone. "She's been a different mum for you than she was for me."

Ezra finally turned to look at him. "But why didn't you ever try to fight back? How could you just let her decide that for you? You ran away one time. You could've done it again."

"I felt like I needed to do what Mum wanted. If I ran away, she'd be mad at me again. Then I wouldn't have a chance at all. I'd never fix what happened with Miss Vivi."

"But what good would that have done? You'd still be gone. Even if you fixed it, you wouldn't get to be with her again. You were in Korea."

"*You* weren't in Korea, though," said Eunjae. He met his brother's gaze. The pain had faded to a dull ache for a while, but now it was fresh again, an open wound for anyone to see. "You were still in that house, so I needed Vivian to come back. I needed her to be with you."

Ezra stared at him, stunned. "It was about me?"

"I didn't say that to make you feel guilty," Eunjae hastened to clarify. "This doesn't mean you have to take sides, or stop loving Mum, or anything like that."

"Have you stopped loving Mum?"

The question hit him directly in the chest. Eunjae swallowed hard. "It could never be that easy."

Cameras whizzed past them, chasing Apollo members around the track. From the grass, Jiyeon caught Eunjae's eye and waved. He waved back, then moved down to sit with Ezra as the sky brightened overhead.

"I'm sorry. I just want you to know the truth, especially about Vivian. She loved you, Ezra. You were her baby. I wish she could see you now. I wish she could've been magic for you like she was for me."

31

J IYEON STUDIED THE BOUQUET in front of her. The colors were vibrant and the stems hadn't drooped. They looked good even after hanging out in a Fall Festival tumbler full of water while she filmed with Kazu. Not bad for an eleventh-hour grocery store purchase.

She tore the cellophane at the seam and rewrapped the flowers with the pages of a newspaper, also sourced from the grocery store. The final touch was a length of yellow satin ribbon that she'd found in her car. It brought an element of whimsy that couldn't be achieved with plain kitchen twine. She couldn't remember where the ribbon came from, or why it was in her car. Janie would call it serendipity. Life was often serendipitous or miraculous, but never merely coincidental. *Maybe magic exists, Yeonnie. Ever think of that?*

She tied a bow, then examined the results. More time was spent adjusting the loops, making them equal in size, yet not so large that they lost their shape. The ends turned out too long, but Jiyeon left them as they were. Those would be pretty as they fluttered in the breeze.

Back when she was Emma all the time, part of her success came from paying attention to the little things: tying a bow, adding a braid, mixing a hint of caramel into a client's brunette balayage. Details often made the difference, drawing the eye and holding attention. Caring about them could set you apart from others posting similar content. Jiyeon didn't mind the extra effort, even though it might be overkill here. She doubted anyone else would be uploading a post like this one.

The idea came from Star-Connect. Fans weighed in daily, and ever since taking over the *Sunshine 24/7* page, she'd been careful to sift through the avalanche of comments. Somewhere in the lengthy chain of responses to Jungwoo's post was a Sunshine who wrote, *Reminder that Hong Namgyu bought flowers for Emma AND everyone on staff???? When will somebody buy HIM flowers????*

Jiyeon thought this was a valid point. Knowing Apollo would film a segment at the high school that morning, she woke even earlier than usual and raced to Lowell's. Thank goodness they had a store in Monroe. It opened at 6:00am just like the Lowell's in Lemon Grove. As long as she hurried, Jiyeon could catch the guys before they left. She'd love to get two posts out of one morning.

She had the bouquet ready. Now she just needed Namgyu to take a break. Did he ever run out of energy? Where did it come from? Nicky and Kazu were no better, running races and arguing about the rightful winner, best out of five and then best out of ten. The rest had slowed down ages ago. Max walked along the track's outer ring, embroiled in another phone call. A sister, most likely, or perhaps all three. Kei, Jesse, and Jungwoo were draped over the bleachers in attitudes of despair.

That's where Eunjae had been when she arrived. The others kept their distance while he talked with Ezra, surpassing Jiyeon's expectations. And she understood how difficult it was, to take that step back, to give space despite wanting nothing more than to run in and help. But he needed to connect with Ezra on his own. No one else could do that for him.

She checked the parking lot. Eunjae had gone driving with Denny and the film crew, more footage for the show. They weren't back yet. In the meantime, Namgyu showed no sign of slowing down. Jiyeon decided it was time to call in reinforcements, setting a course for the bleachers. This brought her past the spot where Simon and Ezra sat in the shade. The former had a book lying open in his lap.

Jiyeon paused to say hello. She'd been meaning to talk to Eunjae's dad, anyway. Opening with the weather was a safe bet, even for someone as high on the reticence scale as Simon. Then she cut to the chase. "We're looking for Mrs. Romero. Do you have any contact info for her? Even if it's not recent, it could still be useful."

After a beat, Simon nodded. "Vivian sent an email, years ago. I can find the address she used."

She hadn't really dared to hope, and this seemed much too easy, but a lead was a lead. Jiyeon left her number and continued to the bleachers. Ezra caught up to her.

"Are you doing another video?"

"Well, I'm trying," she replied. "Namgyu's making it kinda hard to get this done. I might have to run some laps."

"Which one is he, again?"

Jiyeon cleared her throat. "Awwww!"

"Oh. Purple hair. I could go get him."

"No, it should be a surprise. Just need him to come over for a second."

Ezra kept pace with her, lurking like a gangly, teenager-shaped shadow while Jiyeon stopped at the bleachers for some help. She knew the exact brother to ask. Upon request, Kei was kind enough to bawl out, "Namgyu-hyung! You're thirsty! Get some water, big dummy!"

From the other side of the track, a loud gasp. "Aww, I really do need some water!"

Jiyeon leaped into action. She held the bouquet at arm's length, then recorded herself holding it while walking from the bleachers, her hand and the flowers centered in the frame. Later, she'd speed it up and add a title. *POV: Namgyu gave you flowers, so you gave him flowers, too.* Jiyeon could see the post unfolding in her mind's eye. The most important part was his reaction.

He didn't disappoint. Initially, Namgyu scanned the area with a baffled smile on his face, searching for the bouquet's lucky recipient. The smile remained until Jiyeon explained that the flowers were for him.

"Ha! But why? Did I win a game? I do win a lot, but I usually notice when it happens."

"No reason. Sunshines just thought you should have some flowers."

Namgyu took the bouquet. "Flowers for no reason? That's what these are?"

"Uh-huh."

"And they're from Sunshines?"

"Yeah. It was their idea."

"But that's so nice! It's the nicest thing ever!" Namgyu leaned closer to the camera, misty-eyed. "Sunshines, you're the best. This is my favorite day. Aww, I wish I could buy flowers for all of you! But I need to save up because I spent so much money on Keiichi-kun's birthday present, and it was Max's birthday two days before that, they're almost twins, so I really went overboard on my financials this month. That's what Zuzu says and I believe him—"

Namgyu took a breath and Jiyeon rushed to get a word in. "Can I ask you a question? It's easy, I promise."

"Aww! You can ask me any question in the world! It could even be a hard question!"

You'd need a heart of stone to resist Namgyu's mix of sincerity and enthusiasm. She found herself smiling, and although he couldn't understand what was being said, Ezra crept in like a traveler drawn to the fire's glow. Jiyeon pretended not to notice. "Was this always your dream? Did you always want to sing?"

"I didn't dream of singing. Wow, that would be so silly of me. I knew I would sing no matter what!" Namgyu motioned at the members of Apollo. "I dreamed of not being by myself anymore. Did you know my mom and dad both came from big families? Isn't that so amazing? But they didn't have any more kids, after me. That's why I wanted to debut with a group like this. And look how many brothers I got! It's the best. Nobody's life is better. I hope we'll always be together."

The response was unexpected and somehow within the scope of her expectations, all at once. Jiyeon ended that clip and started another. She recorded a message from Namgyu to the fans, basically a laundry list of everything he hoped they'd have, wherever they might be: delicious meals, good friends, warm laughter. Since she'd filmed every piece needed for the post, she let him return to the track for a few more laps.

Ezra stuck around. "I got some videos of the lake yesterday. Can you show me how to make them go in the right order? So it's not boring."

"Sure. Let's see them."

He played the clips for her. She suggested ways to edit the footage, tricks she'd learned and more shots he could add. "We can split it three ways, like this, and put the title in the middle. It's not a busy clip, since you're just panning across the water. Stays readable and won't distract from the text you put on top of it. Does that make sense?"

"Yeah." But his excitement dimmed, and he searched the lot the same way she'd done earlier, looking for Eunjae. "Will he be mad? He doesn't want me messing with this stuff."

"He's just worried. Social media isn't always safe, and it's not always a good place to be."

Jiyeon spoke from experience. Parts of that experience had been painful. Recognizing this, Ezra asked, "Are you mad?"

"No."

She was concerned, but wasn't it better for her to be here? There were dozens of things Jiyeon wanted to change about being Emma, things that were too late to fix now, but it wasn't too late to act as a guide. On this path, intrusion often intertwined with genuine connection. Cruelty coexisted with the incredible kindness of strangers, the stories they told, the joy of being able to help people she might never have reached otherwise. Ezra didn't have to learn that on his own.

"Did you know about Miss Vivi? Am I the only one who didn't?"

Jiyeon wasted a moment trying to find the right words, a configuration of sentences that might soften the blow. But there were no right words, and this would hurt regardless. "I knew," she replied. "Not right away. Eunjae took a while to tell me all of it."

"It took even longer for him to tell me. Everybody knew before I did. It's this big, terrible thing that happened and I didn't know."

"He has a hard time talking about Vivian."

"I get that. And I get why he never wants to talk to Mum, and I get why he left." The bitterness faded. Ezra looked away. "But why'd he stay gone?"

She read the longing in his face, a wish to know and be known in turn. Hadn't Jiyeon seen this before, on an evening in June? Wasn't it the same thing she'd sensed behind a stranger's shy smile? Maybe those books about Molly Merriweather were right to describe time as water, a liquid expanding to fit its container. It ran through your fingers, gone forever. It pooled in the palm of your hand, a mirror so clear that it was possible to see straight through.

"He's here now. You're both here, Ezra." She gave him her warmest smile. "You've got so much time."

*Transcribed from a post by **Emma Han** (@jiye_unnie) on the official Star-Connect channel for **Sunshine 24/7**, later reposted to **Apollo's** social media accounts*

Emma points to the title as it scrolls across the screen: *Let's Fix Your Ponytail! (with a special guest...)* The words fade out, revealing rows of bleachers in the background, flashing silver in the morning sun. She filmed this video on a cross-country track that curves beyond the frame. It's orange, painted with white lines. The shot widens and we see Kazu sitting beside her, arms folded over his muscled chest. His tank top barely qualifies as a full article of clothing.

"What did he say to you?" he asks Emma. "Tell me. You wouldn't push him into the lake for no reason."

Emma replies that she had a reason, for sure. "But we're supposed to be making a ponytail tutorial," she reminds Kazu. "Sunshines are waiting."

Well, say no more. "Sunshines! You ready? Watch this."

What follows is a step-by-step guide to recreating Emma's ponytail from the post with Jungwoo. The screen splits, end result on top and advice on the bottom. We learn strategies for making sure the ponytail stays sky high all day.

When it comes time to teach, Kazu turns his back to us, modeling the steps on his own hair while Emma narrates. He's never cut it shorter than shoulder-length, so there's plenty to work with. An Apollo song plays over the footage.

"You were really young when you left home," Emma says, afterward. "Was this your dream job?"

Kazu chuckles. "You want the honest answer? I had no idea. But I was fighting with my dad every single day, and that made my mom sad, so it seemed like a good idea to leave." His posture slumps just the tiniest bit. "Thirteen years old. Thought I was so smart."

"So your dream was to make your mom happy."

He turns partway, brow furrowed. "You know what? Yeah. Mom's the best."

A picture pops up: Kazu hugging his mother at an Apollo concert in Tokyo. She's smiling, tears shining in her eyes. Like Kazu, she has her hair up in a bun. It's the cutest thing ever. "I bet she's proud of you," Emma points out, gently.

"Yikes. I hope so." He shakes his head. "Man, I can't wait to go home."

Brothers pounce on Kazu, crowding in from every side. What's he doing? Isn't he supposed to be helping her? Don't cry, big dummy. You're going home in two days!

It's difficult to hear Kazu over the noise, but we do hear him revisiting an earlier topic, a dog with a bone. "Tell me what he said. You want me to take care of that for you? I'll do it." He points at someone to his left. "And where were you when this happened? Why aren't you the one who pushed him into a lake?"

"Ah, I was with you. Remember?"

"Oh my gosh, Zu. You'll take care of it? That's *terrifying*, you sound like a *murderer—*"

Emma chooses this moment to step in front of the camera, blocking our view of the fracas. Brightly she says, "That's it! What did you think? Post your ponytail and tag us, okay?"

32

THEY ENJOYED APPROXIMATELY ONE sunny afternoon in Tokyo. Clouds had rolled in by evening, smothering the sky and putting an end to the mellow autumn weather, but of course the wedding would go on as scheduled. Neither the staff nor the bridal party showed much concern.

"It's lucky," Kei explained the next day, as water fell in sheets over the hotel's glazed tiles and sloping roofs. Eunjae and several of his brothers had convened in the shelter of a covered walkway. It was time to rehearse for their performance at the reception, but the usual suspects were late. Jungwoo and Kazu had already gone ahead with Denny. Nicky tended to be punctual for dance practice and very little else, while Jesse... was Jesse. Fervently, Eunjae hoped that their youngest member would show up within the next five minutes. Someone would have to go get him, otherwise. Who had the mental or physical fortitude for such a task? Jet lag was enough of a struggle.

Thunder rumbled. Namgyu looked out at the gardens, humming the chorus of a song intended for Apollo's next album. "What do you think?" he asked. "Like this, or like this? Ha, I can't decide." He sang the chorus two ways, both slight deviations from the guide track, and brothers huddled close to hear the melody.

"Could change it a little more," said Eunjae. "How about this?"

His voice rose above the sound of rainfall and dripping eaves. Max's scowl disappeared. "Hey, that's it. Keiichi, sing it just like hyung did. That line and the next one."

Eunjae heard this and felt a pang of guilt. It occurred to him that Max had been much quieter lately, present but more withdrawn. Things got so busy, with the group decamping to Tokyo for a week. There hadn't been a minute to spare, but Eunjae should've checked on him, especially after the news about Jungwoo.

He'd talk to him after rehearsal. Meanwhile, Kei eyed Max like he was crazy. "Why do you want me to do it? That's the chorus. I never get the chorus. What would be the point?"

"And you'll never get the damn chorus," Max shot back, irate, "if you don't sing it right now. I'll play it for Jungwoo and see what he thinks. It's not like we have to follow all the same old rules we used to, so just sing." He pressed the Record button on his phone. Kei gave up and delivered the verses as demanded. Namgyu came in with the harmony.

The result was something different, something new. But it was still Apollo, and Eunjae realized how much he liked the song, now that he'd heard it this way.

Passing guests expressed admiration. Kei croaked out his thanks, deeply embarrassed. Jiyeon walked up during the last round of bowing, deflecting praise, and then bowing some more. She and her brother had rooms at the adjacent hotel, another Tachibana Group property called Equinox Tokyo. The grounds were connected at several points, allowing guests to come and go.

Drawing Eunjae aside, Jiyeon murmured, "Prism's here. I saw an

Eric in the lobby."

He had no time to react. Jesse had finally deigned to come down from his room, skin perfectly dewy and moisturized, whining about being cold. And how could they be so mad at him for trying to get his full ten hours of sleep? And why was the banquet hall so far away?

The Grand Empress Hotel encompassed multiple buildings, including the wedding venue, a renowned restaurant, and a pair of towers like crystalline shards piercing the sky. These were linked by a garden touted in guidebooks as one of the most picturesque within city limits. Autumn foliage blazed in russet and gold, and a graceful bridge arched over koi ponds dotted with lilies. The scene belonged in a painting, but the paths were uncovered. They'd have to brave the rain in order to make it to rehearsal.

Liveried hotel staff stood at the ready, bowing and smiling, bearing umbrellas wide enough for two. Nicky borrowed one, then approached with a diabolical grin on his face. "It's time, my son. You're up."

Jesse had only been awake for about ten or fifteen minutes by this point, but he was lucid enough to read the writing on the wall. Nicky never grinned like that unless he'd won. It meant the trap was sprung and you'd already been caught.

Struggling was futile. Did Jesse struggle anyway? Absolutely. He fought for his life. This was *bullying!* This was *oppression!* His brothers were merciless, tyrannical beings and he didn't deserve them, he was an *angel!*

Nicky twirled the umbrella, unfazed. "You know how this goes, buddy. Everybody gets a turn. Isn't that right, ajumma? Look at that romantic atmosphere. Rainy day, pretty garden, big umbrella. It's perfect."

"Oh, sure. I see where you're going with it."

Jesse turned to Jiyeon with the pitiful, wide-eyed stare of the freshly betrayed. "Noona, how can you be like this? And why is it my turn? It should be Nicky's turn, or Keiichi's!"

This prompted Kei to step behind a pillar, wary of being chosen instead. That didn't happen. Jesse's fate was written in stone. "Hear me out," said Nicky. "All you have to do is hold the umbrella and walk with her to the banquet hall. You'll have a little chat while the rest of us follow you with the camera. It won't even take long."

"That's too easy," Kei complained, from the safety of his pillar. "Give him something harder. Isn't he supposed to be an actor?"

"Mean! The meanest!"

"Why do you think I gave him the scene that shows up in almost every drama ever made?"

But this was the precise reason Jesse refused to comply. "Nobody else had to do anything like that. It's too much, hyung. I'm not old enough to play a romantic lead. I've got a baby face, that's why they cast me in supporting roles instead."

"Aww, but that's just for now, right? You wanna be one of the important characters someday, don't you?" Namgyu hauled him over to Jiyeon. "You can do this! It's for your future!"

"Yeah, Jess. Think about your career. If you don't practice now, you'll be playing the bubbly junior colleague forever."

"Dead junior colleague," Max put in. "They'll kill you off to keep the plot moving. Happens all the time in those dumb shows Jungwoo loves so much."

"But I like being the junior colleague! And I'm amazing at death scenes, remember when I got stabbed in the MV for *Break Point*, I made that so emotional for everyone and Zuzu even cried for real—"

"Why don't we just go? You guys will be late." Jiyeon pulled her reluctant leading man onto the garden path, deploying the umbrella to the tune of Jesse's panicked howling.

"Hyung!" he cried out, clawing at Eunjae. "Hyung, save me! Tell them you don't like this, tell them you're jealous! Aren't you jealous? Why aren't you ever jealous?"

Eunjae shrugged. "I don't mind. And I've walked with her in the rain before," he added, smiling at Jiyeon, "so it brings back a nice memory, actually."

The standard uproar ensued. When did he do that? Was it recent? Was it today? How did they miss this event? Kei scoffed that it was stupid of Ari-hyung, regardless of when it happened. What if somebody saw and took a picture?

Jiyeon interrupted to ask if Max wanted to get the video for her. "You can hide behind us. Isn't Hazel here? Maybe she won't see you."

"Oh, what the hell, noona—"

"Good!" Jesse crowed. "Torture him, too! Why should I be the only one suffering?"

"Why are you so upset? Isn't she your date to the wedding?"

"Against my goddamn will!"

"But Hazel even posted about you this morning. I thought it was sweet. Did you see it, Eunjae?"

"I did." The actress had uploaded some screenshots of a music video. Dropped by Emerald Entertainment about twenty-four hours ago, it introduced the agency's upcoming girl group, Lumina. Max and Jungwoo were both credited for songwriting and production on the track. It was a pre-release digital single, intended to drum up anticipation and excitement for the girls' actual debut EP in December.

"Congratulations," Jiyeon said to Max. "I saw the song's already gone pretty high on the charts. Can't blame Hazel for being excited."

No one asked, since they'd all seen her post by then, but Nicky pulled it up and read the caption out loud anyway. "SO PROUD OF MY BABY @MX.LEE.MX AND YOU TOO NAMGYU KISS KISS KISSY FACE!"

"Awww! I didn't even do anything and she's proud of me, that's so nice...!"

Agonized groaning. "Do you have to read the fucking emoji too?"

Jiyeon turned her back on Max and his meltdown, looping her arm through Jesse's. She dragged him one step, then another. Borrowing an umbrella for himself, Eunjae took her phone and prepared to follow.

"Eunjae ruined his shoes on that walk," he heard Jiyeon say. "He switched places with me so I wouldn't get splashed. It was sweet. Think you can do something like that? It'll be a nice touch for the video, yeah? We'll slow it down like they do in dramas."

"Awww!"

"Speaking my language, ajumma."

Jesse glanced down at his boots. Gently, he replied, "Noona, please. These are Bottega."

He said this with such finality that Jiyeon couldn't help laughing. Kei lurched after them, swearing under his breath. "Bottega! Did he say Bottega? Those are mine!" The perpetrator let out a squeak but ultimately admitted nothing.

The paths were slick and half-smothered in moss. Stone lanterns shaped like frogs lit the way. Their mouths were wide open, emitting a soft glow. Autumn camellias were in bloom, cherry red, petals and leaves glazed with rain. Even under such dreary circumstances, the place managed to be gorgeous. It was unfortunate that Prism's intrusion soured the effect. Eunjae tried not to worry as Jesse chattered happily about his last drama, a rom-com where he played the younger version of the main lead.

"A script came for me," he confided, as they neared their destination. He'd gotten over his terror pretty fast. "It's one of those hospital dramas. I can't do it, but it sounds fun. I'd look good in those things that nurses wear, right? What are they called?"

"Scrubs," said Eunjae.

"Yeah! Scrubs!"

Jiyeon frowned. "But why can't you do it?"

"Won't have time. Filming starts in January, and we'll probably be promoting for the next album then. Hyungs are waiting to enlist so we can have eight, even if Jaehwan-hyung will still be gone." Stepping over a puddle, he said, "We're worth a lot less when we're not a full set, noona. We're like toys you collect. So I have to pass, but I'm glad they thought of me."

Eunjae paused the recording, dismayed. "We could try and negotiate that. You should've said something."

"For what, hyung? Maybe Jungwoo doesn't care if people are secretly mad at him, but I care. I need all of you to keep liking me or I won't have a place to live when I'm old. But anyway! What did you ask me, noona? If this was my dream?"

And Jesse went on, telling the story of how he was scouted while competing on a quiz show, and how he dreamed of making his grandmother proud. He loved nothing more than to talk about his beloved granny, but Jesse's steps were just a touch too buoyant, and his voice was just a bit too bright.

Eunjae heard regret there, layered beneath forced optimism. It chilled him more than the knowledge of Prism following them across the sea.

33

JIYEON WAITED BEHIND A pillar while her boyfriend posed for photos with seven brothers in identical lavender suits. Eight brothers, if you counted the cardboard cutout of Apollo's leader, Jaehwan. He'd been edited into a matching ensemble at the bride's request.

"Well, he's not dressed like the groom," she said. "That might have been confusing."

Denny lurked at her elbow, draped in black, a living bulwark with arms and legs and a lavender silk tie. His presence kept taking fellow wedding guests by surprise. Some shrieked in terror, much like Jesse when Cardboard Jaehwan came swanning out of the ballroom without warning. Even now, he'd positioned himself as far away from leader-hyung as possible.

Standing next to Denny was a foolproof way of determining which guests were related to Kazu. The whole family had developed an immunity, not even blinking when the guys introduced him as their manager. Jiyeon could see why. Similar hulking figures could be found everywhere she looked, variations of her brother copied and pasted throughout the wedding venue. They monitored from dim corners and guarded critical access points. They patrolled the corridors and carried Apollo's puppy in a bespoke sling provided by Vuitton.

Denny had strong opinions about this sling. He also objected to letting Daisy attend a formal event. Or did they change the dog's name to Anastasia? Jiyeon almost asked, but then her brother grumbled, "These jokers were late for rehearsal, and they'll be late for the performance, too. I needed them in that ballroom seven minutes ago."

"It's still early. I bet we've got at least half an hour." After the ceremony, guests had been funneled straight to cocktails in an adjoining lounge. Not everyone had made it over to the ballroom yet. "Let them do one more before you barge in."

"Do the math, Yeonnie. They take three steps and somebody asks for a picture. At this rate, it'll be another hour to get from here to the table."

"Not if they're running. You know they'll run if they think you're mad."

He gave a disgruntled huff. "I'm not mad at them. They're not the ones giving out exclusive merch at the shop this weekend, of all weekends. It'll be a bloodbath, and I won't be there to barricade the doors in person. I wish Jeannie would torch every box like I asked."

"Mom and Dad wouldn't let her. You know they want to make the fans feel like they're welcome, 'cause they love Apollo, so it's no use fighting it." Resting a hand on Denny's arm, Jiyeon added, "You were right, when you said it'll be over soon. Let's just ride it out."

She said this despite the fact that being here, attending this wedding, was the opposite of 'just riding it out.' Jiyeon understood that Eric came to Tokyo because they'd provoked him. It didn't matter that she hadn't heard from Prism since her plane touched down. She knew they were watching.

Denny issued a moratorium on photo ops and began herding the guys into the ballroom. Jiyeon went with them, trying not to think about Prism, or Leila, or Arthur. She wanted to be free of her problems for just this one fleeting weekend, at least. Why did it feel like she was asking for too much?

Bridesmaids flocked past her, trailed by waitstaff pushing trolleys. Overhead, the vaulted ceiling glimmered with stars. The ballroom was an enchanted woodland divided into four quadrants, each themed to a different season. Pillars became trees bursting with green leaves or shedding drifts of pink blossoms, tiny crystal shards trembling from each bough. The dance floor shimmered like ice under moonlight. This provided a gorgeous backdrop for the next three photo ops, since Eunjae and his brothers didn't like to say no.

Cardboard Jaehwan remained in the hall to greet guests as they came in. The rest of Apollo fell into seamless formation every time someone requested a picture, always leaving a spot between Kazu and Nicky. It was the space they saved for Jaehwan automatically, muscle memory, even though he'd been gone since April. They felt his absence like a phantom limb. And this wasn't limited to their leader; when Kazu and Kei flew out first, two place settings appeared in front of their chairs at dinner, same as ever.

"Are they really okay?" she'd asked Denny, when he met her at the airport. Maybe the faint undercurrent of tension was a figment of Jiyeon's imagination. She hoped so. But weren't they joking even more than usual? And weren't they dodging the topic of Jungwoo's offer from Emerald, treating it like a tender bruise?

"They have to be okay," was her brother's curt response. "Even if he doesn't leave, they can't be together forever. They're nine different people. Sooner or later, they'll have to live nine different lives. I keep saying this 'cause they need to hear it."

And yet: *We're worth a lot less when we're not a full set, noona. We're like toys you collect.*

Suddenly, she couldn't watch anymore. Jiyeon slipped away to find her seat at one of the two tables allotted to Apollo. The napkins were folded into lilies, and the centerpiece was made of real branches painted silver, as if rimed with a thin sheen of frost. She took pictures for her parents and Jeannie. Absorbed in documenting the decor, she was slow to register that someone had taken the adjacent chair.

Fingers walked up Jiyeon's arm, tipped with long, flawlessly manicured nails. "Who left you all alone, unnie?"

She'd seen the movie posters, taped to the fridge and on random walls at each of Apollo's temporary residences last summer. These posters reappeared within hours of being ripped to shreds, as if by magic, so Jiyeon had come to know Hazel's face very well. She had the kind of beauty that stunned on impact. It hit like an uppercut to the jaw, no holds barred. But there was also a softness to her features, something warmer and more welcoming than Max's good looks at first glance. His beauty was built on precise angles, sharp as cut glass.

Jiyeon tried to tell her that it was fine to skip formalities. Why call her 'unnie' when she wasn't that much older? But Hazel waved this away. "Of course that's what I'm calling you. I don't need it getting back to my manager that I wasn't properly respectful. She'd nag me forever."

Under the ballroom's dreamy lighting, it was almost too hard to tell that she'd dyed her hair again, going from the candy floss pink of one role to the luminous platinum blonde of another. "Sorry I tried to stab your boyfriend that one time. You'll forgive me, right?"

"I'll think about it," Jiyeon replied, wryly. It was only a music video, but still.

"Think about it faster. We're outnumbered, so we should stick together." Angling her head in Eunjae's direction, Hazel said, "That's one hell of a haircut. I'm assuming you get the credit."

Jiyeon had to admit that she'd outdone herself. "Some of my best work. Too bad I can't advertise."

"You've made him so much hotter already. I haven't done that with mine yet. Maybe I'll go through his suitcase while I'm here. I could get rid of all the cargo shorts."

This reminded Jiyeon of something Eunjae mentioned at breakfast. "Hey, do you need anything? I heard they lost your luggage."

"Again. They lost my luggage *again*, because I can never fly anywhere without weird shit happening. Thank god the dress was already here. Then Willa wanted me to sneak into this hotel and I told her to very kindly fuck off. I love my manager and I'd die without her, but I'm not scared of Max's fans. If they want a fight, they can have one."

"Did they give you a hard time?"

"They tried."

An announcement rang out from the stage. The bride and groom were due to arrive at any minute. Denny reappeared, dour-faced, glaring at Hazel's updo. It was a variation on the classic French twist, simple and somewhat messy, although Jiyeon assumed that part was intentional. The loose strands were there to give it an artless effect, and the jeweled hair pins added drama. She liked it.

Her brother did *not* like it and made his feelings known with zero preamble. "The weapons policy went out in two different emails, Miss Lim. Hand it over."

"No idea what you're talking about, officer."

"Understood. I'll count to three."

Hazel swiveled in her chair. "And then what? What happens at three—"

"One."

"I don't have any weapons!"

"Two."

"Where would I even put a weapon? Does it look like this dress has pockets? You know they had to sew me into it, right?"

He opened his mouth. Hazel whipped a pin out of her hair and surrendered it to the authorities, pouting horrendously. Goodness, that thing was sharp. Denny speared it through his boutonnière. "And the other one, ma'am."

The second pin seemed like more of a very tiny knife to Jiyeon, not that she was an expert. How fortunate, then, that the members of Apollo had managed to make it to their seats at last. They were the experts. That was practically a katana, what was she doing, why did she have that? Aww, Hazel's hair was still so pretty even when you took the swords out of it!

Hazel threw herself at Namgyu, squealing. She had a clear favorite, and it wasn't Max Lee, who took one look at his girlfriend and tried to leave. His bid to switch seats resulted in a reprimand from Denny. Or maybe it wasn't a reprimand, but Max looked so agitated that it couldn't have been good.

A shutter clicked. Jiyeon turned her head toward the sound and had to smile, because it was Eunjae burning through a roll of film in record time. He'd been so excited to bring that camera. He pointed the lens at her, smiling back.

"Ya," said Kazu. "Why are you so quiet? Shouldn't you tell her she looks nice?"

Jiyeon patted the chair beside her. Eunjae sat down and said, "I did tell her, hyung."

"And that's it? Shouldn't you at least say something about the dress?"

"Ah, I did that, too."

"Idiot. Would Ari take so many pictures if he didn't think noona looks nice?"

"Oooh, but what did he say about the dress? Tell me, my son. I need to know."

Eunjae paused to think. "The zipper works."

Immediate implosion. Max and Jungwoo both fumbled their phones. Hazel stopped pinching Namgyu's cheeks and promising to marry him in her next lifetime. Why would he say that? Why would he have anything to do with the zipper on that dress? Whatever happened to propriety?

"Who else was supposed to zip it up for me?" Jiyeon asked them, puzzled. "I couldn't reach it by myself. And there was something wrong with the zipper when I tried it on the first time."

"Oh my gosh. Ohhhh my gooossshhh, so who helped with Hazel's dress—"

"My manager? Hello?"

Nicky had partially melted out of his seat. "But Max could've helped you with that," he wheezed. "He's a knight in shining armor."

"Gross," Max exclaimed.

"Yuck," Hazel cried out at the same time. The chaos intensified from there.

Looking back, it struck Jiyeon as the most uncomplicated moment of the night, free of tension, light as air. Only later would she realize that Denny hadn't laughed along with them.

34

Outside, rain slicked the city streets and sluiced into gutters, drumming on rooftops and umbrellas. But if you had enough money, weather was no obstacle. You could bring the night indoors, a perfect night with a clear sky, hung with constellations that burned more vividly than reality.

Eunjae had a lot of time to admire this artificial sky; the father of the bride had been sobbing off and on for the better part of the evening. He did a lot of his sobbing on Apollo's Ari.

"Why did you sit there for so long?" scolded Kei. He fussed at the fabric of Eunjae's jacket, declaring it to be a wool-mohair blend requiring meticulous care. "At least he did most of the crying on your shoulder. The suit's holding up fine, but these lapels are faced with silk."

Jiyeon observed this lecture from a nearby bench, catching her breath under a bower woven from branches and fairy lights. She'd only just returned from a round on the dance floor with Namgyu. Before that, it was Kazu. Now she leaned forward, phone up, camera rolling. "So you're saying that tear stains are permanent on silk?" she asked Kei.

"Yes."

"My mom owes you a hankie, then. You let her borrow yours when she cried about Kazu replacing all the chairs in our dining room."

Kei took a break from pawing at the suit. This was a brother with a vast and varied repertoire of frowning faces, each bearing nuanced meanings; by Eunjae's estimation, the current frown had shifted from irritated to thoughtful.

"Of course not," he answered. "I told her to keep it. I think of it like... silk holds on to memories. Tears leave a mark that won't wash out. That happened in the summer, and when summer comes again, the memory will still be there. You'd want to keep that, wouldn't you? If you were crying good tears."

Eunjae smiled. "I think those were good tears."

"Oh, sure. She was really happy. We'd been wanting to replace the chairs forever." Jiyeon smiled, too. "What a nice way to look at it. Hey, was this your dream? To be an idol?"

"An idol." Kei's thoughtful frown remained in place. "I wanted to sing, and I wanted to be good at it. I guess I dreamed of being the kind of performer people wouldn't forget."

Jiyeon had more questions for him, but Nicky strolled over, jacket missing, sleeves rolled just so. His tie was gone, too. "By request," he said, when Kei switched to heckling him instead. "See those aunties over there? This is how they wanted me. The answer's yes if you've got the cash."

"Disgusting."

Nicky grinned. "Now, here's the situation. We've gone viral again thanks to ajumma's last post, so the MV for *Love Me, Leave Me* just hit another milestone for views. Can't remember how many millions we're at now, but people have been watching for that scene. You know, with Zu and the desk?"

"Blech."

"What was he doing on the desk?" Jiyeon glanced up at Eunjae. "Did you do something on a desk?"

"Ah, no."

"Huh. Too bad."

You'd never guess that it was supposed to be winter in this part of the ballroom. Why was it so warm?

"So," said Nicky, clapping his hands together, "what I need is for Keiichi to have some more wine. Ari, make sure he drinks up. We're borrowing Jiyeon for this dance challenge. I'll team up with His Royal Highness while you get the video."

"But she just filmed me!" came the inevitable protest. "Nobody else had to do two videos!"

"Hear me out. I took notes on Eric's social media presentation, and it said the audience loves 'moments of authenticity and vulnerability.' You're very *authentic* after some drinks. Now, since you hate the choreo for this song—"

"Because it's embarrassing!"

"Yeah, so you'll be feeling *vulnerable*. Boom, instant success. I'm a genius." Nicky helped Jiyeon to her feet, then twirled her so fast that she squeaked in surprise. "And it won't even take very long," he added, twirling her again in the other direction. "Thirty seconds, tops. Just the dance break. So easy."

"Ah, it's the hardest part of the dance..."

"Exactly. And Keiichi's good at it, but I'm twice as good. We can't lose." Nicky caught Jiyeon by the waist. He pointed at the wineglass. "I don't see you drinking, my son. You know you'll need every drop to survive this."

Kei declared, emphatically, just how much he hated it here. Waiting for the dizziness to pass, Jiyeon said, "I'm not sure I'll survive this."

"Quit, hyung. You're spinning her around too much."

Nicky responded by dipping his dance partner so low that the ends of her hair brushed the ballroom floor. "Why? Is it bugging you, Ari? Is this finally making you jealous? Because that's my other mission in life, I'll get a reaction if it's the last thing I do—"

He froze. Jiyeon had her fingers curved around his cheek. "Stop bullying him," she said, "or I'll bully you back."

"Whoa, whoa," Nicky exclaimed, swinging her upright. "Watch it, ajumma. You can look, but don't touch. That's how you get invoiced."

"Invoice me, then. I'm gonna go dance with Eunjae."

She broke free and reached for his hand. A song began to play, one that Eunjae didn't know, and the lights dimmed to a watery blue. He checked his watch. "Actually, I thought we could leave early."

It was Saturday here, but Friday at home. Date night. Jiyeon's eyes went wide with surprise, then delight. She stepped closer, still holding on to his hand, cheeks flushed from dancing. A long curl had come loose from the clasp at the nape of her neck. Eunjae brushed it away absently. He wasn't thinking, and it was perhaps the most normal thing in the world, the most normal thing he'd ever done, because who could think in a moment like that one? She was beautiful. She was everything.

But then Nicky said, "Hey, no way. We're all going out to eat after this. I busted my ass to get that reservation. Booked it three months ago."

"What does he care? Hyung's got a new life now. He's been trying to leave us since June."

"We know that's the wine talking, Keiichi."

"It's okay," said Jiyeon, squeezing Eunjae's hand. "We can go with them. There will be other date nights."

That was true, and the disappointment didn't show on her face or in the tone of her voice, even though she must have felt it. She'd grown so used to their plans being displaced, rearranged, set aside. Eunjae couldn't bear this. Apologizing to Nicky, he said, "I'm taking her out. We'll skip dinner just this once."

"Just this once? You're moving to LA. When will we all be in Tokyo again?"

When will we all be here together, again? Everything keeps changing. What if we don't get another chance? He didn't need to say it. Eunjae knew what he meant.

Kei stared down at the tablecloth, running his fingers over the brocade. "Leave him alone, hyung. Let him get caught with a girl in the middle of the night. We're done anyway, without Jungwoo. If he signs with Emerald—"

"He won't."

"You believe him when he says that? Remember when he dragged Ari back to Seoul, remember how he put the job first and his best friend second? I couldn't blame him, then," Kei admitted, "because all our jobs were on the line, not just his. But Jungwoo cares about Jungwoo. That's what it taught me."

Nicky went to pour a glass of water, his smile extinguished. He pressed it into their brother's hand, removing the wine from easy reach, and that was when Denny cut in.

"We need to go," he said. "Emergency. Eric's waiting."

There was something about the way he delivered this message that quelled any potential argument and smothered every question they might think to ask. Jiyeon felt for Eunjae's hand again. Kei shot up right away, offering to find Namgyu, but Nicky barred his path.

"Seems like it's bad news. Keiichi, stay here with Zu." He looked to their manager, who gave a nearly imperceptible nod in response. "Don't tell him about this. Give him another few hours to think nothing's wrong."

He was the eldest present. Kei would've obeyed regardless, but he went without arguing because they could agree on this, at least: Kazu should be able to enjoy his family tonight. If it was possible to shield him from the storm a little longer, it was worth defying Prism's orders. Denny made Kei give up his phone, though. That was also part of Prism's orders.

They hurried out of the ballroom and into a corridor steeped in shadow. This part of the venue had been excluded from the night's festivities by a black velvet rope. Voices seeped out of the fourth door to the left, raised in anger. Jungwoo and Hazel were locked in a tense exchange. Max slouched against the opposite wall. With his shoulders hunched like that, he seemed far diminished from his true height. Hazel loomed larger, by contrast.

"Is it because you don't want to split the credit with him? Is that your problem?"

"Could you cut me some slack? I'm not the asshole you think I am."

"I don't think you're an asshole," Hazel replied. "I don't think of you at all. Not anymore. But if you're telling Max to skip this so that you can keep working with Emerald by yourself, I'll be thinking of you all the time. That's not a good thing. Pray that I'm never fucking thinking of you."

"I'm not the one who told him to say no! He doesn't want to go. He won't leave Ari."

Eunjae stared across the room at Max. What?

"How long will you guys keep this up? I can't believe you'd stay together even when it's holding you back."

"I believe we've heard enough from you, Miss Lim."

Max pushed off the wall. "Shut the hell up. Why are you talking to her like that?" Glaring at Eric, he said, "Keep my phone if you want, but you can't make me stay here."

And then he left with Hazel, wincing when Eunjae called his name. Max wouldn't even look at him.

Eric made no move to interfere. He came to greet the new arrivals, smiling his benign, stock photo smile. "Hello, hello. I apologize for cutting your evening short like this. It's not what anyone wanted." He waved Nicky and Eunjae inside, but prevented Jiyeon from following. "This doesn't concern you, Miss Han. Let me have your phone and Erin will walk you back to your room."

"It doesn't concern me, but you're taking my phone away? I feel like I'm owed an explanation, bottom line."

Hazel turned back for a moment, eyes alight with molten rage. "Oh, it's my fault, unnie. I did some normal girlfriend shit and posted that I was proud of Max. Who knew it would start a war?"

A statement issued by Emerald Entertainment in response to breaking news headlines and rampant fan speculation regarding Apollo, November 2023.

Hello, this is Emerald Entertainment.

Recently, there has been extensive media coverage and online discourse concerning our artists, the members of Apollo. We are aware that internal and confidential correspondence between staff members was released to the public without authorization. Misinterpretation of these materials has affected Apollo's contract negotiations with Zenith Entertainment. We seek to prevent further harm to our artists by providing clarification on several points.

First, the company firmly denies all allegations of attempting to 'poach' talent from Zenith Media or interfere with ongoing negotiations. Our agency has maintained a policy of transparency and professionalism throughout this transitional period for Apollo. The correspondence in question pertained to in-house production roles for Apollo members Park Jungwoo and Max Lee, but no offers or terms had been finalized.

Plans for Jungwoo's continued collaboration with Emerald

Entertainment were initially proposed in October, with the artist and representatives of both agencies in attendance. Similar contractual terms for Max were to be discussed at an upcoming meeting, which Zenith has now canceled.

Second, rumors regarding the termination of contracts and Apollo's disbandment are categorically false. All nine members, including Jungwoo and Max, remain committed to promoting as Apollo and carrying out their scheduled activities.

Lastly, we would like to address increased speculation around the members' schedules in Tokyo. We can confirm that Apollo attended a family wedding as well as other gatherings during their stay. These activities were not conducted in any official capacity, nor were they part of the group's filming schedule for *Sunshine 24/7*.

As the agency, we are unable to comment on our artists' private lives. We ask that fans and media outlets refrain from spreading unverified claims which could damage the members' reputations and careers, as well as their personal and professional relationships. We are prepared to take all necessary legal measures against creators and distributors of malicious content.

We sincerely thank Sunshines for their steadfast support of Apollo since debut. Please look forward to the group's future endeavors.

35

JIYEON WOKE IN AN unfamiliar bed, beneath an unfamiliar ceiling. The sky showed violet through the window, not quite lightless in this hour before dawn. She'd forgotten to pull the drapes.

Remembrance came on a slow wave. This wasn't her room at Langley House. At the moment, this was something of a prison cell. Jiyeon had been told to go to her hotel room and stay there. The night had ended badly. *Eunjae.* She needed to know if he was okay, if Apollo was okay. Where was her phone? She couldn't find it.

Right, it was with Eric. Prism wanted to keep information contained. Liberated from endless digital noise, she couldn't be overly connected and wired and informed. It created new depths of isolation.

Never mind. She had a phone on the nightstand, and Jiyeon knew Eunjae's room number. If she called the front desk at the Grand Empress, maybe they could connect her.

Or maybe not. Maybe they'd tell her the room was vacant. Both hotels were accustomed to high-profile guests and the security measures that came with them, so her best bet would be to figure out the direct number. Well, she could do that. She'd talk to him somehow. Jiyeon sat up, twisting her long hair into a bun. By habit, she tried to use the elastic on her wrist and couldn't find that, either. Of course, because she'd given it to Eunjae, for good luck.

Undaunted, she pushed through possible solutions, everything from trying the front desk anyway to simply getting up and walking over there, Eric be damned. But now there were heavy footsteps thumping down the hall outside Jiyeon's door.

Denny didn't knock. His words were battering rams made of pure, thunderous sound. "Yeonnie, we have to go."

She flew out of bed and threw on a sweater. Fingers on the deadbolt, Jiyeon hesitated. Eric was out there with her brother. She recognized the calm, even cadence of his sentences, smooth as lines read from a teleprompter.

Denny had his suitcase, passport slung around his neck. He wasn't dressed for the weather. He wasn't even dressed to be out in public, not by his own standards. Her brother wore sweatpants only to sleep, but here he was, still in the pair he'd worn to bed. The rumpled t-shirt was old enough to bear the original Wanna Waffle logo, which they'd redesigned more than two years ago. There was a hole in the right sleeve. And it was raining again, but Denny didn't have an umbrella. Nor had he bothered with a coat.

In her head, sirens blared. Something must have happened to their parents, or Janie. An accident, an emergency. "Hang on," said Jiyeon, rushing to pack her own bags. Eric said something about staying in Japan. Words reached her, fragments without context: obligation, image, optics.

Optics. Repulsed, she lost her hold on a tube of lipstick. It rolled into the sink with a clatter. "I understand that you're upset," said Eric, "and there's no question of sending your sister home. We've got a flight booked. Consider that handled."

"We're both going," Denny replied. He came in to help and she could tell he hadn't slept a wink. Since he'd stashed his phone in the same pouch as the passport, she was able to see part of the screen. Messages kept coming in, so many that the notifications stopped showing previews. The sender was Kazu, Kazu, Kazu. They must've allowed him to keep his phone, as leader.

Jiyeon dropped the lipstick again, missing the mouth of her makeup bag entirely. "Denny, what happened?"

He cleared the bathroom vanity, working so fast that she couldn't keep up. "It's the shop," he answered, brusque as always. But this was different, this was worse, because Jiyeon had known Denny since the day he was born. He wasn't just angry. He was miserable.

The shop. What went wrong at the shop?

Eric entered the room uninvited. He'd been joined by one of the Erins, who returned Jiyeon's phone. "This is the earliest flight we could get you," she said, babbling about transportation to the airport and which approved responses were to be given in case of media inquiries. Jiyeon tuned her out. Her battery was at a precarious twelve percent, but the screen was powered on now, flooded with notifications. She scrolled, frantic. Eleven messages from Mom. Eight from Dad.

They'd sent pictures, too shaken to manage much else. The first one hit with such force that Jiyeon had to lean against the nearest wall, seeing stars. She sucked in a breath and forced herself to keep looking.

It was the orange door at Wanna Waffle. The stained glass panels were shattered, reduced to shards on the pavement. Remnants of their father's plants filled the foreground, a carpet of spilled soil and trampled leaves.

Emma had been tagged in dozens of posts across multiple apps.

Most of the content was the same: spilled food, cracked plates, chairs overturned in the dining room. Piles of colorful packaging, long since gutted. Here, half of Apollo smiled from a sign ripped in half. A table had collapsed.

Sunshines had started lining up for the exclusive merch drop on Friday afternoon, with many camping out overnight. And that would've been fine; Wanna Waffle had seen that kind of deluge before. But this time, certain factors were in play. Lumina's music video had broken streaming records, fueling rumors that devoured Star-Connect and social media with the brutal speed of a wildfire. Some were blaming Hazel for posting, but the email leak wasn't her fault, and neither was the severity of Zenith's reaction.

Fan speculation went wild. Max and Jungwoo were leaving the group. Emerald had resorted to sabotage, unwilling to part with proven hitmakers. At first it was just Jungwoo, but now they had the nerve to take Max as well. And Zenith? They'd gotten greedy. They'd have every member of Apollo, or none at all.

Stuck in line for hours, the majority left empty-handed. It took just one angry voice to set things off. A fight broke out, escalating too rapidly to be contained. Maybe they'd never be clear on what the argument was about, but that didn't matter on the Internet. People focused on videos of crazed Sunshines shouting, pushing, shoving. By the thousands, they reposted footage of Joey Han roaring at the crowd.

"He thought they hurt Jeannie," Denny said, dragging Jiyeon out of her feed. "She's fine. Fell down for a sec, but Dad found her. Customers were freaking out, thinking they'd get crushed. No serious injuries reported. Nobody pressing charges, either. For now." He whisked her shampoo and conditioner out of the shower. "Not sure we'll be on the same flight. Eric might try to keep me here, but I'll get going as soon as I can."

She echoed Max's words from last night. "He can't make you stay."

"That's true," Eric concurred, "but the terms of Manager Han's employment are very clear. He has obligations to fulfill. This isn't the time to be leaving Apollo in Tokyo. How would that look? They might be losing two members, and now their manager, too? If he wants what's best for Apollo, he'll stay right here."

Jiyeon locked her phone, banishing the news and the notifications and the pictures, that sickening gleam of glass on concrete. "The guys would want him to go. I know that's what they're telling him in all those messages."

"If that's the case, and the group is fine with him leaving, then management of Apollo will be transferred to Prism. Their agency has no staff members on site. There's also the matter of Emerald Entertainment potentially bringing up a legal breach. The contract requires Manager Han to be present during a crisis, and this qualifies as a crisis."

"He isn't an Emerald employee," she argued.

"There are two binding agreements in place," Eric argued back. "Your brother signed legal paperwork with the agency in order to be allowed access to agency talent and facilities. Even when artists personally choose their own staff, it's still necessary for managers to be cleared through the company."

Denny shook his head. "Yeonnie, let it go. Grab your clothes and get moving."

"What about you?"

"You heard him. I'm their manager. I... I need to stay."

Out in the hall, an explosion of noise. Apollo peered inside, faces drawn and pale. "Let Denny go home," said Eunjae, shouldering past Prism staff. "We'll pay for the flight."

Eric tapped a stylus on his tablet screen, tap tap tap. His demeanor oozed sympathy. "I think he'd rather be here to support you. Isn't that true, Manager Han? You said this in an interview, if I recall correctly. You're very attached to Apollo. They're your friends, and they mean a lot to you. Making friends was never your strong suit, growing up. Now, these friends need you more than ever. I understand why you're so torn. You care about your restaurant, but isn't that just a place? People are so much more important. Your words exactly."

Unbidden, Jiyeon's eyes filled with tears. She would make him take that back. She would smash that stupid tablet to pieces and make him sorry he ever dared to weaponize Denny's feelings about Apollo. She would—

Eunjae took her face in his hands. "Hey," he murmured. "Look at me. Just me. You can't listen to what he's saying, okay? We need to get you out of here. Denny, too. I'll fix this. I'll find a way."

"What about you? What about your contracts?" She'd skimmed the statement issued by Emerald. The agencies were locked in a very public dispute, trapping Apollo in the middle.

"Never mind about us. Jiyeon, the shop... I'm sorry. I'll fix everything."

"That wasn't your fault."

He didn't answer. And then Denny was there, urging her to finish packing. "Staying here won't kill me. Just go."

But it was killing him. The shop had been everything to her brother from the second he walked in. If anyone should be there, it was Denny.

"Boss, we'll talk to Emerald," said Eunjae. "They won't take this to legal. It's a family emergency, so you need to go."

"No." Denny pointed at the door. "Back to your rooms."

"But—"

"Now, Ryan."

No one budged, not Eunjae or anybody in the hall, and then Denny was roaring at Apollo, roaring like Joey in the videos online. "Go!" he yelled at them. "Do what I told you to do! Can't follow a direct order to save your lives. Jesus, I can't deal with this right now."

He pushed a sweater into Jiyeon's arms, a rain jacket, her purse. All the fight had drained out of him. "If I leave, management transfers to Eric. You know he won't treat them like people, Yeonnie. That's not how he sees them, or any of us. We're pieces on a board."

The hallway was empty now. Eunjae kissed her goodbye.

Eric had the gall to pat him on the back as he left. "If there's anything I admire," he mused, "it's how much your manager cares about you. That kind of loyalty is hard to find."

36

P RISM SENT ERIN TO the airport with Jiyeon, but it didn't stop there. Tickets had been purchased for both of them. The only saving grace was that the seats were on opposite ends of the plane.

Between bouts of fitful slumber, Jiyeon flicked through photos. She made note of which repairs they'd be able to tackle on their own and which would need to be outsourced. She tried to remember if they had paint left over from last spring, if the paint chips were at the shop or at Ivy Lane, if there might be flooring samples stashed in the Wanna Waffle pantry. Jiyeon couldn't hold on to any of it, though. And she didn't have the heart to come back to that picture of the door.

If she kept allowing herself to skip it, she'd never be able to assess the damage. Denny had to stay behind, so it was Jiyeon who should handle this. She knew, and she wanted to be doing it, to lose herself in the work. Things needed fixing. She was good at that. But there was so much noise in her head, an unending discordant clash of new thoughts coming in and old worries rising to the surface. On that long flight, even her silenced phone managed to seem loud.

Erin wasted no time upon landing. From the second they deplaned, she launched into a play-by-play of Prism's agenda. The only time Jiyeon got a break was when they were separated at immigration and then again at customs.

"You'll have a late start tomorrow," she said, so magnanimous, "to recover from all the travel and the crazy things you've been dealing with. That sounds good, right? You deserve some rest. Don't worry about your café. We've advised Emerald to send a cleaning crew this week, on behalf of Apollo."

On behalf of Apollo. Did the guys have anything to do with it at all? Were they even aware that the agency made this gesture in their name?

"We don't need help from Emerald," Jiyeon said. Erin paid her no mind. They'd cleared customs by then, and all that remained was to catch a ride out of the airport. She typed as they walked, leading Jiyeon to assume she was arranging a taxi or a shuttle, but no. A lengthy email swooped into her inbox. Erin had spent the flight industriously composing a novel-length schedule overview for Emma Han.

"I've got three tours lined up for you on Tuesday, then two more on Wednesday, with some meetings here and there. I bet you'll have a favorite picked out by Friday!"

"Erin, I need to be at the shop. I can't be out on tours while my parents try to fix this mess by themselves. We'll have to be closed for almost a week, as it is."

Firmly, Erin replied, "Oh, no. I'd say about three days at the most. The cleaners will come through and have you guys operational in no time."

"I said we don't want—"

"Miss Han, the fans will be disappointed if Apollo doesn't make amends in some way. They'll expect the boys to pitch in. Not directly, of course. That's out of the question. But this is almost the same thing!

And I'm sure you don't want to make it seem like your family is resentful in any way."

Resentful? And what about the damage to the restaurant? Prism seemed devoted to glossing right over it, as though Jiyeon's family didn't depend on their business for bills and rent and groceries.

"It isn't safe for the group to show up in person. That would be a very risky thing to do right now." Erin indicated that they should head to passenger pickup. She babbled all the way there. "We've decided the best course of action is to diminish Apollo's ties to this waffle place of yours, now that filming is almost over. There will be some renewed interest when the show drops in January, but we'll tackle that later on."

The signal improved and delayed messages stacked up on Jiyeon's screen. Seeing that so many were from Eunjae, her mood lifted considerably. But then Erin went on to say, "Apollo's done a lot for you and your family. The easiest way to repay them is by sticking to the story we're putting out there. It's the story that puts the boys in the best possible light. So just go on these tours, keep your head down, and avoid giving Sunshines something else to gossip about. Okay?"

They reached the exit, where Arthur was waiting. Well, of course. "Coming with us, Erin?" Jiyeon asked, bitterly. "What if I refuse to get in the car? That might look bad for Apollo."

Arthur frowned. "Don't hold it against her. She's just tired."

"I understand completely! Of course she's tired! Too much excitement. That's why I thought she might prefer a ride from a good friend. Let's chat tomorrow, Miss Han."

The doors opened. A blast of fresh air met the climate-controlled atmosphere of the airport. Jiyeon went outside, fuming. "Drive safe, Arthur," she said. "It's late."

"You really won't get in the car? Come on, Emmie."

"I can get myself home. You've done what they asked, so just let me go. I'm not heading straight to my parents, anyway."

"I don't care. I'll take you, it's fine."

"No. Goodnight, Arthur."

He latched on to the handle of her suitcase. "That mess at the restaurant... I hate that it happened. My family's been really sad to hear about it. They wanted me to tell you."

"Okay. Thanks for that."

"But I'm not surprised, Emms," he continued. "Are you? I mean, shouldn't you expect this kind of thing to go down when you're connected to people like them?"

Flatly, she said, "People like them."

"Apollo. Famous people. Whatever you want to say." He let go of the handle. "No one even knows you're dating Ari, or at least not yet, and this is how it turned out. If you're caught, it could be worse. This might happen again. You should let me help you."

Jiyeon held his gaze for a long moment. "If you want to help me, stay away. If you ever loved me, if you still want to be my friend, give me a break. Please, Arthur."

She called for a rideshare and left him there, rolling her suitcase to the designated area. Her brain rebelled at the idea of calculating the time difference between herself and Eunjae. Still, she replied to everything he'd sent.

In the car, Jiyeon tried to decide if she was disappointed or relieved when he didn't send any messages back. She suspected he'd call if he was able. If he did, she'd start sobbing in the back seat of this nice lady's sedan.

At the end of the ride, the driver eyed Jiyeon's destination with concern. "You sure this is it, honey? Looks like it's closed."

"This is it."

"Got somebody meeting you here? I can stick around. You shouldn't wait alone."

"I'll be okay," said Jiyeon, touched by her kindness. "It's my family's restaurant. I have the keys. Just need to check on something, and then I'll call my dad. He'll come get me."

She had to see it for herself. Maybe she'd expended the bulk of her courage on entering the address in the app, forcing herself to go to the shop instead of running home, climbing into bed, sobbing in the dark. She'd typed it in, though. She'd confirmed her destination without allowing time to second guess, like ripping off a Band-Aid.

Wanna Waffle had been closed since the disaster on Saturday. When was the last time they closed for that long? It had to be those days in June, when Apollo met their fans in this same parking lot and announced that they were free.

Jiyeon managed one step, then another. She followed the sidewalk and turned the corner. The parking lot blurred, the night dissolving into vague shapes and pools of shadow, street lights bleeding into the glow of distant stars. She buried her face in both hands and cried.

The door wasn't always orange. Purchased at an estate sale, it came to them without hinges, coated in a thick layer of dust. Jiyeon loved it, thinking at the time that she'd save it for her own place. When she realized Wanna Waffle needed something special, a memorable and unique detail, the plan changed.

Most of the family was baffled by her fixation on the door. Why did they need to replace the one they had? It worked fine. Her sister came along, though, to wrangle it into the truck they borrowed from Jeannie's uncle. They brought Denny with them to buy paint. Janie insisted on the most garish shade of aqua, and their little brother demanded to know why it couldn't just be 'door-colored.'

Orange. The color she'd chosen for that house she drew in middle school, a color that was bright and happy, evoking warmth in any season. There wouldn't be another door like it on the boulevard. Jiyeon knew that this could draw the eye and make you pause, the way a post could stop you from scrolling, and that was what she wanted. The door was part of her campaign to make the shop feel less like a restaurant and more like a second home. People would come, then. People would stay.

Jiyeon reached out to touch the broken panes of glass, covered with plastic sheets that rippled under her fingertips. The damage wasn't beyond repair. Wanna Waffle would open again, looking better than before. But was this the place where Jiyeon should be? Did the sight of this hurt so much because her heart was here, right here, and she'd been chasing the wrong dream for years and years?

What if this had been the dream all along?

Freddie Dang (Co-host; Producer): I'm just not buying it, Jooney. Why would Emerald set themselves up as the villain here, *again?* There's no way they'd be that stupid.

Jooney Chun (Host): They were stupid enough to lose Apollo.

Freddie: Exactly. They lost Apollo, so now they should be playing it safe. Poaching Jungwoo and Max out of the Zenith deal is not an example of 'playing it safe.' You couldn't play it dumber, and I don't think Emerald's that dumb. They're dumb, but not stupid. (*mutters*) Okay, that made a lot of sense in my head but zero sense when I said it out loud, sorry.

Maisie Chun (Co-host; Jooney's Mom): Why fight about it? Nine of them can make a deal with Zenith, do their group stuff, that kind of thing. The other two can write songs, whatever. Seen it before. One big group contract, nine little solo contracts. Not even a lawyer and I figured that out.

Jooney: Based on the press release from Zenith last weekend, they want all or nothing. They're not willing to let Jungwoo and Max make songs for any competition.

Freddie: It's like they didn't decide they really, really, really want Apollo until the group got crazy popular with those leaks from the show and Emma Han taking over the *Sunshine 24/7* channel. Then Lumina came right out of the gate as monster rookies, and it's thanks to a song by two members of Apollo. Yeah, no wonder Zenith suddenly doesn't want to share their toys after all.

Jooney: Well, when you bring Lumina into the equation... and the way they've patched things up with Apollo since the summer... Emerald Entertainment would need to be very, extremely stupid to ruin its own redemption arc like this.

Freddie: That's why I keep saying there's something shady about this whole thing. I mean, the timing? Those emails just happened to leak on this specific weekend, the day after Lumina's MV? You can't tell me that wasn't strategic. Somebody wanted to start a fire.

Maisie: (*clapping*) Very nice that you're using the college degree now, Freddie. Been waiting forever to see this happen. Real detective work!

Freddie: Auntie, my degree is in journalism.

Maisie: Yeah, yeah. I remember. Went to your graduation!

Freddie: I'm literally using the degree every single day.

Maisie: How? When?

Freddie: Here! On this show!

Jooney: (*laughing in background*)

Freddie: This podcast counts as journalism!

Maisie: That's what you told your dad, eh? It's journalism when you scroll the social media and boom, you see Max Lee didn't go to dinner with the other boys after that millionaire wedding, you see Apollo back in California today—

Freddie: And I reported on it, didn't I? So it was journalism!

Maisie: (*also laughing now*)

Freddie: I quit! I'm quitting, have fun finding a new producer—

Jooney: Oh, but... I hope Apollo's okay. You know?

Freddie: (*sighs*) Same.

37

"Eric wants you on Star-Connect tonight," said Denny. "Couldn't get you out of it, so just keep it short. Don't forget."

Eunjae had forgotten, although it might be more accurate to say that he'd repressed it on purpose. Prism kept pushing him to talk to the fans via livestream, insensitive to his exhaustion. Eric called it 'proof of life' and 'reassuring the audience.'

Reminder issued, Denny left without another word, off to continue doing his work with the same efficiency as ever. Just his work, nothing extra. Their manager barely spoke to them these days. He'd plunged into a deep, wounded silence.

Shoulders slumped, Eunjae stared at Langley House, shining in the late afternoon sun. His gaze always went straight to Jiyeon's window on the second floor. He looked despite knowing she wouldn't be there.

They still had another hour of filming up ahead, even after a full day at the diner. The producers brought special guests, so it was a lot of talking and a lot of pretending to talk. Apollo managed the way they always did, drawing on dwindling reserves of energy, but it was Ezra who got the most screen time. He'd researched their visitors ahead of time.

His list of questions was a mile long, and he asked every single one.

He had questions for Eunjae, too. "Why aren't you guys saying anything about Wanna Waffle?" he wanted to know, when Leila drove him to the house. "Your fans ruined everything. Shouldn't you guys tell them that was wrong?"

Their mother overheard. "The fans are customers. As they say, the customer is always right. Correcting them would be a mistake."

"Yeah, but that was property damage. They should have to pay, at least. If I was a customer at the diner and I punched a hole in the wall, wouldn't I have to pay for it?"

"Someone did pay," Leila replied. She sent her younger son ahead, lingering to speak to Eunjae. "Think about what you're doing to that poor family, Ari. You could do a better job of protecting them. And if they find out about the girl? What then?" She held up a hand, the fingers long and graceful. "No, don't make that face at me. I'm not telling you to put an end to whatever it is you think you have with Emma. As if you'd listen to me! I'm telling you to hide it better. Let Arthur help you. I can't believe you'd let your pride get in the way of keeping her safe."

But he was keeping her safe. It was safer to stay apart. That's what Eric counseled, because there had been another clip buried in that weekend's digital wreckage, discovered on an elderly wedding guest's Facebook page. Sunshines had zoomed in to the point of obliterating clarity, extracting footage that lasted just eight seconds. In an endless loop, it showed Apollo's Ari reaching for someone's hand. There was nothing shy or awkward about it. He'd clearly reached for that hand before. *Emma's hand*, the comments screeched. *Look at the way he's smiling at her. Look at how her hand fits so perfectly in his.*

Prism suppressed the post before it could gain much traction. When Eric made him watch the video and read the comments, Eunjae had just one thought in his head: why would I ever want to hide this?

He was so tired of hiding. And he almost said it to Leila, right then and there, but Ezra cut between them. "Mum, stop talking to him. They've already started rolling. Oh, and I'm staying after. Eunjae said I can, if I want."

Leila smiled, icy and serene. "Best friends now, are you?"

Shrugging, Ezra pulled Eunjae to the cottage. Cameras were aimed at the patio and rigged inside the kitchen. The producers wanted to recreate a scene from the first season of *Sunshine 24/7*, still a fan favorite two years after it aired.

Inside, Max stood at the kitchen counter, holding up a bag of marshmallows like the plastic was porous and the contents were a fast-acting poison. "What is this? What the hell did you buy?"

"I bought marshmallows!" Kazu exclaimed. "That's what you told me to buy!"

Rather than berating him, Max focused his ire on Eunjae. "Why did you let him buy the wrong marshmallows? What are we supposed to do with these? They're tiny, we'd need a million of them. And how are we supposed to roast these on a stick?"

"Ah, sorry," said Eunjae. "The jumbo marshmallows weren't on sale. Hyung bought double of the mini marshmallows instead."

No further explanation was necessary. Max groaned and went back to unpacking the spoils of their grocery run. Discounted spoils, brought down to a fabulously low price using coupons and a borrowed Lowell's rewards card. Jiyeon's was tied to her phone number, and Eunjae had the number memorized.

"I'm leaving if you bought the wrong ass graham crackers, too."

"No, those are right. I put them in the cart while he wasn't looking."

"Edit that out," said Eric, making notations on his tablet. "We can't have any mention of leaving. It's unity, unity, unity. That's our message now and it'll still be our message when people are streaming this in January. Try it again, Max."

So they ran it a second time, grasping at the spontaneity of the first and falling short. Afterward, Kazu explained the dessert menu to Ezra. The dog capered at his feet. Momo had a massive blue bow around her neck, almost the same blue as the hand-glazed tile on the backsplash. Wait, wasn't her name Cosmos now? Jiyeon had posted about Apollo's dog while they were in Tokyo. Sunshines sent names from every corner of the world.

"We're making s'nores. We made them on that last tour, before Hwannie left."

"*S'mores,*" Max corrected him. "Goddamn, hyung."

They assembled ingredients and stacks of plates, learning why these smaller marshmallows were inferior to larger marshmallows. Minis wouldn't roast evenly. You'd have to use a ton just to cover the full surface area of the graham cracker, not to mention the issue of how to melt them over the fire without charring everything else. And that signature gooey texture? You needed jumbo for that.

This lesson on the art of making s'mores came courtesy of Nicky, with additional highly opinionated commentary by Max. The idea of making them in the microwave was Kei's contribution. Brothers booed him away from the fire pit. But in the end, they didn't make the food themselves. At Eric's insistence, the production prepared a tray in advance. All they had to do was eat. No more bickering. Nothing but unity, unity, unity. And that was it for the day, filming complete.

"Aww, let's make s'nores for real," Namgyu said, brokering a truce. Fragile and tenuous as a soap bubble, but a truce nonetheless. Jungwoo stuck around with his guitar. Eunjae invited Denny and received no response.

"Do we really have to use that?" Kei persisted, balking at the fire. "It makes my clothes smell like smoke. The smoke gets in my hair and then I have to wash it. Gyu hogs the bathroom, so then I have to wait, meaning I need to stay up later, and I won't get enough sleep, so then I'll be tired on set tomorrow—"

Ezra studied Kei's face like it would show up on a final exam. "You're the one who wears black," he said, "and you hate it here. You say that as much as the Max guy says he's faking his own death."

"I do hate it here."

A blank-eyed stare. "So leave."

Kazu heard this and prodded Eunjae with his elbow. "Ya. Who taught this kid to be so rude?"

"Hear me out," said Nicky, producing a lighter. "I've got a theory about this. Siblings tend to be opposites, right? Jungwoo's the only musical one out of five kids. Max's sisters are total babes and Max is a big, giant baby—"

"You can fuck right off, hyung."

"Oh, and Actual Ari keeps his rude thoughts up here, in his head, but Aspiring Ari says them out loud."

"Don't call me that!"

"Ooh, my apologies, Ari the Younger."

"Stop."

"Anything for you, Wannabe Ari—"

Suddenly, the fire was blazing. The lighter vanished up Nicky's sleeve and Eunjae shook it out. "Quit, hyung." But it was better this way, with their voices warming the crisp air, and no cameras locked in orbit around them. He preferred Nicky laughing to Nicky gone cold and remote. He preferred Kei complaining to Kei saying nothing, defeated and withdrawn.

The light faded, along with the chatter on the patio. Max scurried inside for blankets, his hoodie, another jacket. "So what are we doing?" Jesse asked, in a small voice. He sat squashed between older brothers, the dog tucked inside his shirt so she wouldn't get cold.

Ezra looked up from his homework. "You guys stopped fighting after you made these marshmallow things, last time."

"You watched our show?"

"I've seen all of your dumb shows. Like, every episode."

Was he indignant or embarrassed? Both? Eunjae couldn't tell. From the corner of his eye, he noticed Max fidgeting with the hem of his blanket. He also had something to say and just wasn't saying it.

"Anyway," Ezra continued, "food is how you fix your problems."

Jungwoo disagreed. "I don't think food will fix this. It's just not that simple."

"Not to you, but you're the one who never thinks anything is simple, right?" The teenager squinted at him. "I think your name starts with a J. Can't keep track. There's too many of you."

The dam finally broke. Max let out a strangled noise that devolved into crazed, hysterical laughter. "This is fucking incredible. If you think we're so lame, why do you know everything about us? I can't stand this kid. Get him the hell away from me."

"I don't know everything about you!"

"Yeah you do, you just said Keiichi's an edgy brat and Jungwoo's an edgy loser!" Max pelted Ezra with a fistful of marshmallows. "Admit it. You watched our shows because you *don't* think your brother is lame."

"I watched your shows because everybody at school asks me about Eunjae," Ezra yelled, seizing a whole bag of marshmallows and volleying right back. "It's research! I have to pretend like I know him! And by the way, you're *all* lame, because you're fighting each other instead of Eric, and your fans trashed Denny's restaurant but you won't say anything—"

Eunjae felt like he'd been sucker punched. Max caught the bag, too shocked to return fire. Wearily, Kazu got between them, braving a potential hail of marshmallows. "Settle down. I agree, but Jungwoo's right. It's not that simple."

"It is. You could just do the right thing, but you won't." Ezra took a breath, then yelled some more. "I wish you'd fight back! I wish you didn't suck!"

38

I N THEORY, JIYEON KNEW what needed to be done. *Just get started*, said the rational part of her brain. The advice had worked for her in the past. But every time the shop's ruined facade appeared in her mind, she wanted to cry again.

She didn't. Jiyeon avoided the shop, letting her parents coordinate with Prism on cleanup, now scheduled for Wednesday morning. She toured four prospective salons chosen by Prism and had a pile of raw material waiting to be turned into content. Daily, she told Eunjae she was fine. Jiyeon told everyone she was fine. This wasn't true, and now she'd been hiding on the back porch at Ivy Lane for hours, getting nowhere with the video she was supposed to edit. But what did it matter?

Stay with Erin. When you're not with Erin, stay home and stay safe. Eric's emails said the same thing over and over again. Jiyeon complied. This was easier than fighting, and probably wiser. What did she even know, anymore? Trudging through empty retail spaces, she evaluated a dream she'd believed in and pursued for decades, now increasingly in tatters.

There wasn't anything wrong with the locations Prism found, even if none had felt right to her. Thanks to all the tours, Jiyeon was forced to confront the truth: she didn't want to open a salon. Her dream had changed. It felt like a betrayal of who she was, of the person she'd thought herself to be. It felt like giving up. And it would help if she could at least figure out the new dream, to adjust her trajectory, to begin again after wasting so much time. She yearned for something else but couldn't name it.

Dully, she checked for news about Apollo. Fans continued to blame Hazel for posting, for merely existing, and for Max's absence at that group dinner on Saturday night. Eric had pushed them to keep the reservation. Later, Eunjae described that joyless meal as the worst they'd ever had together.

Prism took Max's defiance in stride. They made sure to propagate paparazzi photos of him arguing with Hazel up and down the aisles of a convenience store, dressed in full evening attire, both of them beautiful and utterly furious. The gossip machine resurrected articles on Hazel's dating history. Fans criticized the number of villainous acting roles she'd taken, and how often she replied to rude social media comments with reciprocal rudeness. Her idol boyfriend was squeaky clean in comparison.

>> just look at her lol u can tell she's messy as hell
>> fr lol girlie's a psycho
>> It's fake!!! None of that is real!!!
>> Shame on u Hazel for USING Max like this!
>> We know u don't really LOVE him!
>> Max omg you can do better than her

The door slid open on its rails. Jeannie pushed the blinds aside. She slipped through the gap with red-rimmed eyes, a hairbrush in her right hand. In the left, she had a hair tie and some pins.

Jiyeon sat up, freeing herself from the mire because she thought Jeannie had come to be comforted. Even as a child, she'd ask to have her hair braided after a hard day, or in anticipation of anything big and scary that was supposed to happen. On the morning of her uncle's funeral, Jeannie sobbed while Jiyeon combed out the tangles. She'd requested a braided ponytail an hour before her driving exam and a braided updo for commencement. She always said it soothed her.

But when Jiyeon moved to take the brush, Jeannie wouldn't let her have it. "I know how to do this one," she said, sniffling. "I watched your video two million times."

"You're here to braid *my* hair?"

"Yeah, and then we're gonna go fight the twins."

"We're... gonna go fight Steph and Sienna?"

She was an expert on Jeannie's long and adversarial history with Arthur's nieces, both in middle school. The three had a puzzling dynamic, considering how many interests they shared. Stephanie and Sienna Hong were K-pop fans because of Jeannie, who used to be their babysitter. You'd think they'd get along well, but the opposite was true.

"You know they're Sunshines," she said, pulling the brush through. She tried not to tug too hard on Jiyeon's indifferent, flyaway waves. "I got the most obnoxious text message. Just thinking about it makes me so tired, 'cause I wasn't built to be mad all the time, right? Being mad uses up tons of energy that I just don't have."

"Why are you mad? Do I want to know?"

"You have to know! That message was about you and Denny, they saw someone's stupid post on Star-Connect and then one of the biggest Ari fan accounts is spreading lies—"

"Ari fan account. So they only post about Eunjae?"

"Yeah, they post every time he breathes. 'This is what Ari wore to the airport!' 'This is the book Ari was reading on last night's episode of *Shine Bright Apollo*!' If you ever get murdered, I'm reporting them as primary suspects."

"What he wore to the airport," Jiyeon murmured to herself. Did she even know what Eunjae wore to the airport?

"Focus! They're saying... they're saying your whole family took advantage of Ari being sad and lonely. You guys don't really care about him. It's just an act."

Jeannie dissolved into tears, equal parts heartbroken and enraged. Meanwhile, Jiyeon wasn't sure where to start with these accusations. Her family didn't care about him? Based on what evidence?

The search results opened with standard offerings: Emma Han's Instagram account, the official website for *Sunshine 24/7*, a local news feature on Wanna Waffle. Nothing odd until midway down the first page, where a celebrity gossip blog called *K-Star News* had posted about the 'suspicious' and 'concerning' relationship between Apollo and 'unqualified' manager Denny Han.

She clicked the link, heart in her throat. This brought her to a clip of Denny shouting at Apollo to go back to their rooms, embedded in a nine-minute YouTube monologue. Posted two hours ago, it theorized that the guys had been locked up in their hotel and may still be locked up right now, practically held hostage by their manager. Denny Han was a greedy and abusive opportunist. He'd befriended Ari just to use him as the mascot for a failing restaurant.

According to the comments on that video, Denny's sister was no better. Emma Han had used Apollo to stage a comeback from 'the place where washed up Insta girlies go to die.' No such thing as a decent influencer, fans and random Internet bystanders proclaimed. Influencers were the scum of the earth.

On Reddit: Emma Han was cold as ice, rolling around town looking for a new salon while Apollo paid for the damages at her family's lame cafe. She would've been jobless without Ari and Apollo.

And on Star-Connect: That restaurant shouldn't be allowed to reopen. The owners deserve to go bankrupt for leeching off Apollo like this. Did you see how they covered the place in pictures of the boys? These people will do anything to make a buck.

Countless strangers brainstormed how to close Wanna Waffle for good. They could bomb it with bad reviews, report the business as fraudulent, petition Emerald Entertainment to sue. Some even claimed to live in the neighborhood, testifying that the place had gone downhill since June. *We've had brunch there every Sunday for five years now. Thought they were a great family, but now they've gotten greedy. We won't be coming back.*

That hurt so badly that Jiyeon had to stop for a second. But the next comment was even worse: *What were you guys expecting? The manager's a thug. I bet he bullied Apollo into hiring him, it's not like he's got any industry experience.*

"Stay with Apollo," Eric told Denny, that terrible morning after the wedding. He'd banked on her brother's loyalty, the unspoken affection woven into every terse command. He'd pressured Denny to stay because he needed it for the optics. And who would have that footage from Sunday, if not Prism? Who else would be able to post about Jiyeon touring salons when she hadn't even posted about it herself? That had to come from Prism, too.

This was Eric's grand scheme coming together, his narrative progressing as planned. He'd outmaneuvered them completely. And he wasn't done, she realized. That cleaning crew would arrive tomorrow, giving Prism fresh fodder for the official storyline. Apollo was virtuous. Apollo was doing everything they could, and if they fell apart, only predatory outsiders were to blame.

Objectively, it was a job well done. She'd give Eric a medal if she didn't despise him.

Jeannie took the phone away. "Denny's not a thug. They're lying. We can't let them keep doing that." She was really crying now. "Uncle and Auntie said not to come get you, 'cause you're sad and you're tired, but we have to fight. So I'm here, and I'll fight too. I'll go bring the boss back if you want. He has to listen to me 'cause he's named after *my* Uncle Dennis. I have rights. And I hate driving, I've asked for a chauffeur every Christmas since I was four, whatever, but I'll drive." Sobbing, she said, "We have to do something. No, *I* have to do something. This is a Code Violet."

Lizzie and Joey crashed the scene, drawn by the invisible beacon of Jeannie's distress. She cried even more at the sight of them. Eyes burning, Jiyeon got up and hugged her, hard. "We'll fight. Just give me a minute, okay? I need to think. And then I need to call Eunjae."

We're pieces on a board.

That would be Eric's mistake. She decided it then and there. She'd make him regret ever putting them on the board in the first place.

39

W HEN JIYEON CALLED, EUNJAE had to leave the patio, unable to hear over Apollo shouting themselves into a deadlock. He needed to put distance between himself and the outbreak of total war.

"Can you guys be here tomorrow?" Jiyeon asked him, after explaining the situation. "Jeannie's organizing a cleanup. We'll have volunteers helping, but if you came with Denny, that would show fans that you're still on good terms with your manager."

Head spinning, Eunjae wandered to the edge of the property. The valley was a bowl of tumbled stars. "Of course we'll be there," he told her, although he couldn't be certain that his brothers were coming. Eunjae didn't want to consider that eventuality, but so much of what he knew had been obliterated and rearranged.

Halfway to the cottage, while sorting through everything he'd need to say and do, he came upon Max and Jungwoo. They'd both gone searching for him. Unable to agree on who should do this, they didn't make it very far.

"I'm the one who needs to talk to Ari," Jungwoo argued.

"No shit you need to talk to him. Talk to hyung for an hour if you want, but I'm going first. He didn't know about me. I didn't tell him and then he had to find out at the wedding. I know that's fucked up. I have to fix it."

Eunjae jogged over to separate them. "Hyung," said Max, startled. "We saw. Emma-noona sent some links."

"Yeah. Faster that way. Can't waste time."

Eunjae grabbed both of his brothers, marching them back into the fray. They needed to hurry. Every hour that went by was another hour of Prism building a fortress around Apollo, unassailable, shielded on every side. The group would emerge with an ironclad reputation. This protection would come at the expense of people they loved.

The night was clear and quiet, amplifying every sound. They'd gotten loud enough to summon their manager from the main house. That was Denny, demanding a ceasefire. The argument simmered for all of three seconds before reaching a boiling point again.

"We'll talk more when this is over," Eunjae said, "but I'm not mad. I think you should go with Emerald. Both of you."

Jungwoo stumbled on the path. "What?"

He'd wanted to say it for days, but it never felt like the right time, and Eunjae had no speech prepared. He did his best. "Hyung, sign with Emerald. That's your dream. The real dream, the big one. Don't turn it down just because of us, or Zenith, or anybody else. This is your chance, and it's Max's chance, too. Take the offer and stop worrying about me."

No reply. Eunjae had stunned them into silence. Finally, Jungwoo choked out, "I wish you'd yell at me. I wish you'd be mad instead."

"Why the hell can't you be mad?" Max had his hood pulled forward as far as it would go, and he stared at his shoes as he spoke. "Fuck. I hate agreeing with anything he says, but Jungwoo's right. This would be easier if you'd just tell us to stay."

"I can't do that."

"Why not? You fought so hard to get us away from Emerald. Why don't you care? You should care the most."

"I fought that contract so we could all be free," said Eunjae, "and being free means getting to make choices for ourselves."

Months ago, he'd realized that it would never be enough to break from Emerald on his own. Unless he earned freedom for all of them, the victory would be hollow. Now they could move forward, choosing paths that might not run precisely parallel. Those paths led somewhere beyond the horizon, to a place they couldn't even see yet. But in that place, they would meet again. Until then, Eunjae needed his brothers to see that they were free to go, and grow, and keep on growing.

"It's like our old table in the dining hall," he said. "This deal with Zenith, I mean. None of us thinks it's great, but we keep putting up with it anyway. We keep trying to stay together, even when it's not working, because that's what we know how to do. We should stop. Staying together doesn't mean that we have to stay the same."

"Hyung. Are you saying the nine of us are like some shitty table?"

Jungwoo had a hand pressed to his eyes. "The table. Yeah, I get it." With a pained smile, he said, "I couldn't let you leave, but you'll do that for me? I just... I can't stand you sometimes, Ari."

"I can't stand *you*," said Max, easily triggered as always. He kicked at the gravel, face wet, arms crossed tight over his chest. "Fuck. This isn't how it was supposed to go."

"Doesn't mean it won't go well," Eunjae replied. He twisted the fading elastic band on his wrist, always a comfort. "Come on. I think they called Jaehwan-hyung."

He'd guessed correctly. That was their leader's terrifying visage on the screen. "Have you lost your minds? You can't go down there. By all means, send Denny and tell Eric to get over it. That's his family. That's his restaurant. But the eight of you are going to bed, and tomorrow you'll be at the diner, no exceptions."

"Hwannie, it's not right. We should be there to help out. It was our fault."

"One, you don't get to call me Hwannie when I'm pissed at you. Two, you wouldn't be helping. You might even make it worse. What if Sunshines show up looking for you?"

Jaehwan waited, standing in the shade outside the government office building where he fulfilled the terms of his mandatory military service. None of the members had an answer for him, but Ezra blurted out, "Give your dumb fans a broom."

"Why's this one still awake? Don't kids have bedtimes anymore?"

"I'm fourteen, not four. Why would my bedtime be 8:02pm?"

Eunjae hustled Ezra into the cottage, asked him to please stay put for ten minutes, and shoved a random book into his hands. Then he rushed back to say, "Jaehwan-hyung, I have to be there. Denny and his family were kind to me. They've been kind to everyone I've brought to their door, no questions asked."

Denny lifted a brow. "I had questions."

"Ah, right. Sorry about that."

"I still have questions."

Eunjae started over. "Even when they had questions," he amended, "they were kind to me anyway. I love them. I love Wanna Waffle. So I'm going, and I'm really sorry, hyung, but I can't listen to you this time. I'm sorry to cause more trouble. I'll sincerely reflect on the consequences of my actions."

The apologies rolled right off his tongue. Jaehwan regarded him with confusion. Despite knowing this was the equivalent of signing his own death warrant, Eunjae reached over and ended the call, hanging up on someone for the first time in his life.

His brothers stared at him, flabbergasted. Eunjae kept going. Otherwise, he'd crumble like a house of cards, call Jaehwan back, and beg for his miserable life.

"I'm going tomorrow. You don't have to come with me, but I think you should."

Right away, Kazu said, "I'm going." Lowering his voice, he added, "Don't worry about Hwannie. I'll buy him another Baskin Robbins franchise."

"Bribery," hissed Kei. "Disgusting." He didn't opt out of going to Wanna Waffle, though, and neither did anyone else. They had a contract in jeopardy and a pile of unanswered questions about their future, but they could agree on being there in person. They could also agree that Eunjae was a dead man for hanging up on leader-nim when they'd already interrupted his lunch break, but that was a problem for later.

Eunjae turned to Denny next. "Go ahead and leave tonight. Max can drive us in the morning."

"Nah. No telling what Eric's gonna do when he realizes I'm gone."

"Boss, we know you want to go."

"Aww, man," Namgyu said. "If you won't leave, we'll have to make you!"

"Yeah?" Denny replied, nostrils flaring. "And what's the plan there, pal? Kidnapping? Extortion? You take me down with the power of harmonious song?"

"Ha! Imagine if I knew how to do that, I could be so strong, I'd be the strongest—"

Keen to examine the scale of Prism's campaign, Nicky had been scrolling that whole time. He came up for air just long enough to say,

"Listen, Chief. If we drive down together, it'll look like you forced us to go. But if you leave first and we come later, it reads like we followed you out of loyalty. Eric can't say we're prisoners. That's better *narrative positioning*." A big grin. "Don't you love the Prism handbook? I love the Prism handbook."

It was a strong argument. Eunjae capitalized on the momentum. "Go home, Denny," he said. "You're fired."

His brothers' mortification warranted a matching mushroom cloud, curling over the detonation point in a column of dust and debris. They were beyond appalled. First Jaehwan, and now Denny? He'd gone insane.

"You're fired," Eunjae said again. "We're letting you go. You're not tied to us anymore, and you didn't quit, so you're not obligated to the agency. They can only hit you with legal if you quit." He took a deep breath, heart threatening to slam right out of his chest. "And since we terminated your employment, we owe you severance. That's what the contract says."

Nicky hooted with delight. "You're doing this again? You got off on a technicality one time and now it's your signature move? This is my boy, this is my one true son—"

That was the only positive reaction. The others instructed him to grovel at Denny's feet without delay. When he refused to budge, not even Max could take it. "Did you hit your head? You wouldn't be like this if you weren't fucking concussed. I'm driving you to the hospital or whatever they have in this weird little murder town."

"I still don't understand why you think this is a murder town," mumbled Jungwoo.

"You don't understand anything. I can't believe I'm stuck with you. I can't believe I'm actively *choosing* to be stuck with you for the next two years—"

Kei sat bolt upright on his bench. "Wait, you're both going? What about Zenith? What about the contract?"

"It's a murder town," Max maintained, ignoring him. "You get stuck in a place like this and it's automatically a horror movie. It's too cute. It's too nice. That's suspicious as hell and I've been saying this since July."

"Ari-hyung will be in jail stripes forever," Jesse wailed. "I never thought I'd live to see this, I never even thought it was possible—"

Eunjae turned his back on the madness. "Thanks for everything, Den. We'll never be able to replace you, and I don't know how we'll keep going without you, but this is it. Mission complete. Go home."

He braced himself for the worst, but Denny reached out to shake his hand. The noise died down. "Mission complete," their former manager replied. His scowl had unfurled into a smile. "See you tomorrow, Ryan."

40

THE PAINT CHIPS WERE in the drawer under the register, buried beneath layers of junk mail, paid invoices, and the printed instructions for seven different board games. At least Jiyeon knew where to look next time their Friday gaming group disputed the rules for Scrabble. She wanted to send both of her parents to buy paint, just to cut the lecture short, but they were in charge of providing breakfast for the volunteers. The job was too important to reassign.

"Walked back home from the shop," her mother exclaimed again, waving a whisk. "Middle of the night! Walked all the way home with your bags, exactly like a crazy person!"

"Han Jiyeon. Why do this, huh? Jeannie comes to get you, that's it, you listen right away. Dad comes to get you, no. Dad brings you dinner, new magazine, picture of your boyfriend — nothing!"

"Okay, and how did you end up with one of Eunjae's photo cards? Feel like explaining yet?"

"Those cards," said Joey, "are for collecting. I buy the CD, I get two cards. Lucky, too! So many of them, but I get lion boy on my first try?" He pointed at her. "Meant to be. That's what happened, Yeonnie."

Lizzie slotted the whisk into the drying rack with a vengeance. "Why are you so quick to get up when Jeannie starts crying?"

"I thought she needed help."

"This is what I'm saying! Why only come out when somebody else needs help? What about when you need help?"

Jiyeon saw her mother's expression and fell headlong into a memory. Last December, she went to Ivy Lane with her shoes full of sand, no phone, no job, and Lizzie looked just like this when she came to the door. *Went to the beach, no jacket! Middle of the night! Threw your phone in the water, exactly like a crazy person!* No one had ever scolded her so thoroughly. No one had ever held her so tightly.

She thought of how Eunjae might respond. Draping her apron over a chair, Jiyeon went to give Lizzie a hug. "I know. I'm sorry."

"Our Yeonnie, scared of nothing in the world," said Joey. "Nothing, except asking for help. What does your brother call this?" An invisible lightbulb went *ding* above his head. "A-ha! Tomfoolery."

She'd have to hug him later. For now, Apollo had arrived. Jiyeon heard them before she saw them, as usual.

She picked her way over the plastic sheeting laid out on the dining room floor. A breeze whistled through the busted panels where glass used to be, carrying the noise indoors. Who told Jesse he could borrow that jacket? Could this old man buy Jaehwan-hyung a pizza franchise instead of ice cream again? Would it kill him to make an effort? And when would they get to eat breakfast? Some of them were *starving*. Some of them hadn't eaten in *hours*.

She counted only six of the eight. "Where's Eunjae?"

"Whoa, ajumma. That's how you say hi to me?"

"Yikes."

"Aww, Max isn't here either. Why didn't she ask about him?"

"He's not important," sighed Jungwoo, "and neither are we."

Jesse bounced up in Vuitton overalls, warm and cozy in a matching Vuitton jacket. "Oh my gosh. Noona, what if it was one of us instead? You know, when you opened the door that night—"

"Hmm. No."

Six jaws dropped. Six sets of eyeballs popped out of six bewildered skulls. "Wow. She didn't even have to think about it... I've never been rejected so fast in my life..." Was that a shadow on the sidewalk, or Jungwoo's soul leaving his body?

Jeannie herded them into the restaurant. "You've gotta quit doing this," she whined at Jiyeon. "Who just randomly finds idols standing outside? Who does that more than once in their lifetime? I can't cope, okay? I've only had two shots of espresso and it's not enough. I'm just absorbing the caffeine now. No, I'm becoming caffeine. So I energize other people, but I can't make any energy for myself."

The guys were ordered to march into the kitchen. They promised Jeannie all kinds of treats in exchange for breakfast: concert tickets, incriminating photos, a villa in Tuscany. She told them to zip it and prepare for the mission brief. "How dare you ask me for food? Don't you know I've got nothing left to give? Do you think this event organized itself?"

Not long after that, Jiyeon heard Denny and Max come in through the back. She couldn't explain the compulsion to open the blinds; she just knew, somehow, that Eunjae would come around to the front. He'd want to see the door.

She went outside and rushed into his embrace. Eunjae could only hold her with his left arm; he had a parcel tucked under the right, flat and thin, wrapped in brown paper. Seeing the damage in person, he couldn't manage a single word.

"It's okay," Jiyeon told him. "We'll fix it."

"We will."

"Where'd you go?"

"Had to make an extra stop." And then he said, "We've got time. Let's run away."

They couldn't be gone for long, so they didn't run very far. There was a small park down the block, a triangle of greenery wedged between two residential streets. The walk involved a slight uphill climb that took five minutes, give or take, and Jiyeon figured no one else would be around at this hour.

It was still so early, just after daybreak, with the sun obscured by a bank of clouds. Sometimes it managed to shine through, piercing the milky blue light with a glimmer of gold. They didn't talk much on the way there. Eunjae held tightly to her hand, breath fogging the air above the shearling collar of his jean jacket.

In the spring, the park's lone jacaranda tree produced cascades of blue-violet blossoms. Jiyeon used to sit in its shade with Janie, stealing away from the shop for weekend lunch breaks. The last time she came here, Eunjae had just flown back to Seoul and a thick carpet of petals covered the ground. Now the tree was bare, its branches full of sky. Yellowing leaves trembled in the breeze.

They could come back at winter's end. Eunjae would be here, taking a million pictures. She wouldn't need that calendar on the wall in her kitchen because she'd be with him all year round. And there was still so much left to do, a battle they had yet to win, but Jiyeon felt only contentment. They were here together. They'd be here together again.

She'd gotten better at finding silver linings. Janie would gloat, if she knew. She'd be so annoying about it. "There are always flowers," her sister loved to say, regardless of the season, untethered by time and its constraints. The girl read one coffee table book about art history and went on to quote Matisse at Jiyeon forever after.

There are always flowers for those who wish to see them. "You need to get better at finding the flowers, Yeonnie. Just keep looking and you'll find something good." And then her sister would stitch another daisy into the cuff of her sweater, she'd embroider a bouquet on the pocket of Jiyeon's favorite jeans. Janie knew that it was hard for her to see the flowers, so she put them everywhere, well-meaning and heavy-handed in a way that only older sisters can be.

When she left, off to see the world and live a life apart from them, her absence yielded a new lesson to be learned: how to be Jiyeon, without Janie. Sitting with Eunjae, she understood that a similar lesson awaited him, too. He'd have to learn how to be Eunjae, without eight brothers.

If he was worried, if he was afraid, it didn't show just then. He put the parcel in Jiyeon's lap and said, "Look what I got."

Carefully, she peeled the brown paper away. She went so slow that Eunjae had to laugh through his own impatience. "I'm trying not to rip it," said Jiyeon, uncovering the beveled edge of a picture frame.

"Just rip it."

"No way. What if it gets scratched? I still need to bring it home."

"I need to borrow it first. They want it back when I'm done, but it's okay. I'll make two copies."

And that was where Jiyeon stopped. "What is this? What did you do?"

"Offered to buy it. Golden Grove wouldn't sell, though." He shrugged. "Thought that was fair. Can't expect them to break up their collection for some guy."

"Eunjae, you didn't."

But he did. Under the wrap, just a little bit faded by sunlight and the passage of time, Jiyeon saw the house she'd drawn in eighth grade. It had an orange door.

She looked up at him, speechless. Eunjae brushed a tear from her cheek. "When I find an apartment," he said, "it's going on the wall. And when you open your own place, whatever that place might be, we'll hang it up again."

Jiyeon hooked an arm around his neck and kissed him. "I love it. I love it more than I can say. Thank you." But then she was sobbing in earnest, because she had no idea where this picture would go. That certainty was lost to her. "I wish I knew," she whispered. "I thought I knew, and now I don't."

"You don't have to know," Eunjae whispered back, gently. "You've got so much time."

"I said that to Ezra."

"You did. He told me. And I don't know what I'm doing, either. I just know I love you."

The picture frame almost slid right out of her lap and onto the cracked pavement below. "Eunjae. You're saying that to me right now?"

"I am."

"But you've never said that to me before," she stammered.

"I wanted to," Eunjae said in a hurry. "So many times. I mean, all the time, but I wasn't sure if it was too soon." Overcome by belated embarrassment, he added, "Google said I shouldn't."

It was so warm. Jiyeon had never been warmer. Why did she borrow this jacket he'd left in her car? Why did she insist on pretending it ever got cold in California? She would get nothing done today. She would sit on this bench and freak out. And for the rest of this day, for the rest of her life, she would obsess over the look on Eunjae's face when he heard her say, "I love you, too."

This felt like her last love, but it was also the first.

There was still work to be done. Eunjae helped her up so they could walk back. Volunteers were arriving in cars and vans and more than one bus. They came bearing food, ladders, power tools. They fussed over Denny when he emerged from the shop to greet them.

Jiyeon forgot to breathe. She hadn't hoped for such a turnout, what with the short notice and how rough things had been in recent weeks. "But there's so many," she said. "I can't believe it."

Eunjae waited for her, smiling. "Yeah. Kindness comes back to you."

She felt the shift when it happened, like the light changing at daybreak, like every cell in her body wide awake and singing. The dream, the dream. It hadn't changed at all.

It grew.

***A video recorded by Eunjae in July 2023, two weeks before
Apollo's departure from Los Angeles***

To be clear, this is a video of a video. Eunjae has his phone
pointed at the TV screen. He rewinds to the beginning, then
presses play again.

On the day of this recording, we're at the apartment on
Ivy Lane. The living room is steeped in gray. Midsummer rain
drums against the window panes. But on the TV, it's 2005. The
timestamp reads January 10, 9:16am, and this is an apartment
we've never seen. The Han family lived here until Denny started
kindergarten the following year.

Mr. Han narrates the scene. "Here we go," he says, zooming
in on a little girl who pads out of the hallway, yawning. Wavy
hair falls down to her shoulders, rumpled from sleep. Her yellow
t-shirt is several sizes too large, an obvious hand-me-down. She
wears this over polka dot pajama pants that are at least an inch
too short. Joey clears his throat. Then he sings the birthday song
in a rich, booming voice, dragging out the notes for added drama.

"Tenth member of Apollo," remarks Eunjae, from behind his
phone. We hear an older Mr. Han laughing in the background. And

on TV, as the birthday song winds down, the little girl breaks into a smile.

She sits at the table across from her dad. Joey says, "Eight years old! Our Yeonnie is a grown up lady. And for her birthday, she asked us to get her..."

"A haircut!" Again, that dimpled smile. She's missing a few teeth. The tape freezes here, and it's hard to tell if Eunjae hit the pause button or if Jiyeon took the remote and did it for him. He swivels the phone in her direction.

Grown up Jiyeon wears shorts and a blue Wanna Waffle tee. Her eyes are tired, but her voice is warm. "So," she says. "What are you guys doing?"

"Come here, come sit," Mr. Han replies. "Showing Ryan some videos. Remember this? Your birthday."

"Uh-huh." She gestures at Eunjae. "And you're... taking a video of a video?"

He laughs. "It's cute. I wanted a copy."

"First time Yeonnie went to the salon. Got too fancy for haircuts at home. 'No more,' she said to me. 'I want *Miss Gloria* to cut my hair. I want an *appointment.*' An appointment! With Dad, no appointment. Available any time. But did she want that? No."

"Maybe 'cause I wanted something other than a bowl cut."

"Hey," says Eunjae. "That's a classic for a reason."

"There. Did you hear that? Classic. Always in style." Mr. Han claps Eunjae on the back with a very audible thump. It's possible that some organs have been rearranged on impact. "Ryan, you can live upstairs. Neighbors moved out, now the place is empty. I'll talk to the manager."

"He's not moving in upstairs, Dad."

But Mr. Han has the remote now, and the footage takes us back to the past. Eight-year-old Jiyeon gushes about the salon, the chairs that go up and down on hydraulic pumps, the flashing scissors and the hair colors mixed in bowls. She has so many questions. How do they know where to paint the highlights? What happens to all the hair they cut off? And it's so nice there, too. The aunties, they talk the whole time. They know everybody's name. You feel like you're at home.

"Do you think I can cut hair too? And do you think I can make a place like that? I think it's my big dream. Like how Janie's big dream is to see the whole world. But do you think I can do it?"

"Oh, sure," her father replies, without hesitation. "You can do anything."

41

T HEY RETURNED TO FIND Eunjae's brothers arguing vehemently about the dog. Negotiations were floundering. Apollo had been sharing food, clothing, and living spaces for over a decade, but they couldn't share a pet.

"Look," said Jesse, when Eunjae came in. "Ari's a lawyer, so let's make him figure it out. Hyung, who gets to keep Uyu? It's me, right? I'm the youngest. I'll live longer than the rest of you, so she should stay with me. I can't go to your funerals alone. That's so sad, it's just *devastating* to think about."

"Oooh, but we'll still be together at Ari's funeral. He decided to hang up on Jaehwan and then he fired his girlfriend's brother, so my son's not long for this world. Another twelve hours, tops. I put his obituary in the group chat. No paywall, don't miss it!"

Jiyeon blinked at Nicky, then at Eunjae. "You fired Denny?"

"Ah, yeah. Long story."

"Most of us are staying in Seoul," reasoned Jungwoo, in the meantime. "Cosmos should stay there, too. Can't the rest of you just visit?"

Max shot him a dirty look from behind the counter. "That's not even her damn name! Do you know any girl's name or are they just walking, talking, emo song lyrics to you?"

"Aww, I thought her name was Myeonbong, like a cotton ball. Did we change it?" A pause. "Did I change it...?"

Kazu bellowed over the noise. "Quit fighting. She can live with everybody."

"Everybody?" Kei exclaimed. "I don't even want a dog! I never did! She's not *my* dog, this wasn't *my* stupid idea—"

Denny swooped in, gloriously terrifying, a wrathful saint. He went to the panel on the wall and threw every light switch at once. They cowered in the sudden, blinding radiance. "That's enough. Battle stations, now. Don't make me tell you twice."

The members scattered, but Denny told Eunjae and Jiyeon to wait. "Ezra's here," he said, the puppy now curled in the crook of his arm. "Let him know he's in charge of this food safety violation until approximately 1600 hours. Supplies are in the pantry."

"Got it, boss."

"Don't go yet. Just heard that Eric canceled the cleaning crew."

"Let me guess," said Jiyeon. "He's saying you rejected a heartfelt gesture from Apollo and their agency."

"Affirmative. I also abandoned them in Monroe, prioritizing personal interests over professional duties."

While the siblings discussed kicking Eric into next week, Eunjae took charge of Uyu. Petúnia? Milky Way? He wondered if they'd ever settle on a name, or where she'd stay when this was done. So many unknowns remained.

He spotted Ezra down on the far end of the sidewalk, under the shop's striped awning. Surprisingly, Simon had chosen to come along.

He had a bit of paper in his hand, torn from a notepad and marked up on both sides. "I looked through my emails. This is everything I had."

"Oh, yeah," said Ezra, peering over Eunjae's shoulder. "Jiyeon asked if Dad knew where to find Miss Vivi."

Of course she'd beaten him to it. The second he mentioned searching for Vivian, Jiyeon and Denny hit the ground running. He owed them both so much.

Under a letterhead for the Monroe Garden Inn, Simon had scrawled an email address. But there were also names, some phone numbers, and physical addresses spanning both Australia and the Philippines. None of these were current by any means; his last communication with Vivian had been around eight years ago.

"I wrote to her," Simon said, shifting his weight from one foot to the other, unused to such a prolonged conversation with his eldest son. "Wanted to say sorry. The way things ended... it wasn't right. I knew that."

Eunjae couldn't stop the words from falling out. "But you didn't do anything about it. Who cares if you knew it was wrong? You let it happen anyway. What was the point of saying sorry?"

He could've gone on and on, raging at his father so many years too late. *Too late, too late, too late.* It echoed in his head, a painful refrain. Simon nodded at every accusation. He took the assault without trying to defend himself in any way.

It wasn't enough. How could it be? And yet, to continue railing about the past seemed just as ineffectual as this apology, delivered a decade after the fact. The rage disintegrated, a fire without enough fuel to burn.

Weren't they the same? Simon didn't have any fight in him, but neither did Eunjae. Not for the longest time. And he still shied away from confrontations, unlike Ezra.

"When will you say sorry to Eunjae?" he asked their father, always so direct with his questions, determined to drill straight down to an answer. "And me. She was my nanny, too. Just for a little while, but still."

Simon nodded again. "I'm trying."

"To say sorry?"

"Yes."

"Try harder," Ezra said. "I'll help you. No, we can both help you, because Eunjae's really good at apologizing. Jiyeon says it's like, his superpower." He took the dog, scratching her behind the ears. "Weird superpower. Better than nothing, I guess."

Eunjae folded the paper again, sliding it into the back pocket of his jeans. "Ari, they're here," Jungwoo called to him from the doorway. It was time to start. Jiyeon had scheduled an interview with a podcast, hoping to counter Prism's lies with the truth. They'd record right here at the restaurant.

"Saw you with your dad. You okay?"

Eunjae thought about it. "I am," he said, after a beat. "I'm okay."

His brothers had already met the newest arrivals. These visitors had wasted no time getting their equipment into a booth by the window. Eunjae counted two of them. Easiest to spot was the guy by the register, chatting with Max, clad in a wrinkled gray t-shirt. Next to the tallest member of Apollo, this stranger was even taller. He towered over his companion, a young woman in the same shirt, but without the wrinkles. Her face turned a deeper shade of pink with every word Max said.

"Eunjae," said Jiyeon, waving him over. The visitors both turned their heads at the sound of her voice. Or perhaps it was his name that drew their attention; he thought they might have whispered 'Eunjae?' at each other as he went by. That made sense. While his full name was known to the public, it was the stage name that got the most use. They'd expected her to call him Ari, like his brothers did.

She slid over to make room. "This is Maisie Chun," said Jiyeon, indicating the older woman seated across from them. Clad in a magenta tracksuit, she had a cloud of curly, iron gray hair and glasses attached to a silver chain. "She's one of the podcast hosts. That's her son over there, Jooney, and their producer, Freddie. The show's called *Omma Gosh!* and they cover K-pop headlines. It's named after her."

She'd connected with this podcast as Emma, when they invited her to be a guest during their coverage of Seoul Fashion Week. *Omma Gosh!* had grown since then, reaching thousands more listeners, and was especially popular among K-pop fans in this part of California.

"Their episodes tend to be more like casual conversations, no script. I'll sit here, but you guys can jump in whenever you want. Oh, did you guys change your passwords?"

"Yeah. Did that last night." They wanted no repeats of last summer, when Emerald locked them out of their own accounts. Prism had a record of each member's credentials, as Apollo's public relations firm, and they expected Eric to use those if cornered. He'd just call it a necessary tool for image management.

Eunjae drew the mistaken conclusion that Maisie didn't have much to say. She'd kept quiet on her side of the booth, behind the microphones and Freddie's laptop. But as soon as recording began, she hit Apollo with a sharp and unwavering stare, keen as the edge of Mrs. Han's favorite kitchen knife. The bombardment was swift and merciless.

"So, Miss Emma," said Maisie, gaze fixed on Eunjae. "When is the wedding?"

Jiyeon took a moment to process, unprepared for that question. She replied, "Which wedding, Auntie?"

"Any. It can be the wedding of anybody in Apollo, eh? I'm not picky. How about that one? He's the baby, yes? Not too young to get married, though." She crooked a finger at Jesse, snooping from the next booth over. He gave a terrified yip and vanished from view.

Jooney spoke up, fighting the urge to laugh. "Take it easy on them, Ma."

"Yeah, Auntie. Can we avoid offending the biggest names we've ever had on the show? Could you chill out, maybe?"

"Frederica, who needs to chill out? It's not me. Stop looking at the tall boy with the grumpy face. Go to the fridge, put an ice cube on your head. Chill out! Pah!"

Some shooing motions, and then Maisie resumed her barrage. "Now, what was I saying...? Oh, yes! Weddings. We will have eight weddings. No, nine! Nine men in this group, so many. And Miss Emma, you and *Eunjae* go first, already very cozy together so why not—"

A minor scuffle ensued as Jooney went diving into the booth, spouting apologies. Jiyeon didn't catch any of those. She had her hands full just trying to keep her own parents from inserting themselves into the dialogue. Eunjae discovered a great many things in the process, such as when they planned to march him down the aisle ("One year from now! Lots of time to plan a wedding!") and where he would be living afterward ("Apartment upstairs is still empty, very convenient, good location!")

He dumped his jean jacket, eyeing the thermostat with longing. So warm! *Who goes down with heatstroke in the middle of November?* said Invisible Jaehwan, despairing of him. Eunjae considered fleeing to the kitchen, but it was then that Denny signaled to Jiyeon, the shop's security cameras pulled up on his phone. "Perimeter breach," he intoned. "You or me, Yeonnie?"

"I'll go." Jiyeon glanced at Eunjae. This was earlier than planned.

They'd hoped to get at least half of this recorded before Prism caught on.

She got up and answered the door. "Hi, Eric. Why don't you come in?"

42

AT FIRST, JIYEON THOUGHT it was a different Eric. He'd dressed to blend in with their volunteers, a mix of restaurant regulars and family friends. This meant eschewing Prism teal in favor of jeans and a plain sweatshirt, but it was definitely him, armed with his tablet and that wan, forgettable smile. Not branded today, but on brand just the same.

No one said a word when he came in, but Uyu was right outside, barking up a storm. She pulled so ferociously on her leash that Ezra lost his grip on it. "She doesn't like that guy," he said, snatching her up in his arms. Uyu squirmed free, little legs pumping, reaching her quarry in two bounds. Or she might have, if Denny hadn't plucked her from the floor and saved Eric's life in the process.

Namgyu clapped. "Aww, good job, Snowball!" Someone hissed that Prism could use anything against them. Jiyeon drew a deep breath, then let it go. That was true.

She'd thought long and hard about how to offset the damage. It wouldn't be enough to shout the truth by themselves, regardless of the reach they had. Millions of followers or not, Apollo could lose access to their official channels at any time, linked to their fans by digital threads too easily severed. They had to find another way to tell this story. They had to be louder than Eric.

Yet again, she'd found the answer through Emma. Based on Jiyeon's experience online, authenticity was key. Audiences might be transfixed by a pristine, curated product, but it wasn't perfection that sparked connection. Apollo's fans loved spontaneous content even more than they loved high budget, professionally produced music videos.

Eric couldn't control candid moments, and he couldn't control the flow of a conversation. Jiyeon knew of a podcast built on both. She'd liked the atmosphere at *Omma Gosh!* when she joined them as a guest, long ago. They were funny and friendly. When Freddie said they could do it, Jiyeon felt instant relief. Resources. Thank goodness she had them.

Unscripted, unpredictable, potentially messy. They'd have no time to shine this up or even record it in an actual studio. Their episode would give Prism nightmares. Jiyeon made no secret about offering the interview, praying it would goad Eric into action. He'd have to stop them from doing this, right?

"Amazing atmosphere out there," Eric said then, always so congenial on the surface. "What an engaged community. I'm in awe, Miss Han. To build something like this, online *and* in the real world? You should be very proud. What a valuable skill." He motioned to a stack of chairs. "You're free to carry on whenever you're ready, but do you mind if I sit in?"

Max mumbled that he did mind, thank you very fucking much, but Jiyeon bit back every rude thing she wanted to say. She nodded at her brother, who transferred the puppy to Kei, surrendered his own seat... and then planted himself behind Eric like a human doomsday countdown.

Their unwanted guest maintained composure, at least outwardly.

"Please, get back to what you were doing. I'm sure at least some parts of the episode will be allowed to air. In the future, please note that we do require advance notification of any media appearances. There's a process. We'd like to be aware of these things beforehand instead of finding out through social media."

"Could've saved yourself a trip," Jiyeon said, waving at some mahjong ladies through the big dining room window. "This isn't an interview with Apollo. It's an interview with me, and I'm not one of your clients."

She saw it: the tiniest, hairline crack in Eric's composure. "But your contract with the production company does specify—"

"That Prism has to clear any and all media appearances," Eunjae cut in. "Also says she's only required to go through you if the interview relates to Apollo. It doesn't."

"They came to cover the event. Sorry for any confusion."

Eric's smile went taut, a string in danger of snapping. And he probably had more tricks up his sleeve, but by moving to intercept them here, he'd also given Jiyeon the home court advantage. Aunties were streaming into the restaurant now, and uncles in faded baseball caps, and her dad's buddies from the bowling alley. Wanna Waffle had sponsored their tournament gear. The shirts were blue and orange, with a huge waffle on the back.

Apollo members dashed to take the chairs down. Mrs. Garza's grandkids swarmed around Kei, who still had custody of Uyu. They peppered him with questions in English. He inched closer to Max, his eyes telegraphing an urgent wish for subtitles.

"This has to be the whole neighborhood," Lizzie joked in Korean, but Jiyeon knew it wasn't. Arthur was conspicuously absent from this gathering. Hours ago, he'd sent her a message that said, *Hey Emmie.*

Won't be there today. I thought that might be the best way I could help.

It was the closest to an apology she'd ever get from him, so Jiyeon had written back that she appreciated it. *You're helping. Thanks, Arthur.*

His absence meant one less weapon that Prism could use against her. That was a win. And they were still winning, because Eric didn't like the live audience. His gaze darted from screen to screen. Almost everybody had a phone, and almost everybody was using it. They'd generate photos, videos, status updates. Not even Prism could smother that much content before it spread organically, outpacing their efforts.

Eric excelled at polished statements, every word in the right place, the story pieced together in a controlled and orderly manner. But this was a story about real people, happening in real time, and stories didn't come out clean and tidy by default. They just didn't work that way. Life didn't work that way. This was a mess.

Jiyeon reclaimed her spot in the booth, ready to give Eric an even bigger mess. "We're back," Jooney announced. "Folks, it's Waffle Wednesday and we're here with Emma Han to talk about—"

"Sssshh. I'm asking a question. This is journalism. Miss Emma, your brother over there. Single? Married? Tell me."

"Denny's married to the business."

"Oh my gosh," Jesse cried out, swishing a broom back and forth in the background. "That's what I told those girls in Japan!"

"Ha! He did!"

"He told them a lot of gibberish. 'Married desu!' 'Business-shimasu!' That's not even Japanese—"

"I panicked, I thought they wanted to marry *me*—"

"The hell does it matter if he got the point across? Get a life, Keiichi."

Apollo was notorious for hijacking livestreams. One brother's broadcast became every brother's broadcast. They took over with impressive speed, bringing all the chaos she'd come to expect from them. The episode morphed into a Denny tribute. They loved him and he was definitely not available, sorry Sunshines. Also, they loved waffles. Waffles were a superior breakfast food, and their manager was superior to all other managers, and they were going to miss Denny so much. They'd be missing him every day, forever. He wasn't their manager. He was their friend.

Her brother gave them a wordless salute, not trusting himself to speak.

After that, the regulars started chiming in with stories of their own. Remember when Denny was little? Remember when he apprehended that shoplifter in the parking lot? Who else could claim such an accomplishment at the tender age of twelve? Then the conversation shifted to anecdotes about Wanna Waffle: bingo tournaments, breakfast for dinner, traditions kept faithfully over the years. Eric sat front and center, quietly fuming as his precious narrative took on a new and very different form.

He wanted to pull the plug, that much was obvious. He'd sensed the danger. Apollo never appeared on camera directly, and the mic stayed in front of Jiyeon, but the fans would recognize the group's contributions nonetheless. Sunshines could pick them out by their voices, by the backs of their heads, by mannerisms and patterns of speech. Apollo belonged to their fans. Jiyeon knew this, and so did Eric.

They had a room full of people who felt right at home here. The guys were part of that audience, saying whatever they wanted. This didn't break any of Prism's rules. He was livid.

"I remember seeing you here," someone said to Eunjae, then. "It was a Wednesday. You were in that booth over there."

He nodded. "That was me."

"You look happier now."

"Ah, thanks," said Eunjae, smiling. "I love it here. I always will."

"Are you staying for good?"

An auntie from Sunday mahjong took the liberty of answering that question. "Pay attention, Candace. He's marrying the daughter. That's what I heard from Joey."

"Lizzie's daughter? Lizzie-ah, you'll let someone marry Emma? You didn't want anybody marrying Janie—"

"What about the rest of them? What's happening next?"

The members of Apollo searched the crowd for one another. Wordlessly, they seemed to come to an agreement. Kazu was leader, so they let him say it. "We don't know yet," he replied, "but that's okay. We'll figure it out together."

Eric was out of his chair in an instant, gone pale with fury. "Stop recording. I need to speak with Miss Han."

43

IN THE KITCHEN, ERIC said, "I just need to speak with Miss Han."

Eunjae sat down next to Jiyeon. "Go ahead."

"Yeah. Start talking." Denny loomed over the table with the coffeepot in his humongous hand. Scalding liquid sloshed into Eric's mug. No one had ever performed basic customer service with such an undertone of menace.

Eric looked around, halfheartedly sipping coffee. "Isn't there anywhere else we can do this? An office, maybe?"

"Oh, sure," said Jiyeon. "This is our office. Welcome."

This spurred some grumbling. "She's kidding. Get the hell out."

Denny commanded the interlopers to either come in or get out of his sight. Six out of seven eavesdropping Apollo members tumbled into the room. Nicky requested a third option: staying right where he was, thereby absorbing gossip from two rooms simultaneously. Permission was denied.

Last to join them was Ezra. Eunjae didn't want to involve him, but more pressing matters were at hand. They needed to reach a resolution with Eric.

Firing Prism wasn't possible without approval from both Emerald and Zenith, according to the terms. Eunjae wasn't confident that either agency would care about how Eric had achieved his results. After all, the results favored Apollo. But he thought Jiyeon was right, when she insisted they should confront their enemy face to face. Eric preferred to be shielded by screens, operating from a vantage point that made it difficult to see how his actions were hurting real people.

Jungwoo came forward first. "You leaked those emails about my contract. Why? Nothing was final yet. We were still negotiating the terms with Zenith. They were open to it, up until that weekend."

"I didn't leak anything," Eric replied. "How would I do that? Emerald's plans for you and Max were part of internal discussion. The news was leaked by someone from your agency."

"And I'm sure you had nothing to do with that," said Nicky, batting his eyelashes, "just like I had nothing to do with the leaks on set."

"I still can't fucking believe you, hyung—"

"Don't take this out on him. Nicky's my second meanest brother but he's never been evil like Eric. He's not a bad person, he's just trying to be funny. Learn to *differentiate*."

Jungwoo wasn't ready to let it go. "But why? You were supposed to make sure we didn't do anything to make Zenith back out of the contract. Why did you sabotage our chances? They wanted to sign the full group."

"I could've gotten you a better deal. Emerald wronged you and Zenith barely counts as an agency. I had you guys looking great. Of course they started fighting over you, and when the dust settled, you'd have a bigger offer from someone else."

When this answer failed to win him any admiration, Eric said, "Why are you so upset with me? Everything I did was for you. I was doing my job."

"You suck at your job," Ezra huffed. "You couldn't even make them look good without making nice people look bad."

"*Look good?* You think that's all I did?" Here, Eric directed a frosty glare at Eunjae. "Actually, it's not Miss Han I need to talk to. It's you. You're the one who ran away."

"Get off him," Denny grunted. "It doesn't count as running away if you're going home."

"Sentimental. Running away is running away, Manager Han. But I guess it serves you well, to make him feel like this is home. You've benefited from it."

How? Eunjae still felt like he'd done nothing for this family except generate trouble. Drama followed in his wake, a seemingly inescapable side effect of the fame he'd never sought for himself. But he was sick of Prism, sick of fighting. "Don't," he said. Just the one word, and it was plenty. Eric dropped the subject.

"I thought you'd disband," he continued, displaying more emotion than they'd seen from him thus far. "That didn't happen, but the damage was done. This was my chance. Do you know how hard I fought, to be the lead on your account? I knew I could help you stay together. It had to be me. I had a plan and it was going to work."

Jiyeon considered his words. Slowly, she said, "You're a Sunshine."

He'd mentioned it on the day they arrived at Langley House. Eunjae hadn't given it much thought. He figured Eric made a habit of telling clients that he was their biggest fan.

"Don't lump me in with them," Eric replied with a sneer. "I'm not just a fan, collecting merchandise and posting memes. This was my dream, okay? I got an internship at Emerald because I wanted to work with Apollo. They assigned me to a different group, but I've kept up with you guys for years."

"If you want to help us, you could stop going after people we care about."

"See, you keep making that same mistake. Feelings shouldn't be part of this. Feelings are a mess, and that's not what your fans want to see. It's like you forget that you're idols. Do you think fans idolize you for being human?"

"We are human," said Kazu, frowning.

Eric only laughed. "Not to them. You're meant to be more than human, better than human. They want you to smile, they want you to stay together, and they want you without flaws. That's what they pay for. We played that vulnerability angle because it works, but it's a temporary fix. Your audience doesn't want the 'real' Apollo. They want perfect boys they made up in their heads."

"That's not true," Jiyeon argued. "I've talked to so many Sunshines by now. Most of them just want Apollo to be happy."

"Happy and perfect. Which you wouldn't understand, Miss Han, because your success comes from being relatable and approachable."

Relatable and approachable. Pronounced with disdain, like these were points against her, when one of the best things about Jiyeon was how swiftly she could make you feel seen and heard. Eunjae sat up straighter. "I don't like what you just said."

"It's backed by metrics. Emma Han is the girl next door. She's profited from every follower who loved the illusion of being her friend."

Eric was on a tear now, offended by their lack of gratitude. He'd mended their public image. He'd moved mountains in Apollo's name. "That's what Sunshines want from you," he ranted at them. "The ideal illusion. Apollo is a *product*. Apollo is a *brand*. Get that through your heads before you ruin everything you've built."

Kei's shoulders sagged. He closed his eyes. "Are we ruining everything we've built? Is this the end?"

"It's not the end. Take a walk, Keiichi."

Total meltdown. Who the hell called Jaehwan-hyung again? When would Kazu learn to parent them on his own? Complaints were lodged, insecurities aired. From the heart of this storm, Eunjae heard Jiyeon ask a question.

"Eric," she said. "What's your name?"

44

"Your real name," Jiyeon clarified. "It's not Eric. I've always thought you looked more like an Allen, or a Bruce."

Eunjae found her hand under the table. "Bruce. Yeah, I see it."

"It's not Bruce," said Eric. "How is this relevant?"

"I think you should answer her question."

"You're supposed to be nice. Isn't this out of character for you?"

"I'm usually nice," Eunjae agreed, "and you should answer her question."

Brothers weighed in. What was this guy's problem? She'd asked a fair question, and it wasn't even on the extreme end of the difficulty scale. Ooh, had Eric forgotten his own name? Could he perhaps have selective amnesia? They'd played that card already, how boring if they did it again. Hey Chief, what if we put him in a coma for some variety—

Caving under the pressure of too much animosity from too many brothers, Eric muttered, "Trevor. That's my real name."

"Trevor Allen Wong," Denny intoned, reciting the contents of a dossier stored in his head. "Stanford University, graduated with honors. Internships at Emerald Entertainment and Prism Strategic

Management. Offered a permanent position at Prism two years ago, promoted last year. Speaks four languages." He rolled his eyes. "Another one wasted on the entertainment industry."

"Chief, when was he born?"

"Yeah, what year? Tell us."

Denny's mouth twitched. "1999."

"Ha!" said Namgyu. High fives all around. Brothers surrounded Trevor's chair, proclaiming that he could call them 'hyung.' He was younger than every member of Apollo. Everybody was 'hyung' to him. He should show proper respect for his seniors. With immense glee, Nicky declared the establishment of 'an unbroken circle of trust.' The Prism handbook: the gift that kept on giving.

"Not me," Jesse screeched, arms flailing. "He can't call me hyung! Trevor, when in 1999? Before August, right? Please, please, *please* be born before August—"

The Captain confirmed that Trevor's birthday was in May, thus sparing Jesse from having to confront the inevitability of old age. Jiyeon turned to smile at Eunjae. "I knew there was an Allen in there somewhere."

"You both have weird superpowers," Ezra remarked, unimpressed as usual. As for Max, he wanted a refund. *Trevor?* This guy didn't even look like a goddamn Trevor. He had to be lying.

He wasn't lying, and Jiyeon's question had cracked something open, revealing a gap in Eric's defenses. No, Trevor. This was *Trevor*, not a faceless enemy concealed by algorithms and glowing screens. Nor was it an army of Prism henchmen with the same name, parroting the same corporate gospel.

She went for it. "Trevor, you said this was your dream. You wanted to work with Apollo. That's a brand, but it's also nine people. Real people, with families and friends. You're a real person, too. Maybe Eric doesn't care about their feelings, but I think you do."

Trevor stared at his coffee mug. "Eric is me. I did all of those things."

"Oh, sure," Jiyeon replied. "Emma is me, but she's not all of me, just like Eric isn't all of you. You don't have to be famous to have different versions of yourself. Who are you, when it's just you? 'Cause I think there's more to the story."

"Hope you like disappointment," muttered Max. "He's a jackass. That's the story."

"No. He's a fan, and Sunshines don't love you for being a brand. They don't come to your concerts and play your music at their weddings 'cause they care about a product. They care about Apollo, and that's the nine of you." Jiyeon retrieved the coffee pot, pulled a mug from the shelf, and poured Trevor a fresh cup. "You care," she said, "so give the story back to them. That's all we're asking."

Trevor put his head down on the table. He stayed that way for a while. They heard the happy chatter of volunteers coming and going, preparing for lunch, hollering about paint rollers. Raucous laughter filtered through the walls as the audience took over Emma's podcast episode. Eunjae closed his eyes for a moment and thought that it would be okay, regardless of everything hanging in the balance. He'd spent a long time feeling alone, even in a bus packed with brothers, even on stage in a sold-out arena. He didn't feel like that anymore.

He held on to this optimism until Trevor finally lifted his head and said, "I can cancel the rest of the campaign. There's no easy fix for what's already out there, though. It's too late for that." He checked his watch, then the kitchen clock. "Yeah... definitely too late."

"Too late for what?" Kazu demanded. "Ya, call your mom. When I tell her about everything you've done—"

Nicky had it pulled up in record time. "It's bad, Ari."

"Hyung," said Max, grabbing Eunjae by the shoulder and shaking him. "This is America. For fuck's sake, let's sue him."

Eunjae didn't hear anything more. A video looped on the screen, identical to the eight seconds of footage that Eric had shown him before. Here he was at the wedding, reaching for Jiyeon's hand. But that was only the first eight seconds; the rest of the video focused on the elastic band glimpsed just under the cuff of his suit jacket, faded black, printed with flowers that used to be red. They'd spliced in a few clips of Emma Han wearing the same hair tie on her wrist, presenting posts from 2023, 2022, 2021.

He might have taken it better if Prism had stopped there. They didn't. Below the embedded video were still shots of Jiyeon and Arthur on set, and a picture of them exiting the arrivals terminal at LAX. Eunjae knew who to thank for that one. Seeing nothing but bright, blazing red, he blew through the comments.

>> guys, emma went to that wedding w her EX BF

>> literally it's a pic of them leaving the airport together

>> omg no wonder ari's been so sad!!!!

>> this bitch flirted with him at the wedding but went home with another guy

>> She broke Ari's heart

>> I'm not even a fan but that's outrageous

>> did u see that ari's mom unfollowed her on instagram?? bet this is why!

>> EMERALD OUR BOYS NEED HELP

>> THEY HAVE THE SHITTIEST TASTE IN WOMEN

Eunjae made himself read these words again and again. But that was Jiyeon's warm hand on his cheek, calling him back. Calling him home.

"Eunjae," she said, softly. "This went up about twenty minutes ago. Emerald will respond for you, right? I know it's not even 4:00 in the morning there, but it won't be long before they see it. I can tell Colette to deny the claims. That way both sides are saying the same thing. Should I have her wait for the agency, though?"

Colette was her agent. She was asking him when to issue an official denial. His response was automatic, instinctual. "I don't want to deny it," Eunjae told her. "Not the part about you and me."

She lowered her hand, surprised. "We're done hiding?"

Jiyeon's level of surprise was nothing compared to his own; there was a part of Eunjae who couldn't believe he'd reached this point. "If it's okay with you. I know I'm asking a lot."

It had never been normal, for them. That was something Eunjae had failed to give her, although he'd tried, and this would put any notion of normal well beyond their reach. They might regret it. If she didn't want to, if she wanted to keep things as they were—

"Okay," said Jiyeon. "Let's do it."

"Are you sure?"

Her smile was the sunrise. "I'm sure."

Brothers went off, their reactions as explosive as fireworks. Again, he heard none of it. Eunjae went straight to the camera roll on his phone. He knew exactly which pictures he wanted to post.

They'd both been hoping for the right timing. But even though they'd lost the ability to decide when, it wasn't too late to decide how. They could overwrite Prism's version of the story with something better. Something good.

"You don't have to post," Trevor informed him. "A denial from

Emerald should be enough to bury it, and then you just need write a standard apology. 'Sorry for causing concern.' You know how it goes."

He didn't even look up. "I won't apologize. Not for this."

"We'll be fine, Trevor." Jiyeon pushed a Wanna Waffle loyalty card across the table. "Come back sometime. We'll save a spot for you."

"That... sounded kind of scary..."

"Uh-huh."

"Don't talk to her."

"She was talking to me—"

"And you're grateful."

"I take it back," Jiyeon said, wryly. "You made him pretty mad. Try us in about ten years."

Eunjae did look up, then. "Don't."

In the end, they used the same three pictures, stepping outside to take the third together. The light was better behind the shop. Eunjae and Jiyeon stood on the back stoop as the post went live, going over the statement he was sending to the agency. Despite being fired the previous night, Apollo's manager had kindly agreed to handle the rest.

"Hey, I have an idea," Jiyeon said. "Later, what if we did one more post?"

They'd planned it out by the time Ezra came to find them. Leila was with him, imperious in a trench and dark glasses. That was enough of a jolt, but then Simon hurried around the corner from the parking lot. He reached them just as Leila said, "I'm here for Ezra. He'll miss the rest of the week, too."

"Mum, why? I don't want to miss—"

"Last minute casting call. A friend told me about it. It's the perfect opportunity, but we'll have to get you some decent headshots by tomorrow morning. Unless you want to take them for us, Ari? You've got at least one of those fancy cameras with you, surely."

His mother threw that out like a dare. Her words erased color and light, leaving Eunjae with a world rendered in bleak monochrome. He understood that this was Leila's parting shot. The choices he'd made over the last twenty-four hours placed him beyond redemption. She'd given him up as a lost cause once and for all, but Leila had two sons, and she would try again.

"There's an acting workshop two weeks from now," she continued, straightening the collar on Ezra's rugby shirt. "I'll talk to Blackridge. He might even miss the rest of the year, if things go well."

A casting call. Acting lessons. What next? An agent, print ads, a commercial? Jiyeon crossed her arms. "Do you even like acting?" she asked Ezra. "You've never mentioned it."

"Does he have much of a choice? He can't count on his brother to support him forever, especially not now." Cold laughter. "I'm not even sure how Ari plans to support himself. If this is all he'll ever be—"

"Then I'll be happy," Eunjae finished for her.

It wasn't too late. He could stop this right now. He wasn't a helpless kid, and he wasn't like his father, lacking the courage to fight back. Eunjae could win a different future for Ezra. *Don't you see?* he wanted to shout. *Don't you see that I can't let this happen again—*

An excerpt from* Molly Merriweather and the Timeless Prince, *second in a series of children's books* (Molly in Time) *by Robin Ayres

"I really am sorry," said the other Molly. "Time's already split. My future isn't your future. Even if I make a different choice, it won't change anything for you."

Molly choked down a sob. *Don't you see?* she wanted to shout. *I know it's too late to change this for me... but I could change it for you.*

45

COMPREHENDING LEILA'S MOTIVATIONS WOULDN'T have changed how Jiyeon felt about her. Still, she tried to understand. So many theories were plausible. Leila disapproved of Eunjae's decisions, so maybe this was for revenge, or punishment. Maybe she genuinely thought breaking into the entertainment industry would be a viable way for Ezra to make a living.

As of today, Jiyeon had a new theory. Fame was the dream that eluded Leila in her youth. It became the dream she forced on Eunjae.

"Come on," she said now, growing impatient. "We really do need to go, my love."

But the teenager resisted. "Mum, they still need help here. I can't go yet."

"That's sweet, but plenty of people felt sorry for them. They don't need you."

"But—" He looked to his brother, to their father standing on the sidewalk. In what Jiyeon considered to be the most potent surprise of the day, it was the latter who picked a fight on Ezra's behalf.

"He's too young," Simon said. "Ezra should go back to school. We can talk about this when he's older."

"Since when do you care?"

"I cared then, too. I didn't... I didn't say anything. That was a mistake."

This admission hit Jiyeon like a truck. How must it have felt for Eunjae?

Leila stopped in her tracks, so beautiful with the sunlight caught in her hair, setting the strands aglow. Her rage was palpable. Ezra shrank back, frightened by this side of his mother, a side he hadn't seen until now.

Eunjae wrapped an arm around him. He glanced at Jiyeon, holding her gaze for a long moment. She read the sadness in his eyes, but also an unshakable conviction. He'd been so afraid that it would come to this: the cycle repeating, Ezra devoured by their mother's ambitions. None of that fear remained.

He made no promises and no threats. He didn't offer solutions, or warnings, or advice. Despite the complexity of his feelings, Eunjae turned to his brother and said, "What do you want to do?"

Time contracted, expanded, flowed in reverse. Those were Jiyeon's words, the question she'd asked him just hours after they met. *You don't even know what that meant to me*, he'd told her once, later in the summer, when everything between them had changed. *You didn't tell me what to do. You gave me a choice.*

A choice. That's what he'd given to his brother, and Jiyeon understood exactly what it cost him. She loved him so much for it.

Whatever Ezra had expected from Eunjae, it wasn't this. His expression flickered in and out of disbelief. "You're letting me decide?"

"It's your life. You should get to choose."

"You won't be mad if I want to try?"

"If that's what you want, I'll help you. And if it's not, I'll still help you."

For once, Ezra didn't question what he'd been told. He only nodded and said, "Thanks."

"Of course."

"Can I think about it?"

"Yeah. Take as long as you need."

"That's definitely something you should think about before you start," Jiyeon put in. "Look it up first."

He nodded, pensive. "But if I try that thing two weeks from now, I'll have to miss more school, like Mum said."

"I don't know if a few weeks would make much difference when you've been gone for two months already." Eunjae retreated into the shade, out of the glare, and consulted the calendar on his phone. But then he realized that the coming weeks would be empty of obligations, what with *Sunshine 24/7* wrapping up on Friday. His expression lightened. "I could drive you there. I'll just stay in the car, though, so I won't be in your way—"

"You don't even have your own car," Ezra pointed out. "And you don't have a place to live, or a job. I mean, I guess you have a job, it's just going nowhere..." He trailed off. "Wait, you can't stay in the car. I don't know what I'm doing. You have to come with me. I mean, at least to the door."

"At least to the door, then," Eunjae agreed, trying very hard not to smile. *Good for him*, Jiyeon thought to herself. She still wanted to cry. She'd probably have to duck into the pantry and sob it out before they carried on with the rest of the day.

"What about the casting call?" she asked, sending a reply to Denny. He'd been summoning them to lunch for the past ten minutes. "Leila said it was tomorrow morning."

"I don't really want to do that one." Warily, Ezra looked over at his mother, still arguing with Simon. "She'll be mad if I say that, but I don't even know what that show is about. What if it sucks? Or like, what if I'm supposed to play a character who sucks?"

"Let her be mad," said Jiyeon, stoutly. She sent another text to her brother, and one to her mom, glimpsing the preview on the latest of six messages from Arthur. He'd seen the picture of them leaving the airport. "Arthur's saying he tried to call you five times," she told Eunjae.

"Ah, yeah. Blocked him last month."

"You blocked him?"

"I did."

"You don't have to stop being friends with Arthur 'cause of me. I hope that's not why."

Eunjae blinked at her. "Did he ever say sorry to you?"

"Hmm. Not really."

"Then I can't be his friend." Having explained this, he went right back to assuring Ezra that their mother couldn't make him audition. He was still a minor, so there would be paperwork. They'd require signatures from both parents, since it was a shared custody agreement, and it didn't look like Simon would agree to sign. "I'm starting to think he only signed the papers for our show because you wanted to do it."

Frenzied barking interrupted the conversation. Joey lumbered through the back door with Uyu. "This is where you were hiding! Go, go. Listen to Charlie, huh? She's saying, 'Time to eat!'"

"Her name's Charlie now?"

"Oh, they told me that in a letter," said Ezra. "They said the puppy can be Charlie because all the plants are named Charles."

Lizzie shoved the old wooden wedge into place, beaming. "I've been saying this, Yeonnie. Naming everybody Charles, that's how you make it easier. Jane Austen was a very smart lady. Imagine if she picked names for Apollo! Nine boys, all named Charles. Done! Easy!" Still beaming, she patted Eunjae on the cheek, then Ezra, then Jiyeon. Then she went straight to business.

"I'm so happy to meet you," Lizzie announced, taking both of Leila's hands in hers. "Thank you for your two sweet boys. I will take very good care of them. Don't ever worry again, not even a little bit." She led the astonished woman to her rental car. "Drive safe, yeah? Scary out there! Some people drive so fast!"

Neither Eunjae nor Ezra had noticed Denny's arrival. They both yelped when he appeared, laden with potluck food already neatly packaged for Leila's convenience. They yelped again when he told Jiyeon they were ready for the softball bat.

"Sure. It's in the trunk, hang on."

"Softball bat...?" whispered Eunjae.

Joey urged him to go inside, waving to Leila from the doorway. "See you at the wedding!"

"Disregard," Denny said right away. "That's invite-only."

It didn't take long to fetch the requested softball bat. Leila was still there, perhaps somewhat stunned in the aftermath. But it was also true that some people just couldn't take a hint, no matter how warmly you sent them on their way. Jiyeon left her there. She didn't want to ask about Vivian anymore. Best to leave Leila out of it.

By some fluke, Apollo hadn't obliterated the lunch buffet. She ate as fast as she could, and then it was time to take care of the front door.

Half of the decorative panels were still intact. The rest were in pieces, reduced to jagged remnants. It made the door look like a mouth studded with broken teeth. Jiyeon had arranged for a temporary solution until they could have the stained glass made to order. They'd decided to knock out the shattered parts, leaving a clean slate for repairs.

"We'll do four new panels," Jiyeon explained to their friends from the podcast. "Mr. Rivera said he can save the originals and frame them for us. I think it'll look great."

Of course, they wanted to know if the family would try to recreate the old design. She replied that something different had been chosen.

"A circus tent," said Denny, "with eight clowns riding unicycles. Battle dress. Berets, sequins, leather pants. The works."

"Hot clowns. I'll pose for it, Chief. Three easy payments of $3,999."

"Aww, it'll be so pretty! I can't wait to see it!"

"Add some words. 'The sun is always shining.' You fucking loved that one."

The parking lot rang with laughter. As more suggestions poured in, Denny hefted the softball bat, testing the weight and balance. He peered through the haphazard gaps and checked on the tarp that he'd spread on the dining room floor. Most people would find his thoughts inscrutable in that moment, but Jiyeon read her brother like a book. She pried the bat out of his hand. Patting Denny on the arm, she said, "I'll go first."

It didn't take much force to knock her section out of the door. The pieces landed on the other side with an almost musical chime. *We'll fix you up*, she promised in her head. *It'll be okay.*

Denny's turn again, for real this time. Spectators called out encouragement. Jeannie reprimanded the uncles who'd brought out an air horn, citing insubordination. And when their manager still couldn't bring himself to strike, brothers peeled away from the crowd. Brothers were suddenly all around him. They clapped Denny on the shoulder, clung to his arm so he couldn't swing the bat even if he wanted to.

All their different names for him rang out in the brisk November air: Captain, Boss, Chief.

Eunjae left Jiyeon's side to join them. "You've got it, Denny," he said.

As others echoed this phrase, Denny lifted the bat at last. He smashed what was left of the fourth panel to a deafening round of cheering and applause. Jiyeon hung back while everyone else streamed forward, wanting to commit the scene to memory. This was her dream unfolding in vivid color. This was a gathering place, a second home.

She'd helped to build it, before. She would build it again.

The full, uncut version of a video uploaded to Apollo member Ari's social media accounts and the group's official channels in November 2023

The light is beautiful. It's the warm, golden glow of late afternoon, captured just before day gives way to dusk. The sign is dark and the orange door is missing its stained glass panels, but we're looking at Wanna Waffle. You recognize it right away. You've been here before.

We hear talk and laughter. Ari walks a few steps ahead of us, his sweater splashed with paint. "I don't know what to say," he admits. "I thought I did, before we got started."

"Quit overthinking it, Ryan. You're not addressing the United Nations." It's the voice of Apollo's manager, a rumbling baritone that evokes mythical titans and active volcanoes. Emma shushes him from behind the camera. Has he ever addressed the United Nations? No. So he can't really make that comparison, can he? Maybe he should go inside and yell at someone else.

"Oooh, go inside and order us some pizza. How about it, Chief?"

"We can't eat until hyung's done with this video thingy and

I'm starving, I've never been hungrier in my life, I'm *wasting away—*"

This statement comes under fire immediately. First to complain is a teenager whose accent is similar to Ari's, but a bit more pronounced. "You ate enough lunch for three people," he points out. "I watched you do it."

"Hey, now. Is that how you speak to your elders? Jesse's an aging idol actor but he still deserves respect."

Wailing commences. Max stalks into view, brooding, dressed like a rich middle schooler enrolled in art camp against his will. "Hyung, we'll be here all goddamn night if you don't start soon."

"Aww, just tell her everything! Say what's in your heart!"

"I could help," says the teenager. Dozens of comments marvel at Ezra's resemblance to his older brother. Seeing them side by side is like viewing the past and the future in tandem.

Ari smiles, shuffling sideways. "Come on, then."

Now they face us together. The mayhem subsides, and we hear muffled stage directions being issued. The sign above the entrance flares to life. Ari takes a breath, his focus not on the camera, but on Emma. He seeks comfort and finds it there, in an answering smile that we can't see.

Ezra jumps in first. He blurts out, "Miss Vivi, if you're out there, thanks for taking care of us. We've been looking for you. It would be great if we could see you again, maybe someday soon. You could come and visit, or we could visit you."

A round of applause. Mrs. Han is heard announcing that Vivian can come stay anytime, but Mr. Han is very busy congratulating someone outside the frame. "You are very lucky," he tells this person. "Last time a mean boy bullied her brother, we had to pick her up from the principal's office."

Ari laughs, but his eyes are wet. "Sorry it's taken me this long. I've got so much to tell you. There's so many people I want you to meet. And I owe you more songs than I can count, but I've got five we used to sing together, back then. I'll post them later."

"Song Eunjae," says Emma, bringing the camera down half an inch. Or maybe you know her as Jiyeon, since you're a regular here. It's the name Ari murmurs when he pulls her close. She swipes at her tears. "Five songs? You did that?"

"I did."

"Had a lot of downtime in Japan," Jungwoo explains.

"That's what happens when you're in goddamn jail. Thanks, Trevor."

"I'm so happy you did that," Jiyeon says, still crying. She pulls it together long enough to say, "Vivian, I can't wait to meet you. Sorry I'm a mess right now. I thought... since so many people are watching, maybe you'll be watching, too."

"Come cry on me, ajumma. I won't even charge you."

"I'm fine, thanks."

Nicky takes both of her hands. With utmost sincerity, he says, "But you could be the one to fix me." A pause. "Ari, how am I doing? Did that work? Are you jealous yet?"

"Ah, no."

Denny takes over. We're instructed to read the caption for a tip line and other strictly monitored, heavily secured contact methods. Jeannie cries out, aggrieved. A tip line? Is he serious? We learn that this young lady isn't paid nearly enough to spearhead that kind of operation. Spearheading an operation would be detrimental to her health.

"I'm promoting you, Vho. Code Violet."

The audio explodes with raucous, joyful noise. "I'll just keep singing until I find you," Eunjae tells Vivian. He is only Eunjae in that moment, the boy she knew and loved. "This place is home. I found it, just like you always told me I would."

46

Two Days Later

Eunjae paused to hide the sixteenth photo under Jiyeon's windshield wiper. She'd find it later and smile.

The sky was a little lighter by the time he reached the low stone wall on the property's edge. Beyond it was a view of the valley, scattered houses nestled into the slopes, and that telltale shimmer was Lake Monroe. The landscape remained verdant, clinging to its faded greenery in open defiance of winter.

Jiyeon arrived soon enough, following the path from the main house, every footstep crackling softly upon frosted blades of grass. She'd brought a blanket large enough to wrap around both of them. "Out of coffee," she murmured in apology. "We'll have to wait 'til later."

"The diner coffee's better, anyway," Eunjae replied. She nodded, and they sat together in silence for a while as daybreak lit the horizon. A thin curl of smoke rose up from someone's chimney down in the valley. Curled up in his arms, Jiyeon said, "Almost done."

He sighed. "Finally."

Sunshine 24/7 had finished its seventh week of production. The members of Apollo weren't needed for the remaining shots, and most of the eighth week was for tearing down the set, so filming would wrap right before lunch. They could be on the road by early afternoon. Jiyeon had some errands to run, and Eunjae had apartments to tour. Although it was technically a day of endings, it felt more like the convergence of so many things about to begin.

"Ready to meet Gloria and Angie?"

"Nervous. Hope they like me."

Jiyeon laughed. "First the interrogation, then date night."

"Date night," he replied. "That's normal."

She didn't answer, just tipped her face up for a kiss. This, too, was normal. An everyday luxury.

They'd both made an Olympic sport out of avoiding social media, and the Internet in general, since those posts went live on Wednesday. Eunjae didn't even read the statement from Emerald confirming that Apollo's Ari and influencer Emma Han were 'meeting with warm and hopeful feelings.' He only knew the exact verbiage because Nicky turned the announcement into a skit at dinner... and then again at every meal thereafter.

He did read the email from Haewon, signed by both of the agency's founders but sent from her email address alone. It contained their best wishes for his happiness, along with an offer of representation, since he'd opted not to sign with Zenith. *We hope that the terms are sufficiently transparent for you*, they'd written at the bottom. He could hear this line in Haewon's brisk, sardonic voice.

Eunjae had expressed his thanks. Also, that he was on an indefinite hiatus. It was time to get some rest. Few sentences had ever been more satisfying to type.

"Find anything?" he asked Jiyeon, after a while. "Maybe we can go tomorrow."

"Hmm. Sort of. I think there's a place that might work out, but it'll take a lot of renovation. Could be perfect if we knocked down some walls."

Jiyeon listed potential improvements, plans for a bakery case, an airy space full of tables for game nights and studying and birthday parties. She'd add more windows and carve out a small lounge, maybe a conference room for meetings. "Not a restaurant," she'd told him last night, eyes shining. "More like a community center. I'll call it Orange Door."

Plenty of people thought they knew what it was, to be proud of someone they loved. They'd have to work pretty hard to know the feeling better than Eunjae. He was sure of it.

The hour flew by. They parted ways at the cottage, then met again at the diner, just one more time. Although he'd considered himself ready to leave Monroe from the moment filming began, this final day on set still managed to taste bittersweet.

The day's objective was simple: Apollo would work one more Friday morning shift, serving a celebratory pancake breakfast to family and friends. The producers were going for something easy and relaxed.

So much for that pipe dream. Jesse hurtled into the kitchen right out of the stylists' trailer, wild-eyed, one sleeve of his pastel yellow pullover flapping behind him like a flag. He'd spilled lemon water down the front. Throwing himself at Eunjae, he proceeded to cling for dear life. "It's him! He's here, he's outside! Hide me, he's the worst, he's *homicidal*—"

"Could you stop yelling?" Kei snapped at him, ducking under the counter. "What if he hears you? Idiot!"

Max insisted on Jiyeon's immediate evacuation. "Hyung, she can't be in this building. He'll go straight for her."

"Who?"

"A monster, noona. From the actual basement level of hell."

He had a lot more to say on this subject, but Nicky interjected, grinning from ear to ear. "Ari, let her meet him at least once. Rite of passage."

"Ah, no," said Eunjae. Fleeing sounded like the correct response to this state of emergency. Jungwoo thought a barricade would work better. In complete disagreement, Kazu plundered the knife block, intent on arming himself to the teeth.

Realization dawned. "Sunny's here," said Jiyeon. "That's why."

Namgyu explained, lovingly, that she must never say this cursed name out loud. "It summons him. Haha!"

In truth, Eunjae should also be evacuated from the danger zone. As Nicky pointed out, torturing him was Sunny's favorite way of torturing Max. "We're dealing with a master of strategy," he said, chuckling.

"Aww, but Hazel just got here! Wouldn't S-U-N-N-Y attack her instead?"

"Good question, Gyu. Will he rank a fake, stolen girlfriend on the same level as a legit, ethically sourced girlfriend and adjust his target—"

"Shut the hell up, hyung!"

Jiyeon smiled. "Hazel's here? I'll go say hi."

A set of swinging saloon doors separated the kitchen from the main part of the diner. They were shorter than the frame, with gaps at the top and bottom, allowing sunlight and conversation to leak in from the adjacent room. As Jiyeon raised her hand to push through, these gaps filled with sun rays. Cuddly sun rays sewn from plush fabric, engineered for violence.

Eunjae's life flashed before his eyes. He seized Jiyeon by the waist and hauled her out of Sunny's range. There wasn't a second to spare; Apollo's mascot was capable of frightening speed, defying its own unwieldy shape and less than aerodynamic design. The creature came bursting over the threshold as Jesse wailed his head off, begging for rescue in six different languages.

Rescue came in the form of a massive hand, adept with a waffle iron but well-suited for pulverizing boulders as well. Calloused fingers latched on to the intruder. There was a popping noise, and then a hiss as pressure released from a hidden valve. Miraculously, Sunny began to melt. His malicious, starry eyeballs became puddles of nylon. The sun rays drooped like withered petals.

"Ridiculous," said Denny, scowling at the deflated remains of Apollo's mascot. "How many times have I told you to keep your hands off my jester squad during work hours? This is a place of business. I'm running a combination diner and clown orphanage. Have a little empathy for my situation." Their manager yanked Sunny out of the kitchen. "Heads up, Lee," he bellowed over the triumphant whooping, shouting, and singing. "Your girlfriend found Trevor."

"Oh, shit," said Max.

Hazel perched on a bar stool next to Apollo's publicist, legs crossed, twirling a butter knife. She lit up at the sight of Namgyu, but nothing could derail her focus. "Unnie, this is him?" she asked Jiyeon.

"Uh-huh. That's Trevor."

Electric blue nails drummed on the counter. Hazel narrowed her eyes. "He doesn't even look like a goddamn Trevor."

Eunjae wondered why Denny hadn't confiscated this butter knife yet. The boss was usually so stringent about the weapons policy.

Meanwhile, Max replied, "Told you. That can't really be his name. It's a lie."

"Don't worry, baby. I'm taking care of this. A fake name can't save him." Hazel let the knife drop, its blunt edge catching the light. "Said a lot of mean shit about me, didn't you, Trevor?"

"It was for the narrative," he said, fidgeting. "Please don't take it personally, Miss Lim."

"I take everything personally. And did you know I do a lot of my own stunts?"

"I... I did know that..."

"I've got fantastic fucking aim, too."

"Right... the scene with the axe throwing..."

"It's all in the wrist." Hazel kicked his bar stool. "Sit up. This is a job interview."

It was here that Max felt compelled to intervene. "Why?" he demanded. "What do you mean, a job interview? We just need him to release the rest of that footage—"

Wrapping her arms around him, Hazel crooned, "You're so pretty when you're mad at me. I deserve you." And then, while Max squirmed out of her grasp, she got back to Trevor. "Here's what I think, Trevvie. I could kick your ass, but that would be over so fast, if we're being honest. I think my manager's right about it being a waste. You should have a better punishment."

"A better punishment," Trevor mumbled, faintly.

"Awww!"

"Yeah. You made me look so, so bad. You should have to make me look so, so good to make up for it. That should be your main job. Amazing idea, right?"

"How? How is that an amazing idea, this guy's literally the

ringleader of a fucking archvillain association—"

Hazel retorted that Max should stop pretending to be pretty *and* dumb. She'd never known him to be dumb. In fact, he could stand to be a little dumber sometimes, like when he'd beaten her at Crossword Clash ten times in a row and she needed a goddamn morale boost. Could he be a little more sensitive, please?

Brothers chimed in with their unsolicited opinions, unable to contain themselves any longer. Kei unveiled his latest laundry list of reasons for hating it here. Then they all looked on in horror as Jungwoo made the mistake of saying, "Hazel, don't. This is crazy."

Max rounded on him. "Why the hell are you telling her what to do? Who do you think you are?"

"Right? Why don't you fuck off, Jungwoo?"

Caught up in this whirling tempest, Eunjae missed it when Jiyeon quietly slipped away. She stood near the front windows with her brother, deep in discussion over something on Denny's phone. But those were the tracks of tears on her face, he realized. She'd been crying. For how long?

His legs moved of their own accord. "What happened?" he asked, rushing to her side. Ten different scenarios played out in his head like movie trailers, cinematic, complete with ominous soundtracks. At least Eunjae could openly offer comfort now, right when she needed it, instead of having to hide how much he cared.

Up close, he saw that Jiyeon wasn't upset. In fact, she couldn't stop smiling. She showed him Denny's screen.

"Eunjae, it's Vivian. We found her."

San Bernardino
CITY LIMIT
POP 201, 823 ELEV 1040
July

Epilogue

Seven Months Later

At the jump park, Max pays $18.99 for a pair of neon green socks with rubber grips. He scrawls an unrecognizable version of his autograph on a gummy touch screen, signing a waiver that absolves Bounceland USA of any potential sins. He contemplates his own sins. There are many.

First, he allowed Jungwoo to cut the bridge from the song that will soon be playing on the screen above his head. Fuck, why didn't he fight him on that?

Second, he shoved Keiichi into the ball pit and ran. Now his brother will cry and squeal about infectious disease for hours. He'll leave the party in a snit, self-diagnosing dengue fever, dysentery, cholera. Admittedly, Max would push him again if the opportunity came up. It was very satisfying. Sometimes he gets why Nicky is a certified psycho.

His third sin is ongoing. Max pushes it down before it can bob to the surface like a dead body.

They have the whole building to themselves. Denny knows a guy, because he always knows a guy, so theirs is the only party happening at Bounceland this afternoon. If not for certain key details, including the likelihood of contracting a medieval plague, this would qualify as heaven on earth. Delicious aromas of buttery popcorn and melted cheese cycle through the vents nonstop. They have bumper cars and video games and laser tag. The building's made of wall-to-wall trampolines.

He gets why Kazu wanted to throw a party here. It's a place where you don't have to think. You just jump as high as you can, knowing that every surface is padded or elastic or made of foam. Something will be there to break your fall. But Max can't even have fun because, once again, he took a hard pass on self control. The memory burns a hole in his head the way cash burns a hole in Namgyu's pocket.

Overhead, the screen darkens. A ribbon unfurls in the center, forming the shape of a cursive letter L, then tying itself into an elegant bow. The L stands for Lumina. This is the group's first full comeback since their December debut, long delayed and highly anticipated. Max has songwriting and production credits on three of the five tracks selected for the EP.

The same goes for Jungwoo. They've become an established duo, a fact that Max recites any time someone questions whether karma is real. He's certain that karma is what binds him to this brother, that their fates are intertwined because they're both assholes. They belong together. He can't deny it and this makes him sick.

But also, Max is living the dream. He can't deny that, either.

Lumina has four members. The group used to have a fifth. The abrupt departure threw schedules into chaos, and for a while, the girls went to ground. They were a body with an arm hacked off at the shoulder. They crept through the Emerald complex like ghosts. And the member they lost was a vocalist, arguably their best, but Lucie or Yerin could've nailed that bridge, too. For fuck's sake, the bridge was a masterpiece. Max should be jailed for backing down.

"Why's this song so boring?"

This comes from a teenager with golden brown hair and, in Max's humble opinion, the personality of a rose bush that somebody set on fire. That shouldn't be a real personality. It should stay in the realm of edgy tattoos, like the one on Jungwoo's left bicep. Even Jungwoo keeps that covered most of the time and he's a goddamn loser. How is Ari related to this kid? Who forged Ezra's documents at the hospital?

"You're boring," Max shoots back, as Lumina's music video plods through the dramatic intro. "Who does homework at a birthday party?"

Ezra stops scribbling. "Who has a birthday party at an indoor playground when he's this old?"

There's no malice in that retort. Max even detects the slightest hint of affection. That's why he resists the urge to hurl Ezra's backpack into the moat filled with musty, spongy foam bricks. Any moron could tell you that those bricks are crawling with pathogens. Ari-hyung would be sad about his kid brother coming down with some bizarre virus from 1854, so Max refrains.

"I'm serious. Why do you have homework? It's the middle of summer."

A baleful glare. "It's winter in Brisbane. I'm missing the first week of term."

Right. Ezra withdrew from that school in Singapore. He spends most of his year in Australia, with their dad, and comes to stay with Ari during breaks. "Bad timing," says Max. "How long are you here?"

"Just until Saturday."

"You're going to both nights of the concert, then?"

"Might skip tomorrow," Ezra replies, shrugging. "Friday's the last stop on the tour, so that'll be the best one."

This little shit. "Everyone else is doing two nights, but you're not? Get out."

"I have homework!"

Not for long, he doesn't. Max leafs through Ezra's worksheets, then picks up the pencil and starts labeling the parts of an atom in his crabbed, spiky penmanship. It's nuts, how much he remembers. Chemistry was fine because it was full of interesting, oddly beautiful words: valence, molarity, resonance. He memorized the periodic table just for the names.

"They'll never believe I wrote that."

"Not my problem," says Max. The music video reaches its midpoint crescendo. Lumina dances on frozen tundra, their skin and hair dusted with snowflakes. "What's going on with you? Why are you sulking over here?"

"I'm not sulking. I'm doing my stupid homework."

And then he figures it out: Ezra's nervous. Max flips to the next page, a worksheet covered in equations. He skips the hell out of that one. "So you're meeting her for the first time today," he says. "Try not to fuck it up."

Ezra lets him know exactly what he thinks of that advice. He's got a mouth on him, but he never descends to Max's level of mouthiness. Must be related to Ari, after all.

Speaking of Ari, he's sharing a slice of ice cream cake with Jiyeon, still wearing that apron. It was a gift from her family. Max can see it from here, a flash of cheerful orange under the cool fluorescent lights. That's Ari's favorite present this year, no contest. It would've been his favorite last year, too. That's when he was originally supposed to receive it. Mrs. Han approaches birthdays with utmost flexibility. The gift is a year late?

No big deal. Late is better than never.

The apron looks just like the ones they wear at Wanna Waffle. Two names are embroidered under the logo: *Ryan,* in slanting cursive, and then *Eunjae* in Hangeul. When he first saw it, Max buckled under an overwhelming sense of loss. Suddenly, he was a body with an arm hacked off at the shoulder. He crept away from the others like a ghost.

In the life his brother has chosen, he is Ryan or Eunjae but never Ari. In the life they used to live, side by side, always together, the opposite was true. And Max can't help wondering if this means he never knew him, if he spent a decade believing he knew enough but was clueless that whole time. Something about it strikes him as really fucking unfair. He'd like to know Eunjae as well as he thought he knew Ari, but now they live an ocean apart.

Ezra flicks an arcade token at him. "What are you mad about now?"

"Nothing," Max lies, flicking it back.

"You look mad, though."

"Maybe because you're a punk. Maybe because this song doesn't have a bridge and that's why it's boring." He sighs. "Maybe because I was supposed to stay here, but I didn't, and Ari had to do this alone."

"Why are you always worried about him living alone? People live alone every day and they're fine. I don't get why my brother would be any worse off than them."

Max rolls his eyes. "Of course you don't get it. You're a kid."

"You're an adult who acts like a kid," Ezra shoots back, "so you don't get it either. You're not an expert on how to be an adult. None of you act like any regular adults I've ever seen—"

"How would you see any regular adults? You lived at a goddamn boarding school. Adults were outnumbered there, like ten to one. You literally grew up in an expensive daycare situation. Don't even try to sell it like you're an expert on regular adults."

"Didn't *you* grow up in an expensive daycare situation?" Ezra counters. But he stops arguing when Hazel insinuates herself between them, impossible to ignore.

Max's girlfriend is a knockout with warm brown eyes and the face of an angel. She has two ballroom dancing trophies, an affinity for bladed weapons, and a famously short fuse. In her last movie, she punched an ice pick through somebody's skull like you'd pop a straw into a juice box. Then she shoved the guy overboard.

They see each other once a month, if that. After Friday's concert, she'll be gone again, filming on location in Greece. It's a relief, because the heat of Hazel's attention seldom inspires the correct fight or flight response. On a good day, Max *fights* the urge to reach out and scorch himself on the surface of the sun. He *flees* before he can stare back and go hopelessly blind with want. Today has not been one of those good days.

Oblivious, Hazel pinches Ezra's cheeks. This is possible because he's sitting down; built a lot like Ari, the kid probably matched her height at the age of seven. "Who is this," she asks, "and why are we mad at him?"

"You know who he is, Z."

"You're right. I remember everybody who makes us mad."

And then you hire them, thinks Max, never done fuming about this even though ages have passed since Hazel recruited Eric/Trevor as her publicist. She prided herself on combining vengeance with a savvy career move. So much better than Max's half-assed revenge plot from June 2023. But also, Trevor's mom and Hazel's dad were both born in the Philippines, which means they have a shared heritage. "He wasn't allowed to betray me," she'd seethed. "He broke the rules and now he has to pay."

Trevor's an even bigger psycho than Nicky. This hiring decision will surely bite them in the ass. Meanwhile, the guest of honor is due to arrive within minutes. "Better go down there," Hazel tells Ezra. "She'll want to see you."

"He's scared Vivian won't like him," says Max.

"I never said that!"

Hazel's eyes flash. "Why the hell wouldn't she like you? Come on, get up."

They walk him partway, then join Apollo by the lockers. Jesse's with Mr. and Mrs. Han, locked and loaded, ready to take pictures. Keiichi seems intent on drowning Namgyu in hand sanitizer. It smells like lemon, mingling with the scent of expensive cologne. Jungwoo's scribbling away in his dumb notebook. Every experience can be mined for material. Every emotion can be paired with a melody, whether he feels it himself or only knows it secondhand.

Nicky pulls Hazel into a tango, always trying new stunts in case it might make Max jealous. Why the hell would he be jealous? That's not his actual girlfriend.

Max needs to commit. He needs to fake his own death.

She comes back to him soon enough, spinning away from Nicky with a laugh. Her hair is short again, but she didn't have time to renew the fading color before flying out here. This will be remedied by next week. She'll be in character, tearing through Santorini as peerless assassin Gretchen Young. Max will receive eighty selfies a day from hotel balconies and beachside sets: Hazel in shredded evening gowns, Hazel in blood-stained leather. Hazel with a crossbow, winking, blowing him a kiss.

The photos are bound to appear on social media. He'll hit the Like button on every post without fail, because it'll be an earful from Hazel if he doesn't, followed by a second earful from Trevor. This is the narrative. This is the story they're telling. It's the deal they made last summer, and he never forgets it.

Max's girlfriend isn't really his girlfriend. He should quit making mistakes with her in limousines and convenience stores and empty birthday party rooms. They should both get better at remembering that this shit's supposed to be temporary.

"Something's up with you, baby," she says now, peering into his face.

"Just tired. Being on tour is fucking exhausting." And he's still pissed about Jungwoo cutting the bridge from *Everlasting*, and it's annoying that Ezra tried to get out of coming to both concerts by using homework as an excuse, like what kind of teenager does that? How many fifteen-year-olds would rather label a goddamn atom than go to their brother's concert? What a freak.

"It's fucked up," Hazel agrees. "Let's shove him into the ball pit."

Max can't help it. He starts laughing. Then there's a commotion by the doors, and Kazu's already boo-hooing, an absolute sniveling wreck by the time Denny helps Vivian into the lobby. Most of Apollo is no better, but it's Jiyeon who cries the most. She just holds the lady's hand, sobbing, until she notices Ezra hiding behind Jeannie. The kid's picked the wildest time to be shy.

Ari doesn't cry. He looked like this on Monday, when the plane began its descent over Los Angeles. They'd been away on tour for weeks and he was coming home at last.

He's found Vivian again. She's a person, not a place, but she still counts as home.

Max forgets his problems, watching them. He recalls the lyrics of a song written with his brothers, the title track of an album that took them all these long months to put together, through a mess of contract negotiations and conflicting schedules. There's a bridge, a gorgeous one, and not just because the lines are split between Namgyu and Ari.

It won't be this way forever, they sing. *When it's over, everything good is still right here.*

Acknowledgments

This book has had a much longer journey than the two that came before it. I've told everyone who knows me, at least once a week (for 56 weeks), that this book has taken twenty years off my lifespan. I've felt like I'd never finish. I was so sure I'd publishing it as a ghost. It's seriously made me so dramatic, and it's taken a lot out of me, but it's also a book that I'm deeply proud of. Now it's done and I'm here at the end, unable to believe that it's the end. I always save my acknowledgments for last because it feels like a reward; it's so easy to write about the people who helped me get here. Writing is a solitary endeavor, for the most part, but I couldn't turn all these words into a book without the love, support, and immense talent of so many others.

First and foremost, thank you to **Carrie Higa**, world's best editor! I need everyone to understand that you are the only reason why I manage to keep track of which brothers are in the van, which brothers are not in the van, and which brothers I may have forgotten entirely because there's too many of them. (And whose fault is that??? Omg) I love you so much for your care and understanding, and for being my safe harbor in so many ways. Thank you for your friendship. Thank you for not straight up ending our friendship after the one chapter where I switched between 'hair dryer' and 'hairdryer' like 84 times. I'd be nowhere without you!

I do nothing but yell about my artists and how much I love them, but I was born to be an art patroness. Thank you to **Erion Makuo** (@erion.makuo) for another beyond beautiful cover illustration. You always deliver beyond my wildest dreams, and you'd think I'd get used to that after eleven years of seeing your talent grow and evolve, but you amaze me every time. I know you always will. Thanks for giving me the time of day despite being 8000% more famous than I am! Love you bro!

All my love goes to **Joeli** (@joe__lx), who helps me bring this series to life with her gorgeous art and gorgeous face and gorgeous work ethic. Guys, she worked on photo cards of nine men for over a year. I want to adopt her. I want to buy her the whole moon. She's stuck with me forever. I can't live without her. I love you so much, Joey! Thank you for drawing all the men and making them so hot that we temporarily forget they're also clowns. Your power!

Huge thanks to **Enid** (@enid.din) for the beautiful case wrap and title page illustrations in the hardcovers! I remain so very much in love with your art and the feeling of warmth that you bring to every illustration you've done for me. I come to you with a vision and you listen so patiently while also interpreting the commission with such thoughtfulness. You're a dream to work with and I look forward to teaming up again in the future.

Thank you also to **Trishia** (@aartris_) for the chapter art and logos and everything else I've suddenly asked for on a random Thursday. You never disappoint! And I'm so grateful to **Rainn** (@rainnrainy) because now I have a complete set of waffle and pancake stickers!

I LOVE MY ARTISTS!!!

This book is dedicated to **my husband and son,** and since it was meant for the two people I love most, it had to be the best book I could possibly write. I did nearly perish in the attempt, but I feel like it was worth it. This place is home because of you.

Stakeholders have watched over me with love and care throughout this very long process, through three books and a decade of writing before that. Thank you for being tireless champions of my work, for your strength and your kindness no matter what I'm going through. I couldn't ask for more or better. I write about you in the back of every book, but for this one, I have a new stakeholder to thank. **Tara**, I'm so grateful that I found you in the wild, lawless place that is Instagram. "What are we reading next?" A simple question that keeps bringing so much light into my life. Let's be book buying, buddy reading, breadlosing besties forever.

I don't typically ask Apollo for their opinions on anything, I mean they'd just tell me anyway without being asked because they never shut up, but this is an opinion that we share: **Sunshines** are the best fandom, the nicest people, the sweetest and funniest readers in the universe. I'm so happy you exist. Thank you for helping me live my wildest dreams. Thank you for your DMs and your emails and your posts. Thank you for the little notes you write me at the end of Google forms. I love you! Shine bright!

Speaking of Sunshines, I received so many wonderful names for Apollo's dog! I wish I could've used every single name that came in! Thank you to **Amy, Andreia, Cindy, Christy, Devanshi, Laura, Lauren, Nathalie, Rae, and Sheen** for your suggestions. If

I didn't get to include your puppy name in *This Place is Home*, please know I'm doing my best to include it later!

I also need to thank even more Sunshines for being part of my ARC team from the very beginning, since the launch of *This Place is Magic*. There are tons of books out there and it means so much to me that you'd choose to give your time and support to all three that I've sent into the world so far. (I hope you'll come back in the future! Because unfortunately I am insane enough to continue writing novels...) Thank you for being Wanna Waffle regulars: **Alma, Ashley, Cindy, Destiny, Devanshi, Jennifer, Kai, Marie, Rae, Shelby, Sofía, Summer, Tara, and Yuliyana**

I've been fortunate enough to connect with some amazing people since becoming an author. Thank you to the lovely hosts of the **Certified Noonas** podcast for letting me hang out with you virtually for two book launches now, and for your warm friendship that I treasure so much. And I have to thank fellow Houston author **Gabriella Buba** for her friendship as well, along with her big heart and boundless generosity of spirit.

The last paragraph is always for **Ayana** because 1) every book is for her 2) she has to listen to me talk about my writing more than anyone else on this planet 3) without Ayana, there would be no Apollo. She's the one true golden maknae of my life. I am clearly not earning enough to get us a villa in Tuscany so I wish you'd go ahead and rewrite that Naruto fanfic. Babe when??? Saltmates forever! I spade you!

About the Author

Irene Te is a veteran K-pop fan and critically acclaimed author of contemporary fiction. Her debut novel, *This Place is Magic*, was chosen by librarians as the best entry in contemporary fiction for the 2024 Indie Author Project and received the Grand Prize at the 32nd Annual *Writer's Digest* Self-Published Book Awards. When she's not writing, Irene works as a freelance curriculum and instructional designer. She lives in Houston, Texas with her husband and son.

You can visit Irene at **www.irenete.com** or connect with her on Instagram (**@irenewritesthings**).

THANKS
for reading!

P.S. Subscribe to my **monthly email** for the latest updates and exclusive **bonus content**, including extra chapters and short stories!

irenewritesthings.substack.com

9 798990 056688